Praise for Kathryne Kennedy's Relics of Merlin series

"M ... to dis ...

—*Publishers Weekly*

"Superb fantasy... Kennedy will sweep you away into a world of magic, mayhem, and fractured love."

—*Night Owl Romance*, 4.5 Stars

"Kennedy's world is intriguing and filled with pageantry and adventure."

—*RT Book Reviews*

"Enchanting! A feel-good fairy tale set in a spell-binding world."

—*Fresh Fiction*

"Another incredible tale from a very talented author. This series is amazing, and I am completely hooked."

—*The Long and Short of It*

"Set in a Victorian England full of magic, the setting is vivid and unusual, the characters interesting, and the romances are lovely."

—*The Good, the Bad, and the Unread*

"Magic ... refreshing."

—*Single Titles*

Also by Kathryne Kennedy

My Unfair Lady
Beneath the Thirteen Moons
The Fire Lord's Lover
The Lady of the Storm
The Lord of Illusion
Enchanting the Lady

Double Enchantment

~The Relics of Merlin~

KATHRYNE KENNEDY

sourcebooks
casablanca

Published by Sourcebooks Casablanca, an imprint of Sourcebooks, Inc.
P.O. Box 4410, Naperville, Illinois 60567-4410
(630) 961-3900
FAX: (630) 961-2168
www.sourcebooks.com

Originally published in 2008 by Lovespell, a division of Dorchester Publishing Group.

Printed and bound in the United States of America
VP 10 9 8 7 6 5 4 3 2 1

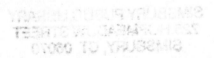

Prologue

Long ago a great wizard was born with magic in his very blood. He lived for thousands of years and went by many names, but the one we know best is Merlin.

Merlin passed his magic down through his offspring, and the power made his children rulers. Some inherited more magic than others, and eventually titles reflected their gifts. In Britain, kings and queens held the strongest power. After the royals, dukes had the greatest magical abilities in that they could change matter. Marquesses could cast spells and illusions and transfer objects but not change them. Earls mastered illusions, while viscounts dabbled in charms and potions. Barons had a magical gift, which could be as simple as making flowers grow or as complicated as seeing into the future.

And then there were the baronets. Part man, part animal, the shape-shifters were Merlin's greatest enchantment… and eventually his greatest bane. For out of all mankind, they were immune to his magic.

Merlin created thirteen magical relics from the gems of the earth, a focus for some of his greatest spells. After Merlin's disappearance, his children tried to find the relics, since these items held the only magic stronger than their own. The relics proved to be elusive until his children discovered that the shape-shifters they so despised could sniff out the power of a relic.

Over the centuries the relics faded to legend. But the most powerful of Merlin's descendants did not forget, and shape-shifters became the secret spies of many rulers.

One

London, 1848
Where magic has never died…

LADY JASMINA KARLYLE SNUCK INTO HER MOTHER'S bedroom like a thief. To her dismay, she realized that she was getting quite skilled at breaking and entering. Jasmina ignored the illusion of slobbering, snarling wolves that her mother had set to protect the chamber from intruders, and began to search the contents of several bandboxes.

She carefully set aside a lovely bonnet decorated with iridescent feathers, a lacquered fan painted with swans, several lace-trimmed handkerchiefs, and a beaded reticule. A glitter of red caught her eye, and she scrabbled for it, scowling with disappointment when she held it up and realized it was only a jeweled button.

She put everything back into the bandbox and opened the lid of another. It was astonishing, really, how clever her mother could be when she set her mind to it. Illusory boxes were interspersed with the real ones, so that her collection looked double.

Fortunately, Jasmina had searched her mother's belongings often enough that she knew where the real items were stored.

The door rattled and Jasmina spun guiltily, waving her fingers with the absent-minded habit she'd developed whenever she cast a spell. She couldn't quite make herself invisible, but her spell would cause whoever entered the room to overlook her presence.

Despite being her mother's maid for forty years, dear Nanette took one glance at the snarling wolves and slammed the door shut again.

Jasmina smiled and continued her search. Nothing in the larger boxes! She moved her search to the smaller, decorative boxes that littered Mother's chiffonier. She shook her head with frustration. There was still the wardrobe to search, and the washing stand cupboard, then beneath the canopied bed—and she hadn't even checked Mother's dressing room yet.

And all for an ugly brooch that looked exactly like—

Jasmina blinked. Nestled among other jewelry, in a pretty box decorated with tiny abalone shells, lay the Duchess of Hagersham's brooch. Her instincts had been correct. Last evening at the Hagersham dinner, her mother *had* been admiring the duke's new gift to his wife with a little too much avarice.

Jasmina held the brooch up to the candlelight, and the large garnet in the center of the piece danced with reflected light. The jewel itself was quite stunning, but the silver figures carved around the sides of it leered grotesquely at her. Ugly little creatures with the most shocking anatomically correct details.

Whatever had possessed her mother to "borrow" it?

Jasmina froze. She could hear the pounding of her heart and realized that the snarling of the wolves had stopped, which could only mean—

"Lucy." Aunt Ettie's voice carried through the closed door. "Are you getting ready for the ball so soon?"

Mother answered, but Jasmina didn't hear the reply. Jasmina shoved the brooch into the pocket sewn into the seam of her dress and sprinted across the room as quickly as her petticoats would allow. Her mother always noticed her, no matter how strongly she cast her spell. She slipped inside the connecting door to Mother's dressing room just as the bedroom door opened, and sighed with relief. Her mother hadn't caught her, thank heavens, which meant she wouldn't have to bear another scene with Mother weeping excuses.

Jasmina crept out the main door and into the hallway and around the stairwell to the safety of her own bedroom. She collapsed on her bed, fighting for breath against the confines of her corset, and dissolved her spell.

A soft tapping on her door, and Aunt Ettie entered. "Well, were we right?"

Jasmina nodded, staring into emerald green eyes that matched her own. But the resemblance stopped there, for Aunt's features were sharp and intelligent, whereas Jasmina's matched those of her mother: soft and innocent.

"Oh dear." Aunt settled her skirts over the arms of the dressing table chair. "My silly, foolish sister. I don't suppose we should tell your father this time?"

Jasmina rose and smoothed the wrinkles from the

counterpane before she carefully rolled it to the foot of the bed. "We have been over this before." Even Aunt Ettie sometimes forgot that Jasmina's doll-like features hid a keen intelligence and a will of iron. "Father wouldn't have the slightest idea how to handle the situation, short of locking Mother away. And it's a woman's duty to keep a man's house a refuge against the rest of the world. Since Mother is unable to do so, that task falls to me."

"I just wish I could do more." Aunt tucked a stray lock of prematurely gray hair back into her severe coiffure.

"Dear Aunt Henrietta, you have already given up all of your prospects to keep our family secret safe. And my magic makes it so much easier to handle the situation."

"I suppose you're right. But it means you shall miss the queen's ball tonight."

Jasmina shrugged and presented her back to her aunt, who began to unbutton the back of her gown.

"If only my sister weren't so…" Aunt left her thought unspoken and pushed the bodice of Jasmina's dress forward. "She insists she's only 'borrowing' from people, and that she has every intention of returning the item right away. She just forgets to."

Jasmina tugged at her sleeves, hearing the frustration in Aunt's voice. She had tried talking to Mother about it as well.

"And then somehow," continued her aunt, "she turns it around and makes me feel guilty. As if it's all my fault, and I'm being quite vulgar for even mentioning it."

"I just think it's something she can't control, and it frightens her," replied Jasmina. "That's why she needs me." Jasmina gasped with relief as the stays of her corset were loosened. "All that matters is keeping Mother and Father happy."

"But you, Jaz. I'm afraid that you'll sacrifice all of your happiness for their own."

"On the contrary. Can you imagine our social standing if Mother's… eccentricity was known?"

Aunt sniffed. "That wasn't quite what I meant."

The door flew open and the subject of their discussion sailed into the room. Mother looked stunning in a pale green ball gown that matched the color of her eyes. Her blonde hair, a shade darker than Jasmina's, was decorated with diamond-studded pins that matched the elegant necklace around her throat. A natural pink blush complemented her smooth complexion, and she'd used only a hint of illusion to smooth the wrinkles from around her eyes. "Jasmina, dear, what are you wearing to the…"

Jasmina stepped out of the puddle of her dress and petticoats and staggered over to her bed, the back of her hand pressed to her forehead.

Mother's full lips puckered in a charming frown. "Whatever is the matter, dear?"

"My head… hurts dreadfully." Jasmina collapsed onto the bedding.

Aunt Henrietta raised a brow at her from behind Mother's back. Jasmina coughed to hide a smile. Mother backed up a step. "I hope it's not catching. You know how susceptible I am to the slightest thing."

"I'm sure it's nothing serious, Lucy," replied Aunt Ettie. "But it seems wise to keep Jasmina at home this evening."

Mother looked crestfallen. "Do you think so? This

is quite the ball of the season. I would so hate for her to miss it. Now, whatever did I come in here for? No matter. Henrietta, you must hurry and get dressed."

Aunt Ettie frowned. "Perhaps I should stay home with Jaz."

"Certainly not. There's no reason for both of you to miss the ball. I will send up her maid with some bitters."

Mother swept out of the room and it felt empty with just the two of them left in it. Mother had that kind of presence.

Jasmina leapt out of bed and knelt in front of her wardrobe, opening the bottom drawer and pulling out the black clothing she'd purchased from a chimney sweep.

"You've become quite the actress," Aunt Ettie said.

Jasmina shuddered dramatically. "Perish the thought." She pulled the rough material of the shirt over her chemise. She barely winced in shame when she pulled on the drawers before stepping into the trousers.

She smeared ashes from the fireplace over her face and surveyed her appearance in the cheval glass. The cap! She pulled it from the pocket of the trousers, stuffed her side curls up into it, and checked her appearance again.

She'd never pass as a boy. She had too much of her mother's features for that. But she wanted to make sure that if a stronger wizard saw through her illusion, he wouldn't recognize her. A chimney sweep walking the streets of London at night wouldn't hazard a second glance, but a woman alone... heavens!

And after all, she planned on sneaking into a duke's house, and her spell didn't make her invisible.

"You look dreadful," pronounced Aunt Ettie. "Why can't we just find some excuse to call on Duke Hagersham tomorrow?"

Jasmina transferred the brooch from her dress to her trouser pocket. "Because it's safer to return it before anyone knows it's missing. Besides, you were caught returning that ring to the baron." Even though the scandal had died down, the rumor that Miss Henrietta Forster was a thief had ruined her chances of marriage.

"But this is entirely unladylike. Not to mention dangerous."

"I've done it before," Jasmina said, "and will most likely do it again. But I don't enjoy it. Please don't make me feel any worse."

Aunt Henrietta sniffed elegantly. Jasmina found it endearing. It was difficult to sniff with elegance; she knew because she'd tried.

Jasmina splayed her fingers, then shook them. Her aunt leaned forward expectantly, her narrow chin jutting out, a look of fascinated attention on her face. Truly, Jasmina didn't need all the hand gesturing or poetry to cast a spell, but it disappointed Aunt if she forgot it.

Besides, it wasn't easy to create an illusion of oneself. She'd use all the props she could get.

> *"Twin of me,*
> *I create thee,*
> *For the night,*
> *You shall be."*

Jasmina made a face. What a horribly dreadful rhyme. But Aunt looked impressed…

The air wavered as a ghostly shape took form. Then Jasmina's hip suddenly burned, a crack of thunder shook the walls of her bedroom, and her body tingled all over.

Aunt Henrietta clapped her hands with delight. "Well done!"

Jasmina smiled weakly and glanced out the window. How odd. No sign of rain. No lightning followed that room-shuddering sound to explain the current that had run through her body. She had never crafted a spell with such… flair. But her illusion looked perfectly created, down to the ribbons on Jasmina's favorite nightgown.

Jasmina took a step forward and looked into her twin's eyes. They stared blankly back into her own. Hmm. Everything seemed fine. "Get into the bed," she instructed. "And go to sleep. If anyone should wake you just mumble and roll over. Can you manage that?"

The illusion didn't answer, of course. It couldn't really think; it just followed her orders.

Aunt Henrietta shuddered. "Truly, Jaz. If you both were in the same room I couldn't pick the real one."

"A royal could. And of course, a baronet—since they're immune to all magic. But my maid won't know the difference, will she?" Jasmina bent over the sleeping woman. Aunt was right, though; she'd done a grand job of duplicating herself. "You will stay in this bed until I come to wake you."

Her illusion smiled sleepily and rolled over.

"Well, I shall require several maids to dress me for the ball this evening," said Aunt Ettie, her mouth curled into a conspiratorial smile. "Shall I make a fuss now?"

Jasmina fumbled in the back of the wardrobe again,

pulled out several items, and stuffed them in her pockets. "Yes, if you don't mind."

Aunt Henrietta gave her a wink, then sailed out of the room in a good imitation of Mother. Jasmina waited until she heard the bellpull and the scurrying of servants running up the stairs before she crept down to the kitchen. She paused for a moment at the stairwell, listening for any sounds coming from the room.

But Aunt Ettie had done a superb job of rousting them; except for Cook humming in the scullery, the basement was utterly silent.

Jasmina's fingers waved and she threw on a don't-notice-me spell. Her hip tingled and she frowned, remembering the burning sensation she'd felt before. She quickly slipped into the pantry using her household keys, then made herself comfortable in the corner of the room. Surrounded by their best china and silver, she settled in to wait for the best time to sneak out. In a few hours, most of the gentry, including the Duke of Hagersham, would be at the queen's ball, and she could navigate the streets of London without being noticed.

For a moment Jasmina wished she were her illusion, safely snug in bed. She dreaded to think how drained she would be after tonight; it would take her months to build her magic reserves again.

If she dared make a light, she would take the opportunity to do an inventory of their tableware. Jasmina hadn't done so in a while; running a household took more effort than one would think. She'd been doing it since the age of ten, when she realized Mother had no head for it and needed her help.

When it grew late enough to venture from her hiding place, she created an illusion of a cat with a wiggle of her fingers, her hip tingling again. Heavens, what was causing that sensation? She dug in the pocket of her trousers and pulled out the contents: her handkerchief, a worn pair of gloves, her household keys, and the duchess's brooch.

The closure of the pin on the back of the brooch had come open, and she realized it had probably been poking her for some time. She refastened the catch before stuffing it back in her pocket.

Jasmina opened the pantry door, made sure to lock it behind her, and glanced around the room. The fire glowed softly, banked for the night, but it provided enough light for her to see that the table and floors had been scrubbed clean, the range had been freshly blackened, and the clotheshorse had clean laundry drying on it.

She smiled with pride on her well-ordered household. She had been taught that the cleanliness of a home showed the moral character of its occupants, and certainly no one could dispute hers.

Jasmina padded over to the hallway that led to the male servants' rooms and made her illusionary cat let out a yowl. She cocked her head, waited another breath, and made it yowl again.

Finally, one of the footmen opened his door and cracked an eyelid open towards the floor. "They fergit to let ya out again, heh?"

Jasmina kept to the shadows, making her illusion curl around his feet, a rumbling purr accompanying the cat's flirtation. When the footman made as if to pick up the animal, she shied it from his reach and toward the kitchen door.

He shuffled toward the back door, Jasmina and her illusion following. He palmed the medallion that released the warding spells protecting the house against magical intrusion and let both her and the cat out. She waited to make sure he put up the wards again and then made her way across the cobbled courtyard, past the mews, and into the alley. She dispelled the cat illusion but continued her don't-notice-me spell.

Jasmina squashed down the feeling of alarm at being alone in the streets at night. She rarely left the house without a chaperone. If it hadn't been for the necessity of learning her way around London to return her mother's borrowed goods, she doubted she'd know anything more than the direction to her favorite shops and park. Indeed, her best friend Ellen had once commented that a lady only needed to know her destination, since her escort or coachman would take her there.

Jasmina shuddered to think how shocked Ellen would be to see her now, skulking through alleyways in a chimney sweep's clothes. Of course, her friend would be even more shocked to learn that Jasmina's mother borrowed things... It was always a choice between two evils.

Jasmina squinted, checking the fingerpost of the street she'd just entered. Mandrake Street wasn't large enough to warrant gaslights and so she took it, keeping to the shadows, grateful for the fog that made her almost invisible. Grateful that the duke lived close to her home in Gargoyle Square.

Not too long ago, she'd had to take a horse out of the mews without waking the stable servants and cast spells over them both. She'd been so exhausted from working that much magic, she'd slept for two days afterward. Tonight she kept to the back streets, eventually coming upon Hagersham House by the rear entrance. The Gothic architecture of the mansion made her feel guilty, with all its church-like ornamentation and stained glass windows of dancing angels.

Jasmina recast the cat-illusion spell and her hip burned quite badly. She wondered if the clasp on the brooch had come open again. She gritted her teeth at the sheer impropriety of her current state.

And then sighed and got on with it.

Her cat yowled at the door for almost an hour. If she employed such inconsiderate servants, she'd have them dismissed. What if they didn't open the door? How would she ever get past the wards a duke kept around his home? Unlike earls and marquesses, a duke had the ability to change actual matter. So his wards wouldn't just make you imagine a thousand bees were stinging you—they might actually be doing so.

Jasmina made her cat yowl louder. A curious dog came from the direction of the mews and began to bark at her illusion. He barked louder when the cat ignored him, and finally getting angry at the insult, charged with jaws open and fangs gleaming. She made the cat larger and it snaked out a paw with claws the size of butcher's knives, swiping at the dog's snout.

The dog believed her cat to be real, so he felt the rake of its claws and let out yip-yip-yips of such pain that he set off the rest of the dogs in the neighborhood. Still, Jasmina felt shocked to notice the blood that welled from the dog's nose. Her illusions weren't usually *that* strong.

Finally someone opened the kitchen door. The butler, by the look of him, his haughty expression twisted with aggravation. "What's going on out here?"

Jasmina had already shrunk her cat back to normal size, but widened its eyes to huge pools of misery.

"Dogs after you, eh? All right, so what are you waiting for, an invitation?"

He opened the door wider, wide enough for Jasmina to get her body through, and both she and the illusion entered the kitchen. The butler shut the door, palmed the warding medallion, and sleepily went back to his room without a backward glance.

Jasmina waited for her eyes to adjust to the gloom, noting that the duke's kitchen wasn't nearly as tidy as her own, and headed up the servants' stairs. If by some chance Duke Hagersham or his wife hadn't gone to the ball tonight, she'd be more likely to encounter them on the grand stairway, and so she used the less conspicuous paths of the servants.

She hesitated at the ground floor, wondering if she should leave the brooch in the dining room, where the duchess had last worn it. But the servants would already have done a thorough cleaning of the room, especially if the duchess had noticed it missing.

Jasmina crept up the stairs to the first floor, went into the drawing room, and pulled the brooch out of her pocket. The fireplace had been cleared. The only light shining into the room came from the gaslights outside. Even so, the gem glowed with a bloodred shimmer in its depths.

She shuddered and stuffed the brooch between the cushions of the settee, wondering again why her mother had chosen such an ugly piece of jewelry.

The sound of muffled laughter made her pause as she stepped out into the hallway, and the wavering light of a candle made her retreat back into the room. Jasmina ducked behind the settee just as a man and woman entered the room.

She recognized the voice of the duke, but the low laughter of the woman sounded nothing like the tittering of his duchess.

"I'm missing a queen's ball for you, my dear."

More soft laughter. "I'll make it worth yer while."

Jasmina heard wet, hungry sounds but resisted the urge to peek around the edge of the settee. Her heart froze at the thought that the duke might see past her spell and disguise.

Jasmina took a silent breath and reassured herself that he wouldn't notice her as long as she didn't draw his attention.

Duke Hagersham gasped, and Jasmina wondered what on earth the woman could be doing to make a man moan so oddly. She heard cloth slithering to the floor and chided herself for her foolishness.

Why else would a man stay home with another woman? She wondered which servant the duke was having an affair with. She wondered how long it would take them to do... well, whatever they were going to do.

Jasmina couldn't risk sneaking out of the room with

the duke in it. She tried to plug her ears against the sounds they kept making, but curiosity kept warring with propriety until she finally gave up the battle and dropped her hands.

Her eyes caught the flicker of movement on the wall, and she realized the couple stood in front of the candle. She could clearly see their shadows. The duke stood with his back to the adjacent wall; she recognized the outline of his hawkish nose and his half-open mouth. The woman knelt in front of him, her hands fumbling with... something. And then it sprang free, and Jasmina could clearly see the outline of its shadow on the wall.

Well, she knew men had them. She'd just never seen one before—and she wasn't now, she reassured herself over the pounding of her heart. It was just a shadow. The woman tilted her head back, the duke trembled, and Jasmina watched as the woman opened her mouth.

Her head moved forward and back until the duke groaned and pulled her up by the arms. Their shadows merged for a moment. Then the woman turned her back to him and bent over. The duke pulled up her skirts, making a lump of shadow over the servant's back, and Jasmina could make out the round curves of the woman's bottom.

Jasmina tensed.

The duke's shadow lunged forward and the woman strangled a scream.

Jasmina's heart lurched into her throat, a rush of... something flooded her veins and in blind panic she leaped over the settee. She sprinted across the room.

Her eyes met those of the duke's for a fleeting second, and then she was tumbling down the stairs, out the door and into the alley before she even registered the expression on his face.

She'd never seen such a look of utter rapture before.

Jasmina didn't pause in her flight until she reached the safety of her own courtyard. She panted and trembled, confused and outraged. No proper woman would behave in such a fashion. No wonder men constantly took up with servants.

She refused to think about the wetness between her thighs—or to acknowledge that she had run only because she'd throbbed and ached when the duke had plunged himself inside the woman.

Jasmina gathered the remains of her magical strength and created the cat. The same footman promptly let it into the house, and she decided to raise his wages.

It seemed like forever, but it had only been a few hours since her family had left for the ball. They wouldn't be home until dawn, and she certainly had no intention of waiting up for them. When she crept into her room, her maid sat snoring in a chair, and Jasmina was so exhausted that she didn't notice the bed was empty until she lay in it.

Her illusions had always lasted until she returned. Perhaps that crack of thunder had interfered with her concentration, and she hadn't created the spell as strongly as she usually did. Thank heavens her maid had fallen asleep and hadn't noticed Jasmina's absence. Or rather, that of her illusory double.

It was the first time her twin spell had failed her, and Jasmina felt a trickle of alarm, trying to think what might have happened. And then another thought struck her: Why hadn't she set off the duke's wards when she'd run out of the house? But erotic shadows kept dancing through her thoughts and carried her into sleep.

Two

SIR STERLING THORN ADJUSTED HIS CRAVAT, FROWNING at the slight yellowish hue of the once white silk. His frock coat showed wear at the seams, his breeches were too light-colored for the current fashion, and despite repeated attempts to shine his boots, they still showed the dull wear of years at the heels and toes.

He tossed his head, throwing the thick black hair off his face. He kept his hair unfashionably long out of pure contrariness. He hadn't come to London to find an heiress to improve his position—not that any of the society matrons would let a baronet near their precious daughters anyway.

Sterling turned away from the cracked cheval glass, annoyed that he'd even bothered to check his appearance. The finest clothing couldn't compensate for being a shape-shifter.

He strode to the worn sideboard and poured himself a finger of brandy. Despite his disdain for society, tonight was the queen's ball and he wished he could make a better impression. Only because he would be introduced to the prince consort, and he was a man Sterling could admire. And whom Sterling hoped would help him.

A knock sounded on the splintered door of his rented flat. Sterling crossed the room in two strides and threw open the door, loosening the worn hinges even further. He stared in amazement.

"Well, brother," said Cecil, "aren't you going to invite me in?"

Sterling's surprise turned into annoyance and he spun, leaving the door open behind him while taking a position near the fireplace. He laid his arm across the mantel and watched his brother and stepmother enter the flat, noting their looks of distaste at the shabbiness of his lodgings.

Lady Ada Thorn settled herself gingerly on an old horsehair chair, her nose wrinkling at the smell of it. Cecil prowled the room with a proprietary air, and Sterling felt his face harden into a mask of stone. "What are you doing here?"

Lady Thorn uttered a small gasp at the harshness of his tone, but Cecil, as usual, appeared unaffected.

"I've come for the season to look for a wife. Mother seems to feel it's time. She also felt that we should come visit you—I say, quite a large place you have here, isn't it?"

Sterling didn't dignify that with an answer. The entire flat would fit in the smallest salon of Thorn Castle, with room left over.

"Still," Cecil continued, "you'd think with the monthly allowance I've been sending you that you could have secured lodgings in a better part of the city. Gads, Trickside is a haven for charlatans—"

"And shape-shifters," cut in Sterling. "Or haven't you noticed the prejudice against our kind?"

Cecil waved an arrogant hand. "Money overcomes many obstacles."

His stepmother had the grace to blush. They must have gone to the shops before coming to see him, for the lady wore a new gown. A matching bonnet framed her silver-touched black hair and brought out the green in her hazel eyes. She looked every bit the part of the prosperous widow.

And Cecil looked quite the dandy, sporting a cutaway coat trimmed in velvet. With his black hair cut just below the ears and his new white cravat adorned with a ruby-studded stickpin, his status of heir to their father's estate was garishly apparent. Although Sterling's shape-shifter abilities also gave him the title of baronet, like most of his kind, the lack of an estate made it an empty title.

"And speaking of money," continued his brother, "when will you give up this foolish quest and return home? The extra expense of putting you up in the city is a drain on our financial resources. Don't you have some grapes to harvest?"

Sterling clenched his fist. Cecil always mocked his vineyards as a foolish enterprise, and it never failed to irritate Sterling, because he had yet to turn a profit.

He should have known they'd come to complain about money. "I'm spending my *sister's* dowry to search for her whereabouts. Not on living expenses, as you can see."

Cecil shrugged, as if he didn't think the flat was too shabby for his brother to live in, although Sterling knew Cecil would disdain to live in such poor surroundings himself.

Lady Thorn cleared her throat. "Certainly it's your sister's money, but your father gave Cecil the right to distribute it as he sees fit. You don't wish to see Angel's dowry diminished, do you?"

Sterling glared at her. Cecil smirked, his onyx eyes glittering.

"I… I mean," tried Lady Thorn again, "without a proper dowry she won't be able to make an advantageous match."

"Madam, what good will a dowry do her, if she's not here to make use of it?"

She lowered her eyes, and Sterling tried to soften his voice. She had only been trying to make peace again. "I do not believe Angel ran off with that sorcerer. She would never have done something so dishonorable. I fear she was abducted, and until I find her and know the truth, I will never stop looking. Don't you worry about her?"

Cecil grunted and flopped onto a velvet settee, splitting the worn fabric and sinking into a hole of stuffing. He appeared not to notice that his bottom had been engulfed by upholstery. "This is the crux of the problem, brother. I think she ran off with that marquess, giving up all rights to her dowry."

"You'd like that, wouldn't you?" Sterling had run out of patience. This discussion had been overly delayed, and if not for Angel's disappearance, would have taken place several months ago. "Then you could have her inheritance as well as mine—"

"I say!" Cecil erupted off the settee, his jackal-form

revealed for a moment: mouth slanted back from curved teeth, nose elongated, ears briefly growing long and wide. He shook himself and resumed his fully human shape. "I never stole your inheritance. Father *chose* to name me the heir. Even though you are the elder son, he trusted *me* to oversee the estate." His voice became smug. "I am just following his wishes."

Sterling wondered if his stepbrother had deluded himself into believing his own lies. Cecil had taken advantage of Sterling's hostile relationship with their father and wormed his way into the inheritance. Sterling suspected that Cecil had purposely made the situation worse by speaking ill of him to Father.

"One day, Cecil, I will find out the truth. But right now, all I care about is Angel. You *will* make available to me the money that Father left her in his will."

"Actually, I think it's time I cut you off." Cecil half-shifted again and howled.

Sterling felt the hairs on his neck bristle in response. He knew it would come down to their animal natures—it always did. He shifted fully, his clothing dissolving into his coat, his stallion form dominating the small room. He tossed his mane and stomped his hooves, the thin walls shaking with the force of it. His nostrils flared, and his ears flattened back.

Cecil cringed and for a moment fear warred with hatred in his eyes. Sterling doubted he would truly stomp his half brother to death. Then again…

His anger drained with the ridiculous thought, and he shifted back to human, resuming his negligent pose by the fireside.

"Perhaps we shouldn't have come," breathed his

stepmother. "You are fighting with Cecil just like you fought with his father. Will there never be peace in this family?"

Sterling shrugged. "The cost to my soul would be too high, madam. Now, if you'll both excuse me, I have a ball to attend." Sterling bowed low to his stepmother. "It was a pleasure to see you, madam. Please let yourself out."

It took all of his willpower not to slam the door behind him.

Sterling strode through the crowded ballroom, the sea of people before him parting like the mares of a herd. But whereas the animals did it to show respect, the gentry made way so they wouldn't soil their persons by the touch of him.

A full moon covered the entire ceiling of the massive ballroom. It hung so low he felt he could reach up and touch it, even though he could see it was just an illusion. Moonbeams radiated from it in transparent shafts of muted light, striking the dancers below in spotlights of iridescent color. Occasionally the moonbeams would swirl around a pair of dancers, curl beneath their feet and lift them a few inches off the floor.

The queen and her prince consort danced together in the middle of the ballroom surrounded by several moonbeams, their love for each other obvious by their gazes. Sterling had been looking for an opportunity to speak with His Royal Highness for over an hour with little success. He had tried not to appear too obvious, but perhaps it was time for a bolder move.

He pushed himself away from the wall; the black void of illusion made him feel as if he had to pry himself out of it. A ridiculous thought, since he was immune to magic, and could see through any spell as if it were transparent. He shook his head, marveling anew at the magic of London. The aristocracy threw around spells as freely as they did their money.

The prince and queen had retired to the refreshment tables, and Sterling strode toward them with determination. He managed to join the crowd surrounding the royal couple, and the prince even turned toward him, lifting an inquiring brow in Sterling's direction.

Sterling opened his mouth to perform the social blunder of speaking to the prince without a proper introduction when he caught a whiff of scent. He turned toward the smell, and another of the prince's admirers immediately captured Prince Albert's attention, but Sterling barely noticed.

It stank, that smell. A hint of it had surrounded the Marquess of Ogreton, the sorcerer who had abducted his sister.

He frantically searched the crowded ballroom, looking for the handsome sorcerer. Sterling's heart thundered in his chest. He'd spent months in the bowels of London's lower districts, suspecting the man had not been a marquess at all, but some baseborn sorcerer who had acquired his magical abilities from an aristocratic love affair. Although rare, it was known to happen. Could it be possible that the man truly might be titled?

Sterling stepped onto the dance floor, ignoring the looks of disdain from the dancing couples. Frustration seized him. Faces spun in and out of his vision.

None of them bore the slightest resemblance to the marquess, and the scent had begun to fade. The only lead he'd managed to get on his sister—

"I beg your pardon," snapped a young man when Sterling bumped into his shoulder and disrupted the pattern of the dance. Why hadn't the fool just gotten out of his way like all the others?

Sterling blinked at the man—truly just a boy, his smooth face as soft as a girl's—and muttered an apology. Then he glanced at the girl the boy held in his arms and froze.

Her eyes glowed an emerald green; her hair shimmered in a halo of white gold around her head. She looked like a proper young lady, with a modest décolletage on her gown of green satin and matching elbow-length gloves. Delicate earbobs and a matching necklace of emeralds screamed sophisticated wealth. Her petite stature, the smooth white skin and softly curved lips, made her appear almost doll-like with innocence.

But not her eyes. For that brief moment when she'd met his stare, he'd seen a glimmer of wickedness quite at odds with her appearance. How utterly fascinating.

The faint odor he'd been following ended with her person, making her even more fascinating.

"I say, would you get out of the way? You're quite disrupting the set."

Sterling looked down his nose at the boy and realized why the fool hadn't avoided him. He could see the were-animal in the boy's mottled hair and smell the earthy scent of predator on him. Sterling half-shifted for a breath of a moment, long enough for the were-hyena to make out his form.

The boy's eyes widened.

Sterling tossed the hair off his forehead and snorted. The boy dropped his arms away from his partner.

Excellent. "May I have this next dance," he said to the girl, making it a command, and swept her up in his own arms, joining the swirl of dancers.

Maybe he shouldn't have done that. The slip of a girl felt every bit the woman in his arms, and his body reacted to the feel of her without a conscious thought of his own. His skin shivered, his muscles tightened, and his shaft began to harden. He twirled her faster, trying to hide his reaction, trying to make sense of it.

Admittedly, it had been some time since he'd been with a woman. His cottage lay in a secluded valley, miles from a nearby village, and he had only one old couple as retainers. After giving up his commission, he'd worked in his vineyards and spent the rest of his time in were-form, ranging the flat, grassy land of Witchshire.

Surely that accounted for his reaction to the soft breast pushed up against his chest, the faint scent of jasmine, the warmth of her small body. He'd never danced with a woman of quality before either. Perhaps the challenge of the unattainable fed his desire.

She looked up at him, her green eyes glowing with a heat that told him she might not be so unattainable. Her parents had best see to it that they married the chit off soon, or they'd have trouble on their hands. But not before he had the chance to find out why she carried the same smell of magic that the marquess had.

"You dance beautifully," she said, her voice a mixture of velvet and… starch.

Utterly fascinating.

"Forgive me for not introducing myself." Sterling relaxed his hold on the girl. "Sir Sterling Thorn, of Witchshire Cottage."

She blushed becomingly. "It's very nice to meet you."

Nice. Not quite the reaction he had to meeting her. When she didn't offer the same introduction he forced the acquaintance. He had little time, after all. For when she figured out what he was—or worse yet, when her parents spied her dancing with him—he knew he'd never be able to get near her again. "May I have the honor of your name?"

Her brow wrinkled prettily, and she frowned, as if she had to search for the answer. "Oh, yes. Jaz."

"Jaz? That's an unusual name."

She shrugged, a delicate movement of her shoulders that made Sterling's gaze stray to her bosom. Just a slight rise of soft flesh, hinting at a fuller figure beneath the yards of green satin...

He must get control of himself. "Is it a nickname of some kind?"

When he met her eyes they glowed with green fire. She'd noticed him staring at the swell of her breasts and she'd reacted with an answering passion. Who was this creature? She looked the innocent, yet had the eyes of a courtesan. Surely, she was too young for that to be true. Could she be masquerading as quality?

She smiled. "You may just call me Jaz."

The orchestra had finished the waltz and they stood for a moment, his arms still around her, staring at each other. Sterling tried again. "Who are your parents?"

"You are very curious." She ran her index finger

across his lips, and he was too mesmerized and startled to move. "So am I."

Her words made him shiver like an eager young boy. His mouth tingled where she'd touched him. He'd lost control of the situation, if he'd ever had it. When the music swelled again, he swept her into another dance, lost in the mysterious depths of her eyes, unable to fight whatever spell she'd cast over him.

He was immune to magic. But this was a different kind of spell altogether.

Her hair shimmered, and he realized that moonbeams had surrounded them. It added to the enchantment of her seduction... and gave them a cocoon of privacy.

Jaz leaned forward, her breath caressing his ear. "Do you believe in love at first sight?"

"No, I... yes."

She gave a throaty laugh, and he buried his mouth in the softness of her neck. She smelled like jasmine and moonlight, her skin soft, hot. He licked her, tasting salt and cream, and he wanted more. How could he make this stop?

"There's so much I need to learn," she breathed. "Would you be willing to teach me?"

He blinked at the audacity of her question. Yes, he wanted to teach her. He wanted to be the only man who ever touched her. But despite what the rest of the nobility thought, he was a gentleman. The lady couldn't possibly know the implications of her request. Her eyes shone with innocence.

The moonbeams released them as the dance ended. Before Sterling had a chance to speak an older man grasped Jaz by the arm and swung her around. "You promised the next dance to me," he growled.

She tried to twist out of his grasp. "I've changed my mind."

Sterling felt a surge of fury when Jaz whimpered as the man tightened his hold. "You heard the lady. Let her go."

The man's eyes widened as Sterling felt the anger of his were-self try to take control of his form. He felt his shoulders widen and his hair whip his face as he blinked against the sudden burn of fury in his eyes.

The other man quickly dropped her arm and melted into the staring crowd.

"Are you all right?" he asked Jaz while the musicians struck up another tune.

"I think so," she replied, rubbing her arm.

As the dancers began to twirl around them, Sterling noticed another man heading in their direction, the fellow's eyes riveted on Jaz with an intensity that promised more trouble.

Then the force of a woman's gaze across the room caught him, and he looked into emerald eyes that matched those of the bewitching creature in his arms.

But the other woman who stood next to her looked more like Jaz, with darker blonde hair and paler eyes, but with the same fine-boned features and petite stature. The taller woman stared at him while she pointed toward the refreshment table, mouthing something to the smaller woman and the man who held her arm.

The couple moved toward the table and the woman's brow lowered with determination as she marched in their direction.

Jaz followed the direction of his gaze and uttered a small gasp.

"Who is she?"

"I… I'm not sure. Yet. But I think… Sterling, you must get me out of here."

He should have been astonished that she'd used such familiar address. But somehow, in the short span of a single dance, they'd passed the barriers of strangers into an intimacy he'd never felt with anyone else before.

Her plea for his help reminded him of Angel, the way his sister would always look to him for rescue from the callousness of their father. A desire to protect the naive beauty overwhelmed him, and he didn't question it.

Sterling clasped her gloved hand and led her through the press of the crowd. They parted for him as usual. He glanced back and frowned. The lecher and the woman still followed them, the woman's emerald eyes glaring at him with determination.

"We'll never manage to hail my hack in time," he muttered.

Jaz squeezed his hand. "I have faith in you."

His heart shouldn't have soared at the offhand compliment, but it did. He didn't want her to reject him. The thought made something twist in his chest. But perhaps it was better she knew now…

"How do you feel about baronets?"

Confusion wrinkled her brow again. "What do you mean?"

Two gossiping women stood in their path, too involved in conversation to notice him. Sterling gently swept them out of his way. They barely noticed.

"All baronets are shape-shifters," he replied. "Were-animals. Men and women who can turn into beasts as easily as you change your gloves."

He risked a glance at her. She smiled naughtily—if such a thing were possible—and eyed him with renewed interest. "Ah. So what manner of beast are you?"

They'd reached the double doors and stepped out into the London night. The early morning fog swirled along the graveled path, partly obscuring the lines of waiting coaches with their drivers nodding off from atop their seats.

Sterling swept her a low bow, ignoring the stares of the red-uniformed guards who stood sentinel beside the open doorway. "Allow me to show you, my lady."

He shifted, watching her grow smaller to his new perspective. He looked for fear and loathing to cross her face. After all, his stallion form was larger than any real horse and his hooves could easily trample a pack of predators to death.

He was a fearsome animal, but Jaz didn't cower. No, her smile widened. Sterling puffed up his chest, tossed his mane, blew hard through his nostrils. He pranced in place and arched his tail.

Jaz clapped her hands, her eyes alight with admiration and… mischief.

The emerald-eyed woman appeared behind Jaz in the doorway. Straggles of gray hair had escaped her severe coiffure, she'd managed to tear the hem of her gown, and her face had shriveled into one giant frown.

Sterling turned his side to the girl, lowered his front legs, and nickered at her. He stood at least nineteen hands high, but Jaz took one look over her shoulder at the woman and vaulted onto his back. Despite her skirts she managed to drape her body over him, and with a shrug he had her positioned so she could grasp his mane.

He took off at a gallop, skidded to a stop when he felt her sliding, then took off again when she resumed her seat. Sterling pounded through the empty London streets, occasionally dodging a late-night carriage, his keen eyes noting shapes in the fog before he encountered them.

Ah, it had been too long since he'd run like the wind! He snorted at the stink of the Thames, reveled in the smell of the salty breeze from the sea. He barely felt the weight of the girl on his back, but his animal-self was acutely aware of the feel of her body, the warmth of her skin.

Sterling shifted when he reached his flat, reaching behind him as he gained two legs, easing the woman down his back. She felt like liquid silk. He led her up the stairs to his room and threw open the door. He didn't think about the shabbiness of his flat. Neither did she, for her eyes never left his, a burning intensity in their emerald depths.

"I should take you home," he said. "But I don't know where you live."

Jaz closed the door behind them. "I suppose that would be the proper thing to do." She turned and closed the distance between them, ran her hands along his arms, settling them on his shoulders. "But I would prefer to kiss my rescuer." She rose to her toes and placed her mouth atop his.

Fire whipped through his body.

She pulled away, that lovely mouth curved into a frown. "I'm not doing it right, am I?"

He couldn't answer. Couldn't stop his arms from curling around her waist and pulling her closer.

"Teach me the proper way to do it," she said, then covered his mouth with hers again.

Bloody hell, the mere touch of her lips made him hot. What would happen if he showed her how to kiss? Because it was obvious she didn't know a thing about it, her mouth motionless over his while she waited for some instruction.

Sterling told himself that a little kiss wouldn't hurt. He tilted his head, opening his lips slightly, allowing their mouths to get closer. She sighed and curled her fingers into his hair. He parted her lips with his tongue, every nerve in his body exploding with reaction. His were-self tried to take over, battling against his human good sense.

Sterling pulled away and groaned. He'd kissed many women before but he'd never responded like this. "I think that's enough for a proper lady to know."

Her green eyes lit with an inner fire. "Ah, but you see, I'm not a proper lady. I want you and that's all that matters."

She pulled his hair, lowering his face to hers, and proceeded to practice what he'd just taught her, slanting her head and opening her mouth. Forcing his lips open with her tongue.

Sterling groaned and tightened his hold, arching her back while he ravaged her mouth, teaching her how to mate with their tongues. The woman was an apt pupil. His desire heightened to a raging inferno and when she tore at his clothing, his traitorous hands started to help her.

He hesitated at the buttons of his breeches.

"I have to see all of you," she murmured. "Please."

Sterling's resolved crumbled. He guided her to the bed and hastily removed the rest of his clothes.

Jaz lay there and watched him with ferocious intensity. She licked her lips when he stood naked before her, not a hint of shyness in her face.

Sanity returned to him for a moment. What did he think he was doing? A gentleman didn't tumble with an aristocrat's daughter without paying the consequences...

"Take off my clothes," she demanded, her voice so husky it made him moan. "The same way you took off yours."

Damn him if he would disobey that order. He rolled her on her stomach and she laughed while he popped off most of her buttons. Sterling frowned at the corset, grabbed a knife from the table and cut the stays, tossing the blade and her ruined corset on the floor when he finished. When the creamy skin of her back was exposed to his view, he couldn't resist running his hands along the curve of her waist, up her smoothly sculpted spine and across her shoulders. He narrowed his eyes at the pins in her hair, searching in the mass of it until he'd removed them all and the wealth of her white blonde curls spilled down her back.

He would have buried himself in her hair, drowning in the scent of jasmine, but she made an impatient noise, one that he had no difficulty understanding. He pulled the dress down her body, crushing the fragile green silk.

She kicked off her shoes and rolled over, and for a moment he couldn't move. She was simply the most magnificent creature he'd ever seen. A sultry smile played on her lips while she slowly removed her gloves. He thought he'd never seen a more erotic display than the baring of her delicate arms. Then she spread her legs.

Sterling felt his shaft jump as he stared at her lovely pink folds. With a groan he leaned forward and slid his hands up her stockings, until he reached the warm flesh of her inner thighs. His touch continued upward, fingers dancing across her ribs to the soft swell of her breasts.

Jaz sighed and arched her back when he stroked her nipples. His blood pounded through him. He had neither the patience nor the control to wait any longer.

He parted her wet, silken folds and eased inside her. After a moment he froze, afraid that he'd hurt her, damning himself to eternity if he had.

"Don't stop," she panted. "Surely, there must be more. Oh, let there be more!"

She wrapped her legs around his bottom with a strength that surprised him, and he gave her what she wanted. She met each of his thrusts with one of her own, groaning his name and thrashing wildly beneath him. Her nails scored his back and enflamed him further, until he could no longer hold back his climax.

Violent pleasure racked his body, on and on until he didn't think he could stand any more. She cried out as well, her hands clutching the bedding, pulling at it with her fists.

He'd never felt anything like this. He wanted to feel it again. And again. His breath sounded loud in the sudden stillness, and he pulled away from her, sitting on the edge of the bed, trying to regain some control.

Sterling glanced down, chagrined to find himself hard again, still wanting more of this strange girl. And he noticed the blood. "You're a virgin," he said.

She giggled. "Not anymore."

He was a gentleman. She was an aristocrat. He could do no less. He turned and met her eyes. They no longer burned with fire, but with a contented smolder that darkened the emerald color to almost black.

Sterling reached for her hand. "Will you marry me?"

Three

JASMINA WOKE THE NEXT MORNING WITH HER bedclothes tangled about her. When she remembered her erotic shadow dreams she felt her face heat, and she quickly scrambled from bed, plunging her hands into the washbowl and splashing her cheeks. She prayed she would never have to look upon the face of the Duke of Hagersham again.

She'd composed herself by the time her maid came to help her dress. Jasmina chose the most demure morning attire, a rose gown with a prim neckline made even more modest by burgundy ruching. The long sleeves had a puffy gauze bouffant style that hid the entire shape of her arms and numerous flounces to disguise the rest of her shapely figure.

Jasmina stared in her mirror and grimaced. She looked even more like a doll in the dress, but at least she appeared every bit the prim and proper young lady. Now all she had to do was clear those shadows from her memory.

She made her way downstairs to the breakfast room, suspecting she'd be the only one up this early.

Her parents and aunt had probably returned from the queen's ball just a few hours ago.

She was shocked to find Aunt Ettie waiting for her at the table, dressed in her best walking gown.

"Goodness, Aunt," said Jasmina. "What are you doing up this early?"

Her aunt raised her head, and Jasmina started at the woman's haggard face.

Jasmina's heart flipped and she forced herself to ladylike calm. "What's happened?"

"I don't know. Tell me that you finished your errand early last night and came to the ball afterwards?"

"Of course I wasn't at the ball—Aunt, what do you mean?"

"Not here." Aunt Ettie rose on shaky legs, handing Jasmina one of her old bonnets. "We must talk before your parents see you. I've had Cook pack us a breakfast basket and the coach is waiting." She grabbed Jasmina's hand and hauled her through the entrance hall and onto the front step before Jasmina had a chance to protest.

"I will come along willingly," Jasmina said as her aunt practically shoved her into the phaeton, "but please, Aunt, with a little decorum."

Aunt Ettie squared her shoulders, settled gracefully into her seat, and popped open her umbrella. "Drive on," she instructed the coachman.

As the horse plodded along the cobbled street, Jasmina opened the cloth over Cook's basket and plucked out a crumpet so light it melted on her tongue. Her stomach stopped rumbling, and she managed to turn a bright smile toward her aunt.

"I know what you're thinking, and it's not possible. The illusion I created could not have attended the ball."

"So you did go to the ball last night, Jaz?"

"I already told you I did not. You must have mistook someone else for me."

"Wearing your green silk gown? With the emerald earbobs and necklace that your mother gave you?"

Jasmina clenched her hands. Mother had given her the jewelry when she'd passed her magical testing. She would have to check her wardrobe when she got home, but she had a sinking feeling her green gown wouldn't be in there. And that her jewelry would also be missing.

Her head started to pound. How was any of this possible?

They had reached Hyde Park and the coachman took the path down Ladies' Mile, the enormous trees that lined the drive providing welcome shelter from the morning sunshine. Aunt signaled him to stop when they reached the entrance to Toadstool Garden, an unpopular area with the gentry and therefore quite private.

She ushered Jasmina along the pebbled path for a time, both absorbed with their own thoughts. Jasmina followed her aunt onto the damp grass and around fungus trunks the size of trees, the fleshy surfaces patterned with the pale colors of the rainbow. The caps shielded them from the sun like enormous umbrellas.

Aunt Ettie finally collapsed atop a smooth boulder. "Now we can talk."

Jasmina sat next to her aunt and arranged her petticoats and skirt, folded her hands calmly in her lap, and prayed for an outward appearance of serenity.

"Jaz, someone who looked exactly like you attended the queen's ball last night. Someone who had access to your wardrobe. Someone who behaved very scandalously." She arched a brow.

"I assure you that after I returned from my errand I went straight to bed," Jasmina protested. "So it is either someone else entirely, which stretches the realm of the coincidental, or my spell went wrong somehow."

Aunt stuck out her narrow chin. "I don't know much about magic, Jaz, but didn't you say your illusion wouldn't fool a royal? Or a baronet? Because they both interacted with your twin as if she were real."

Jasmina gasped. It wasn't possible! And yet her aunt wasn't given to flights of fancy. "Tell me everything that happened," she said, amazed that she managed to keep her voice steady.

"Well, I first caught sight of you—"

"Not me!"

"Yes, of course. I first saw the illusion when she was drinking with the Duke of Banshee's son, but didn't get an opportunity to approach her until she was dancing on a moonbeam with a most handsome baronet."

"A baronet?"

"Honestly, Jaz, if you keep interrupting me I shall never—shoo! Shoo, you spying little creature, shoo! Or I shall slap you with my umbrella."

Jasmina looked around in confusion. A bearded little gnome peeked around the trunk of a lavender toadstool. He tipped his pointed red hat and winked at her before disappearing into a clump of grassy wildflowers.

"The sorcerer should have known when he created a toadstool garden that it would attract gnomes,"

snapped Aunt Ettie. "We'll never eradicate the creatures from the park now."

"Are you sure this handsome man was a baronet,
Aunt?"

"Who, what? Yes, of course I'm sure. I saw him
shift into his were-self right in front of me. And I must
say, what a glorious creature!"

"But shape-shifters are immune to magic." Jasmina's
forehead creased in a frown. "He would have seen
right through her. He wouldn't have been able to hold
her in his arms and dance with her."

"Well, he did. And your twin fooled several other
people as well. Among them the Duke of Banshee and
the Crown Prince. It's why I had to speak with you
before Lucy and Horace did."

Jasmina groaned. "My parents didn't see her, did they?"

"Fortunately not. I distracted them, quite cleverly, I
might add. But they're sure to hear the rumors."

Jasmina hid her face in her hands. She was ruined.
She would be a social outcast, doomed to spend her
days alone in her home. Even if she went out, she'd be
met with cold shoulders and silent stares. She might as
well retire to the country.

Aunt Ettie put a thin arm around her. "It's not as
bad as all that. Other than a few guards and sleepy
coachmen, I'm the only one who knows you left with
him. I can say I saved you from being abducted by the
animal. Enough people saw me following the two of
you out the door."

"Not me," mumbled Jasmina.

"Yes, dear. Of course it wasn't you."

The wind snaked through the trunks of the toadstools,

bringing the smell of musty earth to Jasmina's nose. She sneezed and hoped it would cover the tears in her eyes. She caught a hint of red movement from the corner of her eye when she looked at Aunt. "It's worse than you can imagine. Something went terribly wrong for my spell to be that strong. I can't use my magic again until I find out what happened. What if Mother and Father should need me?"

"For once in your life, Jasmina Elizabeth Karlyle, think of yourself! A woman who looks exactly like you but obviously without your good character is loose among the gentry. What might she do next?"

Jasmina fought panic. "Maybe the spell will fade. But I don't think we can count on that. First I must find out what went wrong with my magic. There's nothing for it. I must go to the Hall of Mages."

"But what shall we tell them?" Aunt's face had paled to the color of fine parchment. "Surely we cannot mention why you needed to create a twin."

Jasmina surged to her feet, holding out her hand to her aunt. "We shall think of some story along the way. Didn't you say I was turning into quite the actress?"

Aunt gave her a wan smile, but took the offered hand and allowed Jasmina to lead her out of the maze of toadstools.

⁓

They arrived at the Hall of Mages in a short time, despite the press of carriages on the way there. They had managed to come up with a serviceable story to tell the head mage. Jasmina had only been to the Hall once, when she'd been tested for her magical abilities and been confirmed as her father's heir. The only requirement for inheritance was magic, regardless of gender, and she was so relieved when she'd shown enough magic to inherit her father's estates. But it had been a nerve-wracking ordeal and she'd hoped she'd never have to enter the doors of the place again.

The coachman stopped in front of the tall building and frowned at them as they departed. Aunt stared him down with a look of her own and a silent signal passed between them. The man would rue the day should he mention their trip to the master of the house.

Jasmina hoped her aunt's intimidation would work; otherwise, they'd have to think up a reason for their visit to tell her father. Astonishing, really, how two women of good moral character had gotten so skillful at evading the truth.

Aunt Ettie's eyes widened with fascination when they entered the Hall of Mages. Jasmina could feel magic seeping from the very foundations of the building, could see it curling like a cloud of multicolored smoke along the raftered ceiling, could hear it hissing and growling from behind the myriad closed doors that lined the huge entrance hall.

A massive desk that looked dwarfed in the marble-tiled entryway sat against the left wall, some pots filled with greenery across from it. A gilded staircase curved upwards to unimaginable heights, and a bank of curved doorways circled the room.

"I have come to see the master," Jasmina said to the clerk. She didn't ask for Prince Albert, although he was currently the master, since it was only proper to use the title he held within these walls.

"Do you have an appointment?" asked the novice, his eyes looking at her owlishly from behind his spectacles.

Oh dear. She hadn't thought about that. "No, sir. But you see, this is rather an emergency."

"That's what they all say," he mumbled.

"A *magical* emergency."

A loud explosion from somewhere within the bowels of the Hall rattled the inkpot on the clerk's desk. His nose wrinkled from the sulfurous odor that accompanied it. "What else is new?"

"Now see here, young man," Aunt Ettie said with a sniff. "I assure you that something evil is afoot in London, and your master will be most displeased if he finds out that you turned away the very girl who created, er, discovered the source of it."

Jasmina felt Aunt Henrietta stiffen with outrage when the clerk was not properly cowed by her dressing-down. Being around such wild magic must have given the man extraordinary strength of character. Heavens, Aunt had brought dukes to their knees.

The clerk picked up a paper and handed it to Jasmina. "Fill this out, please, describing the nature of your complaint in detail. We will notify you when the next available appointment with the master…" His eyes had strayed past her face and he stared over her left shoulder, adjusting his spectacles and squinting. "I say, did you bring that with you?"

Jasmina spun. Across the room stood a collection of oriental vases holding an assortment of plants with rustling leaves. "What?"

"It's that pesky garden gnome," hissed her aunt.

Jasmina could just make out the tip of a red pointed

hat behind the waving fronds. "It must have followed us here."

The clerk cleared his throat and rose. "This must be more serious than I thought. Please wait just a moment, miss...?"

"Karlyle. Lady Jasmina Karlyle, daughter of the Earl of Kraken."

"Yes, yes, of course." The man backed away, his eyes going from her to the potted plants. "I'll just see if the master has a moment to spare."

He practically ran from the hall, disappearing into one of the curved doorways.

"Well, I never," breathed Aunt Ettie. "What set a fire beneath his britches?"

"I have no idea. Why would he be so afraid of a little gnome?" Jasmina walked over to the pots, peering through the greenery. They'd been placed in a circle and she couldn't get behind them, so she shoved her arms between the branches and parted them. "I know you're in there, so you might as well come out. Why is that man so afraid of you?"

"Hmph. He's not afraid of me," answered a high-pitched, gravelly voice.

"Then what does he fear?"

"I smell lots of mischief around you, Lady Jaz. And I like mischief."

Jasmina frowned at his familiarity. The little creature had no right—

"Ouch," she yelped, yanking her arms out of the plants. The little beast had pinched her! Hard enough to bring tears to her eyes. "Why, you nasty—"

"Not advisable," said the clerk, appearing suddenly

beside her. "Ignore him if you can, or he'll just make your life even more miserable."

"What, why?" demanded Jasmina, still blinking away the tears.

The clerk's face softened a moment, staring into her eyes. "Gnomes are attracted to chaos and those who create it. It appears that you are headed into disaster, miss, and he knows it. That's why I'm granting you the audience you requested. If a gnome is hounding you, your magical problem must be dire indeed. Just try not to let the creature make matters worse."

"Oh, dear." Could matters get any worse?

The clerk held out his arm. "The master will see you now."

Jasmina took a deep breath, squared her shoulders, and lifted her chin. She smiled at the clerk and calmly took his arm. He eyed her with renewed appreciation.

"Leave my niece alone, you little pest," Aunt Ettie said, smacking her closed umbrella at the plants. An evil giggle answered her and she sniffed, following close behind Jasmina and her escort. "There should be a warning sign at Toadstool Garden about pesky gnomes following one home."

The clerk led them through a curved doorway and down a labyrinth of corridors lined with stout doors that muffled mysterious sounds. When they reached a door carved with ancient runes of powerful wards, he ushered them into the chamber, then shut them inside.

Jasmina blinked at the man who sat in a leather chair in front of a banked fire. Prince Albert was handsome in a soft, elegant way. Jasmina curtsied, followed a second later by her aunt. She felt surprised by the size of the room; she'd imagined something much grander. It looked like her father's study, full of books and scrolls and well-worn furniture.

"Please rise." The prince's voice was cultured and lightly accented. "Will you have some tea?"

She exchanged a glance with her aunt. Tea with His Royal Highness. Or rather, the Master of the Hall of Mages. She didn't know which title intimidated her more.

Her chin rose a fraction higher and she nodded, taking the chair opposite him and settling daintily on the edge of it. With a calm that required all her years of practicing to maintain, she took the china cup from the servant who handed it to her.

And promptly spilled some in her lap.

The servant laughed, a growl that shook the room, and Aunt Ettie sniffed. Loudly. For the older gentleman wasn't a servant, or entirely a man, for that matter. The fangs that peeked from the corners of his mouth seemed at odds with his distinguished appearance.

A shape-shifter. The way magic seemed to stand still around him—creating a haven of calm—gave her the impression. The rumors that the prince befriended the baronets were evidently true.

The shape-shifter handed her a linen and Jasmina dabbed at the wet spot, blushing furiously.

"Forgive me," said the prince. "I should have introduced you to Sir Artemus, a most trusted confidant. He's reduced to serving me, since I trust him so fully."

The baronet nodded, his golden mane flowing across his cheeks. Aunt Henrietta stared at him with such hunger that Jasmina glared at Sir Artemus until his arrogant grin disappeared and he quit looking at her aunt as if he'd like to eat her alive.

"Yes, well," said Prince Albert, shifting in his chair.

The leather squeaked, the tea tasted sweet and sharp on Jasmina's tongue, and the smell of sulfur had faded to the comfortable scent of sandalwood. She had just started to relax when the master spoke again.

"I understand that you have a magical dilemma?"

"Yes." Jasmina forced herself not to glance at Aunt Ettie before launching into the story that they'd concocted. "You see, my parents are determined that I remain a spinster, so I can care for them in their old age." Which was the truth and an entirely common occurrence. "So when a certain… gentleman of our acquaintance wished to see me"—Jasmina lowered her eyes, as if embarrassed by the admission, when really the thought of lying to this gentle-looking man appalled her—"I created a twin of myself to fool my parents into believing me abed."

Sir Artemus grunted and the prince frowned.

"My aunt accompanied me on my clandestine meetings, of course," Jasmina hastened to add. "And I know it was wrong of me to fool my parents, but you see, I would like to have a life of my own."

The room rang with silence. A muffled pop sounded from beyond the doors. Jasmina tried again. "I wish to have a husband and children."

Aah. Both men suddenly brightened. She'd hit on the right argument, since every man knew that a woman's fondest desire would be a family of her own.

"We're not here to judge you," the prince said. "Only to help you."

Jasmina nodded calmly. "Of course. I can only tell you that when I created an illusion of myself I heard a clap of thunder and that's never happened before."

"And this illusion," Aunt Henrietta interrupted, "attended the queen's ball last night and no one realized what she was."

"Impossible," growled Sir Artemus.

"My aunt is telling the truth," countered Jasmina. "I did not attend the ball last night. When I returned home the illusion had disappeared." Oh dear. If Aunt had been at the ball, that meant Jasmina had met her imaginary lover unaccompanied... But neither of the men seemed to have noticed that particular detail, each absorbed in weightier matters.

"We must consider that she's being followed by a garden gnome," said the master, his voice suddenly ringing with the authority of a wizard. "If we consider her story along with the man who saw us earlier—"

"Sir Sterling," snarled the baronet.

"Exactly!"

"It makes a twisted kind of sense," Sir Artemus said. Jasmina's and Aunt Ettie's heads turned back and forth between the two men. Jasmina hoped they would soon explain what they were talking about, or her carefully cultivated veneer of calm would surely shatter.

"Where is he?" asked the prince.

"I'll find him," replied Sir Artemus, and he strode from the room with a grace that belied his size.

"Now, then." The master settled back in his chair, his fingers steepled under his chin. "You must tell me everything you did that day, down to the smallest detail. Something that you might have dismissed as unimportant could be essential to the problem with your spell casting."

Jasmina glanced at her aunt. Under no circumstances would she reveal her mother's secret. Not even to the Master of the Hall of Mages. So she went over the day, omitting reference to her mother, or the duchess's brooch and her stealing into the Hagersham mansion.

When she finished the prince frowned at her, the curls of hair at his ears only slightly diminishing his threatening appearance. "I'm sure you're not telling me the entire tale."

Jasmina opened her mouth to protest, but the master held up a hand.

"I don't know what you're hiding beyond an illicit love affair, but perhaps if I explain, you'll understand."

Jasmina blushed, but realized she couldn't argue if she wanted to keep her mother's secret. She sighed and let him get on with it.

The master bounced out of his chair, as if he'd held in check a restless energy and had to release it. He paced the confines of the small room as he spoke. "As an earl's daughter, your power is limited to illusions. Yet both a royal and a baronet interacted with this twin. Therefore, the illusion was so powerful we can only conclude that your spell created a real person."

Aunt gasped and Jasmina started to explain the impossibility of it, but the prince continued.

"Even a royal cannot cast such a spell. So the question is: What power can?"

Jasmina suddenly remembered the force that had tingled through her the night she'd created her twin and shivered. "Do you mean to say that someone channeled their power through me?"

"Not someone, but some*thing*." The prince collapsed in his chair. "Are you familiar with Merlin's Thirteen Relics of power?"

Jasmina frowned, vaguely remembering something...

"It's an old legend that's commonly regarded as myth," the prince continued, "and quite dismissed by most of the gentry. The most powerful sorcerer of all time, Merlin used thirteen different jewels as a focus for thirteen different spells. They are the only surviving magic that can overcome a royal's own."

"But that's dreadful," Aunt Ettie said. "If someone with ill intentions acquired one of those jewels, it would be a threat to our entire country."

The prince leaned forward. "Precisely. And that is why, madam, we value our baronets. Since they are immune to magic, they are the only ones who can protect us from these relics."

Jasmina only half listened. The Duchess of Hagersham's brooch! The burning in her thigh every time she cast a spell. The strength of her spells that evening. Could that be why she'd passed through the Hagersham wards without difficulty? But she'd left the brooch in the settee... "Could a sorcerer retain some residual power even after, um, they disposed of the relic?"

The prince smiled, but it didn't quite touch his eyes this time. "Yes. For a time. Have you cast any more spells?"

"No, thank heavens. I thought it would be best to find out what went wrong before attempting any."

"Quite wise. I presume you now remember something more of that evening that you wish to add to your story?"

Aunt Henrietta coughed. Jasmina threw her a look of reassurance. "I did have a certain brooch in my possession. But I returned it."

The prince leaned forward and grasped her hands. "It's important that we get the brooch back, Lady Jasmina. It's the only way you will be able to reverse the spell."

He seemed so concerned for her situation when his own power was threatened that she felt tempted to blurt out the entire story. But Aunt coughed again, and she hesitated. "Are you sure this is one of Merlin's Relics?"

"Quite."

"Can you help me get it back?"

The prince squeezed her hands. "Where is it?"

Jasmina glanced at her aunt. "I returned it to the Duchess of Hagersham."

The master leaned back in his chair with a smile, as if now that he'd been given that vital piece of information he could relax. "Hagersham. Now that's interesting. Lady Jasmina, you must say nothing of this to anyone, for there are many factions in our kingdom who long to get their hands on a relic."

Jasmina blinked. "Of course."

"You will have a better chance of reversing the spell if you find the double you created. Otherwise, I'm not sure if it will work, although of course, you could always try."

Jasmina took a deep breath. "I see. But how will I ever locate her? My illusion went to great lengths to avoid my aunt." Despite what the master said, she couldn't consider her spell a real person. *She* was Jasmina Karlyle, and the other woman a mere copy... or something.

They were interrupted by a knock at the door, and the prince smiled at her. "I think I may have just the man to help you."

Jasmina spun, pulling her hands out of the prince's warm grasp. Sir Artemus entered, followed by another man. A man who took her breath away. Thick, silky black hair framed a strong angular face, and his eyes were of such a deep blue that she felt she could drown in them. Why did she feel as if she knew this man?

"Sir Sterling," said the prince, rising from his chair and nodding at the black-haired man. "May I introduce..."

But he never finished his sentence, because the most astonishing thing happened. Sir Sterling's face lit up as soon as he saw Jasmina.

"Jaz," he cried, and vaulted across the room.

He lifted Jasmina to her feet, wrapped his muscular arms around her, and covered her mouth with his in a kiss quite unlike anything she'd ever experienced. For a moment she responded, melting in his arms as if it were the most natural thing to do. She forgot everything but the feel of his warm lips, the spicy scent of his skin, the heady taste of his mouth.

And then Jasmina realized she was kissing a complete stranger. She pushed away from him and as soon as he relaxed his hold, she slapped his face.

Four

"HOW DARE YOU?" SNAPPED HIS WIFE.

Sterling blinked, staring at the tiny woman before him. She wore a pink gown covered in puffy ruffles that made her look just like one of the china dolls from his sister's childhood collection. Jaz looked genuinely offended by his kiss. Sterling knew he should have refrained from such a public display of affection, but as usual, he couldn't seem to control himself around her.

"My apologies," he said with a sweeping bow.

"I should think so," sniffed the older woman who stood next to Jaz. Sterling frowned. She looked exactly like the gray-haired woman he'd helped Jaz escape from at the ball last night.

The master insinuated himself between Sterling and his wife. "Please allow me to introduce Lady Jasmina Karlyle, daughter of the Earl of Kraken, and her aunt, Miss Henrietta Forster."

Both women gave him a curt nod, and Sterling started to get an ugly feeling inside his chest. Jaz was treating him as if she'd never seen him before. When he woke this morning to find her gone, he had suspected that she'd run back home to her family. It appeared that he'd been right.

Sterling thought he'd be considerate and let her have some time alone with them before he showed up at their mansion and produced their signed marriage document. Evidently, that had been a mistake. It looked as if her family had convinced Jaz he wasn't the man for her. Was that why she was here now, to appeal to the prince for an annulment?

Sterling grinned. She didn't have a chance in hell of getting rid of him that easily. But it would be amusing to watch her squirm for a bit. She deserved it, for leaving him this morning without even a goodbye.

"Please, everyone take a seat," said the master, gesturing at the empty chairs around the fireplace. "We have a great deal to discuss."

Jaz and her aunt sat down across from Prince Albert, but the were-lion, Sir Artemus, stood in a shadowed corner of the room. Sterling picked up the empty chair by the prince and dragged it over next to Jaz, pushing it so close to her that he smashed the ruffles on her gown.

His wife frowned with annoyance and gathered up her skirts with such an air of injured propriety that Sterling smiled down at her. He lost himself in her emerald eyes for a moment, recalling the way they had darkened when he pleasured her the night before. It took all of his willpower not to kiss her again.

She acted such the proper lady when in company and a complete wanton in private. When she licked her lips and couldn't seem to take her eyes off of his mouth, he realized that no matter what influence her parents had tried to assert over her, they had failed. Jaz almost trembled with desire for him.

The prince cleared his throat. "I say, Sir Sterling. Lady Jasmina is not who you think she is."

Sterling grinned. "Isn't she?"

The darling girl leaned toward him, as if drawn by some invisible string to his mouth. If she got any closer Sterling would damn propriety and kiss her again.

Miss Forster huffed and grabbed Jaz's arm, yanking her away from him. His wife's eyes flared with annoyance, then something close to terror as she met his gaze. The wickedness that had shone in her emerald eyes last night had been replaced with a confused innocence; as if she couldn't understand her own reactions to him.

He was acting like a callow youth in the throes of his first passion. But blast, that's exactly how he felt. Sterling looked away from her with a sigh of reluctance and focused on the prince's genteel features.

"As a baronet, I'm sure you're familiar with Merlin's Relics," said the master. "Although we encourage the rest of the aristocracy to view them as nothing but a legend, I'm sure you were told the truth when you acquired your title."

Sterling shook the hair off his forehead. "It's not something that my father thought would ever affect me."

"Your father was wrong. The relics have already affected you. The odor you described on the woman you met last night—that's how you baronets sense the power of a relic. It can sometimes be so strong that it's quite unpleasant. Isn't that correct, Sir Artemus?"

The man growled an agreement.

"It's because of your animal senses," continued the master. "So much keener than a human's, you can literally sniff out the presence of a relic. This woman you call Jaz is a part of this dangerous magic."

Some of the prince's words seemed to be filtering past Sterling's obsession with Jaz and into his brain. Why did the master refer to his wife as if she wasn't sitting in this room? As if the woman he'd met last night had been a different person…

Sterling flared his nostrils. No, she smelled like Jaz. A faint perfume of jasmine and some delicate musk that grew stronger with her arousal. He didn't know what the prince was hinting at, other than that his wife was somehow tangled up with a relic that could be a threat to the Crown. Was that why she looked so frightened? Had she gotten caught up in something that she shouldn't have?

Sterling felt himself shift, a brief flash of stallion rage that made the hair on his head swirl around his face. "If she's in any trouble, I'll take care of her. I'll fix whatever's wrong."

His wife's reaction to his statement was astonishing. She gasped and rose to her feet in one fluidly composed movement. "I will have you know, sir, that I am quite capable of taking care of myself. I certainly don't need anyone trying to take control of my life."

Sterling couldn't help grinning. Her voice and words contrasted so strongly with her perfectly bowed lips and wide-eyed innocence that he almost laughed at her. But the only outward display of her obvious annoyance at him was an increased rise and fall of her bosom, and despite the layers of material she'd covered herself in, he couldn't help notice the swell of her breasts.

Sterling's smile vanished. His memory too readily filled in the rest. One would never guess that her skirts hid such shapely legs. Sterling's gaze traveled up her body, remembering the lush curves of her bottom, the beauty mark on her left hip, the fullness of her breasts in his hands. Her nipples were the precise shade of her gown, and so sensitive that he barely had to flick them with his tongue for her to groan with pleasure.

His wife's eyes darkened to deep emerald green, her pink tongue darting out of her mouth to sweep the fullness of her lips. Sterling wanted her again so badly that he thought he might go mad for the touch of her. He held out his hand. Miss Forster gasped and jumped up from her chair, forcibly holding back her niece as Jaz tried to take a step toward him.

"May I suggest," growled Sir Artemus, "that you explain more quickly, Your Royal Highness?"

"Yes, yes, of course," agreed the master. "It's fascinating though, isn't it?"

Sir Artemus grunted.

"Ladies, do sit down," said the prince.

Miss Forster sniffed and managed to look indignant while she pushed Jaz back into her chair. But before she sat as well, she turned to Sterling and gave him a quick wink before resuming her injured expression. Sterling didn't know quite what to make of that. But he didn't have a chance to register the thought before the prince spoke again.

"This woman," he said, nodding his head at Jaz, "is not the same woman you met last night."

Sterling glanced over at Sir Artemus, and the shape-shifter nodded, as if to confirm that the prince knew exactly what he spoke of.

"You see," continued Prince Albert, "Lady Jasmina crafted a spell last night. An illusion of herself. A twin, you might say."

Every muscle in Sterling's body turned to ice.

"She wasn't aware that she had one of Merlin's Relics in her possession. It made her illusion quite strong."

"I'm immune to magic," Sterling said through gritted teeth.

"We believe," the prince explained, "that the spell crafted into the relic makes the caster's spell quite real." He stood and walked over to his desk, waving his hand over a diamond paperweight. The glow of the jewel faded to blue-black and a sapphire now rested in its place. "Although I used magic to change the composition of this stone, it is as real to you as the diamond was, is it not?"

Sterling nodded.

The master wearily moved back to his chair. "Only dukes and royals can change actual matter, and it saps a duke's magical powers for so long that they hesitate to do it." He exhaled. "Even a royal finds it draining. And no one can alter matter enough to create a living being. Except perhaps with the aid of one of Merlin's Relics. We are grateful that Lady Jasmina did not attempt to create the illusion of a dragon." He smiled at Jaz but she didn't return it. Although she stared straight at the prince, Sterling could feel her watching him from the corner of her eye.

"This is only a guess based on the evidence

presented before me," the prince went on. "Once we have the relic in our possession, we can experiment to learn its true purpose. In the meantime we would like you to assist Lady Jasmina in finding her twin."

Sterling carefully rose from his chair. Sir Artemus pushed himself away from the wall with a casual indifference that didn't fool Sterling for a moment.

No wonder Jaz seemed so confused about so many things. She wouldn't, or couldn't, tell Sterling her full name, yet she'd signed the marriage document with such ease that it seemed to surprise her. Did the habits of the woman she'd been copied from come to her more easily than the memories?

Bloody hell, he was starting to believe all this.

"You should have told me this before I met *her*," snapped Sterling, nodding at Lady Jasmina, who sat so primly upright in her chair.

"I do apologize," said the prince. "But we had to be sure that you were both telling the truth."

Ah, now Sterling could see a bit of Jaz's fire in Lady Jasmina's eyes. They sparkled with indignation that she could be thought a liar. He shook the hair off his forehead and stared at the woman he'd thought was his wife. She was a complete stranger to him, and yet he knew every curve of her body, the taste of her skin, where to touch her to make her cry out with pleasure.

What exactly had he married?

"How can this illusion be a real person?" asked Sterling.

The prince spread out his hands. "We can't be sure that she is."

"So what will you do about her?"

"I will reverse the spell," replied Lady Jasmina.

"The master seems to think that I won't be able to do so unless the illusion is part of the spell casting."

Sterling scowled. "But what will happen to Jaz?"

Lady Jasmina blinked at him. "She will go back to wherever she came from."

Sterling felt a sudden urge to shake her composure. "What do *you* think Jaz is, my lady? Did you split yourself into two? As she gains more of her memory, will that lessen you? What if you become weaker as she grows stronger? Perhaps you will be the one to disappear when you reverse your spell."

Finally her calm broke, and Sterling flushed with shame. Her sweetly curved lower lip trembled, and he fought the need to apologize.

"She's only a spell gone awry. You will have me thinking that I'm not the real me," she whispered.

"Sir Sterling," interrupted the master, "I take it that you came to know this illusion, or twin… whatever do we call her?"

"Jaz," muttered Sterling.

"Only my family calls me that," interjected Lady Jasmina.

"Not anymore."

Sterling got caught up in her gaze again, his pity turning to anger. If she hadn't created that illusion he wouldn't be in this predicament.

The prince cleared his throat. "Well, it would be helpful if you could tell us everything you know about Jaz, Sir Sterling."

Sterling choked back a laugh. He already felt enough of a fool without announcing it to the world. "I didn't know enough to even tell them apart. And

I know nothing of Lady Jasmina to compare their characters." At least not anything he could reveal in mixed company.

"I must assume she's nothing like me," said Lady Jasmina, her back rigid and her face smoothed. She'd regained her composure so quickly that Sterling wondered how she'd come to be so good at it. True, most ladies aspired to show a serene countenance to the world. But few achieved it to her degree.

"And why is that?" Sterling asked, meeting her eyes again. It suddenly felt as if they were the only ones in the room. There were too many similarities between the way he felt with Jaz and the way he felt with this stranger. Sterling had gone from angry to confused. He never lost control of his emotions so easily.

"Because," said Lady Jasmina, her voice full of indignation, "my aunt tells me that she drank too much, flirted shamelessly, and left the ball with you—"

"With me? An animal?" Sterling lowered his voice. "I'm sure the proper Lady Jasmina would never be seen in the company of a baronet. What would all your friends say?"

"Exactly," she replied, heaving a sigh of relief that he appeared to understand. "My parents would never approve. I can only assume that the illusion I created does not have my... proper sensibilities."

"No, she doesn't," snapped Sterling. How could this snobbish girl have Jaz's lovely face and body and scent? It made him angry that he felt drawn to Lady Jasmina the same way he'd felt drawn to Jaz, his hands itching to touch her, his body aching to bury himself inside of her.

Sterling couldn't bear to be near the Lady Jasmina.

"Your Royal Highness," said Miss Forster, "if this Jaz, as she calls herself, has no morals or scruples and if we cannot reveal the circumstances of her existence... well, she may tarnish my niece's reputation beyond recovery. We must find this twin as quickly as possible."

The master smiled at Miss Forster with relief, as if grateful that the woman had interrupted the conversation between Sterling and Jasmina before it erupted into something unpleasant. "Quite right. What do you say, Sir Sterling? Will you help Lady Jasmina find this twin?"

Sterling backed away from the group around the fireplace, folded his arms across his chest, and slid right into the attitude he'd used to handle his father. He saw Sir Artemus raise his brows in appreciation, the prince frown with displeasure, and Lady Jasmina and her aunt blink in confusion.

This morning he'd wanted nothing more than to see Jaz again. Now he didn't even know what, or who, she was. He'd married a creature created by magic, and now he couldn't even be sure if what he'd felt for her had been real. "I think not. My first priority is to find my missing sister, not some foolish debutante's missing ill-cast illusion."

Lady Jasmina gasped. Sterling recognized the familiar spark of fire in her eyes and looked away.

"You said yourself that they all might be connected by magic," said the prince. "I believe that by helping Lady Jasmina, you will also be closer to finding your sister."

Sterling agreed, but he couldn't tell his prince that he felt confused when he was near Lady Jasmina. He had the signature of an illusion on his marriage document. What did that signify?

Sterling shrugged. "What would Lady Jasmina's parents say if she were seen keeping company with me? I don't see how I can be of help to her if my very presence causes her family such... distress."

At least Lady Jasmina had the grace to blush. But that meddling aunt of hers piped up again. "I can arrange it so that you two can meet."

Sterling carefully schooled his expression. "Perhaps now would be the time for you to explain why Lady Jasmina created an illusion of herself in the first place."

"Frankly, sir, that's none of your business," Lady Jasmina said stiffly.

Both women's postures had become so rigid that Sterling couldn't decide who was tougher. He felt an inkling of admiration for them.

"If I recall, Sir Sterling," the prince said with dancing eyes, "you wanted my assistance in finding your sister. I will make the funds available to you provided that you help Lady Jasmina with her own missing person. Are we agreed?"

Sterling frowned. For some reason the master wanted him working with Lady Jasmina. He wondered if it was just to keep the girl out of trouble. Yet the prince seemed to find Sterling's interaction with Lady Jasmina amusing. He doubted if he'd get a straight answer by asking, and instead satisfied himself with knowing he'd have the funds to aid in Angel's search.

"Agreed."

Lady Jasmina narrowed her eyes. Miss Forster smiled with satisfaction.

The prince nodded as if he'd never doubted Sterling's eventual agreement. "Now then, Lady Jasmina. Before I allow you to leave, we must see if any residual relic-magic is still interfering with your spells."

"Yes, of course."

"Let's keep it small, shall we? Just in case."

Lady Jasmina nodded and tapped a finger against her rounded cheek. She stole a glance at Sterling and smiled wickedly. Sterling's gut flipped as he recognized that look. Jaz had given him the exact same smile as she'd lowered her head to his…

Before Sterling's body could respond to the memory, the largest horsefly he'd ever seen buzzed into his face and tried to attack his nose. A magical creation, it couldn't even touch him and yet still he shook his head and snorted, his hair slapping his face. He hated flies.

Lady Jasmina laughed, a tinkling sound that made him think she might not be so different from Jaz after all.

The prince cast a counter-spell. "I can see through the illusion," he said. "What about you, Sir Artemus?"

"Aye."

"So can I," snapped Sterling. "She just caught me off guard."

Lady Jasmina's green eyes twinkled and with a wave of her hand, the annoying fly disappeared.

"It looked quite real to me," Miss Forster said to Sterling with a sympathetic tone. He frowned at her. Of course it did; she was neither a royal nor a baronet. But what bothered him most was her tone, as if she tried to make herself his ally. Blast her, why would the woman do that?

The prince rose from his chair. "I'm sure you'll understand that Sir Artemus and I must devise a plan on how to get the relic back. Would you mind seeing the ladies out to their coach, Sir Sterling?"

He had half a mind to refuse. But that would seem plain surly, and he'd already made a poor enough impression on his prince for one day. With a bow to the ladies, Sterling opened the door of the room and ushered them into the hall. A flash of red disappeared around the corner and out of curiosity he hurried to catch up with it.

When they turned the corner to enter another hall, again he saw a flash of red.

"Sir Sterling," panted Miss Forster, "please slow down."

He caught the look of satisfaction on Lady Jasmina's face and slowed his pace. She expected him to act like a rude boor and his disregard for their smaller strides fit with her opinion of him. Sterling tried not to care what she thought of him but found himself apologizing anyway.

"I beg your pardon. But every time we turn a corner, I could swear that I see a flash of red in front of us. It's probably just an errant spell of some apprentice wizard."

The two ladies exchanged glances.

"Ah. So you know what it is?"

Lady Jasmina stuck her nose in the air but her aunt deigned to answer. "It appears that a garden gnome has decided to pester my niece."

Sterling burst out laughing, surprising himself. It had been so long since he'd managed to laugh about anything.

"It's not funny," snapped Jasmina.

"On the contrary. It's a lot funnier than a fly buzzing about my nose. Do you have any idea what it means to have a gnome trailing you?"

Jasmina sniffed. She didn't do it as well as her aunt; somehow it lacked the dignified disdain that the older woman infused the gesture with. "It's nothing. He's just taken a liking to me."

Sterling continued to chuckle while they made their way out to the drive. He sobered a bit, though, when the horses started to shy as he helped the women into their carriage. If he hadn't had such a firm grip on Jasmina's arm she would have stumbled and injured herself. As it was, when the coach lurched he was able to tug her backwards into his arms.

The bushes next to the drive trembled and Sterling could swear he heard a tiny cackle of glee. He had no doubt that the gnome had made the horses startle. But the woman in his arms distracted his attention thoroughly. She felt so right, so completely a part of him, just like Jaz had felt in his arms. For a moment he held her, his arms wrapped around her tiny corseted waist, her head nestled against his chest. He lowered his nose and breathed in the scent of her.

And suddenly he didn't care that Jaz might be nothing more than an illusion made real. He wanted to see her again. To hold her in his arms and find out if his feelings for her were real. Who could say that the woman he now held wasn't the imposter?

"Let me go," said Lady Jasmina.

Sterling snorted and loosened his hold. Lady Jasmina spun and tried to look him in the eye. Even standing on her tiptoes she couldn't manage the feat and had to settle for craning her neck to look up at him.

"I don't care what the master said," she huffed. "I made this mess and I can get myself out of it. I certainly don't need your interference. And keep your hands off of me."

Then her face smoothed over into that maddening look of serenity, and she spun and scrambled into the carriage without further assistance from him.

Sterling didn't need a garden gnome to know she was heading for trouble. If she didn't remind him so much of Jaz and if he wasn't so desperate to find his sister, he might have left her to her own devices.

Miss Forster wasted no time in giving the coachman instructions to drive on, but she winked at him as they drove away. Sterling realized it was the second time Miss Forster had made that gesture at him. And he still couldn't figure out why. He shifted into his were-form and followed their carriage, determined to keep an eye on the prim and proper Lady Jasmina.

He snapped at a fly that ventured too close to his muzzle. He would never understand women, real or illusionary.

Five

AS THE CARRIAGE ROLLED ALONG PARK LANE, JASMINA popped open her lace umbrella and tried to bury herself under it. Overnight her life had become a disaster, and she desperately tried to think of some way to regain control. And Aunt Ettie wasn't helping.

"He's gorgeously tall, isn't he?"

"Who?" Jasmina replied, staring at the fine mansions they passed without really seeing them.

"Sir Sterling, of course. Such a fine figure of a man—"

"He's a baronet! That makes him only part man."

"Tush, tush. He's more of a man than most of the gentlemen of our acquaintance." The carriage hit a pothole, and Aunt Ettie clutched at her hat, then leaned forward to scold the driver.

Jasmina breathed a sigh of relief. She didn't want to hear about Sir Sterling's finer attributes when she was all too painfully aware of them. It had taken all her self-control to recover from that kiss... and as soon as she had a quiet moment to herself she vowed to relive it. Not that she had any romantic notions toward the arrogant Sir Sterling. Certainly not. It was only that she'd never, ever been kissed like that before. Oh, she'd let a boy steal a kiss or two. But that kiss of Sir Sterling's had been what she'd always imagined a kiss to be like and more. It had been so consuming and intimate, a lover's kiss that spoke of a familiarity with her person.

"Jaz," said Aunt Ettie. "You haven't heard a word I've said."

Jasmina narrowed her eyes beneath the brim of her umbrella. "Please don't call me that."

"Call you—why, I've called you Jaz since you were a baby."

"I know. But that's what *she* calls herself."

"Oh, dear. Yes, I quite understand. It's a bit of a muddle, isn't it? But I'm sure the prince and Sir Sterling will figure it out. Oh, look, the Marquess of Faerlinn is riding his elephant. Such a majestic animal." Aunt Ettie waved at the couple seated in the howdah on the elephant's back.

Marquesses had the power to transfer objects, and Jasmina wondered which prince of India was missing his transportation. Personally she thought the carriage a bit overdone, tented with silks and encrusted with gems. And the gait of an elephant was so ponderous, lacking the smooth prancing gait of a horse. Of course, she'd always had a fondness for horses since she was a little girl. It's why she'd become best friends with Ellen; their mutual infatuation with the creatures had brought them together to spend hours playing in the schoolroom with their collection of china horses.

"Wait until you see his stallion-form."

Jasmina looked at Aunt Ettie, whose chatter she'd

ignored until she heard her thoughts echoed with the mention of a horse. "Whose?"

"My dear, I've never seen you so distracted before. Why, Sir Sterling's of course!"

Jasmina gritted her teeth. Aunt was usually the most practical-minded of women. Whatever had gotten into her to gush over a man? It was true that they didn't often meet shape-shifters among their social circle, and Sir Sterling was the most handsome man she'd ever seen in her life. Sir Artemus was splendid-looking as well. Perhaps all shape-shifters were handsome so that they could get wives.

"Really, dear," continued Aunt, "he's a magnificent, powerful animal. I'm sure that's why—"

"Aunt."

"—Sir Artemus treated him so respectfully. I think even a lion would have a difficult time taking down such a beast—"

"Aunt Ettie."

"—in a fight. Not that I could even imagine such an encounter, of course, or even want to—"

"Aunt Henrietta!"

Aunt's brows lowered and she stuck out her chin. "There's no need to shout."

"I'm sorry. But I would rather not hear any more about Sir Sterling or his were-form. I would rather forget about him. And get him out of my life as quickly as I can."

Aunt Ettie waved at an acquaintance in a passing carriage, then turned her sharp green eyes on Jasmina. "Really? Then I must have completely misunderstood your reaction when he kissed you."

Jasmina felt the blood rush to her face. "You can't seriously think I might be attracted to a baronet? Mother and Father would never approve, even if they wanted me to marry, which they don't. None of my friends would find him even remotely acceptable—oh, this is ridiculous. I will never even see the man again."

Aunt sniffed. "What do you mean?"

"I mean that I plan to solve my own problems, as usual. Without the assistance of the baronet."

The carriage slowed to a stop in front of Karlyle House. Jasmina didn't wait for the footman to help her out. She flew up the front steps just as the butler opened the door.

"Jaz—Jasmina Karlyle," called her aunt. "Whatever do you mean?"

But Jasmina didn't answer. Fortunately, the down-stairs maid waited for her inside the door, complaining that Lady Kraken had requested turtle soup for dinner and that Cook didn't have the ingredients, turtle being so dear, and what were they to do?

Jasmina squared her shoulders and smiled. Now, here was a situation she could control. She sailed into the kitchen, instructing Cook on how to make mock turtle soup. While she was there, another house emergency arose, and then another. By the time Jasmina finished with the household staff, it was time to change for dinner.

She only experienced one bad moment during the meal.

"I had the oddest conversation today," said her mother.

Jasmina lost the grip on her soupspoon and it

clattered back into her bowl. She exchanged a look with Aunt Ettie.

"What was that, darling?" Father inquired. He exuded the polished air of authority common to the aristocracy. His chestnut hair had just the right touch of gray streaks to make him look distinguished, and his brown eyes usually looked distracted, his thoughts primarily focused on new spells to show his fellows at his club.

"Lady Hatter mentioned that she'd seen Jasmina at the queen's ball last night. I told her it was impossible, since Jaz had stayed home with the headache."

"Why is that so odd?" asked Father.

"She kept insisting it was Jasmina. I had to tell her repeatedly that she must have mistaken someone else for our daughter. She was so persistent."

Jasmina noticed that Aunt Ettie sat frozen in her chair too, her eyes staring at the ugly epergne that graced the center of the table. Chubby-faced cherubs held up the candles with their hands, satyrs frolicked in relief around the base, and wilted flowers drooped from the brass cups.

"This is marvelous soup," Lady Kraken said into the silence. "I woke up this morning with such a craving for it."

Jasmina let out a gust of breath and picked up her spoon, noting that Aunt Ettie suddenly became animated as well.

"Where did you manage to find the turtle, Lucy?" Aunt Ettie asked. "It's so rare in the market these days."

Mother smiled rather mysteriously and Jasmina had to stifle her own grin, smothering the flush of pride at making her mother content. The small triumph also gave her the smidgen of confidence she needed to carry out her task this evening. She excused herself from the table before dessert, which might have been a mistake, because Aunt Ettie eyed her suspiciously as she left the room.

Jasmina hurried up the stairs. Finally, she'd be alone to think about that kiss. Her steps slowed and her eyes became unfocused. Her parents had never planned for her to marry, content to have her inherit the title and then let it pass to someone else with an earl's level of magic, allowing Jasmina to care for her mother and father in their old age. She hadn't given it another thought. None of the boys in her social circle had interested her and the few kisses she'd allowed them to steal hadn't changed her mind.

But today... Jasmina shivered, clutching the mahogany handrail of the stairs. He'd possessed her with his mouth, body and soul, until she didn't know which way was up. If that was what it felt like to have a lover—a husband—then she might be missing out on more than she could imagine.

She stared at her white knuckles and relaxed her grip, letting her palm slip along the smooth surface of the rail until she reached the second floor. She told herself to stop being foolish. She could never be attracted to a baronet, even if he kissed her breath away and had the bluest eyes she'd ever seen. Besides, he'd thought he was kissing her illusion, so he hadn't even really been kissing her. Or had he? What, exactly, had Merlin's Relic created with her spell?

Jasmina went into her room and closed the door

behind her. What if the illusion was really a part of her, as Sir Sterling had suggested? Not a duplicate, but one person split into two? She didn't feel any different. Didn't feel as though a part of her was missing. But what if that changed with time?

It didn't matter, she assured herself, beginning to empty the drawers of her dressing table. In a few hours she would set the matter to rights, and instead of questioning everything that she knew, her life would be back to normal. She would be in complete control again, and the memory of Sir Sterling's kiss would fade like a disturbing dream.

Aunt Ettie tapped on the door and slipped into the room. She stood quietly for a few moments before she finally spoke. "We are going next door to play charades with Lord and Lady Wiccens. I thought you might wish to join us to display your acting skills, but I see that you have other plans."

Jasmina looked up from her bed where jars and hairpins and scarves and hair combs lay scattered. She'd arranged her items by color the last time she'd needed to think, but this time she'd decided to organize them by category. Jasmina carefully placed another folded scarf in the drawer she'd chosen for them.

"You're right, as usual," replied Jasmina. "I plan on rearranging my room this evening."

Aunt Ettie sniffed. "And then after that?"

Jasmina widened her eyes in complete innocence. "I shall go to bed."

"Hmph. The last time you organized your room was after your father scolded your mother because dinner was late to the table."

"It was my fault. I should have remembered that it was Cook's day off—"

"That's not the point," interrupted Aunt. "My point is that you always rearrange something when you're upset. So, are you going to tell me what you plan to do? I will be ever so annoyed if you keep me out of it."

Jasmina couldn't help but smile at the grin that softened her aunt's sharp features. "We have always confided in one another, haven't we?"

Aunt's emerald eyes lit up. She rang for the servant and told her to inform Lord and Lady Kraken that she would not be joining them this evening. With a swish of her skirts she sat next to Jasmina to help sort.

"Now, what are you planning? You said earlier that you will never see Sir Sterling again and I can't imagine how you can arrange that, with the prince practically forcing him to help you."

Inwardly Jasmina groaned with relief. "You shan't try to stop me? Or carry on about how handsome Sir Sterling is?"

"My dear, I only want what's best for you."

"It would be best if I never married so that I can continue to take care of Mother and Father."

Aunt Ettie blinked innocently. "Whoever said a thing about marriage, I ask you? It just seemed that you might be smitten with the baronet."

Jasmina tried to think of something negative about Sir Sterling's appearance. She found it difficult. "Did you see the shabbiness of his clothing? I assure you, I am not."

"Of course you're not," Aunt hastily agreed.

"Besides, I have decided to take matters into my own hands. I'm going to get back the brooch and do a reversal spell before that illusion can do any more harm."

Aunt poked herself with one of the hairpins she'd been sorting. "But the prince said he would send his spies to recover the relic."

"I hope to beat them to it."

"But why?"

Jasmina rose from the bed and paced the room. "The prince said they would have to experiment with it first. Do you truly think they'll allow me to cast any spell until they're sure what would happen? And how long will that take?"

In her agitation, Jasmina tripped over a rug and caught her balance by clutching the edge of her washing stand. "The illusion I created obviously has none of my morals—you *saw* the way Sir Sterling kissed me." Her knuckles whitened. "And the prince said I can tell no one of this. What if this Jaz person does more than kiss a shape-shifter? How will I explain it to Mother and Father?" She shook her head, resuming her course about the room. "No, I cannot afford for the illusion to exist for one more minute. I must try to get rid of her tonight."

Aunt Ettie's head had been swinging back and forth, following Jasmina's stomping. "I have never seen you so—well, you certainly have good reason to be—but what about your twin? Didn't the prince say the illusion also had to be present for the reversal spell to work?"

"He said he wasn't sure. But I have to at least try. Will you help me?"

Aunt Ettie rose and enfolded Jasmina in a warm hug. "Of course I— Good heavens, did you see that?"

Jasmina spun. "What?"

"A flash of red atop your wardrobe."

"It can't be," whispered Jasmina.

"How on earth did he follow us through the streets?" Jasmina groaned. "You spying little… we know you're up there. You might as well show yourself." She was shocked when the gnome actually complied.

He swaggered out from behind some boxes to the edge of the wardrobe and sat, hanging his enormously large bare feet over the side. His eyes looked like huge brown marbles beneath bushy brows of the same color. A cone-shaped red hat covered his hair, but his beard and mustache were the same color as his brows, which surprised Jasmina, for most of the garden gnomes she'd seen looked like old men with gray hair. His ears looked almost as large as his feet and when he smiled, his eyes twinkled mischievously.

"Why don't you go home?" Jasmina asked.

He shrugged, his red vest crinkling with the movement, threatening to spill out the pipe stuck in the pocket of it. "It's more fun with you. Shall we go steal something?"

Jasmina's mouth opened and closed. He was right though. For the first time, she'd be stealing instead of returning something.

"That's certainly none of your business," interjected Aunt Ettie.

"Hey, I think it's a good plan."

Which made Jasmina wonder about the wisdom of it. "What's your name?"

"Nuisance."

"And I suppose you have brothers named Mischief and Chaos and—oh, never mind. There shall be no reason for you to follow me after tonight. Everything will be taken care of and you can go back to your fungus patch. So you might as well leave right now." Jasmina walked over to the window and opened it. "Go on, shoo."

He started to whistle.

Aunt Ettie looked around for the nearest umbrella.

"If you don't stop pestering me," Jasmina threatened, "I shall conjure an illusion of the ladies of The Garden Club, and they shall tell you why your kind should be banned from every flower show in London."

The whistling stopped abruptly on what sounded like choking. Ah, she'd come up with the perfect thing to frighten him away with.

"Even if you turn yourself to stone," continued Jasmina, "you won't be able to block out their shrill voices." She rose and opened the window, hoping that she was right and he could still hear everything in that form. "They will chatter incessantly about how your kind detracts from their flower displays. They will discuss in minute detail the silliness of your clothes, the size of your feet, not to mention—"

Nuisance scrambled down from the wardrobe, using the carvings of the wood as a ladder, and bolted out the window. Jasmina slammed it behind him.

Then she immediately felt ashamed. He was such a cute little thing. He'd probably been lonely in that mushroom garden, and it seemed like he needed a friend…

"Don't you dare," warned Aunt Ettie. "He's a troublemaker through and through, and you've got enough problems as it is."

Jasmina shrugged and sat back on the bed. She traced the raised designs of the counterpane with one finger, going over and over the starlike jasmine flowers.

"I suppose you're right," she agreed. "It wouldn't do if Nuisance followed me tonight."

Jasmina went back to organizing the contents of her dressing table, Aunt Ettie helping and occasionally gossiping about some minor indiscretion of one of the members of their social circle, but Jasmina barely listened. She felt horribly guilty about her break-in tonight and couldn't help feeling that now she was officially a thief.

When Aunt began to yawn, Jasmina rose and pulled out her black costume, Aunt Ettie helping her with the stays of her corset and the buttons of her dress. When Jasmina finished rubbing her face with soot, she faced Aunt. "I cannot face the thought of casting another illusion of myself. If we stuff the bed with pillows, do you think you can manage to keep my maid out of my room?"

"It's risky… but I think I can manage it for one night."

Jasmina smiled, gratitude welling in her chest. "Thank you, Aunt."

Jasmina gave her aunt a hug and then cast her "don't-notice-me" spell, escaping the house using her cat illusion. She followed the same streets that she'd taken last time she visited Hagersham House.

Jasmina suddenly stopped. Had she heard an echo of her footsteps? Cautiously she took a few steps, and then stopped again. Something crashed behind her. It sounded like something wooden falling and splintering, but she didn't wait to find out. She broke into a run, her feet flying over the cobblestones.

Jasmina clipped the side of a wooden box holding an ornamental tree and stumbled. Someone, or something, was following her. This time she could clearly hear the echo of footsteps. Only they sounded strange, as if the person had clogs on their feet.

Could it be Nuisance? But he'd had the tough soles of someone who went barefoot all the time. Yet he could be making that noise just to frighten her. Or maybe it was one of the master's spies, sent to keep an eye on her.

Jasmina ran faster, darting between two buildings and through a mews, until she thought she'd lost her pursuer. She stopped to catch her breath, supporting herself with one hand on a wrought-iron fence. She pushed her other hand into her side in an effort to relieve a painful stitch.

She looked up and realized that she'd managed to reach Gargoyle Square. She kept to the trees and shadows as she crossed the square, listening for the smallest sound behind her. By the time Jasmina reached the back entrance of Hagersham House, she'd decided that she'd lost whoever had been following her.

Jasmina suppressed a tiny smile of pride and conjured her cat illusion. This time, the footman let the animal in on the second yowl.

But she experienced a twinge of fear when he spun as she passed him in the doorway, blinking at the spot where she'd just stood. Jasmina darted to a shadowed corner of the kitchen, breathing a sigh of relief when the footman shrugged his shoulders and went back to his room.

She crept up the servants' stairs, wincing at every creak. Jasmina felt guilty and ashamed, because this time she hadn't come to return anything, but to steal. She took a deep breath when she reached the first floor and reminded herself that an imposter was loose in London, using her face and name to do heaven-knows-what.

Jasmina snuck into the drawing room and searched the cracks in the cushion of the settee. As her fingers touched the cool surface of the gem, she grinned with relief that the prince's spies hadn't found it first.

She decided she couldn't waste a moment in returning Jaz to wherever she'd come from. She squeezed the brooch in her hand and began to murmur the rhyme she'd used to summon the illusion. Only this time she chanted it backwards, hoping that the prince was wrong and she didn't need her twin near her for the reversal spell to work.

The sound of thunder filled her ears, her body shivered with an unknown power, and then it seemed as if the magic abruptly turned back on her, slamming her into the settee and knocking the breath from her lungs.

Jasmina blinked, seeing stars. Then she realized that the light was the flame from several lanterns, and would have cried out when the duke spoke if she'd had the breath for it.

"Grab the little thief, men!"

Two burly footmen grabbed her arms, and Jasmina saw the flash of a red hat disappear around the corner of the open door. Next to His Grace stood the duchess, a satisfied smile on her face.

"I told you it wasn't a dream," she said. "That ugly little gnome warned me that someone was stealing my brooch."

The petite woman stalked forward and snatched the jewel from Jasmina's hand.

Six

STERLING STOOD ACROSS THE STREET FROM THE DUKE of Hagersham's house in were-form, his ears perked toward the imposing mansion. A dozen of the prince's spies had followed the girl and were now strategically placed around the house and square. They hadn't made a move to stop Lady Jasmina, nor did they now, as window after window lit up the night.

Sterling snorted with impatience. Why didn't they go into the mansion? For that matter, why had they allowed the girl to go inside at all? Perhaps they thought it might be easier, and better for the prince's secrecy, if they let the girl do their dirty work.

But Sterling didn't have much confidence in Jasmina's abilities as a thief. She'd had more than a dozen people following her, including a stallion and a gnome, and she hadn't known it. What made the prince's men think she could escape the mansion with the relic?

Because he knew that's what she'd come here to get. He heard the thunder of magic and smelled the stench of the relic a short time after she entered the mansion. Didn't the girl have any sense?

Of course, when he'd seen her sneak out of her own home, in the clothes of a chimney sweep, no less, he'd realized that Jasmina's prim and proper manner hid more spunk and depth than he ever would have suspected. He'd almost dismissed her for a real servant… until he recognized the sway of her backside in those trousers.

So he followed her, along with the prince's spies. They knew who he was and vice versa, but pretended to ignore each other.

Sterling stomped his hooves with annoyance, then froze when he heard Jasmina scream. His stallion blood raged, and he couldn't stop the beast from lunging forward, pounding down the front doors of the mansion. His nostrils flared as he followed the stench of the relic up the wide stairs, his hoofbeats only slightly muffled by the carpeted treads. He ducked his head to enter the double doors of the drawing room and came to an abrupt stop.

It took only a moment to assess the scene. The duke's mousy wife held the relic—she reeked with its smell—and she'd been watching her husband and two burly footmen maul Jasmina with a look on her face that no proper lady should wear. When Sterling barged into the room, the duchess took one look at him and spun to flee through another door.

His first urge was to follow her and recover the relic. But he took one glance at Jasmina's face and felt such a fierce, protective rage that he screamed with the force of it. He could see the red blotches—even through the soot on her face—from where she'd been slapped. Her hat had been knocked off, and her white-blonde hair contrasted sharply with her black chimney-sweep disguise. Her shirt had been torn open, and the duke was so involved in ripping off her trousers that he hadn't even registered Sterling's scream of rage.

One of the footmen looked up in time for his face to meet the bottom of Sterling's front hoof. Sterling felt his body knock the duke sideways. The duke slammed into the other footman, and when he spun they both fell flat on the floor. Sterling screamed again and reared, his head almost touching the ceiling.

"No, stop," Jasmina cried, scrambling to her feet on top of the settee. She held out her hands, tears tracking lines of white down her dirty face. Her position on the settee allowed their eyes to meet for a moment that seemed to last an eternity. Sterling slowly lowered his front legs, sidling up to the girl, blowing hard through his nostrils.

"There now," she murmured, stroking his forehead with trembling fingers. "Just take me out of here, will you?"

And the proper lady Jasmina launched herself onto his back, burying her face in his mane. Sterling glanced down at the cowering men, his eyes flashing with promise, and they both scurried backwards, babbling words that cried for mercy.

Sterling spun, ducked out the door, and made his way down the staircase, admiring the way Jasmina clung to his back, as if she were a part of his own body. When he realized that he wouldn't unseat her the way he had Jaz, he plunged over the threshold and out into the cool London night.

He caught the eye of one of the prince's spies and

thought he recognized Sir Artemus. He neighed at the were-lion, looking back toward the mansion before galloping off into the darkness.

When he reached Hyde Park, he slowed beneath the shelter of the enormous trees that lined the lane. Sterling blew hard through his nostrils, inhaled the scent of night-blooming azzinas and headed toward the flowers. Their aroma had a calming effect, and based on the hysterical sobs that still wracked Jasmina's body, she needed it.

Sterling stepped carefully on the gravel path, the crunching sound of his hoofbeats barely disturbing the quiet of the garden. Fog wreathed its tendrils through the thick stalks of the flowers, reflecting the pearly light of the blossoms as they opened their large, white petals to the night. Pollen danced in the glow of the luminescent stigma, releasing tiny puffs of powder, with a scent so intoxicating that even Sterling found his eyelids drooping.

But it worked on the girl. She quit shuddering and lifted her head, her silent sobs reduced to delicate hiccups. "Oh," she whispered. "I didn't even know this garden was here."

Well, he certainly hoped not. The flowers only opened in the dead of night, well past a proper lady's bedtime. Although with her penchant for sneaking around London disguised as a chimney sweep, he wouldn't have been too surprised.

He carried her through the garden for a time, with only the sound of the crickets and his hoofbeats to break the silence. Sterling stayed in his were-form, unsure of what to say. If it was his sister or even Jaz, he would shift to human and offer words of comfort.

But for this woman, so rigid and self-contained, he

had no idea what to say. He couldn't even imagine how her vision of the world she lived in might now be altered. Like so many society ladies, she would have been raised to believe in the honor of gentlemen, in the illusion of safety that her title provided her. He hoped her near brush with ravishment by one of her peers wouldn't break her spirit, and Sterling realized with surprise that he rather admired her courage.

Her words barely broke the quiet of the night.

"He said…" Her voice trembled, and he could hear her struggle to regain control. "The duke said that if I didn't tell him what I knew about the Brotherhood… he would…"

Shudders shook her again and she buried her face in his mane. Sterling froze, uncertain what to do. Then he started to walk again, a slow gait that rocked her on his back until she quieted.

"He always seemed so kind," she mumbled. "We've been to dinner at his home dozens of times. And the duchess, so meek and gentle."

Sterling nickered softly.

"Well." She sniffed, and he could feel her body stiffen as she sat up. "It's astonishing what secrets people can hide beneath their veneer of respectability."

Jasmina began to stroke the side of his neck, and Sterling almost stumbled. It felt as if she had lightning in her fingertips, making shivers of delight run through his massive frame. He remembered Jaz rubbing her palms across his chest. How could two women be so different and yet feel entirely the same?

"I wonder what this Brotherhood is," she continued, "and what it has to do with the relic?"

Sterling snorted and shook his head. He wondered the same thing. He'd never heard of this group, although it seemed that secret societies seemed to develop wherever people gathered. Most of them were harmless groups of men who shared the same interests, but some were political, and if they'd managed to get their hands on a relic...

Jasmina combed her fingers through his mane, distracting him from his thoughts.

"From now on, I shall endeavor to see past a person's title and appearance."

Sterling snorted. Although she'd had a scare, he highly doubted it had knocked that much sense into her.

"But I'm sure Duke Hagersham didn't recognize me. If he had, he never would have manhandled me in such a manner."

Sterling doubted that as well. And he started to get a bit annoyed. Jasmina kept talking as if to herself. As if she'd entirely forgotten that he was a were-stallion and not just any ordinary horse. Amazing, really, how people would babble on to his were-self.

"And it's not as if I don't have any secrets of my own."

Ah. Sterling's ears perked up. Perhaps the lady would oblige him by confessing a few. Like how she'd taken possession of the relic in the first place. And why she'd created her twin.

"At least my reversal spell worked," she mumbled, her body relaxing onto his back. The relic had released so much magic she felt sure her illusion had been dispelled. She took a deep breath. "Those flowers smell so pretty. I wonder what they're called?"

Sterling flattened his ears. Couldn't she stick to one

straight thought? Her mind seemed to jump from one subject to another and he wished she'd get back to her secrets. Not that he was curious about her, of course. Only that it might help him find his sister. And his missing wife.

"I recited the spell backwards, although that shouldn't have been necessary. My intent should have been enough to send that imposter back to wherever she came from."

Sterling mentally swore to himself. He'd smelled the relic and heard the backlash of a powerful spell while she was in the mansion, and he'd suspected that Jasmina had performed the reversal spell. But he'd hoped it hadn't worked. He wanted to see Jaz again, to find out why she affected him as no other woman had. To know that she was somehow a real person. The thought of never experiencing the delight of her body and the fire of her passion again left him feeling desolate.

He'd traveled the length of the garden path and reached the entrance to the lane. Sterling froze in indecision. The girl continued to sway on his back, the shock of her fright and the properties of the flowers combining to lull her into a trance.

He felt torn between curiosity and anger. Anger at Jasmina for banishing Jaz before he had a chance to really know her. And curiosity about Jasmina. The girl had created his wife, after all. Surely there must be some of Jaz in her. Sterling snorted and shook his head. He just couldn't imagine the young lady on his back having the same qualities as the woman he'd made love to. The spell must have twisted more than just the nature of the illusion.

And yet. He recalled the way Lady Jasmina had melted into his arms when he'd kissed her in the Hall of Mages. She'd responded just as passionately as Jaz; indeed, he hadn't even known they were different persons until later. Perhaps her proper exterior hid a smoldering fire? What would happen if he kissed her again? If he shifted back to a man, took her back into the garden and kissed her beneath the glow of the azzina flowers?

"You nasty little beast," snapped Jasmina.

Sterling stomped his front hoof in surprise, turning his head to roll an eye at her. Had she read his mind? How had he forgotten that this woman had also slapped him senseless after he'd kissed her? He shook his back, tempted to dump the little lady off of it. But she held on as if she were molded to his body.

"I see your hairy toes sticking out from beneath that pile of leaves," continued Jasmina. "If it weren't for you, they wouldn't have caught me."

Ah. Sterling followed her gaze to a trembling bundle of azzina leaves, just as a set of hairy toes curled back beneath them. So, the gnome had gotten into the house before her? And alerted the duke to Jasmina's presence?

Sterling's stallion blood roiled. That gnome had almost gotten Jasmina violated. Something she might not have overcome. The little pest might be more than just a mere nuisance if he continued following Jasmina.

Of course, now that Jasmina had banished her twin, she would no longer require Sterling's assistance. It wasn't as if the gnome would be a bother to *him*. So why did he feel such anger at the little creature? Why did he feel as if he couldn't walk away from her unless he knew she'd be safe?

Why did he feel such rage at the peril the gnome had exposed her to?

Sterling's animal-self took over, and he reared. Jasmina gasped with surprise but held on like a burr.

He charged the leaf pile and stomped it with his front hooves. Then he spun and kicked with his back legs until shredded leaves filled the air.

The gnome had run before Sterling could do any damage, but he hoped he'd at least given the creature as much of a scare as Jasmina had experienced at the duke's hands.

He tossed his head with satisfaction. Now, to lose the gnome for a while. He spun and lunged forward, satisfied that the girl still hadn't lost her grip. Indeed, she seemed to lean forward in anticipation of his run.

His hooves barely touched the ground as he tore along the lanes and pathways of Hyde Park. He took a moment to admire Jasmina's riding skills before he lost himself in the sheer abandon of his reckless run. The wind streamed through his mane and the trees blurred beside him while he galloped as if the hounds of hell were after him. He only slowed when he felt sure that the gnome could never have followed; his chest heaved and his breath blew hard through his nostrils. That had felt grand.

He took a sedate pace as he traveled through the empty streets of London to the girl's home. He had time to regret not kissing her. It would have been interesting to discover if she really did have a bit of Jaz in her. But perhaps it was for the best. He didn't belong in her social circle, and she'd never accept a baronet as her husband, no matter what passions might flare between them.

But when he reached her house and she slipped from his back, he couldn't help feeling pleasure as her warm body slid along his. She stood for a moment, looking him in the eye, her fingers still tangled up in his mane.

"Thank you for saving me," she whispered, her face softening for a moment. "And for that wild ride… and for scaring Nuisance."

He blinked.

"The gnome." Her smile lit her face and Sterling couldn't resist nuzzling her shoulder, then her neck, whickering softly in her ear.

She shivered. "Aunt Ettie was right. I could easily fall in love with your were-form. I've always adored horses."

Sterling shuffled his hooves. So, she hadn't forgotten that he was truly a man, after all. She just liked his were-self better. Only half of him felt insulted.

Then he watched her make a startling transformation. She let go of his mane and smoothed back her wild hair, her face smoothing as well. Her back stiffened, and her shoulders squared. Like a carefully cultivated mask, her features hardened into the proper Lady Jasmina.

"So I'm quite glad that we shall never see each other again," she said. "Goodbye, Sir Sterling." As if they stood in a crowded ballroom and she'd given him a well-deserved cut direct, she turned and disappeared around the side of her mansion.

Sterling stood frozen for a moment and then threw back his head, tossing his mane with a show of contempt. He'd be glad never to see her again too. She'd done nothing but disrupt his life with her spells and headstrong notions of fixing her own problems.

Although he had to admit that he admired her.

He turned and headed toward Trickside, the tidy mansions in their neat squares fading into the ramshackle brownstones where he rented his flat.

Yes, he admired the way she'd decided to recover the relic herself. The way she'd rallied from the treatment of the duke and his men. Not many of the women he knew could have managed it. Sterling stepped over a drunkard and wondered how she'd managed to develop such strength of character.

Before he could speculate further, he quickly banished Lady Jasmina from his thoughts. After all, he would never see her again. And the woman he'd known as Jaz had never been real. He'd be better off forgetting them both.

But as he headed up the rickety stairs to his door, he still couldn't banish the desolate feeling that had come over him when she bade him goodbye.

The next evening Sterling walked up the steps of the Wiccens' mansion and avoided looking at the home next door. He told himself again that he'd accepted the invitation from the Lord and Lady Wiccens for the same reason he'd accepted all the others: to discover the whereabouts of his missing sister.

It had nothing to do with the fact that the Lady Jasmina lived right next door. He had no desire to see her again. Yet when he stepped inside and exchanged greetings with Lord and Lady Wiccens, he quickly scanned the entrance hall, looking for a pair of emerald green eyes. And when he didn't see them, he hurried up the stairs to the drawing room, studying the knots of people, a disappointment bordering on anger rising inside him when he didn't spy a head of white-blonde hair.

The girl wouldn't be so rude as to decline an invitation from her next-door neighbors, would she?

"Ah, Sir Sterling. What an… expected surprise."

Sterling spun and stared into the golden eyes of Sir Artemus. The were-lion grinned, revealing the sharp incisors at the corners of his mouth. Sterling snatched a glass of port from a passing servant's tray and threw it down his throat. It burned all the way to his stomach, and he felt much better.

"I could say the same of you," Sterling replied. "Not many baronets accepted the invitation, I see." Indeed, they appeared to be the only shape-shifters in the room, and he'd already noticed the alarmed glances cast in their direction.

Sir Artemus shrugged, his massive shoulders tightening the seams of his jacket so that they appeared in danger of splitting. "Because of the prince, it would be a mistake not to send our kind an invitation. It amuses me to occasionally accept one just to keep the upper classes on their toes."

Sterling nodded, although he doubted the man's words. Sir Artemus was here for a reason, and he wondered how difficult it might be to find out why. Glasses tinkled and conversation flowed freely, accompanied by a pianoforte being played badly in the background. He didn't think they'd be overheard, but still, Sterling lowered his voice. "Did you recover the item without further incident?"

Sir Artemus raised one golden brow. "Did the lady arrive home safely?"

"Yes, she's safe and sound… no thanks to you."

The man actually laughed at him. "She's quite a skilled thief, you know. We figured she could get the relic out of the house with less fuss than we could."

"You figured wrong," snapped Sterling.

"Unfortunately, yes."

Sterling frowned. He'd been talking about the assault on Lady Jasmina, but he had a feeling the other man spoke of something else. "You did recover the…"

And then she walked into the room. Sterling could no more tear his eyes away from her than he could have ripped out his heart. She looked quite different from the ragged urchin he'd rescued last night. Her hair had been twisted into tiny curls that bounced on her cheeks, and she wore a charcoal-colored dress that made her eyes look like smoky emeralds. If she hadn't held her nose in the air with haughty correctness, he might have made a complete fool of himself.

"You're drooling," murmured Sir Artemus.

"So are you."

The were-lion shrugged again. "For a different reason."

"You didn't get it, did you?" Sterling narrowed his eyes. "You're still spying on her because you failed to recover it, and she's the only link to it you have."

Jasmina and her taller aunt had been talking to the round-faced Lady Wiccens. Lord Wiccens had been showing off his latest batch of potions—small vials of colored liquid that exploded into puffs of sparkling starbursts whenever the pianoforte hit the higher notes. Sterling hadn't heard the question, but he clearly heard Lady Wiccens, for she'd raised her voice above the explosions, and the song fortuitously ended at that moment.

"Haven't you heard, dear? The Duke and Duchess of Hagersham have disappeared. It's terribly droll of them, to leave without a word to anyone. It's quite the subject this evening, to speculate on their whereabouts and destination."

Sterling watched Jasmina's face relax with relief. No, he didn't suppose she'd want to encounter Duke Hagersham so soon after last night. And it also gave him the confirmation he needed.

"They escaped with the jewel," he murmured to Sir Artemus. This time he didn't make it a question.

Another shrug. It was Sterling's turn to laugh, and he had the distinct pleasure of watching the other man bristle in response. So, the were-lion had managed to let his quarry get away, with the relic no less. No wonder he looked so out of sorts.

And then Lady Jasmina looked at him and the laughter caught in his throat. They stared at each other until a gentleman's back cut her from his view. Sterling took a deep breath. He reminded himself that this woman wasn't his wife. That he hadn't slept with her. He'd made love to an illusion, and any attraction he might feel for Lady Jasmina was only that. An illusion. But he couldn't stop his hands from twitching to feel her soft skin. Couldn't stop the longing to strip off her clothes like he had that night, to taste the sweet saltiness of her skin again, to release his passion within her silken folds…

The gentleman blocking his view moved out of

the way and Jasmina's aunt glanced over at him. Or rather, at Sir Artemus. The were-lion growled low in his throat, licking his lips as if contemplating a delicious morsel.

Miss Forster grabbed her niece's arm and towed her toward them. Jasmina struggled to escape her aunt's grasp, muttering protests all the while, but the other woman appeared not to notice, her eyes glued to the inviting gaze of Sir Artemus.

"Mother and Father would not approve of my talking to baronets," said Lady Jasmina.

"They're not here, dear," replied her smiling aunt.

Sterling would swear that Lady Jasmina's slippers were smoking in her efforts to backpedal away from them.

"Sir Artemus, Sir Sterling. What a pleasure to see you again." Miss Forster held out her hand and Sir Artemus gave it a lingering kiss. The older woman nearly swooned, Jasmina gasped, and half the guests in the room gave their little group mingled looks of disgust and turned their backs.

"You're creating a scene," Jasmina scolded.

"It's a beautiful evening." Her aunt carried on as if Jasmine hadn't spoken. "Shall we all stroll along the balcony?"

The were-lion still held the older woman's hand, and with a smile that had his incisors glinting in the candlelight, he smoothly curled it around his bent arm. "It would be my pleasure, madam."

Jasmina looked as if she wanted to flee again, but her aunt held her firmly in place with her other arm. The four wove through the throng of guests, out the double doors and onto the moonlit balcony. It overlooked Mandrake Square, with its interlocking fountains and white-pebbled pathways through trees fashioned into various flowing shapes.

"What a lovely evening, Miss Forster," growled Sir Artemus, looking down on her with glowing eyes.

"Oh please, call me Henrietta, won't you?" She giggled.

Jasmina gave a grunt of disgust at the same time Sterling did, and she glanced at him in surprise.

"Sir Sterling," said Miss Henrietta Forster. "Would you mind keeping my niece company while I show Sir Artemus the view from the far end of the balcony? Oh, and I would clasp her arm quite securely, if I were you. She's been feeling a bit faint this evening."

Sterling grinned and did as she bid, placing Lady Jasmina's arm firmly within his grasp. Sir Artemus wasted no time in leading the older woman away, a low purr of anticipation rumbling within his throat.

"Let me go," hissed Jasmina.

"You heard your aunt," Sterling replied, unable to suppress a smile. Jasmina was so prim that he couldn't resist the urge to discomfit her. "Besides, the damage has already been done. You've been seen talking to a couple of animals."

She had the grace to blush.

"But don't worry. I'm sure you'll recover from this one minor slip to your reputation."

"I've had several of them recently," she replied. "It will take me months to repair the damage."

"But I'm sure you're up to the task."

She turned her face up to him then, looking so bewildered by the upheavals in her life that he felt an instant pity for her and almost let her go. But the moonlight washed her cheeks with pale color, sparkled in her eyes and highlighted the curve of her brow and the sweep of her lips. Her beauty took his breath away.

"What are you doing here anyway?" she asked. "Usually your kind shuns society functions."

"I was invited."

Bloody hell. She licked her lips to snap at him again and his groin jumped in remembered delight. He turned toward her, closing the distance between them until he could feel her breath when she spoke.

But she didn't back away. "I told you I never wanted to see you again." She moved a bit closer, as if her mouth was drawn to his.

Sterling smiled. Unlike Jaz, she didn't know what she wanted. But something deep inside her responded to him, and he felt a flicker of hope. Maybe a bit of the woman he thought he'd married really existed in her. "So you thought I came here just to see you?"

She blinked.

"You forget about my sister, Angel. I am hoping to find a clue to her whereabouts."

Jasmina's shoulders relaxed. "And Sir Artemus? Why is he here?"

An errant breeze blew a curl across her face. Without thinking, Sterling reached up to sweep it back. His hand froze in the act. He'd forgotten how soft her skin felt and he couldn't resist the impulse to stroke it. He swore that for a moment she leaned into his caress, and then—

"Oh, I beg your pardon," said a familiar voice from the doorway, and Sterling's blood turned to ice. He looked up to see his brother standing with his arm around a redheaded girl.

"You have rotten timing, Cecil," snapped Sterling.

Seven

JASMINA HAD NEVER BEEN SO GLAD TO SEE ANYONE IN her life. The man standing in the doorway blinked stupidly at Sir Sterling, long enough to allow her to recover from… well, she couldn't be quite sure. But her heart had been beating entirely too rapidly, and Sir Sterling's hand had left her skin tingling where he'd stroked it.

And she'd desperately wanted him to kiss her.

Jasmina would have a stern talk with Aunt Ettie after tonight. Her aunt's fascination with Sir Artemus would surely hurt her family's reputation, and she'd exposed Jasmina to the attentions of this handsome were-stallion.

After she'd performed her reversal spell, she'd been sure she'd never see him again, and relief had warred with her disappointment.

Because she'd already half-fallen in love with his were-self. And the man was entirely too handsome for her own good. His black hair reflected the glow of the moonlight, which only served to enhance the hard angles of his face. His lips looked entirely too full and inviting, and his eyes kept trapping her with some kind of promise in their depths that she couldn't resist.

Yes, it was entirely Aunt Ettie's fault that Jasmina felt the need to kiss a man so completely unsuitable for her.

Jasmina pushed away from her captor, and he let her go. He seemed completely focused on the intruder in the doorway. She resisted the urge to run while she could, feeling an unreasonable desire to find out why Sterling had such an astonishing reaction to the other man.

Cecil certainly didn't look very imposing. He stood not much taller than the petite woman beside him and he dressed splendidly, with a velvet coat and a white cravat fastened with a ruby-studded stickpin. Jasmina thought the girl with him looked familiar—certainly not of her social class, but a minor baron's daughter.

"Forgive me, sir," Cecil finally replied. "But I'm afraid you have me confused with someone else."

Jasmina felt Sterling's shock like a tangible thing. He cocked his head, that heavy mane of black hair sliding across one eye, and rocked back on his heels.

"What new game is this?" muttered Sir Sterling.

The redhead swept her haughty gaze over Sir Sterling. Jasmina winced. She'd noticed the ragged tear in Sterling's jacket, the frayed edges of his breeches and the worn toes of his boots. The other woman obviously noticed the same details. Her look of scorn made Jasmina bristle. What right did she have to look so disdainful? As a baron's daughter, she'd only have some minor talent, more of a gift than true magical ability. Jasmina tried to recall the woman's name. It was difficult to keep track of all the barons.

"Cecil, do you know this man?" asked the redhead in a screechy voice. Ah, that triggered Jasmina's memory. The Honourable Blanche Liliput, a baron's daughter indeed, with the magical gift of—what was it? Something to do with birds.

"I'm afraid he's mistaken me for someone else," replied Cecil. His onyx eyes pierced Sterling with a startling intensity and for a moment Jasmina saw his body waver into some kind of dog. But one with incredibly large ears and an even narrower face than his human one.

Heavens, another shape-shifter! She'd managed to live her entire life without encountering a single baronet, and now they appeared to be crawling out of the woodwork.

Sir Sterling grunted as if he'd been punched in the stomach. He muttered some curses that Jasmina pretended not to hear as Cecil took Miss Blanche's arm in a firm grip and steered her back inside the drawing room.

"Who was that?" whispered Jasmina.

Sir Sterling looked down at her, his dark blue eyes almost black with some fierce emotion. "My brother."

"But he said—"

"I know what he said, the little whelp. Excuse me, Lady Jasmina." He bowed to her, an elegant sweep of his lithe body. "I must find out what kind of game Cecil is playing." He left her without another word, disappearing into the crowded drawing room.

Jasmina resisted the urge to call out to him. His absence made the moonlight less bright, made the sounds of the fountains playing in Mandrake Square an irritating gurgle instead of the soothing splash they'd been but a second ago.

Why would his brother pretend not to know him?

She stiffened her spine, then smoothed her dark skirts. It was entirely no business of hers whatsoever. Who knew what sort of antics a pack of animals got up to? She should just be relieved that he'd finally left her alone. That they'd been interrupted and he hadn't gotten a chance to kiss her.

"Why so glum, dear?" asked Aunt Ettie as she and Sir Artemus approached.

"What do you mean?"

"Why, you just now sighed so forlornly."

Jasmina lifted her chin. "I did no such thing."

Sir Artemus grinned, his eyes alight with mockery. Jasmina frowned as fiercely as she could, silently relieved to have someone other than Sir Sterling to focus on.

"Why are you here, Sir Artemus?" To Jasmina's intense satisfaction he took a half step back, dropping Aunt Ettie's arm. "And don't tell me because you were invited—I won't be put off again so easily. Baronets rarely attend the functions of the socially elite."

Aunt Ettie studied Jasmina's face with wariness, and Sir Artemus looked like a trapped animal seeking a way to escape. Goodness, she must be more frustrated by the encounter with Sir Sterling than she'd thought.

"Well?" Jasmina tapped one slippered foot beneath her skirts.

"I, um, don't have authorization to reveal anything to you."

Jasmina looked pointedly at her aunt. "So this is strictly business, is it?"

Sir Artemus flushed, and Aunt Ettie turned an inquiring gaze on him.

"Well, yes, it was supposed—"

"Then you'd best be seeing to it," suggested Jasmina. "Although I can't imagine why you'd be skulking about my neighbor's home when you have the—" She'd almost said relic, but even here and now she shouldn't utter such a secret. "—*artifact* to experiment with."

Sir Artemus turned red beneath his golden skin, and Jasmina gawked. She'd been so relieved to hear that the Duke and Duchess of Hagersham would not be at the dinner tonight that she'd failed to consider the implications. What had Lady Wiccens said? That the couple had mysteriously disappeared?

"You didn't recover it, did you?" she whispered.

"Oh, dear," Aunt Ettie exclaimed.

"It was in the room," continued Jasmina. "I saw you and your men enter their home when I left. How is it possible that the duke and duchess managed to get away?"

"They cast a spell with the most powerful magic in the kingdom," growled Sir Artemus.

Jasmina covered her mouth with her hand. Thank goodness she'd been able to perform the reversal spell before the Hagershams had spirited away the relic.

"But why are you *here*?" she asked again, sweeping her arm at the mansion. "Surely, there's no one here involved with the—"

Sir Artemus quickly bowed with a grace that belied his powerful body. "You are far too clever by half, Lady Jasmina. A wise man would end this conversation, and despite what you may think of me at this moment, I am not a dunce." He turned to Aunt Henrietta and kissed her hand. "I don't often mix business with pleasure, madam. But you made me forget myself."

And then he left the balcony, with Jasmina and her aunt staring at each other with expressions that, given different circumstances, would have had them giggling at each other.

"Your behavior toward the man was quite vulgar," Aunt Ettie finally said.

"He wouldn't know the difference," Jasmina replied. "Besides, we have bigger things to worry about."

Aunt Ettie really had a right to be annoyed with Jasmina. After all, her aunt hadn't shown interest in a man since she'd been jilted many years ago. But surprisingly, Aunt quickly dismissed Jasmina's behavior to the were-lion and raised her brows in alarmed curiosity. "What do you mean?"

Jasmina took a deep breath. "I think Sir Artemus is here to spy on me."

Aunt sniffed.

Jasmina lowered her voice and leaned closer, her words dropping to a mere whisper. "The duke said something to me last night. He asked me what I knew about the Brotherhood."

Aunt placed a hand above her heart and widened her eyes. "The what? Why didn't you tell me this earlier?"

"Because I thought that once I performed the reversal spell I wouldn't be involved in this mess anymore."

"Is that pesky gnome still around?"

Jasmina raised her voice. "Nuisance?"

The hanging vines that covered the balcony shook, and a snicker of laughter reached their ears.

"You should have known better," sniffed Aunt.

Jasmina groaned. "I didn't think that the duke recognized me, given his behavior. But what if he did? He thinks I know something about his nefarious Brotherhood, and *he* knows that *I* know what that brooch really is. If they think I know too much about whatever they might be planning… if they're planning something… which I highly suspect…"

"What, what?" Aunt clasped Jasmina's shoulder with her thin fingers.

"They might think it safer to—" Jasmina barely breathed out her last words, "get rid of me."

Aunt Henrietta shivered. "Nonsense. You're being overly dramatic."

"I do hope so."

"Come along now." Aunt Ettie laced her fingers through Jasmina's and led her to the drawing room. "I think a glass of punch—heavily laced with rum—is exactly what we need to regain our level heads."

Jasmina didn't comment that neither one of them had ever touched a drop of anything stronger than overly steeped tea and just allowed Aunt to tow her along. Her mind whirled with implications, including the presence of Sir Sterling. Was he spying on her too? Did he think his sister's disappearance could be tied to this mysterious Brotherhood as well?

After the cool air on the balcony, the stuffiness of the drawing room hit her like a warm shroud. Jasmina trudged through it, trying not to glance around the room for a glimpse of coal-black hair and deep blue eyes. But the guests had already lined up by order of precedence to go downstairs to the dining room, and

Aunt Ettie quickly ushered her into line. Right behind them, thank goodness, stood her best friend Ellen and her long-time friend Ferdinand.

Jasmina felt so happy to see a friendly face that she hugged Ellen before she had a chance to properly greet her. Ellen's eyes turned as cold as glass as she studied Jasmina from head to toe. With a deliberate swish of her skirts, she turned her back, giving her own best friend the cut-direct.

Aunt Ettie tugged at Jasmina's hand before she had a chance to poke Ellen in the back and demand the reason for her cold shoulder. Jasmina had to concentrate on keeping her skirts lifted high enough to avoid tripping as she navigated her way down the stairs, so she didn't have a chance to talk to Ellen until after they had been seated at table.

Jasmina still hesitated, pretending to study the dinner choices carefully written on the card in the silver menu holder next to her plate. Had Ellen seen her on the balcony with Sir Sterling? Had she seen the shabbiness of his clothes and recognized him as a shape-shifter? They had both been raised with the same sense of propriety, but surely Ellen wouldn't shun her so easily?

Not her very best friend, who had spent so many hours with her in the nursery, playing with their collection of china horses. Who had given the first ride on her new pony to Jasmina. Who had sworn, despite Ellen's childhood friendship with Ferdinand, to never marry.

No, Jasmina decided. It would take much more than a brief association with a baronet to destroy their friendship.

"Ellen," Jasmina whispered. "What's the matter with you?"

At that moment, Viscount Wiccens decided to treat his dinner guests to his latest creation. The bottles of potion scattered among the plates and glasses and bouquets of flowers ornamenting the table suddenly began to steam, and multicolored pillars of vapor rose to the ceiling. Jasmina looked up with the rest of the diners as the mist coalesced into forms that looked like a cross between a lily and a butterfly.

They fluttered back down from the gilded ceiling, landing atop guests' heads and shoulders and on the tips of several large noses. Jasmina joined in the applause while attempting to dislodge one of the apparitions from her forearm. On the front of its segmented body sat a head that sprouted two long antennae with extraordinary eyes at the tip. They blinked innocently at her while she shook her arm.

Aunt Ettie sat on Jasmina's other side, deeply engrossed in a conversation about the feathered bonnets displayed in the new milliner's shop on Bond Street. Jasmina listened to some of the conversation when she suddenly froze, an odd feeling creeping over her. The flying flower winked and started to crawl up her sleeve and into her hair, settling itself just on top of her sausage curls. But she barely paid it any attention, her gaze drawn to the very far end of the table.

Sir Sterling was staring at her.

A proper lady would quickly slide her gaze past his. She would never acknowledge his stare for so long that other people might happen to notice.

But Jasmina lacked the power to pull her eyes away

when their gazes locked. Something about the way he looked at her made her insides melt and her breath quicken. She remembered the way he'd saved her honor and the wild ride he'd taken her on through Hyde Park. She remembered the kiss he'd given her when he'd thought she was her illusion and how her body had longed for him to kiss her again on the balcony.

Jasmina felt her cheeks grow hot, and she resisted the urge to squirm in her chair. His blue eyes danced with humor at her rising color, but still she couldn't look away.

Oh, how she really wished she'd never seen him again.

Another man a bit farther up the table laughed. Sterling's eyes narrowed, and he turned toward the sound, releasing her from his gaze. Jasmina took a deep breath, trying to still the shaking of her hands and the fluttery feeling inside her stomach.

She turned to see what had torn his attention from her. The man he'd called his brother sat with the redhead on one side of him and an older woman on the other. The woman looked remarkably like Cecil—she surely had to be his mother. But Sterling must have gotten his looks from his father, because he didn't resemble the woman at all.

If Cecil and his mother felt Sir Sterling's gaze, they didn't acknowledge it. They treated him like a complete stranger, and Jasmina couldn't help glancing back at Sterling with a puzzled frown.

What an odd sort of family he had.

She didn't know what expression she had on her face, but it made his mouth soften and his eyes melt to a liquid blue. Jasmina's pulse started to race again.

"Have you no shame at all?" Ellen whispered.

Jasmina turned and blinked at her, still slightly dazed. What might she have done if he'd smiled at her with that devil-may-care grin of his? She probably would have made a complete cake of herself, and in front of the very cream of society!

"Thank you, Ellen," she whispered back to her friend, who gave her a puzzled glare and turned back to her soup.

Jasmina looked down. Her pheasant soup had cooled; tiny lumps of congealed fat floated on the surface. She grimaced but followed her friend's example, concentrating on the meal.

She could feel his eyes on her throughout the second course of larded partridges and through the removes of compote of apple and apricot tart and plum pudding. Jasmina took small bites of each, her stomach so fluttery by now that she dared not eat more than that.

But when dessert was served, her love of ginger ice cream made her glance up at the small silver bowls atop the tray the butler carried. She swore her head swiveled of its own accord down the table to where Sir Sterling sat. He'd leaned over to talk to Sir Artemus, and she took advantage of his distraction to study the breadth of his shoulders, the wave in his hair, the strength of his hands. He held a wine goblet by the stem and she marveled that his strong fingers hadn't broken it. Jasmina remembered how he'd caressed her cheek, so gently that she'd barely felt his touch, and yet a tingle had traveled from her cheek to her toes. And vaguely, in the back of her mind, she remembered other things…

"I don't even know who *you* are anymore," Ellen hissed.

Jasmina reluctantly quit staring at the delectable Sir Sterling and faced her friend, who leaned toward her with her hand hovering over her mouth to hide her crooked teeth.

"I don't understand why you're so angry with me," Jasmina replied. "You have to admit the baronet is handsome, and you've admired your own fair share of unsuitable men."

"I suppose you mean to tell me that you've only just *admired* that shape-shifter's good looks?"

Jasmina glanced down at her melting ice cream. She had yet to take a bite. "Are people gossiping about me already?"

"How can you sit there so innocently and tell me it's nothing but gossip?"

Jasmina inwardly groaned. Had someone seen Sterling and Jaz together after they'd left the ball? Heaven knows what they might have been doing—in public, no less. And then Aunt Ettie had practically forced him on her tonight and they had surely been seen on the balcony.

Jasmina couldn't tell Ellen about her bungled spell or the relic or anything. And she'd reinforced whatever gossip Ellen had heard by her own behavior this evening. She couldn't fault her friend for being angry with her.

"Oh, Ellen, I don't know what's happening to me," whispered Jasmina. "I never even wanted to see Sir Sterling again, but then he was here this evening and I can't seem to control myself around him—"

"Do you think I even care about that animal?" snapped Ellen. "Though after your behavior last night with Ferdinand, nothing would surprise me."

Ferdinand sat on the other side of Ellen and seemed to shrink in his seat.

Jasmina felt such a twisting in her chest that she struggled to breathe. "What are you talking about?"

"I'm talking about you and Ferdinand in Spellsinger Gardens cavorting with tree nymphs…" Ellen's voice was strangled.

Jasmina thought she might swoon. Tree nymphs were notorious for their sexual escapades and it testified to Ellen's anger that she even mentioned them, since they were not spoken of in polite society. While she had been risking herself to recover the relic, her illusion had been causing her reputation as much harm as she could.

"I thought you had no romantic interest in Ferdinand," said Jasmina.

"That's entirely beside the point. Your behavior is the issue! Mama has already told me that I'm not allowed to see you anymore." Ellen's breath hitched, and she blinked back tears. "Oh, Jasmina, why Ferdinand? Anyone else and I might have forgiven you."

Unfair. Jasmina had no idea Ellen was in love with Ferdinand. How astonishing. They had both sworn to be spinsters together until their dying day. Jasmina felt a bit betrayed that her friend hadn't confessed her true feelings to her. Still, she desperately wanted to tell Ellen that she'd never do such a thing. That she'd created a twin with a mythical relic and it had been only an illusion that had dallied with her sweetheart.

But Jasmina could do nothing of the kind. It would be a betrayal of her country. Not to mention that Ellen would never believe her.

A flying flower chose that moment to land next to Ellen's plate. With a viciousness that surprised Jasmina, her friend slapped her hand down and squashed it flat. Ellen calmly wiped the mess from her hand with a napkin, and with a composure that Jasmina admired, returned her attention to her dish of ginger ice cream.

Jasmina felt Sir Sterling's gaze on her again. This had to be one of the worst moments of her life, and she didn't want him witnessing it. She kept her eyes glued to her dish of melted cream, swirling the mass with her dessertspoon.

How would she manage without the companionship of her best friend? How could she possibly repair the damage her illusion had done? And then a horrible, dreadful thought occurred to Jasmina.

"Ellen," she whispered.

Ellen studiously ignored her.

Ferdinand leaned forward to pluck a fig from the silver bowl in the middle of the table, caught Jasmina's eye, and turned purple. Jasmina could hear Ellen's teeth grind.

"Please, Ellen, I need to know. What hour of the night was she—I—with Ferdinand?"

Ellen pushed away her dessert and started to arrange the lace on her sleeves.

"Please, Ellen." Jasmina's voice broke. "If my friendship ever meant anything to you, please tell me."

"Can't you keep track of your own dalliances?"

Ferdinand leaned toward the two of them. "Keep

your voices down. Ellen, I told you that nothing really happened. You shouldn't be so hard on Jasmina."

Ellen's mouth opened and closed like a fish and for once she neglected to cover it with her hand. "Don't you dare speak to her."

Ferdinand's pudgy face purpled again when he met Jasmina's eyes, but with a strength of character she hadn't known he possessed, he defied her friend's command. "We just got a little wild from drinking too much brandy. I have vowed to stay away from the stuff from now on and suggest you do the same." He gave her a quizzical look. "It changes you into an entirely different person."

Jasmina could only imagine what her illusion had done with Ferdinand. And she didn't want to pursue the thought. "What time did we part?"

Ellen gasped.

"My memory is a bit fuzzy too," he confessed. "But I left you at the Gardens shortly after dawn."

Ellen made a strangled sound, rising from her chair so quickly that the footman had to lunge forward to catch the back of it. She covered her face in her hands and ran from the room.

Jasmina couldn't move. The implications of what Ferdinand had just said overshadowed her concern for her best friend's pain. The reversal spell hadn't worked. The illusion was with Ferdinand long after Jasmina had performed the spell in Hagersham House. She still existed. She would continue to wreak havoc in Jasmina's life.

Ferdinand mumbled something and excused himself to follow Ellen. Jasmina realized that the conversation in the dining room had come to a complete stop and when she looked up, every pair of eyes were upon her.

"My heavens, what's happened?" asked Aunt Ettie.

Jasmina could only shake her head. She signaled for the footman to assist her with her chair, and with a calm that took all her years of practice to maintain, she walked from the room, through the entrance hall and out into the courtyard.

A fountain of marble adorned the center of the cobbled courtyard, with water pouring out of the mouths of jugs held by cavorting mermaids. Jasmina took several deep breaths, trying to maintain her composure, but a litany kept repeating through her brain: *I failed, I failed. The imposter is still loose in London.*

A streak of color captured her attention. Lord Wiccens had put some kind of potion in the fountain. Wisps of gold and silver light swirled through the liquid, broke through the surface to weave their way around the carvings. One gold tendril sneaked over the side and tried to wrap itself around Jasmina's waist.

She backed up into the solid warmth of a male body. Jasmina spun and stared up into the handsome face of Sir Sterling.

Eight

"Are you all right?" he asked, his face so close to her own that she could feel the warmth of his breath. She backed up again.

"I'm fine. How dare you follow me?"

He ignored both her words and the tone of her voice. He picked up her hand and held it between his own. "You're trembling. What did that gentleman at the table say to you?"

"Nothing," she mumbled.

"If he has insulted you in any way, he will pay for it, I promise you." He lifted her hand and kissed the back of it, his warm lips sending shivers through her. She snatched her hand back.

"You take entirely too many liberties, Sir Sterling."

"You have no idea, my lady," he whispered.

Jasmina's eyes widened. If she'd had any doubts before, she didn't now. He'd been intimate with her body; only it hadn't been hers, but that of her illusion. An unreasonable surge of jealousy overtook her. Ridiculous. But the thought of him touching another woman, even though that woman was her double, almost made her gnash her teeth. Oh, how she wished the reversal spell had not failed!

"Leave me alone," she whispered.

"I would if I could," he replied, wrapping his arm loosely around her waist, pulling her toward him. His mouth lowered to hers.

Jasmina's heart longed for him to kiss her, had wanted him to since he'd first introduced her to the pleasure of his lips. But her mind refused to allow her to give in to such weakness. She must get control of her life back, and he threatened that goal more than her imposter did.

She twisted out of his arms, the fleeting brush of his lips finally spurring her to do what she'd longed to all evening: She fled. She ran into Lord Wiccens' garden, to the path that connected their neighbor's house to her own. But she stumbled and went down in a tangle of skirts right beside Lord Wiccens' hothouse. It allowed her to think for a moment. She couldn't go home in her present state. Mother and Father would ask too many questions.

Jasmina opened the door to the hothouse and felt the humid warmth soothe her as it so often had as a child. She wove her way through the stands of plants, dodging poisonous barbs and delicate petals and pollen-heavy stamens. Lord Wiccens experimented with plants; grafting and transforming, always trying to create new combinations for his potions. The outcome could result in some beautiful creations, but more often than not in grotesque parodies of nature.

Jasmina found her old hiding place by instinct, the glass of the building diffusing the moonlight to a weak glow. She crawled into the pile of burlap sacks that

Lord Wiccens used to cover his plants in the early spring and huddled into a ball. She pounded her fists against the padding.

She had always led such a comfortable, predictable life. Certainly, there had been ups and downs, but she'd smoothed over any minor problems that threatened to disrupt her family's serenity. She'd even managed to handle her mother's dreadful borrowing habit with cool efficiency.

But now she'd lost her best friend and failed to solve the problem of her bungled spell. Even if she managed to repair the damage already done, the imposter was still loose about London, creating even more complications for her to unravel.

What had she ever done to deserve this? She'd only tried to be a good person, good daughter, and friend. Yet her life wasn't her own anymore. Jasmina took a deep breath. She'd come here to gather her composure, not to feel sorry for herself. But still…

She couldn't even control the inappropriate longing for an entirely unsuitable man.

"Poor Jasmina," whispered a squeaky voice.

"Stop following me," she scolded.

A large potted palm shifted its leaves, and a giggle was the only reply.

Jasmina sat up, determined to ignore the garden gnome, as attention only seemed to encourage him. She wrapped her arms around her waist and tried to think of what to do. Somehow she would have to find the Duke and Duchess of Hagersham, borrow the relic from them, find her imposter, and perform the reversal spell again. She refused to be daunted by the enormity

of the task and focused instead on her determination
to regain control of her life.

Unfortunately, she knew just where she had to start.

As soon as she thought of the handsome Sir Sterling
she thought she heard his voice, as if she'd conjured
him up herself. Had he followed her here, even after
she'd rejected his kiss? Well, he was nothing if not
persistent. There was no denying that she needed his
help in order to solve her problems, but she couldn't
allow him to touch her again. She would just have
to make it very clear that she had no interest in him
whatsoever. That whatever had happened between
him and her illusion had nothing to do with her.
She must make it clear that she could never become
involved with such an unsuitable man.

She started to crawl out of her hiding place, had just
opened her mouth to call out to him, when she heard
another voice. A decidedly feminine voice speaking in
breathless tones.

"…I took a breath of air and saw Lord Wiccens'
hothouse and thought I'd see the gorchids he's so
proud of. What are *you* doing out here, Sterling?"

Jasmina reflexively cast her don't-notice-me spell and
burrowed deeper into the sacking. The woman spoke
so familiarly to Sir Sterling that she wondered about
their relationship. She had no intention of announcing
her presence and instead shamelessly eavesdropped.

"It doesn't matter," he replied, avoiding the lady's
question. "It appears I've been given the perfect
opportunity to speak privately with you."

A whisper of silk, a nervous shuffle of slippered feet. "I
can't imagine why you would need to talk with me—"

"Can't you? Tell me, Lady Thorn, what manner of game is your son playing?"

Jasmina scooted forward, parted the leaves of some grassy plant, and tried to make out the figures at the far end of the dim hothouse. Yes, the woman Sir Sterling spoke with had the same outline as the woman who'd sat next to Cecil at dinner. But why hadn't he addressed her as mother? Unless—

"I-I don't know what you mean," replied Lady Thorn, backing toward the door.

"I mean, dearest stepmother, that Cecil pretended he didn't know me."

"I really think you should speak with Cecil about this."

Sterling's dark form closed the distance between the pair. "I intend to. But I can't guarantee that Cecil will emerge from the discussion unscathed."

The small woman's breath caught on a hitch. "I so wish you would just trust your brother's judgment... oh, very well. Cecil thought that it would be best— just while he courted a wife—you see, that we..." Her voice trailed off.

Jasmina leaned forward, her ears straining. The leaves of the palm tree rustled again.

"It's not that we're embarrassed by your appearance," continued Lady Thorn. "We know your father's castoffs are all that you can afford. It's just that Cecil wants to make a good impression. Despite being a baron's daughter, or perhaps because of it, Miss Liliput is rather particular."

Sterling grew very still. "Cecil would rather his fiancée didn't meet the poor relations until after the wedding."

"If you weren't so insistent on finding your sister—"

"What does Angel have to do with this?"

Lady Thorn started to back toward the door again, her arm floundering for the handle. "Cecil isn't the only one who thinks she might have run away with the marquess, Sterling. Not everyone believes that she was abducted."

Jasmina could feel Sterling's rage from across the room. In the gloom she saw his human form waver; saw the hint of an elegant muzzle and a sleek equine shape. The dark outline of the woman slipped out the door, but Sterling made no move to stop her.

His human shape solidified, and he let out a breath that Jasmina heard clearly in the sudden quiet. Her heart flipped a bit as he hung his head, his long hair falling over his face. How dreadful to have one's family disown you. She'd never consider doing such a thing. Even if her mother's habit of borrowing things were discovered, she'd never disown her.

Jasmina realized that she defined everyone else's family by her own. Despite their differences, they had always been loving and loyal and faithful to one another. She couldn't imagine what it would be like not to have that sort of support, that solid foundation that was sometimes the only thing one could rely upon.

She tried to stop the thought from entering her head but it pushed through anyway:

Sir Sterling Thorn needed her.

The palm leaves rustled again, and Jasmina scowled up at the foliage. Sterling glanced toward her hiding spot, and she cringed back into the sacks. She thought he might be embarrassed that she'd heard such a dreadful conversation and wanted to spare him any further humiliation.

Palm fronds shook. "Over here, Sir Sterling!"

"Shh," whispered Jasmina, turning and glaring at the little red cap that bobbed among the foliage.

"Who's there?" Sterling called out, making his way through the rows of plants.

"Lady Jasmina!" answered the gnome.

Jasmina clenched her fists. If she ever managed to get her hands on that little scamp... "I'm going to spell you a nose that looks like a big cucumber," she threatened.

"Where are you?" asked Sir Sterling, waving aside the foliage as he made his way right to her.

"Oh, dear, stop that," warned Jasmina, crawling from her hiding place with as much dignity as she could muster. "The leaves of that plant will make you break out in horrible red splotches."

He froze, not a foot away from her, and studied the stalks of the fuzzy looking growth. "Really? How do you know?"

"I, um, had a dreadful experience with that particular herb when I was a little girl." Jasmina winced, remembering the several days of agony she'd endured from the disfiguring patches. "Actually, I'd suggest that you don't get too close to any of Lord Wiccens' creations. He's made some interesting transformations."

"Dangerous ones?"

Jasmina nodded. "Some."

"Then what are you doing hiding among them?"

"I wasn't hiding. I was thinking. There is a difference."

She could feel his smile in the darkness. With

infinitely more caution he made his way through the plants, until he stood next to her bed of sacking.

"She was eavesdropping," interjected Nuisance.

That did it. She disliked using her magic to harm others, but the gnome had gone too far. Jasmina waved her fingers at the tree. "Go find a mirror, Nuisance. And when you've apologized for your behavior, perhaps I will remove the spell."

She heard a small gasp; then the leaves rustled and shortly after, the door to the hothouse opened and closed.

"What did you do to him?" asked Sterling, closing the distance between them until she could feel the heat of his body. Jasmina backed up, her heels smacking into the bottom edge of the stack of burlap sacks. Perhaps getting rid of Nuisance hadn't been such a good idea. She could already feel her body reacting to Sterling's nearness.

And she already regretted her temper. "I just altered his appearance a bit."

Sterling chuckled. "Warts?"

"Oh, no. Just… well, I'm already ashamed that I did it, no matter how much of a bother he is." Jasmina tried to edge her way around the man, but with the sacking on one side and garden implements on the other, he all but blocked her escape. "I'm going to remove the spell this very minute, and then I'll go find him and apologize."

Jasmina raised her hands to perform the reversal spell, but Sir Sterling captured her fingers in his own warm grasp. "No, don't. At least, not right away. Perhaps it will discourage him the next time he gets the urge to tattle on you." He stepped closer to her until she could clearly see his handsome features in the gloom. His dark blue eyes glittered black; strands of his dark hair had escaped his hair tie and fell about his face, softening the hard angles of it. "*Were* you eavesdropping on me?"

Jasmina swallowed. "Not on purpose, I assure you. I often come here to think." She would not confess that he'd managed to get her so flustered she couldn't go home. "I'm dreadfully sorry about your family. They are treating you quite appallingly." Now, what had possessed her to blurt that out?

His face hardened. "It's none of your concern."

He was right. His problems had nothing to do with her. Then why did she have the overwhelming desire to erase that awful mask of indifference from his face? Why did she feel compelled to restore his usual charming demeanor? She'd started this and now she couldn't seem to stop. "What your family thinks of you doesn't matter in the slightest. What matters is what you think of yourself."

"I'm completely aware of that fact, Lady Jasmina."

"I only wanted you to know that I think their behavior is dreadful. Really, what right do they have looking down their noses at you?"

He held her hand to his mouth and kissed the tip of her finger. "I appreciate your concern."

His mouth felt so warm on her fingertip. So soft. She knew she should pull her hand away but since she couldn't quite manage to do so, she just pretended to ignore it. "I'm only stating what's right and fair. It has nothing whatsoever to do with you personally."

"Of course not." He opened his mouth and her finger slid inside. The sensations that coursed through her body from that slight contact shook her. His tongue felt sandy yet soft, and his mouth a hot haven of—oh, she didn't know, but even the rasp of his teeth felt sinful. She really should tell him to stop.

"Which brings me to something I feel compelled to discuss with you." He suckled her finger. Jasmina's toes curled. Something astonishing happened to her lower body that she'd never felt before, and yet it somehow seemed familiar. A curious tightening sensation.

He dropped her hand; she suppressed a moan. What on earth had come over her? The darkness shadowed his face but she thought she detected a slight twitch of his lips. And she felt his features soften a bit when he reached out to caress her cheek. Some of the frostiness had melted from his demeanor, as if touching her erased the hurt that his stepmother's words had caused.

Splendid. Now if she could only withstand the delicious torture, he'd be his old self in no time.

Jasmina knew they'd be forced to see each other again, but she wasn't quite ready to tell him about her failed reversal spell yet. "Should we ever meet again," she mumbled, for his fingertips had traced a path to her mouth and she spoke against them, "I must make it completely clear that I'm not interested in you romantically."

His hand faltered.

"Even if I had the desire to marry, it couldn't be to someone like you. Regardless of what happened between you and my illusion, I must insist that you remember I am not her. I cannot welcome the attentions of a shape-shifter. It would be entirely improper."

His face froze again. Oh dear, she'd just managed to soothe him and now he appeared as disgruntled as before. All she'd accomplished was to make her own heart beat faster and her lips tingle from where he'd touched them.

"I confess I had forgotten," he said stiffly. "Since you appear identical to Jaz, you must allow for an occasional lapse. I will attempt to be vigilant in reminding myself of your true feelings for me."

Jasmina fought the urge to touch him. She'd handled this very badly. But really, she had no experience with men, especially those of a lower social class, and it might take her a while to get the knack of expressing herself properly.

"You know nothing of my true feelings," she replied. "I don't care one jot about the condition of your clothes or that you change into an animal. But I can't say the same for my mother and father, and their opinion of my behavior means the world to me."

"Didn't you just tell me that the only opinion that matters is one's own?"

His voice dripped with contempt. Jasmina opened her mouth, then snapped it shut. She couldn't stand to have him look at her like that. And she felt like such a hypocrite for thinking that his situation couldn't possibly mirror her own because of his social status.

She'd never been made to feel like a snob before. She'd always been around others who felt and acted the same way she did. Who shared the same ideas. He'd upset her way of thinking entirely.

"It appears that we both have family issues to overcome."

Sir Sterling looked down his beautifully sculpted nose at her. Sometime during their conversation he'd planted his fists on his hips and created an invisible wall between them. Even worse, that dreadful look of bored indifference had recaptured his features.

"The difference between us," he drawled, "is that I'm willing to overcome mine."

Although he put up a convincing charade, Jasmina felt she'd wounded him, perhaps even more deeply than his stepmother had. That hadn't been her intention. She fought against the knowledge that he needed her with the conviction that he was a dangerous man and she should keep her distance.

"The difference between you and Jaz," he added, "is that your twin was ruled by passion. And you, my lady, are ruled by a cold heart."

Jasmina flinched. She knew he'd meant his words to hurt, to wound her as she'd wounded him. He'd managed to do so quite admirably. It infuriated her. "If you mean that I have morals and values, sir, I quite agree."

"Is that what you call them?"

Now he purposely baited her. Yet she noticed that his hands had loosened and he'd lost that look of bored indifference.

"I have passion," she snapped.

"Then you hide it well beneath that prissy exterior."

Good heavens, had he just called her prissy? Jasmina stood on tiptoe, threw her arms around his neck, and did what she'd wanted to do all evening, drat him. She kissed him, with the same fervor that he'd kissed her when he'd thought she was Jaz. Something like jealousy inflamed her, and she strove to outdo that first kiss, forcing his mouth open with her tongue. A tiny part of her mind wondered how she'd known how to do that, but she was too lost in delicious sensations to really care. She plunged her fingers through his hair, dislodging the thong that held it bound. With a grin of delight she twisted the thick strands around her hands, pulling his head back with a harshness that made him groan. She kissed his neck and sucked at his skin until he groaned again.

Somehow his mocking words and need for a loving family and pursuit of her all evening tangled up into something stronger than Jasmina could define. Something broke inside her and she realized that she'd lied to him. His lack of title, his ability to shift into a horse, and his tattered clothes only made him more appealing to her.

Somewhere deep inside she knew she wanted him. Wanted him in a way she shouldn't even have been aware of.

It infuriated her even more. He'd managed to break her control, something no one had ever done before. Jasmina pulled on his hair until he fell to his knees and her body bent over his. Somehow she'd known that he'd allow her to do this. And it was much better. She could reach his lips again.

With a ferocity that scared her she closed her mouth over his and forced it open, sweeping her tongue inside, seeking to somehow possess him—but it wasn't enough. She knew there was more, another way to meld her body with his, to claim him for her own.

And she knew exactly how to go about it. Just as she also knew what he looked like without his clothing: the small scar on his chest, the smooth ridges of his stomach, the hard planes of his thighs and the dark curly hair that sheltered the swollen hardness of…

Jasmina gasped in astonishment and tore her mouth away from his. She remembered how familiar he'd seemed to her when she'd first met him. But this was ridiculous. How could she know what his naked body looked like? Or did she just have a vivid imagination?

The dratted, beautiful man smiled up at her. "It seems there's a bit of Jaz in you after all."

His words brought her thoughts to a screeching halt. What an absolutely dunderheaded thing to say.

"How would you feel if I told you that my reversal spell didn't work?" she snapped. "That Jaz still exists out there somewhere?"

Oh, how she wished for total darkness. But enough moonlight shone through the glass roof for her to see the sparkle in his eyes at her words. "My— Jaz still exists?"

Jasmina slowly untangled her hands from his hair and took a step back. "Yes."

Sir Sterling stood, his height intimidating her so that she shook at the thought of what she'd just done to him. He smoothed back his tousled hair and she clasped her trembling hands together. Had she really yanked him to his knees? What had possessed her?

"I have to see her again," he muttered. "I have to find out…"

Lady Jasmina's eyes narrowed. "Are you in love with her?"

"No… yes… I don't know."

Jasmina felt like laughing or crying or tearing her

hair out. The man had fallen in love with an illusion. He'd pursued her only because he desired her twin and she was an available substitute. She wanted to curse him for an idiot but the sudden envy that flared in her overwhelmed that feeling. She should curse herself for an idiot.

She took a deep breath and willed herself to calmness, vowing never to let the man break her control again. Her shoulders squared, her nose went into the air, and she adopted the most ladylike demeanor in her arsenal.

"You wanted to know what the gentleman at the table said to me." She couldn't resist the desire to hurt him back. "Ferdinand inadvertently told me that my spell didn't work. He said he'd left his lover near dawn, which was sometime after I'd performed the reversal spell at the Hagershams'."

Sir Sterling grabbed her by the shoulders. "His lover?"

"Yes. And despite what Ferdinand thought, you and I both know that *I* wasn't his lover. Perhaps you shouldn't flaunt Jaz's passionate nature, sir. It appears that she can't seem to control it."

He stared down at her haughty face in confusion, as if trying to find the woman who'd just kissed him so willingly. "I don't know how you manage to put on that mask of indifference so easily, but you're quite good at it."

"Release me, sir."

His hands dropped.

"Since it appears that I will be forced to accept your assistance in finding my illusion," said Jasmina with admirable calm, "I would like to repeat my earlier sentiments. I am not attracted to you, and you must not confuse me with my illusion again."

He stared at her as if his thoughts were miles away. Probably thinking about Jaz. Jasmina squeezed her hands until they tingled.

"If I agree to help you," he finally said, "will you give me your promise that you will allow me to speak to Jaz before you do the reversal spell?"

"Why? She's nothing but an illusion."

"Again, that is none of your concern."

Jasmina flinched. "Her behavior doesn't deserve such loyalty." She pushed past him, calmly heading for the exit. He didn't answer her as she made her way past the snapping doidums and carefully avoided the powdery leaves of the chifern. By the time she opened the door of the hothouse into the cool of the London evening, her eyes had started to burn, and she had to blink rapidly to clear her vision.

What a dreadful evening. She'd never felt so confused in her life. One minute rejecting the man and the next practically leaping on him; and then ultimately having her pride injured and a bit of her heart bruised by his obvious desire for an illusion she had created!

The earth tilted a moment and Jasmina shook off the dizziness. She marched to her front door, brushing past the butler when he opened it. She still carried her don't-notice-me spell and vowed to go straight to bed without delay. She prayed that things would look better in the morning.

But the dreadful night still wasn't over.

As she passed the drawing room she heard the

sound of raised voices. She tried to ignore them, but then she heard her mother call for her. Why did Mother always have the uncanny ability to see through Jasmina's spells? Jasmina groaned and removed the now worthless illusion.

Jasmina stepped into the drawing room and frowned. Mother and Father sat on the velvet settee opposite Aunt Ettie and… "Lady Wiccens?" blurted Jasmina. "What on earth are you doing here?"

She hadn't meant to sound so rude, but the woman had left her own dinner party, and surely all the guests had not departed yet.

"I felt it my neighborly duty to inform your parents of your aunt's behavior," said Lady Wiccens, her round face pinched and her watery blue eyes gleaming.

"Aunt Henrietta?" gasped Jasmina.

Aunt Ettie's narrow face looked even sharper with suppressed anger. "It appears that Lady Wiccens doubts my abilities as your chaperone."

"Where have you been?" demanded Father.

Jasmina reeled. "I… I walked home. Through the gardens. I needed some fresh air." She'd never seen her parents this upset.

"Well, if you'll excuse me," said Lady Wiccens with righteous triumph, "I have to get back to my guests."

She left the room, but they all ignored her.

"You weren't concerned for my safety, were you? I've played in Lord Wiccens' gardens since I was a child."

Mother looked confused and Father furious. Aunt Ettie seemed almost beaten, and that worried Jasmina the most.

"Lady Wiccens was kind enough," said Aunt, her

voice dripping with sarcasm, "to inform your parents of my particular attention to a baronet."

"Oh, Henrietta," said Mother. "We don't mind that you've finally shown an interest in a man. It's just that, well, couldn't you have chosen someone more acceptable?"

"What I want to know," snapped Father, "is what you were thinking when you forced our daughter into the company of the other animal."

Aunt Ettie looked ready to explode with words, but instead she swallowed them and abruptly nodded. "You're quite right, Horace. I never should have left her alone with the man. I will not fail in my duties as chaperone again."

"You'd best not," warned Father. "Or I will be forced to replace you with someone more reliable."

Jasmina gasped. "Father, surely you can't be serious. I assure you that Aunt had the best of intentions."

"What?" He jumped up from the settee. "You shouldn't be acknowledging one of those creatures, much less be seen talking with one. If I didn't know you any better, I would believe some of the nonsensical gossip that's been said about you lately. But you've always shown such a level head that I've given you the benefit of the doubt. But don't push me, young lady, or I shall lock you in your room and toss away the key!" Father spun on his heel and stomped out the door.

Jasmina stood in openmouthed stupor. Father had never spoken that way to her before.

"Really, dear, I'm surprised at you," said Mother. "Entertaining the attentions of a man when you know we expressly forbid you to marry. I thought you wanted to never leave this house?"

"I don't. My feelings on this matter haven't changed. I know how much you and Father need me."

Mother's face relaxed. She rose, all silk and lace and perfume. "You know I could never get along without you, dear."

Jasmina nodded and allowed her mother to kiss her cheek before she left the room.

"What was that all about?" Jasmina asked her aunt as she collapsed on the overstuffed chair next to her.

"I want what's best for you, and they want what's best for them," muttered Aunt Ettie.

Jasmina had never felt so exhausted in her life. Her world had been turned upside down and she wondered if sanity would ever return. "Oh, Aunt, they were right. It was very bad of you to leave me alone with Sir Sterling. And you could have chosen someone more appropriate than Sir Artemus to set your cap on."

Aunt Henrietta sniffed. "Don't you start in on me too. I have not set my cap on anyone, and I did what I thought was best at the time. Did Sir Sterling find you in the garden?"

"Aunt!"

"Never mind, dear. I was just hoping, that's all." Aunt laid a finger aside her nose, her forehead wrinkled in thought. "In the future I will just have to be more circumspect where your parents are concerned. What did Ferdinand say to you that upset you so?"

If Jasmina hadn't been so tired and confused by the evening's events, she would have asked her aunt why she seemed so keen on the prospect of Sir Sterling courting her. Perhaps the handsome faces of the shape-shifters had blinded Aunt to their lowly social status. But Aunt didn't know that Sir Sterling was in love with her illusion, and Jasmina had no intention of discussing it. "Ferdinand gave me the most dreadful news."

Aunt sniffed.

"It appears that my reversal spell didn't work." Jasmina rose to her feet, too tired to stay and discuss the matter fully. "And that illusion I created is behaving most shamefully."

"I suppose this means that you will be forced to accept the assistance of Sir Sterling in finding your twin?"

Jasmina nodded, clutching the door frame for support. "The prince was right. Apparently the illusion must be in the same room for the spell to work—or at least in closer proximity. And since Sir Artemus failed to recover the relic, I'll have to find that too."

Jasmina expected her aunt to be horrified at the news. But when Jasmina bade her good night, she noticed that Aunt Henrietta wore a most gleeful smile on her face.

Nine

STERLING SAT AT THE RICKETY ESCRITOIRE TRYING TO concentrate on his correspondence. But his mind kept replaying images from last night. He should have known that Lady Jasmina's prim exterior hid a volatile passion. After all, he'd made love to her twin.

He tossed the letter aside and rose, pacing the small confines of his flat. The question still begged to be answered: What, exactly, was Jaz? A physical copy of Lady Jasmina only? A duplicate of the original?

Perhaps the spell had gone more wrong than anyone realized. The two women were indeed similar, yet vastly different. Lady Jasmina had brought him to his knees with a passion even stronger than his wife's. The lady had possessed him body and soul and he couldn't say the same of Jaz. He'd lusted for her, yes, and paid for it by marrying her. And yet his memory of her paled in comparison to the reality of Lady Jasmina.

Sterling tossed his head. He'd pursued Jasmina relentlessly, at first confusing her with his wife. She'd frustrated him with her proper behavior, battling the desire he saw in her eyes with her social upbringing. But he had to admit that the chase had thrilled him; the challenge of cracking her calm demeanor had made him even more determined to kiss her. He'd used every persuasion he could think of, even baiting her by comparing her to Jaz. And then she'd turned the tables on him.

His scalp tingled from the memory of her pulling on his hair. He'd allowed her to possess him; indeed, he hadn't had the will or inclination to stop her. And that had never happened before.

Sterling paced back to his desk and crumpled several letters in his fist. Half of the letters from his informants had seen his wife with several men, each time in compromising situations. Whereas Lady Jasmina had to be goaded into losing her control, it seemed that Jaz had none at all.

He wished that Lady Jasmina's reversal spell had worked. Then he wouldn't feel compelled to track down Jaz and try to find out what manner of woman he'd married. But he owed her that duty, regardless of her behavior.

He just wished he hadn't brought that hurtful look to Lady Jasmina's face when she'd told him that his wife still existed. But perhaps it was better this way. He couldn't afford to become involved with the real woman when he had her magically created twin to contend with.

Sterling tossed the crumpled letters back onto the worn escritoire. At least one of his informants had finally managed to find out where Jaz was living. He would have his answers tonight... and he hoped a lead on the whereabouts of his sister, if Jaz was still somehow involved with the relic.

Sterling glanced out his darkened window and began to untie his cravat. He'd sent a messenger sprite to Miss Forster, asking her to bring her niece to the Troll and Tankard pub near the London Docks, but he couldn't be sure that they'd be able to meet him. He wasn't even certain that he really wanted Lady Jasmina with him tonight, but he'd promised the prince he would involve her. And the prince had fulfilled his own promise in providing more funds for Angel's search.

His lips twisted as he pulled out a black coat and trousers from his doorless wardrobe. Why did the important women in his life all manage to go missing? Sterling pulled on a shirt gray with age and buttoned his coat over it. With the black trousers and no cravat, he should be able to blend in with the night. He filled his pockets with items he felt might be necessary for tonight's task, then tucked several weapons about his person that could be employed with minimal noise. Stealth would be called for this evening.

He left his flat, surveyed the empty streets, and shifted to his stallion form, his clothing melding into his coat, the weapons a bit trickier. His hide was tough in a few spots, and if he carried anything too large it just wouldn't shift. When he neared the dock, the stench of the Thames grew worse. He tried to snort the smell of it from his nostrils. Light spilled from row after row of shabby buildings. The West End might be silent after midnight, but the East End came alive. The Troll and Tankard looked to be doing some jolly business tonight. As he neared the tavern, a sailor was ejected bodily through the open door. Sterling had to step around his unconscious figure. He stayed in the shadows between the pub and a warehouse, vowing to wait only a few minutes for Lady Jasmina and her aunt to show.

The longer he waited, the more he realized that he'd been mad to ask the lady to join this venture. She'd never make it down the street without being molested. He decided he'd take Lady Jasmina home if she managed to come tonight. And that meant waiting several more hours and perhaps missing the opportunity to find Jaz.

Sterling pawed the dirt alley with his hooves in frustration. And then he spied two more drunks waddling down the street toward the tavern. Something about the pair seemed familiar.

The flash of a red, pointed hat following the pair convinced him. He gave a soft whicker, alerting them to his location in the alley. A whispered argument ensued and the taller sailor, who was most certainly Jasmina's aunt, turned reluctantly back around, scrambling atop the horse they'd been leading.

Lady Jasmina walked toward him. He could see the vague outline of the spell she'd cast to disguise her appearance and admired her handiwork. A bandanna wrapped around her head contained her seemingly cropped blonde hair. The sailor's jacket showed no hint of a womanly figure, although the striped breeches displayed rather shapely legs for a man. The narrow face and hawk-like nose displayed an expression of a man it wouldn't be wise to tangle with.

Although the jagged scar running from temple to jaw might be a bit much.

Sterling shifted to human. "I should have known you'd be smart enough to come in disguise."

Lady Jasmina shrugged. "I thought I'd mix my illusion with some real clothing, although I can't imagine that there'd be too many of the aristocracy slumming the East End this late at night."

"You'd be surprised."

She gave him a quizzical expression. "I smudged my face with enough ashes to be unrecognizable in case I ran into anyone who could see through my spell. My hair is tied in a tail at the back of my head—"

"Cor," slurred a man coming into the alley. "Wot, can't a man take a piss in private?"

Sterling looked down at his muddy boots and winced. He should have suspected...

The sot started to open the trousers of his pants; Jasmina's eyes widened on a gasp, and Sterling grabbed her hand and pulled her from the alley. He shifted, bending his front legs, and she didn't hesitate to climb on his back.

Sterling walked to the far end of the docks, keeping to the shadows, until they stood across the road from an old, dilapidated warehouse. He shifted back to human and pulled her with him behind a stack of crates.

Jasmina eyed the building with disgust. "Surely my twin hasn't taken up residence here?" she whispered.

Sterling tried to breathe through his mouth. The odor of rotten fish made his eyes water. "My informant said that a woman fitting Jaz's description has been seen coming and going from this building. I just hope he's right, because we're going to go to a great deal of trouble to find out."

"Do you have a plan?"

Sterling smiled. Despite the fact that Lady Jasmina had probably never been in the East End of London in her life and that she'd had a man almost relieve himself in her presence, she'd gotten right to the heart of the matter. And even though she currently lurked behind filthy crates on a stinking street, she maintained her cool demeanor, as if she were sitting down to tea in her own parlor.

Lady Jasmina made a jolly good partner-in-crime. He didn't suppose she'd be flattered if he told her that, though.

"Look at the shadows flanking the building," he murmured. Jasmina's eyes narrowed at the forms of two men.

"Now, about every hour the two guards meet up—bloody hell."

"What is it?"

"It's that pesky gnome. If he pulls any of his tricks tonight—" Sterling couldn't finish his sentence because the men had already started to move.

"Stay here," he commanded, slipping from beneath their hiding place and using the shadows for cover. The foggy night aided him. Sterling had no difficulty coming up to the men unawares, a cigar carelessly held in his fingers. "I say, do one of you chaps have a light?"

One of the men immediately fished in his pockets, but the other scowled and reached for his blackjack.

Sterling didn't give him time to raise the weapon. He half-shifted, using his stallion strength to knock the two men's heads together. He snorted with relief when they both sank to the ground.

"Well done," whispered Jasmina from behind him. "I shudder to think where and why you learned such a trick."

"I thought I told you to stay put."

She ignored him. "Now what?"

Sterling dragged both men deeper into the shadows of the adjacent building, where he bound their limbs and gagged their mouths. Lady Jasmina eyed his bulging coat pockets but restrained from asking him what else he might have hidden in them besides ropes and gags and a cigar.

"Can you cast a spell to look like the smaller one?" Sterling asked, nodding at the two guards.

"I think so." She dropped to her knees and ran her hands a few inches from the guard's face. Bless the girl for not asking any more questions. They needed to get back in front of the door before the replacement guards arrived.

Sterling tossed his head. "Well?"

As Lady Jasmina passed her hands over her face, the hawkish nose and jagged scar were replaced by bushy black brows and pockmarked skin. Her clothes shimmered and changed as well, although there hadn't been much difference between her disguise and the guard's own clothing.

Sterling started to think that he'd done the right thing in asking the lady to accompany him tonight. She stepped forward and he blinked at her new appearance, still unsettled by her masculine guise. Thankfully, he could see right through her spell to the smudged-faced woman beneath.

He unbuttoned his jacket and rolled it into a ball. Sterling stared into her smoky green eyes while he stripped off his shirt. Her breath caught as her gaze traveled over his naked torso, and he grinned. He'd ignited something in the Lady Jasmina and he doubted she was even aware of it.

"You might want to turn around."

He could see her blush even in the dim light. She spun and he admired the straight line of her stiffened back while he changed into the taller guard's clothing. He stuffed his long hair up into the cap and pulled it low over his brow. "What do you think?"

Sterling thought he heard a high-pitched giggle and searched the shadows, but didn't see that telltale flash of a red cap.

Jasmina turned and cocked her head. "As long as they don't look too closely, you might pass for the other guard."

"Good." Sterling hesitated. "Are your magical reserves up to the task? I wouldn't want you harmed by draining yourself."

Jasmina looked surprised by his concern. Had he made her think he cared so little for her? "I'll be fine."

Sterling nodded, and they both walked back to the door just in time. Sounds of locks from the other side rattled and it swung open, two burly men grunting at them as they took over guard duty. Jasmina grunted back and Sterling just shrugged as they passed the other two men through the door, Sterling closing it quickly behind them. That should take care of the gnome, if he still followed them.

They stood inside a long hallway of crumbling brick and old spiderwebs. Fairylights illuminated the tunnel, the globes of enchanted dust providing little deterrent against the gloom.

Sterling took a deep breath. "Relic-magic," he muttered. "But it's old." Jasmina shivered and he glanced down at her, hoping her courage wouldn't fail her.

"What good will it do to find my illusion," she whispered, "if I don't have the relic to reverse the spell?"

"Wouldn't you prefer her locked up at the Hall instead of going to balls and soirees wearing your face?"

Lady Jasmina squared her shoulders and marched down the corridor. Sterling caught up with her in two strides, pulling his cap down even farther. He opened the door at the end of the hallway and they entered the storage area of the warehouse. Boxes stamped with labels of their contents littered the enormous room. Sterling lifted the lid of one half-opened box and glanced at the duplicate statues of Egyptian gods that lay nestled in sawdust. No doubt they were touted and sold as original antiquities.

"Stay behind me," he whispered. Off to the right amidst the crates shone a curve of light, where Sterling thought additional guards might be. But he didn't think Jaz would be in the storage areas, so he headed to the left, where the offices were located. It took them over an hour to search the unlocked rooms, and none of them looked like sleeping quarters.

Sterling's neck started to itch. So far, it had been

too easy. Not a single guard patrolled this area and it made him twitchy. Then again, they hadn't found a hint of his wife and perhaps there was nothing here to find.

"This one is locked," whispered Jasmina. Sterling nodded, pulled a lock pick from his pocket and set to work. Lady Jasmina raised a brow but didn't say a word about his finesse in opening the door. He remembered the way she'd broken into the Duke of Hagersham's mansion in her chimney-sweep disguise. Now that he thought about it, she appeared to be awfully skilled at breaking and entering herself.

He didn't have time to give it further thought as the door lock clicked and swung open. Sterling headed down the dark narrow stairway, Lady Jasmina hard on his heels. The air grew chillier the farther they descended. The musky scent of earth and damp made it hard to breathe, and the darkness became absolute when they reached the bottom of the stairs.

"Light," whispered Sterling. "But not near us."

He saw Lady Jasmina nod and felt a glimmer of admiration for her. She didn't ask questions, just did what needed to be done. A dim light flickered five feet in front of them. Sterling blinked. More doors. Many more doors studded the circular, earthen-hewn under-ground chamber. He gritted his teeth in frustration and realized that despite Jaz's unconventional nature, she wasn't likely to live in this underground cell.

Sterling turned to head back up the stairs when a sound caught his attention. He half-shifted to stal-lion, using the keener ears of his were-self, and heard more shuffling.

It could just be a rat. But he had a horrible thought. What if Jaz was being held here against her will? What if she'd gotten involved with whoever owned this warehouse of fraud and had done something to anger him?

His imagination was working overtime.

Still, he circled the room, pausing before each door, half-shifting and listening within before moving on to the next one. At the thirteenth door he heard sounds of breathing. He worked on the lock, but it was more complicated than the ones upstairs.

He heard the door at the top of the stairs squeak open.

"Someone's coming," he warned Jasmina, his hand steadily working the lock. Sterling heard her mutter a spell, then a furious pounding from the top of the stairs.

"Rats," she whispered.

Sterling smiled. The pounding turned to thumps and then a curse and the sound of running feet. He glanced up at her.

"Ogre-rats." She grinned. "Big, ugly hairy ones."

Their eyes held for a moment, a timeless second that seemed to go on for an eternity. The glitter of humor in her eyes changed into something else, some longing that he felt reflected in his own soul. But then the lock clicked open and he remembered his wife. He pushed the door open.

Jasmina blinked and waved her hand, throwing her ball of light into the room in front of them. The chamber stank of urine and blood and other smells he refused to identify. A small figure huddled in the far corner, a young girl with black hair and thin limbs.

Sterling's heart squeezed and he shifted uncontrollably.

With an iron will he suppressed his were-self, forcing his voice to low tones. "Angel?"

The girl opened her eyes and stared at him. Eyes that looked glazed with shock. That glittered a pale green in the mage-light. Sterling's heart sank. Angel had blue eyes. For a moment he'd thought he'd found his sister, and the disappointment cut him like a knife.

The girl whimpered and tried to shrink into a smaller ball. Lady Jasmina stepped cautiously forward, holding out her empty hands. "We won't hurt you, see? We've come to rescue you."

The girl shook her head. "You lie. You're one of them."

"No, it's only an illusion." Jasmina ran her hand down her face, removing the spell. "See? I'm not really a man."

Sterling stepped between Lady Jasmina and the girl. "She's a shape-shifter. Your illusion didn't work on her."

"But I don't understand…"

The girl pointed an accusing finger at Jasmina. "You're that lady. The one with the man who stole me."

"No, child. That wasn't me. It was… my twin sister."

"Lady Jasmina," whispered Sir Sterling, "can you please give me a bit of room?" Again she didn't ask questions, just did as he asked, yet he had a feeling it was due to the shock of having a child fear her. Or the knowledge that her twin had been involved with the abduction of the girl.

Sterling shifted, lowering his equine head and blowing gently at the child. When she smiled he shifted back to human. "I'm one of you. You can trust me. What's your name?"

The child sat up, words falling from her mouth like a dam bursting. "Mary Rabins. I can change into a rabbit, just like my ma. She works at the Hook and Claw Inn an' I was helpin' with the wash an' this man and lady come an' took me an' said they needed to expera... eperamen—"

"Experiment," interjected Lady Jasmina.

Mary's mouth clamped shut. Sterling sighed and held out his hand. "Come, child, and we'll take you home. You want to go home, don't you?"

Her eyes filled with tears and she nodded her head. Sterling gathered the slight form into his arms and Mary cried out. He studied her exposed skin, but couldn't see any signs of bruising. Had they already experimented on her? How and why?

He didn't have the time to ask her any more questions. Perhaps when he brought her to the prince they'd be able to find out more.

Lady Jasmina led the way up the stairs, peeking around the door left ajar by the guard she'd scared with her illusion of ogre-rats. She waved a hand for Sterling to follow and they stepped out into the warehouse, weaving their way through the stacked crates.

Sterling's neck started to itch again. The silence felt too heavy. He half-shifted, bringing a smile to Mary's face, and listened with his were-senses. Something up there, on top of that crate just beside Jasmina.

"They're over here," shouted a tinny voice. "Quick, quick, before they get away!" A small figure with a nose like a cucumber and ears like a mule jumped up and down atop the wooden crate.

Sterling let out a vile oath. That bloody gnome.

He'd forgotten all about him. So much for making a stealthy exit. Now whoever had kidnapped the girl would be warned, and by the time he told Sir Artemus about it, the warehouse would be cleared out and a new base established. How had the little monster managed to get in anyway? Too late to think about it now. He turned and handed Mary to Lady Jasmina. Jasmina sagged beneath the child's weight, and when the girl wiggled to be let down, the lady gladly set her on her feet.

Sterling pulled both knives from his boots and crouched in a fighter's stance. "Run," he snapped, wondering why Jasmina just stood there. Then three guards rounded the corner of stacked crates and he didn't have time to think of anything other than defending their lives. They hadn't drawn their guns yet—blades were much quieter when avoiding the notice of the police. Sterling responded in kind, throwing both his own knives at once. He hit the man on the left in the leg, temporarily downing him. But his other knife embedded itself up to the hilt in the crates behind his attackers.

"You missed," squeaked the gnome.

"Only one of 'em," growled Sterling. He pulled the other knives from his sleeves and crossed them defensively as one of the guards swung at him with his sword. Sterling heaved the swordsman away from him and spun, blocking a swing from the second man.

"Bravo," yelled the gnome.

Then both of the guards backed up, including the one on the ground, who crawled backward on his knees. Sterling turned around. Behind him stood an illusion of two snarling hellhounds, their long fangs dripping foam and their faces twisted in such furious menace that they even made Sterling wince. With a mighty leap the hounds jumped over him and snapped at the guards.

He stuck his knives in his waistband, strode over to Lady Jasmina and picked her up, kissing her with such gratitude that he left her face a becoming shade of pink.

"We make a great team," he murmured.

"Er, Lady Jasmina," called the gnome from atop his crate.

"Haven't you caused enough trouble, Nuisance?" she replied, staring at Sterling with the most delightful warmth in her eyes.

"Duck!" he screamed.

Sterling heard the panic in the gnome's voice and carried Jasmina to the ground with him. A bullet whizzed over their heads and sent splinters flying from the crate behind them. And he'd bet that those bullets were silver.

He dragged Jasmina behind the crate. "Mary," she gasped.

The child sat where they'd left her, huddled into a ball of fear again. Sterling cursed and shimmied across the floor. The idiot guards shot at the illusory dogs, so most of their bullets flew above his head. But based on their sword-fighting ability, he wasn't about to gamble on their sharp-shooting skills.

He dragged Mary to safety, pulled the child into his arms and followed Lady Jasmina, who didn't need to be told to run this time. They reached the door where they'd entered, the troublesome gnome right behind them. "Two guards waiting outside," panted Nuisance.

Sterling looked down at Jasmina. She nodded, even though her face showed signs of magical exhaustion. The door flew open and another hellhound charged out, slathering and snarling with enough menace to send the guards outside running. Before they gathered their courage and pulled out their own pistols, Sterling handed the child to Lady Jasmina and shifted, lowering his front legs and snorting with impatience.

Jasmina slid onto his back like water over a smooth rock, but the child and the gnome scrambled and kicked his ribs, and Sterling shook his mane with annoyance. Finally he felt them settle, and he took off at a canter, Jasmina managing to keep his other two passengers on his back.

Sterling galloped over London Bridge and along Basilisk High Street, all the way to Westminster Road, then slowed to a walk the rest of the way to the Hall of Mages. A were-stallion had extraordinary speed and strength compared to a regular horse, but he did have his limits.

He went to the back entrance of the Hall and shifted as soon as his charges climbed off of him. Sterling rapped on the door and told the novice who answered to fetch Sir Artemus. The were-lion appeared at the door with remarkable speed, his shirt half on and his eyes still blinking sleepily. "What do we have here?"

Lady Jasmina wobbled on her feet, her face white with exhaustion. Sterling grasped her arm and brushed past the baronet with Mary following. Nuisance had disappeared.

"Tea, I think," said Sterling. "And some scones for the little one."

Sir Artemus raised a golden brow but led them into a parlor while he presumably went to roust a novice to prepare a tray. Sterling led Jasmina and the child over to the fire, where they collapsed onto a settee.

"Are you all right?" he asked Jasmina, worried at the pallor of her skin. Right now, the child looked in better condition than the lady.

"Too many spells," she murmured, staring into the flames. "Too many distressing discoveries."

Sterling glanced at the child.

"I wanna go home," Mary said.

He nodded. "You will. But first you must eat, and then talk to the prince. Wouldn't you like to meet His Royal Highness?"

"No. I wanna go home."

"Perhaps you could bring her mother here," suggested Lady Jasmina.

The child thought about it a moment. "All right."

Sterling smiled at Mary, relieved and a bit surprised by the child's resiliency.

Sir Artemus entered the room. "I'm sure you're going to explain your late-night visit." He glanced over at the sailor clothes Jasmina wore, then pointedly at the child. It wasn't a request.

Sterling tossed the hair off his forehead. "I found a lead on my... Jasmina's illusion. In a warehouse that held the old taint of relic-magic. We didn't find Jaz, but we found this child held captive in a room."

Sir Artemus frowned.

"She was kidnapped by Jaz and another man,"

Sterling continued. "They told the child that they wanted to experiment on her, and I thought the master would like to speak with her, in case she overheard anything else."

"I want my mama," wailed the little girl.

Sterling nodded. "A Mrs. Rabins. She works at the Hook and Claw Inn."

"On Wonderland Road. I know of it. I'll send for her now." Sir Artemus hesitated. "In the meantime, I suggest you take Lady Jasmina home. She looks ready to expire."

"I'm fine," she insisted.

Sterling shook his head. "No you're not." He held up a hand as she looked ready to protest. "I promise I'll tell you if we find out anything else." He stepped over to the settee and gently lifted her to her feet.

A novice entered the room as they were leaving, and Sterling watched Mary's face light up at the treats on the tray. She'd be fine.

"One more thing," Sterling said as they stood outside the door. He didn't think it was a coincidence that Mary had been abducted and that she was a shape-shifter. "Sir Artemus, have other shape-shifters besides my sister gone missing?"

He looked surprised enough that Sterling believed his reply. "No, not that we've heard of." He glanced at Mary stuffing tarts into her mouth. "But we're a private lot. Perhaps I'll do some sniffing around."

Sterling nodded. "I'll be back," he promised.

Then he led Jasmina out into the early gray dawn of a London morning.

"You'd better get me home fast," she whispered, her voice faint with fatigue. "Or I'm in for it."

Sterling bowed. "As my lady commands. Are you sure you aren't too tired to keep your seat?"

She gave him her most dignified glare. He shifted while laughing and welcomed her weight on his back. He galloped through the streets, startling a few ambitious costermongers. She dismounted on the service street behind the mews of her home. She wavered on her feet for a moment. Then her head lifted, her spine straightened, and she took a few steps forward.

Sterling nickered, worried that the drain on her magical reserves had been too much for her. She turned, stared into his eyes a moment, then leaped toward him, wrapping her arms around his equine neck, tangling her fingers in the thick hair of his mane.

Sterling froze. She hugged him hard and then spun on her heel, disappearing around the corner of the stables. A surge of unfamiliar warmth overtook him. Beneath that priggish exterior beat a heart braver and kinder than any he'd ever known. He could live a thousand years and never meet another woman like Lady Jasmina Karlyle.

Why did he have to go and marry her twin?

Ten

Jasmina listened to the birds outside her open window while she finished her daily correspondence. She sealed her last letter with a blob of red wax and sat back with a sigh. "Why did you save my life last night, Nuisance?"

She heard a rustle from the top of her wardrobe. "If you die, I won't be having any more fun, now will I?"

Jasmina turned in her chair, arranging the ruffles of her white skirt. She clasped her hands in her lap and looked up at the garden gnome, suppressing a smile. He looked dreadful, with that huge pocked green nose and furry ears. "You've come very close to killing me, you know."

His large brown eyes shimmered. "That was before."

"Before what?"

"Before I got to know you. Not that I really wanted to kill you, mind." He tugged at his ear and winced at the furry texture. "I just get carried away. Will you get rid of these ears now?"

"I suppose it's the least I can do." Jasmina waved her fingers. The mule ears disappeared, although the gnome's own ears weren't much smaller. The little man felt them and grinned. Then he crossed his brown eyes to stare pointedly at his cucumber nose, and this time Jasmina burst out laughing. "Oh, dear. I'm terribly sorry, you just… with your eyes crossed…"

Nuisance kicked his heels on the top of the wardrobe door and glared until Jasmina removed the cucumber illusion. He scrambled down from the wardrobe and stood in front of the cheval glass, tilting it downward. "There are several lady gnomes who will be grateful."

Jasmina pushed her hand over her mouth. Granted, his nose was no longer green, but it was still quite generous. And lumpy.

"I'm considered quite a catch, you know."

She nodded frantically, wishing he'd stop talking. She felt ready to burst into laughter again and it might hurt his feelings. Jasmina wanted to continue whatever sort of truce she felt they'd reached.

"Handsome, I am. To other gnomes, that is." Nuisance peeked bashfully at her. "Not sure about humans. Do you think I'm handsome, Lady Jasmina?"

Oh, heavens. She couldn't speak. Jasmina nodded again, tears burning her eyes. She felt sure lady gnomes considered him handsome. After all, most male garden gnomes looked a hundred years old. Youth had to be to his advantage. But he couldn't be more than two feet tall, and his bare feet had black hair curling up from the toes, and ears as big as saucers still stuck out from the sides of his head.

Jasmina removed her hand from her mouth and, with an extraordinary force of will, stuffed the laughter back down her throat and changed the subject. "I do wish you'd stop following me. Isn't there some lady gnome that's missing your, ah, attentions?"

"Of course. But she wouldn't be half as fun as you."

She resisted the urge to throttle him. "Do you call nearly getting shot *fun*?"

His brown eyes twinkled. "Wasn't it grand? And did you see Sir Sterling fight with his knives? I haven't seen that kind of swordplay in decades."

Jasmina sighed. He had a point. Sir Sterling had been magnificent, all flashing steel and rippling muscle and savage grace. Just the memory of his bravery made her face hot. Made her want to squirm in her chair. Made her want to possess the man, to tame him and make him her own…

Nuisance cocked his head at her. "Looks like you enjoyed it too."

Jasmina scowled in the best imitation of her aunt. "Don't be ridiculous."

The gnome harrumphed and hopped up on her windowsill, pulling his pipe from his pocket. Before she had a chance to protest he'd packed and lit it, a stream of smoke curling about the room. Father enjoyed the occasional cigar, and Jasmina had already wrinkled her nose in anticipation. But surprisingly the smoke smelled heavenly, like a meadow of sunflowers on a hot day.

"I think you like the animal," accused the gnome.

Jasmina breathed deeply. "Nonsense. I have no interest in men. And even if I were to marry, it could never be to a shape-shifter."

Nuisance nodded with satisfaction. "Still, he's got more style than most of your snobbish circle."

Jasmina wished the little scamp would cease his

prattle about Sir Sterling. The baronet had risked life and limb to save her, and she'd never forget it. She'd tried desperately not to think about him. His tenderness made her feel cherished. His bravery made her feel safe. She didn't want to feel those things. It made her question her desire to never marry—made her question the opinions of society.

Made her insanely jealous of her own illusion.

Mercifully, Aunt Ettie chose that moment to knock on her door and peek around the frame. "Your parents are waiting, Jasmina. Did you forget they were taking us to the—" Her eyes followed the trail of smoke to the window. "What are you doing here, you little beast?" She entered the room and waved her closed umbrella threateningly.

Nuisance took a puff and defiantly blew a smoke ring.

"He was just leaving," said Jasmina, rising from her chair and smoothing her bodice. "And I don't think you really want to follow me today, Nuisance."

He nervously eyed Aunt's swishing umbrella. "Why's that?"

Jasmina plucked her own umbrella from the stand and chose her favorite sun bonnet, the one woven with tiny white silk roses around the band. "Because we are going to the annual rose show." She smiled when Nuisance choked on his pipe.

Jasmina quickly checked her appearance in the glass. Her white day dress of smooth lawn would keep her cool in the sun, and the ruffles on the skirt and over the bodice would flutter with every small breeze. She tied her bonnet ribbon under her chin. "Just imagine. Real Garden Club ladies everywhere. One could only guess at their reaction to a garden gnome amongst their prized displays."

Nuisance dumped the ashes from his pipe over the ledge of the window and slipped it back in his pocket. "I suppose there are a few ladies back in Toadstool Garden who've been longing for a visit from me."

Jasmina glanced at Aunt Ettie and sent her a warning look not to laugh. "That sounds like an excellent idea. Aunt, shall we go?"

Aunt Ettie shifted her gaze from Nuisance to Jasmina with a frown puckering her brow, but didn't say a word until they'd reached the bottom of the staircase. "I don't like the look that gnome was giving you."

"Whatever do you mean?" Jasmina thought Aunt would be happy that Nuisance seemed to be more accommodating.

"Oh, my dear girl. Didn't you notice? Why, he looked absolutely smitten!"

"Then perhaps he'll give me less trouble."

Aunt sniffed. "I'm not sure if a garden gnome in love is any better than one intent on mischief."

"You exaggerate," replied Jasmina as they reached the front door. Aunt Henrietta followed Jasmina out to the waiting carriage without another word. Mother and Father already sat inside, obviously impatient with the delay.

"Did you forget to check the time, dear?" asked Mother. "You're usually quite prompt."

"I do apologize." Jasmina took her seat across from them and looked out the window. She seemed to be doing a lot of apologizing lately. "But there was some correspondence I had to attend to."

"Oh, of course," said Mother, aware that half of Jasmina's "correspondence" involved instructions to the staff on the running of the household.

Father told the coachman to drive on, then gave her a nod of approval. "You've always been a responsible girl."

Now, why did his comment make her cringe? Usually such praise would fill her with satisfaction.

Jasmina forgot all her worries when they reached St. James's Park and entered the arch of magically blooming flowers that served as the entrance to the show. She breathed in the perfume of thousands of roses, and her eyes feasted on the riot of colors and blossoms. Just past the prince's private pavilion two paths of sparkling gravel branched in opposite directions, winding through arbors and refreshment tables and flower displays that sported engraved placards proudly announcing the horticulturists.

Father chose the path through the naturally grown flowers first, since the magically grown displays always overshadowed them and stole some of their glory. They strolled through lilac-colored roses of such variety that Mother had to exclaim over each one—to the delight of Father and the annoyance of Aunt Ettie. Jasmina followed them quietly—as was her habit—soaking up the calm aura that nature seemed to inspire in her, when suddenly she felt… something. A heightened awareness, a pull of her senses.

She looked up, scanning the knots of people winding their way through the paths ahead of them. Over the tops of a border of red roses, beneath an arbor covered in a bloodred variety, stood Sir Sterling Thorn. He leaned a hip against the latticework, his arms crossed over his broad chest, his full-lipped mouth curled in a sardonic grin. His black hair shimmered in the sunlight and his eyes sparkled like deep blue sapphires.

Jasmina felt herself drowning in his gaze. She remembered the last time she'd seen him, when he'd been in were-form and she couldn't resist hugging the stallion. Did he realize how much she'd admired him for his bravery? That her gesture had been an impulse she couldn't resist?

She couldn't let him know how much her feelings toward him had altered. As soon as they found the relic and her twin, she would never see him again. It was ridiculous to allow herself to feel this way about a shape-shifter.

The calm she'd felt had shattered. Her heart raced in a staccato rhythm that made her part her mouth just to catch a breath.

Sir Sterling's grin broadened.

Jasmina reached inside herself for the mask that had always served to hide her emotions and struggled to put it in place. Her palms broke out in a sweat. If only he'd stop staring at her! Why did this connection exist between them? As if her body responded to him despite her resistance.

"Jasmina, are you feeling all right?"

Thank heavens. Aunt Ettie's face cut her off from the baronet's view and allowed Jasmina to regain control of herself. "I'm perfectly fine," she replied, with only a hint of shakiness to her voice.

Aunt Ettie clasped her arm and tugged her along to catch up with her parents, leaning close to whisper conspiratorially. "Don't look now," she warned.

Jasmina plastered a smile to her face. Had Aunt Ettie felt Sir Sterling as well? But no, Aunt's next words cautioned her against someone else entirely.

"It's the Honourable Blanche Liliput."

"So?"

"She's with her shape-shifter fiancé. And she's such a dunce that she's making a beeline for your parents."

Good grief. Jasmina saw the redhead towing a black-haired, jackal-faced man along with her. And she remembered his name. Mr. Cecil Thorn. "It's his brother," she whispered back.

"Whose brother?" asked Aunt Ettie, her eyes already alight with the anticipation of the meeting. Miss Blanche was the worst sort of social climber, always trying to encroach on the upper classes, and although Mother and Father had always been polite to her, she should realize that a shape-shifter on her arm would doom her.

"Blanche's fiancé is Mr. Cecil Thorn. Sterling's brother."

"Oh." Aunt Ettie's face sagged in disappointment. "That certainly takes all the fun out of it."

Jasmina patted her shoulder. "Don't worry. Sir Sterling quite despises his brother. It appears that Cecil won't acknowledge their connection because of the gossip surrounding their missing sister."

Aunt perked up. "Excellent. Then they shall both deserve what they are about to get."

Mother and Father were discussing a particular variety of the pink French rose when Blanche dropped to a deep curtsy in front of them. Neither of them even glanced at the girl. Cecil cleared his throat. Aunt Ettie sniffed.

Jasmina had experienced so many of these exhibitions of social status that she'd learned to ignore them. Usually her parents gave the cut direct, and only occasionally was her family on the receiving end of such a slight. Either way, she'd always taken her cue from her parents and hadn't given it much thought.

Unlike Aunt Henrietta, who enjoyed the discomfiture of a presumptuous social climber.

Miss Blanche had finally unfolded herself from her curtsy, her face pinker than the surrounding roses. "Good afternoon, Lord and Lady Kraken."

Mother and Father continued to stroll along and the silly Miss Blanche actually walked backwards to keep in front of them. "I would like to introduce my fiancé—"

"Lord Kraken," Mother said, her eyes never for a second landing on the couple, "I think I should like to see the magical exhibitions now."

"Mr. Cecil Thorn," continued Blanche, raising her voice an octave higher.

"Excellent idea," Father replied, steering Mother in the direction of another path.

Several ladies standing near them stared in horror at the impudence of the young couple. One of the younger girls pointed at Cecil and giggled. His face turned pinker than Miss Blanche's and he roughly grasped his fiancée's arm. "You said you knew them," he snarled.

Jasmina blinked at the hostility in his voice, allowing her eyes to meet his for one dreadful moment. Sterling's brother glared at her with such venom that she stiffened her spine and pulled her skirts away from the couple. She wished she could have given the girl a brief nod, since Blanche suffered only from mere silliness. But Cecil did not. Obviously his animal nature extended to his man-form, and he lacked the qualities of gentlemanly behavior that Sir Sterling showed an abundance of.

"Oh, my," breathed Aunt Ettie. "It always amazes me how well your parents *do* that. I've never been able to pull off such a cut with that much polish."

"Good," said Jasmina. "It shows that you're a bit kinder. Would it have harmed them to give Miss Blanche a nod? I admit that Cecil deserved a snub, but she's just a foolish girl trying to fit in…" She trailed off, amazed at her own newfound sympathy.

Aunt Ettie grinned and nodded her head, the egret feathers in her bonnet flapping crazily with the movement. "It does my heart good to see that you finally realize your parents aren't perfect—that perhaps their needs and opinions aren't necessarily your own."

"I-I meant nothing of the sort," said Jasmina, almost running to catch up to her mother and father. She just wished she didn't now know that a gentleman's character wasn't determined by his title. Her ill treatment by the Duke of Hagersham had driven that point home. Even more revelatory had been the equally unexpected kindness of Sir Sterling Thorn.

But her aunt didn't need to know that.

Jasmina trailed after her parents, Aunt Ettie glued to her side, a smug grin on her face that Jasmina refused to acknowledge. Instead she lost herself in the creations around them. None of the flowers were illusions or magical creations; they had to be real for the show. But magic was used in their growth, and unlike Viscount Wiccens' greenhouse, all had been grown for their beauty and not their herbal value.

Mother gasped and exclaimed over a rose display that appeared to be blooming before their very eyes. Jasmina watched as a blue rosebud opened its petals and waved in the breeze for several minutes. Then the rose dropped its leaves, wilted to brown, and the stem sprouted a new growth just below the old one. Jasmina examined the green sprout in amazement as the entire process repeated moments later.

Despite her concentration on the magic of the blue rose, she felt Sir Sterling's stare again. She didn't have to turn around to know it was him. She felt his attention through the tingle of her skin, the flutter of her belly, the frisson of heat that curled between her legs.

Preposterous! She could not allow this man to upset her so. Aunt Ettie gave her a questioning glance and Jasmina smiled weakly at her, struggling to regain control. She would not allow other people to notice her state of mind.

Jasmina tried not to think of him. They passed a vine that grew roses large enough to sleep in… and an image of her naked body curled up inside with an equally naked Sir Sterling popped unbidden into her mind. That was the second time she'd imagined him without his clothes on. How did she manage that when she'd never seen a naked man before in her life?

She scanned the pathways around her, ready to do battle. She still felt painfully aware of his presence and hadn't managed to fully regain control of herself.

Therefore, he had to leave. It would never do if Mother and Father noticed her anxiety.

Her eyes met his as if they'd been snared in a trap. He stood next to a mound of tiny white roses, the spent petals floating on the breeze and surrounding him in a summer snowstorm. He looked like some deity from one of her books, and she couldn't stop the smile of admiration that curled her mouth. She'd had every intention of glaring at him, of waving her hand to tell him to leave her alone. But Jasmina could only stand, frozen to the spot, a low moan rising in the back of her throat.

Aunt Ettie squeezed her arm. Hard. "My, I think the heat has made me a bit dizzy." She dragged Jasmina along behind her. "Excuse us, Horace, but I think I need some refreshment."

Father nodded distractedly. The Marquess and Marchioness of Faerlinn had deigned to stop and talk to them, and he proudly exchanged pleasantries with his peers. Mother exclaimed over the Marchioness's ruby necklace, all the while glancing about to see if any of their acquaintances bore witness to their conversation with a titled couple a class above their own.

Aunt Ettie purchased two glasses of lemonade and forced Jasmina to drink hers. "Whatever is the matter with you?" asked Aunt between sips.

The cool, tart liquid seemed to revive Jasmina from the spell Sir Sterling had put on her. And everybody said that baronets didn't have any magic. "Sir Sterling is here."

"Aah," breathed Aunt Ettie, as if that explained everything. "Where?"

"The next path over, standing next to the miniature roses." Aunt Ettie turned.

"No, don't look now," warned Jasmina—too late. Aunt Henrietta waved at Sterling, who bowed in recognition.

"Now you've done it," snapped Jasmina.

"Don't be a goose."

"He's coming this way." Jasmina set down her glass and turned to flee, but her parents blocked her way.

"Feel better now, Henrietta?" asked Father.

"Quite."

"Then let's carry on." Father patted Mother's arm where it crooked around his own and continued down the path.

"I-I think I'm not feeling very well," said Jasmina to her father's back.

He looked over his shoulder, annoyance creasing his brow. "Not you too?"

Jasmina cringed at the look he gave her. Father hated to be inconvenienced. "I'm sure I'll be fine," she hastily assured him. He nodded and continued walking. The path straightened out before them and Jasmina glimpsed Sir Sterling. Heading straight for them.

"Then again…" she said. This time Father ignored her, and Mother was so busy chattering about the furry rose exhibit that Jasmina doubted she'd heard her.

Sir Sterling didn't alter his course. She didn't dare look in his eyes, knowing that she'd be doomed if she did. Mother's voice faded to silence as she noticed the baronet directly in their path. She slowed her pace to walk alongside Jasmina and glanced sharply at her, which made Father frown, his eyes going from his daughter to the baronet.

Surely, they didn't know? Other than Lady Wiccens mentioning that Jasmina had been seen talking to a baronet, her parents couldn't have any idea of her relationship with Sir Sterling. Could they?

Jasmina glanced at Aunt Ettie, the older woman's eyes suddenly widening in understanding. But Jasmina had not forgotten the threat her father had made about replacing her aunt as Jasmina's chaperone. To lock Jasmina in her room and toss away the key.

Jasmina lifted her chin, her parents smiled, Aunt Ettie grimaced, and they all walked on. They were going to do it. They were going to snub Sir Sterling, and she would have to go along with them. After everything he'd done for her, surely she couldn't manage to cut him. But she couldn't disappoint her parents, or humiliate them by acknowledging a baronet in public. But maybe Sterling had more sense than to approach her?

Jasmina glanced up. His eyes met hers for a moment, that rakish smile of his lighting up his face, and she stopped breathing. He bowed, a low sweep to the ground.

And they all sailed past him as if he didn't exist.

Jasmina started to breathe again, wishing that she'd stopped permanently, for she'd never felt more ashamed of herself in her life. She didn't dare look over her shoulder at Sterling, afraid of what expression she might see on his face.

Mother and Father chatted on as if nothing monumental had happened, but Aunt Ettie sent Jasmina a look of apology for encouraging the baronet toward them. As they walked on past the peacock roses and the roses of spun gold, Jasmina felt something tear inside of her. She'd always taken into consideration her parents feelings before her own. But she had to live with her own conscience too, and she made a decision. Sterling was a good man. A brave man. She'd never slight him in public again, despite how her parents would feel about it.

She fought the urge to run back after him and apologize. That would only create a scene. But next time. Next time she would give him the public acknowledgement he deserved.

"I think the lemonade *was* bad," said Aunt Ettie. "My stomach is quite uncomfortable. Are you still feeling unwell, Jasmina?" Jasmina nodded with relief, even though Father looked annoyed again.

"There's no reason to inconvenience yourself, Horace," Aunt assured him. "Jasmina and I will take the carriage home by ourselves, and I'll have it sent back for you."

Since Father's outing would not be interrupted, he gave them both a smile and told Mother not to worry over a little stomachache, and steered her quickly toward the next display.

"Thank you," sighed Jasmina.

"It's my fault that you were put into that impossible situation in the first place," replied Aunt. "I should never have waved at him. It was quite gauche of me."

Jasmina didn't reply, too intent on seeking out Sir Sterling. If she should happen to overtake him she could apologize. But she hadn't felt his eyes on her since their brief encounter, and she didn't spy a gentleman with thick black hair. She blinked back tears.

"You there," snapped Aunt Ettie. "What do you think you're about?"

Jasmina glanced up in surprise at a hovering messenger sprite. The winged creature settled on her shoulder and whispered in her ear before taking to the sky again with a buzz of iridescent wings.

"Well, what did she say?"

"It's a message from Sir Sterling," replied Jasmina, her heart pounding with excitement.

"Of course it is, but what does he want?"

Jasmina took a deep breath. "He wants me to meet him in the bog."

Eleven

"The bog?" asked Aunt Henrietta. "Ugh. That exhibit has been closed for months. Why ever would he want to meet you there?"

"Because it would be deserted."

Aunt Ettie sniffed. "Of course. Well then, let's be off. I can always tell Lucy that we began to feel better and tried to rejoin them but couldn't find—do stop shaking your head at me, Jasmina."

"I'm going alone."

Aunt looked torn between alarm and glee. "Are you sure?"

"Yes. I need to apologize, and I'd rather do that in private."

"Naturally." Aunt Henrietta glanced around. They stood near the entrance to the garden show, the prince's pavilion just beginning to fill with his courtiers. A dirt path to their right led into a stand of trees sheltering a small gazebo overrun with vines. She grasped Jasmina's arm and casually sauntered over to the small structure. "I will wait for you here. If you are gone longer than one hour, I will be forced to come fetch you."

Jasmina stared at her aunt in amazement. An entire hour? It was one thing to allow her charge out on a mission to return one of Mother's borrowed jewels, but quite another to willingly let Jasmina go meet with a man for such a length of time. Perhaps her parents were right. Perhaps she needed a more responsible chaperone.

Jasmina huffed and lifted her skirts, making her way through the forest path toward the lake. She was the one who wanted to meet Sir Sterling alone. Did she really want Aunt Henrietta to protest, or was she too frightened to take responsibility for her own decisions?

The path ended at a wall of bulrushes and grasses twice her height. An old sign with the words Exhibit Closed hung crookedly between two posts, marking the entrance to a trail already overgrown with plants. Jasmina ducked under the sign and noticed the ground lay covered in recently cut leaves. She avoided the sticky sap oozing from the sliced plants, her footsteps squelching in the soggy ground. Her best walking shoes soon became saturated, and she hoped they weren't ruined. Insects buzzed around her face, the growth nearly met above her head, and Jasmina had started to feel panicky from claustrophobia when she stumbled into a clearing.

The grasses gave way to enormous plants that formed a circle around the clearing, a few misshapen trees growing among them. Smaller plants grew on the ground beneath them, their shiny green leaves glittering in the sunshine in a prism of colors. Jasmina bent over to study one, reaching out to touch the tiny hairs that glittered with drops of moisture.

"I wouldn't do that," said Sir Sterling from behind her. If he had expected to startle her, he was sorely disappointed. But she did pull her hand away.

"Why not?"

"Those are carnivorous plants. Those shiny drops on the ends of the hairs trap insects. Then the leaves curl around their prey and release a substance that allows the plant to digest the insect."

Jasmina rose and turned, meeting his dark blue eyes. They glittered a hard cobalt, lacking the usual eager warmth she'd become accustomed to. His jaw looked equally rigid, his expression one of bored annoyance.

"I suppose you want to know what Mary said," he snapped.

Jasmina blinked. She'd been so intent on forming a proper apology that she'd completely forgotten about last night's adventure. But now her heart leapt with hope. Had the child revealed her twin's whereabouts? She licked her lips and stepped closer to him. He still had tiny white rose petals trapped in the strands of his hair, and she didn't resist the urge to run her hand through the thick black mass, creating a tiny snowfall.

He took her hand and pushed it gently away. "Mary overheard Jaz and the man who'd kidnapped her speak about a Brotherhood." His voice sounded husky.

Sterling walked toward the center of the clearing, as if he wanted to put as much distance between himself and Jasmina as he could. "They kidnapped Mary and who knows how many other weres to find out the secret to our immunity to magic. They will only discover that it's in our nature—but how many shape-shifters will they harm in the process? The same relic-stench surrounded your twin and Mary and the man who kidnapped my sister. And the Duke of Hagersham disappears with the relic and mentions a Brotherhood. I intend to find out how they are all connected."

"Since my illusionary twin appears to be involved as well, I suppose I shall have to help you," said Jasmina absentmindedly, still trying to form her words of apology for cutting him. Could a man even forgive such a blow to his pride? She doubted Father ever would. She closed the distance between them, grimacing at the sucking sound her shoes made on the wet ground. It felt like walking on a soggy carpet.

"That won't be necessary." He tossed his head and stood his ground, although she could tell he fought the urge to back away from her. "From what Mary said, their lair is in the Underground City beneath London, and it's not a place I would take a proper lady."

"I'm not exactly a proper lady," whispered Jasmina, standing so close to him she could feel the heat of his chest. "Not anymore."

He studied her, his eyes as hard as crystals. "My dear, you are the most prim little miss I've ever had the misfortune of meeting."

He was so angry. He purposely ignored the invitation in her eyes. Undaunted, Jasmina ran her hand up his chest, curling her fingers about his neck, stroking the back of it with the pads of her fingers, somehow knowing that his skin was sensitive there. Perhaps she didn't need words. Perhaps if she kissed him he might forgive her.

"Your hair looks like white gold in the sunshine," he said dispassionately, as if commenting on the weather. "And your eyes lighten to the shade of spring grass."

Jasmina smiled, bending his head down to hers. He didn't resist, just stared at her in fascination until her mouth touched his. For a moment he stood as rigid as a statue, but when her tongue pushed open his lips he groaned and his arms came around her, pulling her hard against his warm body. He took control of the kiss, pushing her body backwards as if he couldn't get close enough to her.

Jasmina felt the earth shake and held on to his shoulders for dear life. Oh, how she could get used to this. This complete arousal of her senses. He tasted like the finest of wines; he smelled like spice and sunshine and roses. Her fingertips felt every bump in the weave of his coat fabric and the tops of her hands tingled where his silky hair brushed over them. The back of her waist burned from the heat of his hands, and she reveled in the feel of his taut muscles enfolding her. Jasmina surrendered herself completely, aware of nothing more than Sir Sterling Thorn.

His lips moved to her throat, and his breath against her ear made her shiver. "I thought you asked to meet me so you could find out what we discovered from Mary." His chuckle against her neck made the earth move again. "But you yearn for me, don't you? I've lit a fire beneath that proper demeanor and despite your abhorrence for my nature you can't help yourself, can you?"

Jasmina loosened her hold on his shoulders and wrapped her fingers in his hair. Had her actions today made him think she actually abhorred him? Oh dear, he needed her to tell him how she really felt. She tugged gently and he allowed her to pull back his head so she could stare into his eyes. "I do not abhor you. I think you are brave and kind and—wait a moment. What did you say?"

His face had just started to soften from her words, but now his handsome features froze in distrust. He straightened and let go of her. "What do you mean?"

"I mean… you said…"

The earth shook again.

"You said that *I* asked you to meet me here." Jasmina frowned up at him. "But I received a message from *you*."

The ground gave a roll so hard that Jasmina almost lost her balance. Something flickered in Sterling's eyes, and he grabbed her hand. "It's a trap," he growled, pulling her nearly off her feet as he lunged for the exit path through the grasses.

They'd only managed to make it halfway out of the clearing when Jasmina glanced behind her. The soggy peat had formed a depression where they had stood, and suddenly the ground completely gave way. A burp of rot puffed up through the tear in the middle of the meadow. She found herself struggling uphill as the earth collapsed behind them. "What's happening?"

"Sinkhole," gasped Sterling, tearing at the peat with his hands, their bodies now almost parallel to the ground. "Aided by magic. But natural."

Which meant he wasn't immune to it. Jasmina frantically thought of a way to save them, wishing she had the power of a marchioness to transport them out of here, or the magic of a duke so that she could change actual matter. But what could her illusions do against such a thing?

Jasmina couldn't find purchase with her feet; they kept slipping out from under her, and despite Sterling's strength they started to slide backwards. It felt as if he would tear her arm completely out of its socket. She took another look behind her and wished she hadn't. A black hole seemed to be swallowing the meadow, an endless drop down into muddy waters that would surely suck them under and slowly suffocate them. She scrambled her feet even faster, clutched his waistband with her other free hand, and stifled a scream.

Sterling managed to grasp the drooping limb of one of the scraggly trees and halt their backward slide.

"Now what?" she asked.

"I'm open to suggestions."

The earth dropped again until Jasmina could no longer feel it beneath her. How could he sound so blasé? Oddly enough, though, his tone calmed her. "Perhaps I should scream for help?"

"What, and alert your parents to the fact that their estimable daughter had a private rendezvous with a lowly baronet?"

Jasmina's feet flailed on thin air. Was the man completely mad? "Help," she screamed. "Somebody help us!"

The meadow had entirely disappeared, only the round circle of growth ringing the black hole. She dangled from Sterling's arm, while he in turn dangled from what appeared to be a completely unsatisfactory tree branch.

A red pointed hat suddenly popped over the edge

of the pit. "I'm here," called Nuisance. "Lady Jasmina, have no fear! I will rescue you."

Sir Sterling snorted in derision. Jasmina almost laughed with relief. "Nuisance! Thank goodness you followed me anyway. Go get someone to help us."

"Quite unnecessary," puffed the little man. "I'll just go back and get that rope that held the warning sign, which you should have heeded, by the way..." His voice faded as he apparently trotted off to suit his words to action.

Sterling cursed. Jasmina agreed. She had little faith in the gnome's ability to rescue them and so she didn't hesitate when a magical solution suddenly occurred to her. With a mumble and just a faint wiggle of her fingers, flames burst up in the air behind them. Terror fueled her magic and the fire raged so high it pierced the clouds.

"Now you've done it," muttered Sterling. "That should bring half of London down upon us."

Jasmina opened her mouth to reply when she felt her body drop a good inch. Had she heard the creak of wood? She looked up at the tree limb and saw that it had started to peel away from the trunk.

Sterling cursed again. "Lady Jasmina, I want you to let go of my hand—"

"You cad."

"Don't be ridiculous. When it comes to you, I'd rather die first than see you come to harm. Now listen, transfer your hold to my waistband."

Her other hand already held his waistband. If she transferred her hold his trousers would support all of her weight. She had a sudden vision of his pants dropping down to his knees and it didn't titillate her in the slightest. "Will it hold me?"

"If it doesn't, I promise that I'll be falling right behind you, love."

Her heart did a little flip over the endearment. And her mind scowled ferociously. He had to choose this moment to say such a thing? When she couldn't think about the implications or enjoy the sound of the word on his lips?

"Now do it," he commanded.

Jasmina transferred her hand to his waistband and it sagged beneath her weight, but held. She swallowed.

The man didn't wear any drawers.

As soon as she let go of Sterling's hand, he started to pull them upward, using only the strength in his arms. If she hadn't been so terrified, she would have cheered in sheer admiration. Then the sound of splintering wood reached her ears and she silently prayed for him to hurry. He grunted with the effort, pulling them up hand over hand, faster than she would have thought possible, but not fast enough. His arms had just reached the edge of the hole when the tree branch tore away completely.

Jasmina looked down—she couldn't help it. The sun shone on the surface of the mud at the bottom of the pit and things slithered in it. Things with scales and teeth and long tentacles.

She closed her eyes.

But they didn't fall. She cracked a lid upward and almost cried with relief when she saw that Sir Sterling had managed to grasp several naked tree roots. Again they rose, until he reached the edge and heaved his body half over, reaching down and flipping Jasmina up to lie next to him.

"Why didn't you wait for me?" demanded a squeaky voice and Jasmina looked up into the scowling face of her gnome. She didn't have the breath to reply to such a preposterous statement.

"Look, I brought the rope and everything." Nuisance tossed the old, frayed rope down next to her. With a withering glance at Sir Sterling, he disappeared back into the foliage. Jasmina showed the rope to Sterling. He eyed the tattered strand with skepticism. She knew it had less chance of holding her weight than the band of his trousers.

"You might want to get rid of that," said Sterling, nodding at the column of fire that spewed upward from the pit. With a wiggle of her fingers Jasmina dismissed the spell, hoping now that no one had taken notice of it.

"Let's get out of here." Sterling stood, holding his hand out to her. "Can you walk?"

She nodded and clasped his hand, allowing him to help her to her feet, marveling at the warmth that flowed through her at his touch. Her legs felt wobbly but managed to carry her with a little help from her rescuer. Jasmina desperately tried to hide the tears that fell down her face by pretending they didn't exist. She straightened her crooked bonnet and held her head high, taking delicate steps along the path despite the squishy sounds her shoes made.

"We've made someone nervous," he said, his hand a slight pressure on her arm.

She feared if she answered him her voice would break.

"That trap was meant for me," he continued, apparently lost in thought. "It would have been easier to set a magical one. However, since you also received a note to meet me there, I have to assume that someone wants you dead as well."

Tears had blinded her eyes, and he steadied her when she stumbled.

"You'll need someone to watch over you."

She could feel his eyes studying her as he waited for a reply. After several minutes of their squelching shoes and the wind sighing through the grass above their heads as his only response, she felt his arm snake around her waist. His voice lowered to a husky whisper. "Jasmina, love. It's all over. There's nothing to cry about."

They had almost reached the end of the tunnel of grass. Jasmina could just see unfiltered daylight ahead. She planted her feet and turned to look up into his face. Did he really think she was crying over their near brush with death?

"That's not—" she started, but her voice cracked and she had to struggle to maintain her composure. She tried again. "First of all, I'm not really crying. My eyes are just watering. And secondly, they are not watering because I was afraid. I am certainly made of sterner stuff than that."

His black brows shot up, and the right corner of his mouth twitched. Somehow both his arms had made their way around her waist, and he pulled her close, his face inches from her own. "Then pray tell, my lady. Why are your eyes watering?"

"Because." Oh, drat, her voice broke again. Jasmina

took another breath. She released her words with a rush. "My family and I cut you dreadfully today. And then you saved my life again before I even had a chance to apologize. You are one of the best men I know, and I'm ashamed of how I treated you."

He gathered her close, and she didn't hesitate to burrow her face in his shoulder. "That's why you're upset?" he whispered. "Because of some silly social convention?"

Jasmina nodded, scratching her nose against the weave of his coat. She felt his body shudder and lifted her head to stare at him, her eyes narrowed in suspicion. "Are you laughing?"

"Perish the thought. But I've just realized that I will never understand you."

Still, his lips kept twitching, and Jasmina's heart lifted a bit. "You forgive me, then?"

His hand skimmed over her cheek, smoothing the hair away from her face. Her coiffure had come completely undone, and she must have lost her favorite bonnet sometime during their struggle. It should have upset her, but all she could think about was how his blue eyes sparkled at her, how warm his arms felt as they held her securely within his embrace.

"There's only one way to guarantee my forgiveness," he murmured, his mouth lowering to hers.

Her heart skipped a beat. "And what would that be?"

"Kiss me."

Tiny jolts of lightning sparked through Jasmina's body as she rose on her toes and curled her fingers around the back of his head. *I'm sorry*, she said with her mouth, slightly opening her lips and pressing them against his. *I want you*, she said with her hands, smoothing them down the back of his muddy coat. *I wish you wanted me and not my illusion*, she said with her entire body, rubbing the length of her against him.

He pulled his head back for a moment, his eyes searching hers. As if he'd heard her thoughts and wanted to see them reflected in her face. He did the oddest thing then, a half nicker, half growl, as if his were-self and the human one fought for dominance. Or as if they'd both come to a complete accord.

Sterling lowered his head so quickly, so smoothly, that the force of his kiss stole her breath. He lifted her off her feet and she felt the world spin as if his kiss had become a dance. And Jasmina danced with him. Beneath the grasses of a bog. Muddy, scratched, and wet, with the smell of damp earth and tepid water filling her nose.

It was nothing short of heaven.

When Sterling finally set her on her feet it felt as if the ground shook, and she looked up in alarm, hoping it wasn't another sinkhole. Then she silently prayed for one when she saw the crowd gathered at the edge of the bog.

Jasmina's hands stole to her hot cheeks; then she hastily dropped them, smoothing the skirts of her dress, dismayed at the number of rents and the amount of mud that covered her once-white ruffles. She stiffened her spine and raised her chin, clasping her hands calmly in front of her.

"Well done," whispered Sterling.

She spared him a glance. He'd crossed his arms over his chest, a cocky grin across his face, exuding such an air of arrogant nonchalance that she echoed his sentiment right back at him. Then boldly faced the crowd.

"It appears that they are unharmed, Your Royal Highness," said Sir Artemus, who stood at the prince consort's side.

Aunt Ettie stood next to the were-lion, a look of apology and relief etched on her angular face. Next to Aunt stood... her parents. And the Marquess and Marchioness of Faerlinn. And behind them what looked like all the guests of the rose show.

"What happened?" demanded Prince Albert.

Sterling shrugged, the worn seams of his muddy coat threatening to split. "A sinkhole, I believe. Of a most... natural occurrence." His words hinted at more, and the prince narrowed his eyes and nodded at Sir Artemus.

The were-lion turned and growled at the assembled onlookers. "We have the situation in hand. Return to the gardens and we'll be along shortly."

Jasmina stared down the looks of censure cast in her direction as the crowd slowly drifted back through the forest. But she took a breath before meeting the eyes of her parents. Father glanced at the marquess as the man put his arm around his marchioness and led her away, and whatever her father had seen on the other man's face made him purple with rage. His brown eyes glittered and his mustache trembled as he looked at her. "Come here."

Jasmina froze. For the first time in her life, she was afraid of her father. Her chin rose a fraction higher.

"My lord," said Sir Sterling. "Your daughter has done nothing wrong."

"You dare even speak to me? You rake... you libertine... you animal! Jasmina, come to me at once."

Mother had started to cry. Aunt Ettie stared at Father as if she'd never seen him before. Jasmina took a step forward and then steeled herself, for she'd made a vow and intended to keep it. She turned back to Sterling, sweeping a low curtsy to him, muddy skirts and all. "Thank you," she whispered.

Sterling took her hand, and Sir Artemus physically restrained Father from attacking the baronet. Sterling placed a kiss on the back of her hand, as if they'd just finished a waltz in Buckingham Palace instead of narrowly escaping death in a bog. "It was my pleasure, my lady."

Father sputtered, fighting the restraint of the were-lion. "Jasmina, you will come to me this instant."

"Yes, Father." She slowly walked to his side, her shoes squishing loudly in the silence, her muddy petticoats sticking to her legs.

Jasmina had never imagined that her father would look at her the way he did now. Her stomach sank to somewhere down around her feet. Father had always adored her and treated her with respect. How had she allowed him to be so enraged with her?

She didn't need her illusion to destroy her life; she appeared to be doing a fine job of it herself.

"Father, I can explain," she started, but a glance at the prince warned her to say no more. She couldn't explain anything to her parents, not when it involved the safety of the realm.

"Horace," interjected Aunt Henrietta, "surely you are overreacting. There's no harm done, really. I'm sure Sir Sterling realizes that he's damaged Jasmina's reputation and will do the right thing by marrying her."

Jasmina blanched. How she wished Aunt Ettie wouldn't try to help.

Father had gone very still in Sir Artemus's hold. "Are you mad?" he hissed. "My daughter will never marry an *animal*. You are dismissed, Henrietta. As of this instant, you are no longer Jasmina's chaperone, do you understand me?"

Aunt Ettie took a step backward, her face white with shock. Mother's sobs shook the forest. Sterling tossed his head, his were-form shadowing his human one. Sir Artemus held her father so tightly that his knuckles had turned white.

And from somewhere within the tall grasses she heard the muffled laughter of Nuisance.

Prince Albert's voice cut through the tension. "Enough. Enough, I say, Lord Kraken. I see that your prejudice of my baronets runs as deep as the rest of your peers, and I'm appalled by it."

Some of the anger drained from Father, and he lowered his eyes. But Jasmina knew that her father's feelings would not be changed even by the words of his prince.

"She is my daughter, and I know what's best for her."

Sir Artemus finally released Father, although the were-lion continued to watch him. Jasmina's father adjusted the cuffs of his coat and cleared his throat. "My apologies, Your Highness. I may have over-reacted to the situation. But I had always assumed my daughter was a proper young lady." He turned and glared haughtily at Sir Sterling. "You, sir, will stay away from my daughter. I will have no more insults to her reputation."

Jasmina opened her mouth to protest that Sterling had never been anything but a gentleman when the were-stallion threw back his head and laughed. Jasmina frowned. Couldn't Sterling see that he only infuriated her father even more?

Sir Sterling glanced at her, his blue eyes as hard as ice and his mouth curled into a sneer. Oh heavens, he just didn't care. He didn't give a farthing for her father's opinion. Before things could get any worse Jasmina took a step closer to her father, allowing him to drape a proprietary arm about her waist. Sterling laughed again.

"This is intolerable," said Father.

"Quite right," agreed the prince. "Sir Sterling, stop baiting the man."

Sterling tossed his head and smiled even wider. He stared at Father for a moment and something passed between them that Jasmina faintly grasped. Some silent challenge that made her shiver.

Father led her through the forest, her mother and aunt bringing up the rear. Jasmina wished she could have stayed behind with the three men and been privy to their discussion. Now that the enemy had made such a bold move, what did the prince plan to do about it? Then she looked up at her father's face and realized she had best deal with one problem at a time.

Silence reigned until they arrived home and entered the privacy of their drawing room.

"How dare you embarrass me?" demanded Father, slapping his hand on the mantel of the fireplace.

Jasmina took a deep breath. "It wasn't intentional, I assure you." She tried to keep her voice calm and soothing.

"You will not leave this house until I feel that I can trust you again. Is that understood?"

"I… I… yes, of course, Father."

His brows lowered. "You have gravely disappointed us, daughter."

Jasmina's heart sank. She had never expected to hear those words from her father. She'd spent her entire life trying to do nothing but please him.

"I'm sorry."

"You will go to your room and not come out until I say so."

Aunt Ettie sniffed. "Isn't that a bit extreme? Surely you cannot expect her to decline all of her invitations at the height of the season."

Father looked as if he might have an apoplexy. Jasmina wished Aunt would just *stop* trying to help.

"She's my daughter and she will do as I tell her. And you!" Father took a step toward Aunt Ettie. "You are lucky that I'm still allowing you to stay in my home. And neither of you will leave this house unaccompanied, do you understand?"

"Of course they do," interjected Mother, sailing to Jasmina's side. "Come along, dear. Let's get you out of those muddy clothes. Henrietta, you'll need to change for dinner as well. Horace, please sit down and I'll have the maid bring you a brandy."

Jasmina watched her mother in amazement while they all scurried to do her bidding. She'd handled that amazingly well. When they reached her room, Jasmina gave her mother a grateful hug.

Mother took a step back and frowned. "Where do you keep the household keys?"

Jasmina blinked. "They... they are in my rose-wood desk."

Mother swept over to the escritoire and placed a delicate hand atop the shelf of cubbies. "Which one, dear?"

"The one on the far left."

She removed the keys from the small drawer and placed them in the pocket of her skirt. "I'll ring for your bath."

"Yes—but Mother, why are you taking the keys?"

"It's for the best, dear. Just until this matter is settled. Don't you think?"

Without waiting for an answer she sailed out the door. Jasmina collapsed in a puddle of torn and dirty skirts, her mouth open in disbelief. She'd had the run of this household since she was ten. It had never occurred to her that she'd done so on her mother's sufferance and that it could be taken away from her at any time.

This was a more devastating blow than her father's disappointment. Her chest squeezed so tightly she felt dizzy. She'd lost everything that mattered to her. And even worse...

Jasmina clenched her fists.

Even worse was that Mother now wore a new ruby necklace around her pale throat. The same ruby necklace the Marchioness of Faerlinn had worn earlier today.

Twelve

STERLING STOOD IN THE BEDROOM OF HIS FLAT, TUCKED A final knife in his boot, and reached for the leather cord to tie back his hair. He caught a glimpse of himself in the mirror and smiled, imagining what Jasmina would have to say about his clothing. For the past week he'd searched the Underground beneath London, the city of a thousand tunnels created by black magicians. Tonight would be no different, and he'd dressed in his work clothes, the rough material patched and mended in several places.

Then he thought of Lord Kraken and scowled. Lady Jasmina's father surely wouldn't approve of a man who got his hands dirty. The definition of a real gentleman meant he didn't work. Yet at times Sterling had helped harvest his small vineyard. Despite his father's mockery of the enterprise, and now Cecil's, he was determined to make the venture a success. He'd grafted the grapes on his own and knew they'd make the sweetest of wines. Once he had enough funds from the first few harvests to afford more help he'd burn these clothes. But for now, they helped him blend in perfectly with the citizens of the Underground.

He raked his hair back from his face and tied the leather. Why was he thinking about the old man anyway? He should be used to the way the gentry treated him by now. And yet over the past week he'd thought of nothing but the Lady Jasmina and her father. The brief flash of defiance she'd shown in curtsying to Sterling, and the old man's utter refusal to consider a shape-shifter as a husband for his precious daughter, had him smiling one minute and furious the next.

Sterling had given that little scene more importance than it warranted. He didn't give a farthing what Lord Kraken thought of him, yet he'd be hanged if he'd follow any orders from him concerning Jasmina. Not that he had any intention of marrying Lady Jasmina. He had already married her illusion.

He froze with a sudden thought, his tattered jacket halfway on his shoulders. Jaz was an exact duplicate of the lady herself; he had *her* signature on his marriage license. Ergo, he might even be considered already married to the Lady Jasmina. He laughed as he thought of the look on Lord Kraken's face if he ever found out about that license.

Sterling shrugged his coat the rest of the way on. It didn't matter. Nothing mattered but finding his sister, and he'd already been distracted enough by Lady Jasmina. He should be grateful to the old man for keeping his daughter confined in her home. Now he no longer had to worry about her safety and was free to search the Underground without the lady's interference.

Although she had made a jolly good partner when they'd gone into that warehouse…

"Enough," he said to his reflection before heading

for the door. He didn't relish the thought of crawling through crypts again to get to the entrance to the Underground. Trudging through the filth and sludge of the dark city, trying to wring information from the terrified inhabitants. The place reeked of relic-magic, but he couldn't pin down one scent stronger than any other to trace it to the relic.

He was sure that was why his heart leapt when a messenger sprite whispered in his ear just outside his building.

"Dear Sir S., Our mutual charge will escape tonight on an errand of great importance. Protect her. H.F."

"Can't the girl stay put?" he snapped, scaring the sprite and sending her buzzing up into the dark night. After what had happened in the bog, he couldn't help wondering if this might be another trap. Or if Jasmina might be heading into one. Still, it was an opportunity to see her again, and he tried not to think too hard about the smile curling up the corners of his mouth as he searched for a shadowed alley. He shifted to stallion, his unshod hooves and black coat and uncanny speed allowing him to travel the foggy London streets almost like a shadow. He mentally thanked Aunt Henrietta for her cleverness in not only knowing where to send him a message, but keeping abreast of her niece's activities despite Lord Kraken's dismissal of her as Jasmina's chaperone.

Someone wanted Jasmina dead. She shouldn't be roaming the streets at night. What could be so important that she'd take such a risk?

Sterling leaped over a cart, dodged a carriage and flew around the corner of Mandrake Square. He'd gone about his own business of searching for his sister, safe in the thought that Jasmina wouldn't dare leave her home. He'd seen the look of pain on her face when her father had chastised her and realized that the man's opinion meant everything to her. He felt sure Jasmina wouldn't dare take a breath after that without the old man's permission. She desperately wanted her father to think well of her again, so Sterling had never imagined she'd defy his orders.

The thought that she intended to do so tonight pleased him immeasurably.

The windows of Karlyle House were black, the only illumination coming from the gaslights on the street and the lone fairylight above the front door. Sterling could see the magical wards in the gloom. The old man had strengthened them since Sterling had last been here. To keep Lady Jasmina safe, or imprisoned? Either way, she must have found some way to escape undetected, but he still snorted in shock when he saw a slim, shadowy form shimmying down a rope from the roof of the three-story mansion.

Sterling kept to the shadows, debating whether to drag her back inside her house or just follow and protect her. Since she'd likely escape again and he enjoyed her defiance, he decided to allow her to complete her late-night errand. Besides, he was curious about where she was going.

With a deft flick of her wrist, Lady Jasmina unhooked the grapple from the roof and stepped aside as it fell to the ground. Sterling wondered where she'd learned the skill, or better yet, where she'd managed to practice with the climbing rope. But he didn't have

time to ponder further, because she'd wrapped the
rope around her waist and slunk around to the back
of the mansion.

He followed her again through the foggy streets of
London, down alleys and over fences, usually in were-
form but sometimes shifting to human to manage
some tight squeezes. Sterling kept an eye out for a red
hat and for the prince's spies that they'd agreed she
needed for protection. But it seemed that for once,
Lady Jasmina had managed to lose her troublesome
gnome. And either the prince's spies were very good,
or she'd managed to elude them as well.

She finally paused before a crenellated mansion,
unwinding the rope from her waist and swinging the
grapple thoughtfully. He really hoped she'd decide
to spell her way into the home through the servants'
entrance, because the sight of her dangling twenty feet
off the ground had made his gut clench with fear.

Lady Jasmina swung the grapple and missed, nearly
thwacking her head in the process, but on the second
try she hooked a notch in the stone and began to climb
with a swiftness that made Sterling snort in appreciation. He kept to his were-form, his sight and hearing
so much keener, standing still as a statue with his ears
cocked toward the mansion.

If she got caught again, he'd have to break down
another aristocrat's door. He relished the prospect.

An eternity later she climbed back down the
rope. A cry wasn't raised; the lights in the mansion
didn't flicker on. Sterling allowed himself to relax
and squashed down an irrational feeling of pride.
If Nuisance hadn't betrayed her to the Duchess of

Hagersham, Jasmina would have managed to steal the relic back.

And it suddenly occurred to him that she might be stealing from whoever owned this mansion. But that was ridiculous. Her family had plenty of money, didn't they? But then, what was she doing sneaking into the house in the first place?

Sterling allowed her to keep a street ahead of him on her way back home, only turning the corner when he could be sure that she wouldn't see him following. There were more layers to Lady Jasmina Karlyle than he could have imagined. Perhaps the illusion she'd created wasn't so far off the mark after all.

Perhaps he'd fallen in lust with Jaz, but he felt dangerously close to falling in love with the mysterious Lady Jasmina. He quickly dismissed the thought.

"Psst."

Sterling's hoof froze in the air. That voice seemed to come from right next to his head.

"Up here."

His eyes swung up to the foliage of one of the trees that lined the street. Nuisance hung from a lower branch by one arm, rather like a monkey.

"They've got her, Sir Sterling."

He didn't stop to ask the gnome any questions. Sterling lunged forward into a full gallop, just in time to see two dark figures pulling a slight form inside one of the shop buildings. He'd get to smash down a door tonight after all.

Sterling put action to the thought, mentally thanking Nuisance for being such an unshakable pest. He would have walked right by the abandoned shop if he hadn't known where to look. The old wooden door caved in with a satisfactory crash. The two men holding Jasmina dropped her like a rock, pulling knives from their sheaths and charging him before he had a moment to evaluate the situation.

Their knives had been coated with silver and when Sterling lashed out with his hooves, one of the foot-pads managed to slice his foreleg. It burned like hell. Sterling screamed in fury, his stallion blood raging, his were-senses heightened.

The two men didn't stand a chance. Within minutes they lay on the planked floor in a rapidly spreading pool of blood.

He snorted and pawed the floor, snapping the wood. If they hadn't reacted so fast they never would have cut him. He shook the fury down and shifted to human, noticing the spell that wavered in the air, half-formed. "Snarling hellhounds again?"

Jasmina gave him a wobbly smile. "It worked last time."

Without thinking he held out his arms to her, and without thinking she rushed into them. She smelled like jasmine and ashes. He ran a finger through the gray soot on her cheek and then found her mouth, kissing her with all the fear he'd felt for her and all the longing of an entire week without her.

He'd been fooling himself, and tonight had shaken the realization from him. When he'd seen those men grab her, a rage had washed through him that he'd never experienced before. The thought that she might get hurt, that he might never see her again...

She shuddered, then melted into his arms, returning his kiss with a passion that almost surprised him. Almost.

Sterling set her back on her heels. "What do you think you're doing, running about London in the middle of the night when you know there are men who want you dead." It wasn't a question.

She blinked those large eyes of hers, her doll-like face looking entirely too innocent for his comfort. "It was necessary."

"And I managed to save your life. Again. That entitles me to some answers."

She squared her shoulders and settled that mask of composure over her features. She was so *good* at that. This time, somehow, it managed to calm Sterling as well.

Jasmina glanced over at the bodies on the floor. "We can't talk here."

Sterling backed up and shifted to stallion, lowering his front legs, grunting a bit from the pain of his cut. She slid on his back without another word, molding her body to his as if she were a part of him. He cantered through the streets in the direction of his flat, surprised she'd actually agreed to give him some answers. Several times he tried to alter their course toward a park or Jasmina's home, but his hooves unerringly took him back toward Trickside. Sometimes his were-self knew his heart better than he did.

He wanted Lady Jasmina. He'd lusted after her illusion, but that was a paltry thing compared to how he wanted the real woman. He wasn't quite sure when she'd become so precious to him. When she'd helped him rescue Mary? No, before that, when he'd rescued her from the clutches of the Duke of Hagersham and she'd shown such fire and strength.

He tossed his head, prancing for a moment. No,

surely it had been when she'd slapped him after he'd kissed her in front of the prince. But no matter. He wanted her to share with him things she would never share with anyone else. She would be his, body and soul, despite society's objections, despite her father's wishes... even despite her very own misguided sense of propriety.

The confusion Sterling had felt since he'd met this woman and her magic cleared from his mind. She already belonged to him; she just didn't know it. His only task was to force her to realize it.

Sterling finally stopped in front of his dilapidated building, shifting to human before she dismounted, catching her arms and sliding her from his back. She felt like a sunbeam moving down his body.

"Where are we?" she whispered.

"My flat." He watched her face, waiting for her reaction. A gentleman did not take a lady to his private apartments unless he planned on seducing her. Which he had every intention of doing.

She took a shaky breath. "This is entirely improper. Surely there must be another place where we could talk—what is that on your arm?"

Sterling glanced down at the bloody patch. "Just a scratch. But the knife was coated with silver. Weres are, shall we say, sensitive to the stuff."

Her hand went to her throat. "You could bleed to death because of me."

Sterling's eyebrows rose. Sometimes shallow cuts bled a lot, but apparently she was unaware of that fact. He didn't attempt to enlighten her.

"It must be cleaned and washed," said Jasmina, her concern for his welfare evidently overriding her objections to entering his apartments. "Quickly, take me to your room."

Sterling grinned and led her up the stairs, past the drunken oaf who slept in a huddle of rags, careful to open his door gently, still unsure that the worn hinges would hold. The fire in his hearth had gone out. He'd left a window open, and the room was freezing. Without any gaslights on the street, the room was also pitch black. Fairylights never lasted long around him, and he smacked his shin against a table before he found the candle. He hesitated before lighting it.

What would the lady think? He still wore his working clothes, even worse for wear with the blood soaking his arm, and the flat was probably unlike anything she'd ever been exposed to in her pampered life. He lit the match. This was his life. Lady Jasmina would just have to get used to it.

Her eyes reflected the small flame of the candle within their liquid depths. She glanced around the room, seemingly unconcerned about the shabbiness of the flat, and sprang at him. "Help me get this coat off. Do you have any brandy? Never mind, I see the decanter. Get that shirt off too—whatever is it made of, burlap? Never mind, where is the washstand?"

"In the bedroom."

She didn't bat an eye, just tugged him along with the candle in one hand and his arm in the other. Sterling submitted to her ministrations, amused and becoming aroused at the same time. A novel sensation. She appeared not to notice that he stood next to her half-undressed, her entire being concentrated on the cut along his forearm.

She washed his wound, her fingers gentle and deft. He remembered the way they'd felt sliding into his hair, curling along the back of his neck. How had she known that his skin was most sensitive there? Sterling leaned forward and nuzzled her hair, breathing in the soft, flowery scent of it.

"Do you have any bandages?" She sounded breathless.

"No." His voice sounded husky.

Jasmina glanced up at him, shadows playing along her face. She looked stunning in candlelight, even with her face covered in soot. He took the face flannel from her hand and poured fresh water over it, wrung it out and gently washed the ashes from her cheeks. She froze, so still he couldn't even see the rise and fall of her breath. He dropped the cloth and traced the contours of her face with his wet fingers, slipping down her tiny nose and across her rounded cheek to her soft chin. When he reached her lips she shivered, her mouth parting on a desperate gasp of air.

For a moment she turned her face and leaned into his hand… but quickly pulled away, her expression demure once again. She stared at him with wide eyes and walked away, returning with the decanter. She poured the brandy on his arm, and Sterling gritted his teeth at the fiery pain that dashed away his amorous thoughts. "Well done," he murmured.

She ignored him, too busy tearing a dry linen cloth into tiny strips. Jasmina bandaged his arm, and Sterling closed his eyes, overwhelmed by sensory overload.

"Are you all right?"

"Don't be ri—"

"Perhaps you should sit down."

He glanced enthusiastically at the bed, but before he could take a step, she turned and took the candle into the sitting room. He tossed his head. Lady Jasmina's proper demeanor was like a wall of bricks that he had to break down one by one. He remembered the way she'd kissed him in the bog... but that had been just after he'd saved her life. And before her father had seen them together. Her resolve to win back the old man's affections may have filled the chinks in the wall that he'd managed to destroy. No matter. He would make her his, and his heart leapt at the challenge of it.

He followed her, collapsing into the overstuffed chair in front of the fireplace. He watched as she lit and banked the coal as if she did it every day, when he knew she had an army of servants to do the task for her. He smiled when she bent over, the trousers she wore revealing the shape of a lovely backside. No wonder women hid their bodies beneath layers of skirts. His hand itched to feel those curves, and he bloody well couldn't take his eyes off of her bottom until she stood up and turned around.

Sterling shifted uncomfortably, his trousers suddenly tight.

She took off her cap and shook her head, blonde curls spilling around her shoulders. "Shall I make us tea?"

He nodded eagerly and she bent over again, setting the kettle on the hob while he again contemplated the appeal of her bottom. When she finally stood and glanced around the room, he'd managed to work himself into a fine state of arousal. And all he'd done was look.

She dragged the rickety chair from his desk over to

the fire and gingerly sat, apparently sighing because the thing didn't collapse beneath her. "I'm perfectly aware that I owe you an explanation. You must think that my actions are terribly foolish."

He didn't answer. He couldn't. His blood raged, and he didn't trust his voice. His hair fell over his eyes and he left it there, watching her from behind that screen. Even in a chimney sweep's coarse clothing, with her hair in disarray and a bit of soot still smudged across her nose, she looked every bit the lady.

"It's just…" Her voice trailed off as she stared into the fire. "It's a family secret and I've never told anyone else." She folded her hands in her lap and glanced over at him. "Does your arm feel better?"

He nodded and she smiled. The building creaked and the wind rattled the shutters. He watched her watching him. Sterling realized he must help her or she would never speak. He leaned forward, wincing at the tightness still in his trousers, hoping she wouldn't notice. He didn't want to scare her. He wanted all her secrets, not just those of the bedchamber.

He reached out and put his hands over hers. "I will tell you one of mine and then you shall tell me yours."

Jasmina nodded, her eyes shining within her beautiful, composed face.

"You wondered why my stepbrother wouldn't acknowledge me. He says it's because of Angel, but it's more than that, you see. After my mother died my father remarried and his new wife desperately wanted her son to inherit. She was always kind to Angel and me… yet in little ways she made us feel as if we weren't quite part of the family anymore. Father's were-form was a stallion too, and our personalities were, shall we say, combustible."

Sterling tossed his head, clearing the hair away from his eyes, watching his words put another crack in that wall of hers. Her shoulders had loosened and she leaned toward him, unaware that her rigid mask had slipped.

"We had always fought, you see. I never agreed with the way he treated the tenants, the number of women that he took to bed in my mother's home. Before I joined the army we had another fight and by the time my service was over, I was no longer welcome back. I had given Cecil too much time to work on Father." His hands tightened on hers and when Jasmina gave a little gasp of pain, he quickly released them. "Oh, Cecil assured me that he was trying to heal the rift between Father and me. But in truth he made it worse. He told me to stay away until Father's anger cooled, all the while filling my father's head with lies about me, telling him that I stayed away because I never really cared for him at all."

Sterling stared at his hands. He hadn't meant to tell her all of it, but once he'd started he couldn't seem to stop. He shrugged, shaking off the betrayal. "Cecil has always wanted me out of his life so he could assume the inheritance and title without any trouble from me. This situation with his fiancée only gives him a good excuse."

"But why don't you do something about it?" she whispered.

"Because I am partly responsible. And because my father is dead. The time that I could have done something about it is past. My only regret is that my father and I were deprived of a relationship. Even as flawed as it was." He glanced up, and her eyes shone with pity. He didn't want her pity; he wanted her heart, so he didn't confess how much his stepmother's rejection had hurt him. And how a small part of him still longed for Cecil's affection. "Besides, I have more important things to worry about right now. Like my sister, Angel. And you."

"Me?"

Sterling rubbed his bare chest absentmindedly. "You and your troublesome illusion."

At the mention of Jaz, her back went stiff again. "I'll make that tea." She rose to go to the fireplace.

His hand shot out and grabbed her arm. "Don't."

She said nothing, just stood calmly in his grasp.

"I told you one of my secrets, and now you owe me." She hung her head and Sterling grimaced. The woman could try the patience of a saint, and he was far from that. He would break through that reserved exterior if it killed him. He only knew one way to shatter her control, and he didn't hesitate. With one fluid motion he rose to his feet, kissing her until he felt her melt against him. He gathered her in his arms, wanting to carry her into his bedchamber, but knowing he'd have to wait.

Sterling didn't just want to make love to her. He wanted Jasmina to make love to him as well.

He sat back down in his chair, her stiff little body cradled on his lap. Sterling removed the pins from the bun at the back of her head until the rest of her silky locks tumbled into his hands. He stroked them, feeling her slowly relax. "Come now, your secret can't be any worse than mine. I can't imagine that you've ever allowed your temper to get the better of you."

"Of course not."

He smiled at her offended tone. "Then what is it? Why did you learn how to break into other people's homes? Why did you take such a foolish risk tonight?"

She laid her hand on his bare chest, tucked her head beneath his chin. "You could ruin my family with my secret."

He continued to stroke her hair. "You can trust me."

The coals shifted on the fire and a breeze curled through the room; he'd forgotten to shut the window, which was just as well. The cold helped control his desire. She seemed to be thinking, her fingers tracing an idle pattern across his chest, making his skin tingle. He gently covered her hand, fearing she would drive him mad. "I've saved your life more than once, Lady Jasmina. What else must I do to earn your trust?"

She made a sound—half sob, half laugh. "If it were only my own secret… but, you see, it's about my mother." Sterling bent his head and kissed the top of her hair. She sighed. "My mother 'borrows' from her friends, you see. Mostly jewelry. She can't help it, and she has every intention of returning the pieces. But she usually forgets, and so I have to return them for her."

Bloody hell. He'd never imagined such a thing. The charming Lady Kraken, a sneak thief? And Jasmina's father had the audacity to treat Sterling like— "Does your father know?"

She sat up, bumping his chin, her face wide with

terror. "Of course not. No one knows, except me and Aunt Ettie. And now you."

"Does respectability mean so much to you?" asked Sterling.

"That's hardly important. What matters is that it means a great deal to my mother and father. It's their *world*."

She looked frightened and on the edge of regretting that she'd ever told him. He stared into her smoky green eyes, the firelight playing across her face, making a shadow from her long lashes. This proper young lady had learned how to break into mansions. She dressed as a common chimney sweep and risked her own purity to protect her mother and family. How many other women in the world would have the courage and daring to do such a thing?

"I'll never tell another soul, Lady Jasmina. You have my word. And now that I know your secret, I could even help you."

Her hand fisted beneath his. "I don't need any help. I can take care of my own family. And I was doing just fine, until Merlin's Relic altered my spell. Now I have absolutely no control over my life." Words spilled from her lips like a dam bursting. Sterling froze, afraid she'd realize she'd let her wall down. Afraid she'd brick it back up again.

Jasmina's voice lowered. "And now I've lost my best friend, my father's respect, and the peace that I've always maintained in my home." Tears ran down her cheeks, and she swiped them away. "And the very worst thing is… Mother took my keys!"

"What keys?"

She looked at him in amazement, tears glittering in her eyes and sparkling on her cheeks. Some women looked dreadful when they cried, but not Lady Jasmina. Tears softened that perpetually haughty expression of hers, making her rounded features look exceedingly vulnerable.

"The keys to everything. To the house and the cellars and the pantry. I've been running the household since I was ten."

"Why?" He kept his voice soft, as if talking to a newborn filly.

"Because I'm good at it. Because Mother needed me to do it." She sniffed, staring at him as if he were an imbecile. But he wasn't as obtuse as she thought. He started to get a glittering of understanding about the Lady Jasmina.

"And now she doesn't need you?"

She reared back as if he'd struck her. "Of course she does! This past week has been dreadful. The maids are slacking on their work, and the footmen's uniforms look sloppy. And Father is in even worse humor. How am I ever going to get back in his good graces when his dinner is cold and his port and paper are never waiting for him when he gets home?"

"Indeed," murmured Sterling, wiping the tears from her cheeks. She stiffened at his touch, but the fist beneath his other hand uncurled and he laced his fingers in hers. "But I beg of you to consider that I need you even more, Jasmina."

She huffed. "You don't need anyone to look after you. You're strong and brave and…"

He smoothed the hair back from her face, curled his

hand around the back of her neck and tilted her head up. "Look at me. No, not at my chin, but in my eyes."

"I don't want to." Her lower lip stuck out enticingly.

"Why not?"

She shrugged, refusing to answer.

"Jasmina." He said her name like a caress, putting all the desire he'd suppressed into that one word. Her eyes flew to his and her lips parted. But still she resisted, afraid of the need he'd allowed to reflect nakedly in his gaze. "Jasmina," he said again, his voice a husky whisper, lowering his mouth to her own. Gently he touched his lips to hers until she opened to him. Until she moaned and melted into his embrace. Then he clutched her like a drowning man, as if he needed her more than he needed air to breathe. Her shirt was half-untucked from her trousers, and he slipped his hand beneath it. He sucked in a breath. She hadn't worn a corset, just some sheer underthing. Sweet warmth, silky skin. She trembled in his lap, and his shaft swelled again beneath her lush bottom.

Sterling held her in the crook of one arm, smoothing his hand along her tiny waist, inching higher and higher, until he cupped one perfect breast in his palm. She gasped in his mouth as he deepened the kiss, his tongue playing with hers. His fingertips sought the peak of her breast, circling the pad of his finger over it until it hardened and she squirmed in his hold.

He pulled his head back, staring at her passion-glazed eyes, her flushed face. "I need you," he whispered. "And here's what you're not going to like. You need me too."

Thirteen

STERLING PULLED JASMINA CLOSER AND SHIFTED HER body, until the back of her head lay against his shoulder and he could reach the lobe of her ear with his mouth. He suckled, shifting his hand over to her other breast, his fingertips caressing until it hardened as well.

Her back lay against his chest, her body draped over his legs, her heels touching the floor. He wanted this moment to be about her, but he couldn't help a bit of selfishness. He undid the buttons of her shirt with one hand and when her fingers fluttered up to stop him he gently pinched her breast, making her arch her back and moan. Her hands gripped the arm of the chair until her knuckles turned white and Sterling smiled, making short work of those buttons.

He frowned when the firelight revealed her undergarment, not the skin that he so desperately craved to see. He suppressed a curse, loosing her breast for a moment, ripping the thin material down the front. Sterling gazed at her hungrily. Full breasts, hardened to rosy peaks. A tiny waist. Skin that glowed in the firelight with a shimmer he might have thought was magic if it hadn't been for his immunity. Jasmina made a sound of protest, but he quickly slipped his hands over her breasts, whispering in her ear how beautiful she was. How much he needed to see her.

He knew every inch of her body, of course. But Sterling didn't for a moment confuse the woman in his arms with her illusion. He knew the depths of Lady Jasmina. What she hid beneath that proper exterior and why. He didn't just want to satisfy his lust for her; he wanted to make her a part of him so that she couldn't imagine being separated from him. He wanted to make her deliriously happy.

Sterling smoothed one hand down to her waist, to the top of her trousers, stopping just beneath the waistband. He pulled them down, so he could see the beauty mark on her left hip. Then he quickly slid his hand lower, groaning at the feel of her wiry curls, seeking the small nub that would make her realize just how very much she needed him.

Her heels slammed against the floor and she bucked, her bottom slamming against his shaft, making him groan with the pleasure of it. Bloody hell, was she that sensitive? He gritted his teeth against his own need and stroked his fingertips up and down her nub, feeling it swell beneath his hand. He kept his touch gentle even though she tried to increase the pressure by pushing up against him.

Sterling kissed her neck and fondled her breasts and never stopped his gentle strokes. He couldn't get enough of touching this fascinating woman. He wanted this moment never to end, but she started whimpering and thrashing with need. He regretted and delighted in the knowledge that he would have to bring her to fulfillment.

But not before he offered her a taste of more to come.

He cupped the throbbing, wet place between her legs and leaned slightly forward, until he could feel her hot opening. His shaft jumped eagerly, as if it had a mind of its own, and he had to wait for a moment to bring himself under control.

"Sterling." It was half a command, half a plea.

He closed his eyes, plunged his finger inside her, heard her gasp in surprise but tighten around him. He wished it were his shaft buried inside of her— visualized it while he pulled his finger halfway out, plunged it in again, his palm rubbing her nub until she rode his hand with a wildness that stroked her bottom over his lap, creating a friction on his shaft that he couldn't ignore.

Bloody hell, he was never this sensitive.

When Jasmina cried out with her release, he had to grit his teeth to hold back his own as well. She arched her back and he steadied her body between his lap and hand. She shook, trembled, slowly came back to earth, her harsh breathing reverberating in the quiet room.

Sterling gathered her into his arms. He'd never thought to experience the same passion that he'd shared with Jaz, but he'd surpassed it, surely. The real thing was so much better than the illusion.

And he hadn't even taken her to his bed yet.

He kissed the corner of her mouth, the side of her nose, memorizing the feel of it, wanting to explore every inch of her. Her eyes fluttered open, and she stared at him without her mask of propriety, her face reflecting only wonder and delight.

"That was…" she started, searching for words, grinning impishly.

He couldn't resist the lure of her smile. He covered her mouth with his, tasting that sweetness, his hands searching for the opening in her shirt, touching those perfect breasts again. The dear girl really had no idea. He couldn't wait to truly show her what making love was all about.

She wrapped her arms around his neck, fumbling with the leather tie holding back his hair, and his scalp tingled when she finally untied it and buried her fingers in his hair. She pulled her mouth away from his and he allowed it, feeling his hair flowing over his forehead, across his cheeks. Jasmina brushed it back, running her fingers through the black strands.

"It's unfashionably long," she said, just a hint of primness in her voice.

He raised a brow.

"Don't ever cut it," she murmured, giving it a tug.

Sterling grinned, lowered his head and kissed her so hard she was bent halfway over the side of the chair. He had to get up; he had to have her. Now. He supported the back of her head with one hand and rose with her in his arms, still kissing her, still unable to satisfy his need for the taste of her.

He strode to the bedroom door and kicked it open. Odd, he hadn't remembered shutting it. But right now he wasn't sure he could remember his own name. Until he took her. Until he buried himself inside her and made them one whole, new being.

A candle cast a bright glow by the bedside table. He knew bloody well that he hadn't left one burning in here...

"Hello there." Nuisance sat in the middle of the bed, smoke curling from the pipe stuck between his lips. "I think this has gone far enough, don't you?"

Sterling cursed.

The gnome choked on a drag. He blinked up at them through watery eyes. "Impressive."

"Get out."

"Hmm. Don't think so. It's my duty to protect the lady's virtue."

Sterling very gently lowered Jasmina to the floor, took two menacing steps toward the little pest and winced. He could barely walk; his trousers were so tight, his body so aroused that he saw red for a moment. "Get out or I will hurt you."

The gnome laughed. Sterling had warned him. He lunged at Nuisance, gripping him around the neck, perfectly willing to toss him out the window. The gnome shifted into his natural state. The weight of the rock unbalanced Sterling for a moment, and he flopped onto the bed. He rolled the gnome-shaped rock over the edge, looking hopefully at Lady Jasmina.

"He can still hear and see in his rock form," she said. She'd already managed to button her shirt and was tucking it in her trousers.

Sterling rolled off the bed, picked up the rock and heaved it out his window, knowing that it couldn't be damaged from this height, grinning when it hit the ground with an audible *thunk*. He slammed the shutters closed and spun, his hair flying around his face. "Undo those buttons."

Her chin rose. "Certainly not. He'll be peeking in the window or he'll manage to sneak under your bed."

A giggle sounded just outside the closed shutters and Sterling collapsed on the edge of the bed, his hands curled into fists. "There must be some way I can get rid of him," he mumbled.

He heard her soft footsteps, felt her hands smoothing his wild hair. It did funny things to his body. Painful things. "Don't," he said. "Jaz, please don't touch me right now. I just need a minute…"

She gasped. The bloody gnome giggled again. He looked up into her horrified face. "What?"

Lady Jasmina turned to ice. She gathered dignity like a shroud and managed to look like a prudish spinster at an elegant soiree. "I think you should take me home now, Sir Sterling."

He rose to his feet, clasping her rigid shoulders in his hands. "Don't look at me that way, love. Don't hide behind your wall again when I've just managed to break it down."

"I don't know what you mean." But her façade had crumbled a bit and she looked up at him with eyes suspiciously wet. "I had thought… I had hoped that your kisses were for me tonight, sir. Not for some illusion that only an idiot would fall in love with."

And then he realized that he'd called her Jaz. Did she truly think he was in love with her illusion? After tonight, surely she realized… but perhaps not. He pulled her to his chest, hoping to melt her with the heat of his body. "First you should remember that your illusion is a duplicate of you—it's perfectly understandable that I would be drawn to her. But she is nothing compared to the real thing, do you understand?" He held her from him, tipping her face up when she refused to look at him. "Yes, I may have lusted after Jaz, but it's you I pleasured in my arms tonight. It's you I want to make love to."

A snort from the direction of the window. Sterling fought down his temper. There must be some way to get rid of that gnome short of killing him.

Her face had lost none of its rigidity. "I wish I could believe that."

Sterling tried to tamp down his impatience, but bloody hell, he'd been stretched to the limit of his endurance tonight. How many men would ever have to convince a woman that they weren't in love with her magical image? How could a woman even be jealous of such a thing? He stared at her bruised lips, the smoky emerald of her eyes. Did she really care for him enough to *be* jealous? "It's too easy to shorten your name to Jaz. It was only a slip of the tongue."

She raised a brow. He dropped his arms so he wouldn't be tempted to shake her. He raked his fingers through his hair, his animal-self having reached its limit. "Damn it, woman, I love you."

The words had just tumbled from his mouth without thought. But as soon as he spoke them, Sterling realized how absolutely hopelessly he had fallen in love with the Lady Jasmina. She was so beautiful… and frustrating and prim, and would complicate his life enormously. But heaven help him, he couldn't live without her. How had he thought her mere illusion would ever suffice?

Her eyes widened, and her hands flew to her cheeks. "There is no reason to shout at me."

"I wasn't… did I…" Blast it, words weren't going to work. She would never really believe he was in love with her. She would always think he desired her illusion, and wouldn't allow herself to trust him enough to return his feelings. "What can I do to convince you?"

"Find my illusion."

Sterling spent the next week in the dank warrens of the Undergound, fruitlessly searching for his sister, the relic… and Jasmina's bloody illusion. But the denizens of the Underground were like terrified rats, scrambling just to stay alive. Giving him answers about the wizards that ruled the dark would ensure certain death.

But tonight he would solve at least one of his problems. Nuisance. Sterling blew a breath from his nostrils, stirring up the dust below his hooves. The London fog had cleared for a change and Hyde Park looked serene in the starlight. Sterling headed for Toadstool Garden. It appeared that the gnome had developed an affection for the Lady Jasmina, and Sterling decided it was worse than the little creature's earlier penchant for just being a pest. Especially considering Sterling's own pursuit of the lady.

Sterling shifted to human when he reached the outskirts of the growth of toadstools. The huge fungi cut off the starlight beneath their tops and he narrowed his eyes, trying to peer through the gloom. The garden hadn't been tended for years; weeds and grass grew between the stalks, and trash littered the wild growth.

"I can't believe I'm doing this," he muttered as he pushed his way through the weeds. The musty smell of the toadstools tickled his nose, and the weeds made him itch. He heard rustlings and giggles when he passed the outlying toadstools. He paused in a little clearing and took a deep breath. "I'm looking for Nuisance's girlfriend."

He just hoped the little pest had one. But judging from the dead silence around him, he'd been wrong. Surely in such a small community they would know of the little gnome? "Or perhaps a young, attractive gnome who might wish to be Nuisance's girlfriend."

Another ominous quiet followed. He wondered idly if there was such a thing as a young, attractive female gnome. With a snort Sterling sat on the damp ground. He'd gambled on the hope that he could sweet talk a girl gnome into romancing Nuisance, but maybe he'd overestimated the gnome's attraction. Bloody hell, who could judge these things, anyway? "Surely, someone might be interested in the where-abouts of a single, virile male gnome?"

The grass to his left rustled and a little man with silver hair and knobby knees stepped out. "Yer looking for Trouble, mister."

Sterling tossed back his hair. "It's sir, not mister, and I'm not looking for trouble. I'm just looking for a girl gnome to ease the lonely existence of a friend of mine."

The little old man hobbled forward, his knobby knuckles clutching a cane intricately carved with archaic symbols. "Ayup, that's what I said. You be looking for Trouble."

"I'm not…" Sterling grinned. "Where might I find this Trouble?"

"The thirteenth toadstool on your left." He pointed with his cane. "That-a-way. I caution you, though, she's a right vicious female. She's been in a spittin' temper ever since that young rascal left. It's the only reason I'm helping you, mind. We could use a break from Trouble."

"But I thought you garden gnomes thrived on chaos."

The old man had the audacity to look indignant. "Sir, you got a lot to learn. We gnomes would rather cause other people problems than live with our own."

Sterling shook his head, then turned to search for Trouble. When the little lady finally emerged from beneath the thirteenth toadstool, she shouted up at Sterling with one finger waving wildly at him. "I told that Nuisance if he stayed put I'd give him enough children that he'd never want for mischief or mayhem. But what does he do? The first chance he gets he runs off!"

Sterling stared down at the tiny woman. Stiff brown hair stuck out from her head like a hedgehog's spikes. She had lovely liquid brown eyes, but her ears stuck out like saucers, her nose was rather lumpy, and she had long, hairy toes. For a fleeting moment Sterling didn't blame Nuisance for running off, but then again, the little gnome was an equal match for this girl's features.

"I don't care whether he ever comes back," finished Trouble with a stomp of her bare foot.

Sterling squatted. There must be some way he could encourage her to pursue Nuisance. "Some men get frightened when they fall in love. Perhaps that's why Nuisance ran away."

"Hmph." But that did seem to sway her for a moment. Then her wide mouth thinned. "Nope. He just went off to have a wild time and expected me to sit here and wait for him to come back. Well, I'll have you know that I have other prospects."

"But none as—shall we say—appealing as Nuisance?"

She hung her head and watched her toes dig up dirt, but not before Sterling saw a glimmer in her eyes. He couldn't believe he was about to do this…

"I mean, most of the gnomes I've seen are old and gray. Nuisance is young and, er, handsome and dashing." He would burn for the lies streaming from his tongue, but Sterling reminded himself it was for a good cause. His own. "Seems a shame for you to let him get away."

She shrugged. "He'll come crawling back, and when he does…"

Sterling almost felt sorry for Nuisance for what this little gnome appeared to contemplate. But he needed Nuisance preoccupied now, not later. When they recovered the relic and Jasmina's twin, he was sure he'd never see Jasmina again. The lady needed to fall in love with him now if he ever had a hope of making her his. He knew Jasmina didn't want him in her life, but she desired him in her bed. That was Sterling's trump card—and he intended to play it.

"I suppose," said Sterling, trying to look innocent, "that Nuisance might come back. But it seems he's developed a fondness for the lady who created the chaos he so loves—"

"What?" Trouble's head snapped up. "He's fallen for a human woman?"

Sterling had hoped to make her jealous, but he hadn't expected her to burst into tears.

"Oh, my." She hiccupped. "He must be awfully lonely to have fallen for one of those big, ungainly human women. I had no idea... you must take me to him, sir. He must be desperately in need of a proper companion."

Sterling blinked, feeling his smile waver, but quickly offered to show her where she could find Nuisance. He shifted to stallion, allowing the little gnome to scramble up his tail and straddle his neck, feeling her tiny fingers grasping his mane all the way to Mayfairy. He shifted back to human in Mandrake Square and pointed up at Jasmina's window.

"Will you give Lady Jasmina a message for me?"

Trouble fisted her knobby hands on her hips. "The woman who's trying to take my Nuisance from me?"

"Ah." Sterling crouched down next to her. "But you see, the lady is in love with me. She just doesn't know it yet."

She nodded her spiky brown head. "Like Nuisance is lovin' me but don't know it. Well, with your looks I fear your task will be harder than mine. I mean, you have such a small nose and a square jaw and your hair isn't coarse at all. But I'll do what I can. What's the message?"

Sterling fought back a smile. And then he pondered his message. Words didn't appear to work with Jasmina, but if he said them often enough, maybe she would come to believe them. "Tell her that you're a gift from me. That I love her. That I will come every night and wait beneath her window until she comes to me."

Trouble rolled her eyes. "Couldn't you have kept it shorter? Oh, never mind, I'll try to remember it all."

With a puff of dust she disappeared into the shadows. Sterling shifted to stallion, but even his keen eyes couldn't make out the form of the gnome as she scrambled up the side of the building—although he did see a spiky silhouette for a brief moment in front of Lady Jasmina's window.

Sterling pranced into the street beneath a gaslight, tossing his mane and stamping his hooves, pausing every so often to glance up at her home. A light flared in her room, and he held his breath as he saw the slim outline of her shape appear at the window.

The light went out and Sterling galloped to the side of her house, staring up at the roof. She must have found a weakness in her father's magical wards up there, and he expected her to use the same escape route this time. But nothing moved, except the wind whispering through the trees and a cat foraging in the dustbins. Sterling checked the back of the house, then the front again, and waited until dawn started to tint the sky with red before he finally gave up.

He hung his head and wearily made his way home. She hadn't come to him. She surely understood the implications of his gift—that they would finally be alone to finish what they'd started together.

She still thought he was in love with her illusion. His only hope was to find Jaz to prove that he really loved Jasmina.

Yet Sterling wasn't entirely sure how he'd react when he saw Jaz again. Would he find that he loved the illusion just as much as he did the real thing? He stomped his hoof, cracking a cobblestone. He told himself angrily to stop doubting his feelings. How could Jasmina trust them if he couldn't manage to do so himself? It was impossible to love an illusion.

Just impossible.

Fourteen

JASMINA SLOWLY MADE HER WAY DOWN THE STAIRS IN answer to her father's summons. The maid had looked terrified and she could only imagine Father's mood if that was any indication. Though Jasmina had been an example of the perfect daughter the last few weeks, Mother would still not return the household keys to her, and Father had dismissed several of the most loyal of their household staff for incompetence. He would never think to blame Mother's management on the recent chaotic state of his home.

Jasmina paused at the foot of the landing to check her appearance in the large gold-leafed mirror. She smoothed her hands down the front of her pale green gown and adjusted the cashmere shawl about her shoulders. Her green eyes stared calmly back, her face smoothed of any worry lines, and her cupid mouth relaxed into a gentle smile. Jasmina resisted the urge to grimace. Sir Sterling was right: she was very good at looking composed when she felt anything but.

For the past few weeks she'd had to endure the arguments and sullen silences of the two gnomes who now occupied her bedchamber, because she'd vowed not to leave her room until her father bade her. Unfortunately the gnomes had resolved their differences rather quickly. She'd hoped that meant that they'd go home, but Nuisance had still refused to leave. *Then* she'd had to endure the sounds of the two creatures making up. They had no shame in making love wherever and whenever the urge struck them, and Jasmina had resorted to plugging her ears with cotton to keep out the sounds they made.

Too bad she couldn't also block the shadow dreams of the were-stallion that disturbed her sleep.

She knew perfectly well why Sterling had sent Trouble—he needn't have bothered giving her a message. With Nuisance distracted, they wouldn't be interrupted the next time Sterling tried to make love to her. Jasmina glared at her reflection. As if there would be a next time. Did he honestly think she would believe him when he said he hadn't confused her with an illusion? Especially when she knew that he had already taken Jaz to his bed—

"Dawdling won't make this any easier," barked Father from inside the drawing room.

Jasmina's breath hitched, and she turned and entered the room, taking in Father's rigid stance by the fireplace and Mother's fidgety fingers on the arm of a plush wing chair. She didn't know whether her father had purposely created the illusion of flames licking the walls, or if he was so angry that he'd lost control of his magic. But she could almost smell the fire and brimstone.

Jasmina calmly waited for him to speak while gray

smoke traced a sinuous path over the plush carpet at her feet. She refused to feel intimidated. She'd refused every invitation even though she'd longed to go to some of the events. She'd stayed in her room as her father had asked, and it wasn't her fault if his meals were late or burnt. She had been extraordinarily good, all for the sake of earning back Father's respect and affection.

So why was he so angry?

"It has come to my attention," he finally said, his words clipped and low, "that you have disobeyed my instructions not to leave this house and behaved in a manner unsuitable to your upbringing."

Jasmina opened her mouth to protest, then just as quickly snapped it shut. Somehow he had found out about her visit to the Faerlinns' mansion, and she couldn't tell him why she'd had to disobey his direction that once. And that it had only been once—good heavens, what if he knew that she'd gone to Sir Sterling's flat?

Jasmina swayed on her feet. Mother sprang from her seat and put her arm around her waist to steady her.

"You didn't think I'd find out about it, did you?" His brown eyes glittered and the walls erupted in new flames of blue-black. "Not that I would ever step foot inside Spellsinger Gardens myself, but I have single gentlemen friends who talk, Jasmina." His mouth twisted, and she could swear she saw tears in his eyes. "And they saw you cavorting—with barely a stitch of clothing—and with tree nymphs of all things. How did I fail so badly in raising you?"

He turned his face away, one hand covering his

eyes, and Jasmina thought she heard her heart break for him. How stupid of her to forget about the illusion. She'd foolishly assumed that Jaz had gone Underground and would stay there.

Jasmina took a step toward her father with this dreadful, twisty feeling inside of her chest. She held out her hand in entreaty or sympathy, she didn't know which, but flames wrapped around her arm and she quickly snatched it back. Her shawl had fallen to the floor. She left it there, feeling uncomfortably warm even though she knew that Father's version of hell was only an illusion.

How easy it would be to tell him! Just blurt out that she'd created an extraordinary illusion of herself with one of Merlin's Relics. Father could be trusted with the secret. At least then he would know the truth, and when one of his friends accused him of having a wayward daughter…

Jasmina's head slumped in defeat.

Father would tell them everything to defend the family's name and social position. She hated to admit it, but he didn't have the strength of character to resist, even if it meant imperiling the safety of their country.

"It appears that I cannot trust you to keep your word," said Father.

Jasmina didn't reply. There was absolutely nothing she could say to him anyway.

"It also appears that you behave even worse without the influence of your aunt, but you obviously still need a firmer hand. Therefore, I have decided to remove you from London, at least until the worst of the gossip dies down. And until you prove yourself trustworthy."

Jasmina's spirits had lifted at the mention of Aunt Henrietta. It would relieve so much of her loneliness to have her aunt to confide in again. But what did he mean by a firmer hand? She lifted her head and met his eyes, which somehow looked older and sadder than they had just yesterday. Oh, how she wanted to apologize… but it would be meaningless.

"I have decided we are to take a tour of the Continent."

Mother let out a little squeal of delight and threw herself into Father's arms. The flames in the room snuffed out as if they'd been smothered by Mother's happiness. "Oh, Horace, what a wonderful idea."

"Now, now," admonished Father. "This is supposed to be a punishment. It's the only way I could think of to remove Jasmina from the unsavory acquaintances she's acquired in London and to keep my eye on her at all times. At least until her former good sense reappears." But when he looked at Mother, his mouth quirked into a grin. "But I'm glad the idea appeals to you."

"Oh, Paris," crooned Mother. "And the canals of Venice and the skybridges of Foressia. Oh dear, we have nothing to wear."

Father glanced at Jasmina. "You can purchase new frocks in Paris. I want to leave as soon as possible."

"But, dear, we will look like complete provincials. Surely we can take a few weeks to update our wardrobes."

Mother stood on her tiptoes and kissed Father's cheek. He nuzzled her hair and smiled. "Just a few weeks." He enfolded Mother in his arms and glanced up at Jasmina, his smile somehow turning sad. "Go tell your aunt."

Jasmina nodded, picked up her shawl, and left the room without glancing behind her. The fire on the walls had faded to a warm glow, and she closed the doors of the drawing room behind her, grateful that her mother could so easily temper her father. Jasmina had never thought she'd need her mother's protection from her once-adoring father.

A fuzzy brown head popped up from behind a Grecian vase. "My, that was jolly good," crowed Trouble.

"I told you," replied Nuisance. "She's better fun than two ants fighting over a crumb."

Jasmina rolled her eyes, sweeping past them and up the stairs. What other creatures in England would sit and watch two ants fighting? Ugh. But she had no time to bother with the two annoying gnomes. She had just run out of time. She couldn't leave London now, with that illusion still running loose and Sterling and the prince's spies having absolutely no success in tracking down the relic.

She could no longer afford to obey her father's wishes. It hadn't been successful anyway, with her illusion haunting Spellsinger Gardens and running about with tree nymphs. Surely that was worse than her association with a baronet. And she needed Sir Sterling to find Jaz so that she truly could put her life back in order. *Then* she would contrive a way to put herself back into Father's good graces.

Jasmina tapped on Aunt Ettie's door before opening it. Aunt's room boasted a huge canopy bed of carved cherry wood layered in yellow ruffled bed coverings. The walls were papered in silk with huge bouquets of yellow flowers; yellow rugs brightened the dark marble floor, and bursts of that same color peppered paintings and knickknacks until the room almost glowed. Jasmina always felt like she was stepping into sunshine. Aunt sat in a stiff chair before her open window, looking older than Jasmina remembered her. But when she turned her head and saw Jasmina, her eyes lit with a youthful fire. "You're not supposed to be in here, you know. But I'm so glad you are."

The kindness in her voice made Jasmina's eyes burn and she launched herself across the room, collapsing in a heap of skirts and petticoats beside Aunt's chair. Jasmina buried her face in the soft flounces of her aunt's favorite morning dress. "Father decided you aren't such a bad influence after all."

"Ah, I see." Aunt stroked the top of Jasmina's head. "And what momentous occurrence made him deduce that?"

"That wretched twin." Jasmina's voice was muffled by fabric. "In Spellsinger Gardens… with tree nymphs."

Aunt sniffed. "Well, I must say, tree nymphs are quite worse than baronets. Lascivious creatures, with no conscience whatsoever. Really, how could anyone even compare the two? Why, Sir Sterling is the most respectable man—"

Jasmina lifted her head and sighed. "Please don't start, Aunt. You've made it perfectly clear how much you admire the baronet. And that's why I came for your help."

"What's happened?"

"Father is taking us on a tour of the Continent… oh, how could you possibly look so pleased? Don't you realize what this means?"

"That you won't see Sir Sterling for months and you're afraid he might forget you?"

Jasmina blinked. She hadn't thought of that and despite her irritation with Aunt Ettie's one-track mind, she realized Aunt's words made her feel feverish with jealousy. If she didn't find and banish the illusion before she left, Sterling might find her. Would he become entranced by her illusion again? How could she compete with a woman who had already shown him her charms?

But weren't they just an imitation of Jasmina's own charms? She shook her head. This was entirely too confusing. She refused to think about him because she remembered the way he'd made her body feel with just the touch of his hand. How she'd felt vulnerable and out of control... and totally alive.

"Please, Aunt Ettie, focus on what's important. This means I only have a few weeks left to find this illusion and get back control of my life. Heaven knows what trouble this Jaz could cause me while we're gone."

"Yes, dear, of course." Aunt patted her head, then glanced up over it. "Those two nasty little gnomes are shedding their clothes behind my fainting couch. However have you managed them the past few weeks?"

Grunts and squeals of pleasure followed Aunt's words. Jasmina groaned. "If I break them up they'll only be at it again someplace else. It's best to ignore them. I've been using cotton in my ears."

"Quite wise, I suppose. But a young, innocent girl like you should not have to be exposed to such behavior." Jasmina flushed guiltily, for she no longer felt as innocent as Aunt supposed. Aunt Ettie picked up a pillow embroidered with yellow roses and launched it across the room. A squeal of surprise followed. "The next volley will be my glass figurines, and if you turn to stone I shall drop you out the window myself."

"That kind of hurts," Nuisance whispered to Trouble. "Let's go to Jasmina's room." A giggle, a flash of color at the door, and they were blessedly gone.

"I think it was better when I only had Nuisance to deal with."

Aunt Ettie's sharp features softened. "I'm sure Sir Sterling meant well when he sent you Trouble."

"She does distract Nuisance, but she was supposed to take him back to the Toadstool Garden." Jasmina rose to her feet. "Instead she appears to have joined him in delighting in my problems."

"The nature of gnomes, dear. Now, didn't you mention that you wanted my help regarding the handsome Sir Sterling?"

Jasmina rubbed her eyes. "I need you to send him a message."

Aunt didn't ask how Jasmina knew that she was capable of getting in touch with Sir Sterling. Instead, Aunt narrowed her green eyes and asked, "Why don't you just go to him tonight when he comes to your window?"

"You don't miss much, do you, Aunt?"

"Just because Horace forbade me to see you doesn't mean I haven't been keeping an eye on you. Why don't you go to him?"

"Aunt!"

"Did you two have a fight, or..." Aunt's eyes lit up with hopeful glee. "Perhaps a lover's spat?"

Jasmina tried not to squirm. "Certainly not. And I don't want to give him the wrong impression by going to him as if I were his lover."

"I see," huffed Aunt. "Very well, what message do you want me to send?"

Jasmina walked to the window, playing with the yellow tassels adorning the drapery while she stared out onto Mandrake Square. The cobblestones in front of their mansion looked rather cracked and misshapen. "I want him to take me to the Underground with him. I'm forced to disobey Father and search for the relic myself."

Aunt studied her with eyes that saw too much. "I will send him a note and contrive a way and place for you to meet him. Will that do?"

Jasmina watched a matched pair of blacks trotting in front of a smart little curricle and thought of her were-stallion. His incredible beauty surpassed that of any ordinary beast. His extraordinary strength and speed made her feel as if they flew through the streets of London. She thought of his black mane and silky tail because she couldn't think of the man. She would come undone.

If only she could be sure he was in love with her and not an illusion.

❧

The coach rattled to a stop in front of an old graveyard, and Jasmina turned to Aunt Ettie with amazement. "Are you sure this is where he said to meet him?"

Aunt peeked around the curtain, sniffed and nodded. "The sign says Thieves Chapel."

Jasmina stared dubiously at the slice of bark that had the letters etched into it with what appeared to be ax strokes. The sign had been nailed to a rough-hewn post staked near an overgrown road, which led up a hill to a crumbled ruin of old stones. Wooden crosses, gravestones, and mausoleums ornamented with stone gargoyles surrounded the old building. Even in the sunshine the place looked ominous. "Do you suppose everyone buried here was a thief?"

Aunt Ettie waved a hand. "What does it matter, dear? They're all dead. Turn around, now, so I can get at your buttons. Getting you changed in a carriage will be a task, but you can't go crawling through tunnels in your skirts."

"There are tunnels?" asked Jasmina, struggling out of her gown.

"I can only assume, dear. Now, into your chimney-sweep clothing… who could have imagined the costume would come in handy so often? Perhaps I'll have a pair of trousers made for myself."

"If I had my choice I would never don another pair of trousers again. I *like* being a lady, Aunt. It perplexes me that I'm forever being forced to act otherwise."

"But you do it so well, dear. I will return for you at six, so don't be late. And I shall have picked out the loveliest material for your new gowns. And of course slippers and gloves and—"

"Yes, yes, Aunt. But where am I supposed to go?" Jasmina shoved her side curls up into her cap.

"Why, into the chapel. I thought that was obvious."

Jasmina breathed a sigh of relief. She wouldn't have to walk through the graveyard on top of all those dead bodies. She cast her cat illusion and slipped from the carriage, glancing at the coachman to see if he noticed. But he appeared half-asleep until Aunt rapped smartly on the carriage door and it lurched forward.

Leaving Jasmina standing all alone. In a thieves' graveyard.

She made her way up the weed-choked path, catching the faint sound of voices coming from the warehouses surrounding the churchyard. Despite still being in the city, she felt isolated, as if she walked a trail through some ancient moor and if she screamed there would be no one to hear her.

"Stop thinking about it," she muttered, "and just get on with it."

The chapel walls appeared to be more intact than they'd looked from the bottom of the road. Two oak doors still hung from their frames and she pushed one open, entering the chapel, where the lack of ceiling allowed even more weeds to flourish.

"You look as beautiful as ever."

Jasmina blinked at the shadowed alcove toward her right. His voice did odd things to her stomach, and when he stepped into the sunshine his appearance did even odder things to her heartbeat. The tattered clothes he wore didn't detract one bit from his handsomeness. Nothing could hide the wide breadth of his shoulders, the straight lines of his body, the silky black of his hair, nor the deep blue of his eyes.

She stared at him hungrily. Surely it had been years since she'd last seen him and not days. He seemed unwilling to break the silence as well, just continued to gaze at her as if he could reach into her soul and capture it for his own.

Jasmina wrenched her eyes from his and lowered them. His hands lay carelessly at his sides, those long fingers twitching a bit, as if he longed to reach out to her. She couldn't help the flush that rose to her face when she remembered the feel of his fingers on her skin. How he'd touched her… where he'd touched her. His gentle strength and how he'd played her body like some instrument of pleasure.

It made her feel shy. With a baronet. Ridiculous. Jasmina took a deep breath. "What are we doing here?"

"There's a crypt below the chapel that leads to the Underground City. There are other entrances, but all of them are even more unpleasant."

"Let's get on with it then."

He moved toward her. "You're serious? You want to help search for the relic?"

Jasmina's head snapped up. She stared at his chin. It was a strong, rugged chin. "Whyever else do you think I'm here?"

"I'd hoped it might be a ruse." She could hear the smile in his voice, and her eyes lifted of their own accord to his mouth. "I hoped that you wanted to see me again. That you were just afraid to come to me at night."

"I'm not afraid of you."

"Are you sure?" His arms swept around her shoulders so quickly she barely had time to blink. Then his mouth covered hers and she barely had time to think, for a moment so lost in the glorious sensation of his warm mouth that all she could do was hold on and kiss him back.

Her good sense returned and she turned her head, trying to push him away. His mouth swept to her ear and Jasmina shivered. "You're afraid of what I make you feel," he murmured, his tongue doing wicked things to her ear. She had never imagined…

She stiffened her back and he sighed, allowing her to step away from him. "I assure you, I'm here only to find the relic and that blasted illusion of mine. Perhaps this was a bad idea."

"You're still angry at me for calling you Jaz."

He had a half smile on his face and Jasmina clenched her hands. He looked so smug. "Father has decided to remove me from the bad influences of London." She swept her gaze pointedly at his attire. It looked to be some kind of common field laborer's garb. "He is taking my family on a grand tour in less than two weeks' time. I have to get rid of that illusion before I leave."

Those deep blue eyes narrowed and he regarded her thoughtfully. "You don't have to go anywhere. Marry me."

Jasmina sputtered. She couldn't form a coherent word.

He shifted a bit, the outline of his were-stallion appearing to breathe smoke. "You still don't believe that I love you."

"What happened between you and my illusion?" Astonishing, that only those words managed to escape her lips.

"It doesn't matter. She was nothing *but* an illusion."

Jasmina crossed her arms over her chest. "We can't

be sure of that. What if she proves to be something else? What will you do then?" His lips narrowed and his eyes looked troubled. She tried to squash the feeling of disappointment that rose inside of her. "You don't know. I think you are confused, Sir Sterling, and I'm not sure anything will change that unless and until we find your Jaz."

He didn't argue with her. That disappointed Jasmina even more, and a slow burn of anger grew to replace the dreadful feeling of disappointment. She wished he'd been sure of whom he'd been proposing to before he'd said those words.

Sterling led her to the back of the chapel where a portion of the roof still stood and stopped before a large slab of stone. He half-shifted, moving a stone that would take ten ordinary men to manage, revealing a pitch black hole beneath. "You'd best get rid of the cat and disguise yourself as a man."

Jasmina glanced down in surprise. She'd forgotten that she still held the illusion. She waved her fingers and cast her spells, using a final one to send a ball of light down into that black hole.

"Get rid of it," he said. "We don't want anyone to know we're coming."

"Why not?"

"Mugged, raped, tortured—take your pick. It's worse than the East End down there."

He was just trying to frighten her. "But we won't be able to see where we're going."

Sterling gave her an arrogant grin. "Have you forgotten what I am?"

Of course not, but Jasmina hadn't realized that his

were-talents were so formidable. Could he really see in that blackness? When he lowered himself into the hole, she decided she would just have to trust him. No, she realized that she did trust him. If not with her heart, at least with her life.

Her experience crawling down rooftops made the climb negligible for her, but when they reached the bottom and she stared at the wall of black before them, she balked.

"Put your arms around my back," whispered Sterling. "And stay close. There are pitfalls and chasms."

Jasmina nodded wordlessly and did as he asked. She was sure she slowed him down, but he never complained. There were times during that blind journey when the weight of the earth surrounding them felt like it was crushing her. When she couldn't breathe and had to fight the urge to turn and run back the way they'd come, mindlessly screaming to get out. She shivered with the inner battle against a terror she'd never felt before.

"Are you sure you want to do this?" he asked her more than once.

But Jasmina would only tighten her grip on his solid back and answer with a breathless, "Yes."

She felt the cavern before she saw it. Her senses seemed to recognize an opening, and she pushed against Sterling's back to hurry him on. When he stepped from the tunnel, she blinked against the comparative brightness. Fairylights flickered from the ceiling far above them, imitating the night sky. Stone houses constructed from the excavations of thousands of tunnels littered the enormous floor of the cave, most of them without roofs. Around the buildings flowed streams of water like an enormous spiderweb. They appeared to carry away the refuse of the citizens just like the Thames did above.

Jasmina had heard of the Underground, the same way she'd heard of the East End. But it was like some fairy tale of another land far away that she'd never expected to visit. She wondered how anyone could live down here and then realized that many wouldn't have a choice.

"If I had enough magic to change the world I would," she whispered.

"But we don't. We can only change a little bit at a time."

He had stepped beside her, laying his arm casually around her waist, and when she glanced up at him his face looked so serious and troubled that her heart twisted. Jasmina closed her eyes against the surge of longing she felt for him. He was such a good man. Entirely unsuitable as a husband, of course, and half in love with an illusion, but still, the longer she stayed in his presence, the more she came to admire him.

Sterling led her through the city, stopping to talk to several people he'd obviously gotten to know while searching for his sister. Most of them had hideous deformities as a result of magical experimentation. Something that was never allowed above-ground, but here...

A small boy with three eyes and a lipless mouth tugged on Sterling's worn jacket. "Yer shtill offerin' a reward fer the tunnel?"

Sterling squatted. "Yes. Have you found it?"

The boy nodded, looked at Jasmina suspiciously, then jabbed his thumb over his shoulder. They followed the lad back to the outskirts of the city, Jasmina feverishly wishing she had the power of a duke so that she could fix the child's face.

Black holes covered the sides of the city cavern and, after a breathless walk, the boy pointed to one of the openings. Sterling raised a brow but didn't say a word, just tossed the lad a shilling and watched him disappear back within the warren of buildings.

Sterling gestured at the openings. "Some of them lead to nobles' Underground homes, some to dead ends and traps. There are thousands of them, so I doubt the boy is right. But I could never search them all in my lifetime, so any lead is better than none."

"Why would any noble choose to live here?"

Sterling shrugged. "They can practice black magic without repercussion. Many of them have homes above ground too, where they lead seemingly upright lives."

Jasmina nodded, thinking of Duke Hagersham and how thoroughly he'd managed to deceive her peers. Then Sterling picked her up and ducked inside the cave as a group of men made their way toward them. They all carried weapons and many of them walked with a lurching gait. She forgot to be afraid of the darkness until they were well inside the tunnel. "Will they follow?" she whispered.

"No."

"Why are we stopping?"

"The tunnel branches in three different directions." He set her back on her feet. Jasmina wavered in the darkness without a point of reference to focus on, latching on to his jacket for balance. "We'll try the left. Come closer, and follow me the way you did before."

"No."

His voice growled with irritation. "Don't tell me the idea of staying close to me bothers you. I know better."

"I meant," replied Jasmina, matching her tone to his, "that you should let me choose which way to go."

She could feel his surprise. "Why? You've never set foot down here, and I've been exploring for weeks."

"I–I'm not sure. I just have a sudden feeling that we should take the tunnel to our right."

He shrugged, his jacket lifting in her hand, and took the direction she suggested. He paused at every intersection, waiting for her to decide which way to go. Jasmina was glad he didn't ask any more questions because she couldn't explain it. She had no idea why one way felt any different from another, but it did.

Sterling stopped again. "A door."

"In the tunnel?"

He grunted and she could feel his body moving while he smoothed his hands over the door. He paused, rummaged in his pocket, and she heard clicking sounds as he picked the lock.

"Where did you learn to do that, anyway?" she whispered.

He hesitated, then murmured, "The military. I was a spy."

Ah. Well, that explained quite a bit. She wanted to ask more, but this was a foolish place to have a discussion. She heard the tumble of the lock. When Sterling opened the door, Jasmina cast an illusion of light and threw it forward into the room. It burned her eyes and she blinked quickly, looking for danger. But if there had been guards they'd left their post. Some kind of game lay abandoned on the table, the miniature characters slumped in relief atop the playing board of guillotines and hangman's nooses. Three chairs and a keg of ale surrounded the table.

Several more wooden doors faced them, and Sterling turned to her with a lift of his brow. Jasmina closed her eyes, then pointed toward the one directly across the room.

He quickly applied his lock picks and opened the door. Sterling stared inside for a moment, his expression changing from amazement to horror so quickly that Jasmina caught her breath.

"Angel," he breathed. And then he disappeared inside the cell.

Fifteen

JASMINA SLOWLY FOLLOWED STERLING INTO THE ROOM. Rough-hewn walls, a dirt floor, and a stink more pungent than the Thames made her grimace. A black swan sat in the corner of the room, her head tucked beneath a wing. Sterling sank to his knees and held out his arms. The swan shifted, becoming a thin young woman. The baronet gathered his sister in his arms as if assuring himself that she was real.

Even through the grime and rags that she wore Angel was lovely, with hair as black as her brother's, but eyes of such a pale blue that they seemed to glow as she blinked up at Sterling's face.

"I knew you would come," she whispered, her voice gravelly with dryness. "I never doubted for an instant."

Sterling gave his sister such a tender smile that Jasmina felt envious of their closeness. What would it be like to have the same faith in a man that Angel obviously felt for her brother?

"Oh, Sterling," continued Angel. "The marquess said we were just going for a walk. I know I should have brought my maid with me, but he seemed so kind. I never thought he would… would…"

"Hush," whispered her brother. "It doesn't matter and this isn't your fault. Understand?"

Jasmina must have made a noise, for suddenly those pale blue eyes were directed at her, and Angel raised an accusing finger. "She's with them."

Sterling shook his head. "No, she's with me. Lady Jasmina has a… twin. Angel, are you well?"

"I'm thirsty," she rasped. "And I've never *really* been hungry before, Sterling. It truly hurts."

Jasmina took a step back as she watched the expression that fell over his handsome face. She heard a sound behind her and turned. "It's the guards."

Jasmina didn't even bother to cast a spell. She felt Sterling shift behind her and had the good sense to just step out of the way. A flash of seething black muscle passed her, and the three guards went down one by one. They never stood a chance. Within moments Sterling's were-form stood over the prone men, stomping the ground and bridling with unchecked violence. Jasmina waited for him to shift back to human but he raged on, circling as if looking for more enemies. She called out to him and he turned, those lovely eyes now a dark red, his nostrils flaring and his black mane flying around him. He looked like a stallion from hell and if she hadn't known his gentleness, she would have been terrified.

"Easy," she breathed, taking a step toward him. "It's all over now."

Sterling stomped and displayed a wicked-looking set of teeth, but Jasmina didn't hesitate. She placed a shaking hand on his sleek neck and smoothed the bristling hair. He froze for a moment, then shuddered, leaning his head on her chest, nearly knocking her over. "You've had your revenge. It's time to take care of your sister now."

He finally shifted back to human, his arms wrapping around her and holding her close, his heart still thundering with a staccato rhythm. "They hurt her," he said through gritted teeth.

"Sterling?"

Jasmina turned to find his sister watching them with puzzled eyes. Angel swayed on her feet, her ragged bodice clutched together with her fists. Sterling caught her before she fell, his speed still amazing to Jasmina.

"Let's get you out of here," he murmured, and gathered up the emaciated woman in his arms.

Angel glanced at Jasmina. "There are others here." Jasmina nodded and searched the guards, found the keys, and unlocked the rest of the doors. She didn't expect the relic to be here, or her twin, but she looked anyway. Sterling hadn't moved a muscle, determined to protect his sister with his body, but his eyes followed Jasmina intently. Hoping that her twin might be here? Jasmina threw him a dark look.

A ragtag bunch of prisoners entered the guard-room, blinking against the glow of her light, keeping their distance from their rescuers, especially Jasmina. Sterling assured them that she wasn't Jaz, and although a few looked skeptical, most took him at his word. Sterling then strode across the room, carrying Angel as if she weighed no more than a feather. Jasmina quickly grasped the back of his jacket.

"I'll have to put out the light," she told the others who followed them, glancing back over her shoulder. Some of them had shifted to their were-forms; a wolf, several rabbits, a hawk and a hog. Jasmina stifled a nervous laugh.

It was quite a menagerie that made its way through the dark tunnels and back to the Underground City. Sterling had chosen a clever entry into the city, for the tunnel that led to the chapel opened onto the backs of several buildings. They weren't noticed, thank heavens. Jasmina could only imagine the cacophony this group of weres would cause if they'd been attacked by anyone. She stifled another hysterical giggle and realized that perhaps she was more tired than she'd thought.

Jasmina had to argue with Sterling for ten minutes when they reached the crypt in the chapel. He still refused to let go of his sister, but he finally relinquished his hold and Angel managed her way up the sides of the shaft quite nicely.

"You certainly aren't going to gallop in broad daylight through the streets of London with your sister in such a state," she told him when he evidenced every intention of doing so. He shifted to stallion in reply. "Sir Sterling, I don't think Angel could stay on your back if she tried."

His blue eyes studied his sister and he slowly shifted back to human. "Do you have another idea? I need to get her to a doctor."

Angel shook her tangled hair. "I just need something to eat. What of my friends?"

Sterling blinked in surprise at the other weres. "I

think the prince would be interested in talking to them as well."

Jasmina walked to the outer door of the chapel and peered outside. It felt like years since they'd gone beneath the earth, but she could see Aunt Ettie and the carriage waiting for them at the end of the road. "I think we can fit some of them in the carriage," she said, turning to find that only Sterling and Angel stood behind her. "Where did they go?"

Angel shrugged. "They are simple people. Like us, they have a title but none of the wealth or land to make it meaningful. The thought of speaking to royalty made them flee. But don't worry, they shall find their way home." She swayed, as if her words had weakened her, and Sterling snatched her up in his arms again.

Jasmina worried that Angel might expire on the spot. She looked so dreadfully weak. Jasmina couldn't cast an illusion to hide Sterling and his sister, but fortunately she only had the coachman to worry about. She really didn't want him bringing home tales to her father. So she quickly cast a spell over his eyes until they entered the carriage.

Jasmina glanced at Sterling. "To your flat?"

He shook his head. "The Hall of Mages. I want her seen by a doctor and I want her kept safe until I find *them*."

Jasmina had no doubt whom he referred to. He would make Angel's abductors pay for what they'd done to her. She gave instructions to the coachman and sat back, studying the hard angles of his face. She ached for him. For the guilt she saw when he looked at his sister. For Angel's pain that he took upon himself.

Her poor aunt hadn't uttered a word since they'd entered the coach.

"Aunt Ettie," said Jasmina, "may I introduce Miss Angel Thorn?"

Her words released the dam around Aunt's mouth. "Oh, my! You found her. Well, of course you did. I quite see the resemblance to you, Sir Sterling. You poor dear, you look quite famished. Whatever did they do to you, child?" Jasmina wasn't quite sure if it was her aunt's kind tone or genuine concern, but suddenly Angel's eyes started to water, and she threw herself across the carriage into Aunt's arms. Aunt looked surprised, and then her own eyes started to tear, and she patted and cooed to Angel the rest of the trip.

Jasmina scooted out of her seat to give the two ladies room and sat next to Sterling. It felt like sitting against a sun-warmed rock. She could feel his tightened muscles almost vibrate with unleashed fury. "She will be fine."

He continued to stare straight ahead.

"We will find those responsible."

No reaction, not even a blink of those dark blue eyes. Jasmina glanced down beside her. His large hand clutched the edge of the seat, his knuckles white. She cautiously laid her hand next to his. The carriage jostled over a pothole. She carefully placed her fingers over his. He loosed a breath, and some of the tension went out of his shoulders. His lips quirked as he turned over his hand, clasping her lightly but with a firmness that didn't relax until they'd reached the Hall of Mages.

Jasmina instructed the coachman to the back entrance, and she helped her aunt assist the still teary-eyed Angel from the coach while Sterling announced their presence. Sir Artemus answered the summons, raising a golden brow at their party.

"You're making a habit of this," he growled at Sterling. But before the were-stallion had a chance to respond, he moved forward. "My dear Henrietta, let me help you."

Sir Artemus assisted both of the women into the same parlor they'd brought Mary to. "Tea," he said to the novice who'd followed them. "And a tray of food, I think."

"And a bath," added Jasmina. "Aunt, can you fetch my dress from the carriage?"

Aunt Ettie disentangled herself from Angel's arms and rose. "Of course, and I picked up several other dresses from the modiste today. I will see what might be appropriate for Angel." She gave the girl a gentle smile before she left the room.

Sterling sat next to Angel and Jasmina stood behind the sofa, feeling a bit left out. Sir Artemus took a chair facing them. "Your sister, I presume?"

Sterling nodded. "I want a doctor. I want you to keep her here for her own protection, until I find those responsible for this."

Sir Artemus nodded, but kept his golden eyes fixed on Angel. "Do you know why you were taken?"

Jasmina gave her best imitation of Aunt Ettie's sniff. "I hardly think this is the time for questions. My friend has been treated dreadfully."

Angel gave her a grateful smile, but shook her head,

as if what she had to say was more important than her own welfare. "They are making an army."

A profound silence followed her words. Jasmina could hear the faint ticking of the clock on the mantel. Then Sir Artemus let out a breath and leaned forward. "How do you know this?"

Angel swallowed. "They sent in some of their soldiers to see if they could harm me. They said they'd made the creatures with relic-magic, but how can that be? Because the soldiers felt real to me. They could hurt me, yet I was immune to all of their other spells and black magic."

A strangled sound escaped Sterling's throat, and Jasmina fought the urge to go to him. Instead she went to Angel, warming the girl's cold hands with her own. "They have one of Merlin's Relics that enables them to somehow copy people. Did the men look alike?"

Angel frowned. "Yes. Sometimes they sent more than one man and they did look very much alike. They also sent other creatures. Trolls and giants and elves. But they couldn't seem to understand the slightest thing. They were easy to defeat."

"The copy lacked the original's intelligence? So they are forced to duplicate only men," said Sir Artemus, thinking aloud. "Did you see their army? How many men? How many other creatures?"

"N-no. They never let me out of the prison-cave."

Sir Artemus waved a massive hand. "It's all right. You did well. We know that this army will withstand the defensive spells of even a royal, since relic-magic is stronger than any other on earth. But because of their experiments we also know that

were-kind can fight them just like ordinary men."
His voice trailed off. "But how can I prepare against
an army I can't find?"

"It doesn't matter," interjected Sterling, "when
they can replace their soldiers by the score."

"We don't know that. Spells always weaken the
caster; it may take days to create so many soldiers. And
since they're hiding them it sounds like that's what
they are doing."

Angel shivered and Sterling wrapped his arm
around her. "That's enough," he snapped. "We can
discuss this later."

Fortunately a novice arrived with a tray and a
hipbath, several water-bearers behind him. While
Angel dove into the food, the servants prepared her
bath, and when Aunt returned with the clothing she
shooed all the men from the room. It took some time
for Jasmina to clean up herself and then Angel. She
winced at the other woman's skeletal figure, the bones
so prominent she could have counted Angel's ribs.

"There, dear," said Aunt, arranging the silk tie
around Angel's dress. The material hung from the
girl's shapeless body. "Don't worry now, I'm sure
you'll fill it out in a few weeks."

Angel nodded, eyeing the pastries left on her tray.
While Aunt helped Jasmina with her buttons the
other young woman crept stealthily toward the table,
feeling at the seams of her new skirts. Angel quickly
wrapped several crumpets in a linen and stuffed them
in her pockets, frowning when she realized Jasmina
and Aunt Henrietta were staring at her. "They will
take the tray away."

Jasmina nodded as if the statement were entirely reasonable.

Angel shrugged her bony shoulders. "I might be hungry later."

Aunt gave her a tremulous smile. "You can just ask for more, dear. They will soil the dress…"

Jasmina hushed her aunt, took one of the smaller boxes that had once held a pair of new satin slippers, and joined Angel at the table. She gathered the rest of the food, arranging it between sheets of linen, then replaced the lid and handed it to Angel. "You can put it beneath your bed. Just in case."

Angel nodded, clasping the box to her chest, giving Jasmina a rather awkward, sideways hug. "I don't know when I shall ever take anything for granted again. Thank you."

Jasmina's eyes burned. Sterling's sister needed her so very much. Suddenly she desperately wished that Angel were her very own sister. That she had the right to care for her. She'd buy her pretty things and arrange her hair and make sure she never worried about—

"She would sneak me food, you know," whispered Angel.

"Who?"

"Your… your twin. I just thought you should know."

Jasmina smoothed the front of her gown. She'd thought her illusion was a copy of herself who lacked a soul and proper morals. It upset her to hear that Jaz could be kind. She couldn't afford to like her twin, not when she had every intention of destroying her.

Jasmina turned away but Angel grasped her arm, lowering her voice even further. "And he loves you."

Oh, heavens, Sterling's sister wasn't finished with her confidences. Jasmina wanted to run but her feet stayed glued to the floor. She didn't bother to ask Angel whom she referred to. "I don't know what you mean. How can you possibly have determined such a thing on such short acquaintance?"

"You don't know what you've done, do you?" Angel's pale blue eyes widened. "You conquered his beast, Lady Jasmina. No sane person would even approach a were-stallion in full fury. Yet you did, and brought him back to his human form. He must love you very much."

Jasmina felt tempted to tell Angel about Sterling's relationship with her "twin," but decided now wasn't quite the time. Instead she hid behind her mask of propriety and patted the other woman's arm.

Angel's sudden frown of puzzlement turned to alarm. "You won't hurt him, will you? Sterling and I... we haven't had much love in our lives, my lady. Please don't be careless with his heart."

"I declare," interrupted Aunt Ettie, having finished bundling up their dirty clothes and advancing across the room with a look of determination. "You both look so serious. Whatever are you talking about?"

"My brother," replied Angel.

"Oh, yes, he is the bravest of men," breathed Aunt. "So incredibly handsome too. It appears that all were-kind are exceptionally attractive people. Why, Sir Artemus—"

Before Aunt Ettie could continue with her rapturous declarations about the were-lion, Jasmina quickly strode to the door and threw it open. Sir

Sterling lounged against the wall opposite the door, his muscled arms folded over his broad chest, one leg crossed in front of the other in the most casual of attitudes. But she wasn't fooled.

"Your sister's injuries will heal with time," murmured Jasmina. "She has suffered deprivations, but I'm sure she will overcome them." He straightened, the hard angles of his face softening with relief. "I shall come to visit her tomorrow, if it is all right with you."

She blinked and with that uncanny speed he suddenly stood in front of her, his warm hand clasping her own. Sir Artemus approached from down the hall with several novices, but that didn't deter Sir Sterling in the least. He brought her hand to his mouth and kissed it, his soft lips lingering on her now tingling skin. "I thank you for the care of my sister, Lady Jasmina."

Jasmina glanced down the hall. Sir Artemus gave her a cheeky smile, and the novices' mouths dropped open. She removed her hand from Sterling's grasp and lifted her nose. But her voice was soft when she replied, "You are most welcome, sir."

Sterling nodded and swept past her, joining his sister on the sofa, placing a protective arm around her waist. Jasmina studied them a moment, feeling such warmth in the simple act of it that she knew without a doubt she loved them both.

How utterly devastating.

As Sir Artemus passed her she touched his arm. "What of this army?"

His golden gaze swept her. "Do not worry, Lady Jasmina. I assure you that the Corps of Were-kind will defeat them." His glance strayed from her to Sir Sterling. "I suggest you focus your energies on the problems that only you can solve."

That night Jasmina dreamed of shadows and hot skin and the sound of her own laughter. She woke with a start, kicking the covers off her sticky body. She rose and opened the window, breathing in the fresh air. The fog lay like a blanket of white over Mandrake Square, the night moonless and still. She knew what she had to do.

Jasmina touched the fairylight by her bed, the weak glow just enough to allow her to change her clothing. Aunt Ettie had washed her chimney-sweep disguise, and although worse for wear from her trip to the Underground, at least it smelled clean. She wrapped her rope and grapple around her waist and started to tiptoe from the room.

"Where ya going?" asked a sleepy voice.

Jasmina huffed, glancing at the two small shapes curled up behind her settee. "None of your business."

She heard the patter of feet, and Nuisance yawned hugely up at her. "Listen, I already missed all the excitement from today." He sent a scornful glance at his sleeping bedmate. "And I've never been to the Underground, blast it."

Jasmina shuddered to think of the trouble he could have caused if he had followed them earlier today. "I'm sorry that I slipped from the house without telling you of my plans."

Nuisance stuck his finger in his ear and probed.

"Well, then, I suppose that's all right. So, where ya going now?"

She debated telling him the truth. If he followed her he'd find out anyway. "I'm going to visit Sir Sterling."

"At this time of night?"

"Yes."

"Oh, ho! I know what you're planning and I suppose I—" He glanced again at his bedmate, who interrupted her snoring to wheeze and roll over. "I suppose it wouldn't be fair of me to interfere."

Jasmina rocked back on her heels. "Nuisance, don't tell me you've acquired a conscience. You will destroy my faith in all gnome-kind."

"Hmph. You best get going before I change my mind."

And with Nuisance's blessing Jasmina snuck up to the attic, to the trapdoor where Father's wards were weakest. She anchored her rope and shimmied down, flipping the rope when she reached the ground to dislodge the grapple. She stood for a moment, tempted to go back to her own bed.

Then she turned and jogged down the empty street. Sterling might not be home. He might be back in the Underground, searching for the relic and her illusion. Jasmina broke into a run at the thought of him finding Jaz before she had a chance for a fair fight.

A light glowed in his window. It drew her like a beacon. She snagged the roof and prayed no one heard the soft *thunk* of her grapple, then began to climb. When she reached the window of his flat Jasmina pushed open the shutter and froze.

Sir Sterling *had* gone to the Underground tonight, and it looked as though he'd run into trouble. His black hair was clouded by dust, a dark bruise bloomed on his cheek, and a red mark marred the absolute perfection of his broad chest. His broad, very naked chest.

He sat in a bath, his skin gleaming by firelight while he washed the cut and inspected the wound. He seemed to dismiss it as insignificant and reached into the water, picking up a cup and dousing his head. With his eyes closed he lathered his hair with suds, the muscles in his arms rippling in the most fascinating way, the frothy soap running down his face and neck.

Jasmina swallowed. Hard.

When Sterling started to rinse his hair Jasmina took advantage of the moment to crawl over the window-sill. She stood, unable to take her eyes off of him. She could see his chest and the tops of his knees. The rest of his body was covered by sudsy water, and she felt the blood rush to her face as she longed to see what the rest of him would look like.

But somehow she knew what he looked like, as an image of his naked body flashed before her eyes.

She blinked, and the image faded. She had to content herself by studying the muscles of his shoulders, the sleek lines of his back. Jasmina took a few steps closer, truly fascinated by the way the water slid over the two large muscles that framed his nipples. One drop of suds quivered on his left nipple and she wanted to catch it with her finger. Instead it slid over the tip and slowly ran down his ribs, diffusing in the water below.

Sterling smoothed the wet hair back from his face and turned to look at her. Her stomach flipped. How long had he known she was there, watching him? He didn't say a word, just continued to gaze at her with a question in his eyes.

Jasmina took a deep breath and reached for the buttons of her shirt. The look in his glittering eyes changed, became more intense; it seemed to radiate a heat that she felt from across the room as she slowly unfastened her top.

Her shirt puddled on the floor, followed by her trousers. Cool air from the open window fluttered the back of her thin chemise and chilled her bottom when she removed her drawers. Despite her resolve Jasmina could not remove the protection of her underclothes. Foolish, really, since the material was so sheer that he could probably see every bit of her anyway. Still, she left the chemise on as she approached him.

He appeared to be shocked into immobility and silence. Good, that's exactly how she preferred it. Jasmina ran her hands over his slick, wet hair, loving the silky texture of it. When she explored the smooth skin of his back, his muscles tensed beneath her touch and she smiled. She found the bar of soap floating on the surface of the water and quickly lathered her hands.

She heard him suck in a breath. When she smoothed her soapy hands over his shoulders, he groaned and their eyes met. Jasmina almost abandoned her plan at that moment. What she saw in his midnight-blue eyes shook her to the core. If she continued with this there would be no going back. Not for him.

Certainly not for her.

Sterling leaned against the angled back of the tub, and her hands followed with little thought from her. She'd never imagined the feel of soap across a man's skin; the slippery smooth texture made her palms sensitive to the contour of every hardened muscle.

Jasmina ran her hands over his nipples. The hardened nubs sent tingles of pleasure across her palms. His wound appeared shallow, but she avoided touching it, afraid to hurt him. She smoothed soap through the black hair of his chest, then followed the path it made down to his waist, beneath the water. His stomach sucked in at her touch, and her hands brushed against something smooth and round.

She looked up at him and leaned forward, bending over the tub, her breasts brushing against the edge of it. Jasmina touched her mouth to his and then pulled back, staring into his eyes. They burned with a feverish tenderness. She kissed him again, this time deeply, until she twined her tongue with his.

His arms went around her so quickly she didn't have a chance to protest. He pulled her atop him in the tub, his hands tangling in her hair, his mouth hungrily devouring her. Her knees lay between his legs, only the thin barrier of her chemise separating their skin. For a moment all Jasmina could do was succumb.

His wet hands lowered, meeting the bare skin of her legs, sliding back up beneath that thin material to clasp her bottom and push her onto his hard arousal, his tongue battling with her own. Jasmina grabbed the sides of the tub and pushed away from him to catch her breath, to regain control.

"Don't," she said.

One black brow went up. "Are you sure?" he said through gritted teeth. He knew. He knew she wanted control, and his voice said it would probably kill him.

"Yes."

He nodded. He would allow it anyway. Jasmina gave him a wicked smile and stood up between his legs. Her wet chemise molded to her skin; she could feel it sticking between the folds of her legs and across her breasts. Sir Sterling groaned.

"Stand," she instructed, and he came out of the water so fast it poured over the sides of the tub and raced across the wooden floor. Jasmina rescued the bar of soap and started lathering her hands again. He closed his eyes and seemed to whisper some fervent prayer, but Jasmina was too busy studying every inch of his magnificent body to pay much notice. She ran her hands across his chest again, this time continuing down the sides of his waist to his slim hips, feeling the bone and muscle. A part of her felt she was discovering new territory, but another part of her seemed to know exactly what she would find. She shook off the confusion and concentrated on her task.

Lady Jasmina leaned forward and curved her hands over the small dips in the sides of his bottom, to the full, round back of it. She ran her slick hands over the twin mounds, feeling him tremble from the effort it took not to move. She refused to pity him. Her fingertips swept up the curves to his lower back, and she felt two more very small dips there. How absolutely wonderful.

Jasmina went higher, explored the ridges of his spine and finally caressed his shoulders again, running her hands down the taut muscles of his arms. Back up to his chest, to play with his nipples again.

Sterling let out a sound. Something like a strangled curse. Jasmina kissed him then, an apology and a promise, before she bent down and lathered her hands once more to continue her explorations. The man felt so incredibly beautiful.

She smoothed soap over his waist and tried not to look at what lay below it yet. Not until she could touch it too. She rubbed his hips, then his thighs. Muscle upon muscle. Sterling stared straight ahead, his face clenched in concentration, and since she couldn't reach his lips she kissed his neck, lapping up a few drops of water with her tongue.

Then she leaned slightly back and closed her hands around his shaft. She felt so frightened that she never would have managed it if she hadn't been in complete control. Sterling did curse this time, a word quite unsuitable for a lady's ears, but Jasmina absently forgave him. She measured him with her hands and wondered how she'd ever manage him. But she knew she could… didn't she?

She explored his thick ridges and the round smooth end of him. The heavy sacs that hung beneath. Then down his legs again to his calves. Jasmina rinsed her hands and reached for the bucket warming by the fire. She poured half the contents over his body and the rest of the water into the tub, warming it a bit.

"Sit down."

He took a deep breath and then sat. Firelight played across the planes of his cheeks and the firm line of his nose. He'd spilled out so much water earlier that it now barely came to his waist. His shaft jutted from the water and Jasmina shivered for a moment, then slowly peeled away her sodden chemise.

Sterling watched her through narrowed eyes, his

full mouth thinned in determination, his hands gripping the sides of the tub until the muscles in his arms and shoulders bulged. Jasmina very carefully placed a foot on each side of his hips. She lowered herself to her knees, grateful that there was just enough room on each side of the bath. She sat astride the length of him, the hard line of his shaft lying flat against his belly, and closed her eyes for a moment.

It would hurt. She knew that. But somehow she also knew the pleasure that would follow.

Jasmina took Sterling's hands and lathered them with soap, guiding one to her breast and the other to the place where he'd touched her before. He groaned with relief and started to massage her, his fingers sliding gently across her nub, the slick feel of his touch sending ripples of pleasure through her. Anticipation built throughout every nerve in her body, centering on the rhythmic pressure of his hand. She throbbed and shook and he threatened to take away her control. Jasmina rose slightly on her knees, scrambled for the soap again and lathered the tip of him, then swiftly lowered her weight.

She closed her eyes and whimpered.

Sterling froze beneath her and when she opened her eyes he was frowning in concern. Jasmina blinked away tears and raised herself up again, the water creating a sucking motion, rippling around her, adding another sensuous element to the movement.

His hands began to move again, caressing her, adding the distraction of her pleasure against the pain as she plunged him inside of her again. And again. Until there was no longer any pain, just a burning need that made her take him in deeper each time she lowered herself.

"Jasmina." He stared into her eyes.

She moved her body forward, shifting him in and out but at a different angle. Water splashed up his waist and over her hips and she thought she might scream from the sheer pleasure of it. Her body suddenly imploded, taking her completely by surprise as wave after wave of incredible delight washed over her.

Sterling said her name again and then thrust against her, his body wracked by his own tremors, his eyes fixed on hers so that she could read every moment of his pleasure within their dark blue depths.

Jasmina sagged against his warm, wet chest while her breathing slowed, a delicious feeling of languor spreading over her. His arms wrapped around her, and he held her until the water grew cold, whispering endearments while he pressed warm kisses against the top of her head.

Jasmina slowly rose, her knees protesting. Tomorrow they would remind her of this night. She dried off her body with a cloth, sneaking glances at Sterling's magnificent frame still stretched out in the tub. His head was flung back, his eyes closed, as if she'd sucked the life out of him. Jasmina smiled while she dressed.

"Stay the night," he said huskily.

She turned to look at him. He still had his eyes closed, his head flung back. The temptation to kiss his throat nearly overwhelmed her. "You know I can't."

"Then kiss me before you go."

Jasmina shook her head. "Then I shall never leave. Look at me."

He rolled his head toward her and slowly opened those brilliant eyes.

"Who am I?" she asked.

He frowned for a moment, then quirked his lip as comprehension dawned in his eyes. "You are Lady Jasmina Karlyle."

"And you shall never forget it." Jasmina turned and grabbed the rope still dangling outside his window. As she climbed over the sill the husky sound of his voice reached her.

"I never have, my lady."

Sixteen

THE NEXT DAY JASMINA COULD BARELY KEEP HER EYES open for her fittings. Normally she felt quite content to stand for hours and allow the modiste and her swarm of fairies to wrap gorgeous fabrics around her body. But her knees hurt and her eyes felt gritty and without anything specific to do, she had entirely too much time to think.

"What do you think of this material, dear?" asked Aunt Henrietta, who sat comfortably on an upholstered bench across from her. Jasmina glanced over at the ceiling-to-floor mirror. The fabric had been magically enhanced. Tiny sparkles of gold peeked from the weave of the emerald green cloth, creating starbursts of light that flared whenever she moved. "It's a bit… spectacular."

Aunt nodded. "Imagine how you will sparkle on the dance floor. We'll take that one as well."

The modiste nodded her head and slipped a speculative glance at Jasmina while the flutter of fairy wings swept the material from the room. Aunt appeared to be excited by their trip, but Jasmina only felt a desolate emptiness at the thought of leaving London. Because she hadn't found her twin, or because she wouldn't see Sir Sterling for months?

He was so incredibly beautiful. She hadn't realized the full extent of his physical... charms until last night. She'd thought to brand her image in his brain, but instead it was his features that haunted her.

The way his eyes turned smoky when she touched him...

His face taut with pleasure...

Shadowed by firelight...

Softened with tenderness as his mouth lowered to hers...

"My lady?"

Jasmina opened her eyes. The modiste looked at her expectantly while Aunt Ettie frowned at the material the fairies tried to drape around her. The cloth seemed to have a mind of its own, snaking around her waist and flowing sensuously over her shoulders. It had been woven so tightly she could barely discern the nap in the dark green material. It kept fluttering against the fairies' hold, as if it flew in a wind... created by the gallop of a black stallion.

Jasmina smiled at the plump modiste. Like most women of her profession, she had an uncanny ability to discern the tastes of her clients.

"Ah, the lady likes it?" murmured the modiste. "See how it flutters with every breath? Yet no magic went into the making of it."

Which meant it would keep its beauty in the presence of a shape-shifter.

"It's such a dark green it's almost black," objected Aunt Ettie.

"I'll take it," said Jasmina. The fairies fought the material all the way from the room, then brought several other selections, which Jasmina ignored, allowing Aunt to choose.

Something about last night worried at the back of Jasmina's mind. She just couldn't overcome thoughts of Sir Sterling to allow herself to fully consider it. The feel of his skin beneath her palms. His head thrown back, that black silky hair cascading over the tub and the shadow of his handsome profile. The way she'd known exactly how to pleasure him.

Jasmina's knees buckled beneath her.

Several of the little fairies dropped the cloth and snatched at her chemise, holding her upright. Their lovely pointed faces stared at her in concern, their shimmering multicolored wings beating furiously beneath her weight. She straightened and thanked them.

"My, the time has flown," said Aunt. "It's near dinner already and we still haven't visited the milliner." She waved her hand, and the fairies quickly dressed Jasmina while Aunt sighed with exaggerated dismay. "At this rate we may have to delay our departure to finish our wardrobe purchases."

She winked at Jasmina, who smiled weakly in return.

Jasmina followed Aunt from the shop and closed her eyes when she entered the privacy of their coach to hide the wince of discomfort as she sat. Another reminder of her night with the baronet.

"I fear that a few more days may not help, Aunt. Neither Sterling nor the prince's spies seem to have any success in finding the relic or my illusion. It's like looking for one particular grain of sand on a beach."

She felt Aunt Ettie pat her hand. "Now, dear. Sir Sterling found his sister, did he not? I have faith that he will find the illusion as well. He's a decidedly stubborn man."

"If it wasn't for me I doubt if we would have found Angel," mumbled Jasmina. She froze as her mind suddenly raced. She *had* known where to find Angel, which turns to take, *as if she'd been in those tunnels before*. And Angel had said that her illusion brought her food. Jasmina had also known exactly how to make love to Sterling, as if she'd done it before. And she knew that Jaz had made love to him.

But none of those things were within the realm of her experience.

"Angel looked rather well, today," said Aunt Ettie, interrupting Jasmina's thoughts. "She's putting on weight surprisingly fast."

Jasmina nodded distractedly. Could it be possible that she was accessing her illusion's memories? That somehow they were linked?

"If we hadn't spent so much time visiting her today we might have managed the milliner too." Aunt was smiling speculatively at her. "It's just too bad Sir Sterling didn't put in an appearance... despite our rather prolonged visit."

The carriage rocked as the coachman clambered down and then opened the small steps. Jasmina climbed out and raced into the house, distracted with her new ideas. What if she tried to concentrate on her illusion? Would she be able to connect with even more of Jaz's memories? She didn't stop to wonder how or why it would be possible, she just did it.

And she felt the connection. Just bits and pieces of Jaz's memories. A tenuous yet tangible link that might enable her to find her illusion.

Aunt Ettie watched her with a worried frown. "Your mother didn't... you didn't have an errand last night, did you?"

Jasmina blinked, taking a moment to comprehend her Aunt's words, and then blushed. Good heavens, she could imagine Aunt's face if she told her of her errand. Jasmina shook her head.

"It doesn't look as if you slept well, then. Why don't you take a rest? I'll make your excuses to your mother and father and have the maid bring you up dinner on a tray."

Jasmina gave her Aunt a grateful hug and dragged herself up the stairs. After the first rush of adrenaline at the thought that she might be able to find her twin, all the strength seemed to flow from her body. She wanted to send a message to Sir Sterling immediately, letting him know that she thought she could find Jaz. But they wouldn't be able to search for her until tonight, and she needed her strength. It could be the most difficult evening of her life.

She didn't bother to remove her gown, just collapsed on the bedcovers and closed her eyes. She had no idea that making love to a man would be so exhausting. Thoughts scurried through her brain, but they stayed disconnected, and she fell asleep dreaming of Sir Sterling. Of how much she loved him. Of how she hoped he would choose her instead of her illusion.

But she dreamed of a tunnel, and she was running for a light shining at the end of it. Within the glow she could see Sterling standing next to her illusion, his eyes fascinated by the low-cut gown Jaz wore. A gown that Lady Jasmina would never dare exhibit herself in.

Sterling took a step toward the illusion.

"No," cried Jasmina. "You don't love her, you love *me*."

The illusion laughed, her pale blonde hair swirling loose around her sweet-looking face. "You're too late. He chooses me."

Jasmina finally got close enough to grasp Sterling's arm. "Doesn't our night together mean anything to you at all?" But he still wouldn't look at her. If only he would look at her!

The illusion laughed wickedly. "I showed you what to do. Why would he want the copy when he can have the original?"

And Sterling gathered Jaz up in his arms and kissed her. Jasmina's heart twisted with pain and fury and—

She woke to tears in her eyes… and the most dreadful smell. Jasmina strained against a weight on her chest and threw on a spell of light in panic. Nuisance sat between her breasts, his large brown eyes staring owlishly at her, his breath foul enough to wake the dead.

"It's about time you woke up. I have the most delicious news!"

Jasmina groaned and pushed the gnome off her chest. "What time is it?"

"Close to midnight, I imagine. Your dinner is cold."

Jasmina glanced at the tray of food sitting on her occasional table. Her stomach rumbled and she sat up, reaching for an apple that didn't appear too brown. She bit into the ripe fruit, the sweet flavor bursting in her mouth, watching the gnome as she chewed.

Nuisance flopped on his back. "Don't suppose you stopped to wonder why we weren't following you today."

Jasmina chewed thoughtfully. She'd thought that Nuisance was so distracted by Trouble he had lost interest in her. She should have known better.

The gnome stood and flung himself backward again with another *flop*. "We found another human with a penchant for trouble. Only she brings it on herself." He scrambled to his feet again. "Did you know your mother steals things?" *Flop*.

Jasmina choked and reached for a glass of water. "She only borrows things," she managed to say.

Nuisance spread his arms and legs atop her bedding, swinging them as if making an angel in the snow. "Ho, ho, that's a jolly good one. Did you hear that, Trouble? When the gentry steal, it's called 'borrowing.'"

A giggle came from underneath the bed.

"It explains a lot about you, though," continued Nuisance.

Jasmina carefully set down the apple core and wiped her fingers. Her back stiffened and she calmly regarded the gnome. She didn't need another one of her mother's indiscretions to disrupt her plans. She didn't want to take the time to return anything tonight. With her luck, the owner of the pilfered item would probably reside clear across London.

She told herself to quit thinking about it and just find out the worst. "How do you know my mother borrows things?"

Nuisance opened his mouth, glanced at her face, and swallowed whatever cheeky remark he'd been about to make. "We followed your parents today, see. They've been discussing *The Taming of the Shrew* and I wanted to see it."

A snort of disgust from under the bed.

"And it was jolly good," continued the gnome, "until the taming, of course." He cocked his large ears and blew out a breath of relief when a satisfied "hmph" sounded from below. "Anyway, after the performance, as Lord and Lady Kraken were entering their coach, guess who knocked on their crested door?"

Jasmina clasped her hands together so she wouldn't be tempted to throttle the little man. "I can't imagine."

He leaped to his feet again, bouncing happily. "Miss Blanche Liliput and the insidious Mr. Cecil Thorn!"

Jasmina groaned. Why did it have to be Sterling's brother? And that silly Blanche? Miss Liliput would delight in exposing the faults of her peers.

Nuisance hopped a jig. "Imagine the futile attempts of your father to cut them. Imagine how skillfully they evaded the rebuffs. Oh, the sniveling and pretensions of Miss Liliput were genius! Still, if it hadn't been for the cameo that she wore, your mother never would have continued the conversation."

"She didn't." Jasmina's knuckles whitened. Of course she did. Normally Mother only borrowed a bit of jewelry once or twice a year, and only when she was especially unhappy. Had her disappointment in Jasmina caused this sudden rash of borrowing? Guilt made her chest tighten. She would have to return the cameo tonight, and she'd already slept through half of the evening.

She had planned to meet Sir Sterling when he came to her window and ask him to take her to the Underground. But after that dream she'd had... "Did the were-stallion come to my window tonight?"

"Why? Planning another tryst?"

"Never you mind. And stop sniggering."

Nuisance tried, his lips contorting. "Sir Sterling has already come and gone."

Jasmina huffed in relief. "Then I'll have to go to the Underground by myself—after I return that pin."

Nuisance clapped his hands in delight as soon as she mentioned the Underground, and surprisingly, Jasmina felt glad that the gnome would follow her. She wouldn't be alone in that wretched place. And she might as well admit to herself that she was relieved Sir Sterling wouldn't be with her when she confronted this twin of hers. Maybe she could just complete the reversal spell before he ever saw Jaz. Then she wouldn't have to worry about whom he'd choose.

But first, she'd need the relic. Jasmina closed her eyes, frowning in concentration. Could she sense the relic the same way she'd sensed Angel? If her illusion knew where it was...

"What are you doing?" asked Nuisance.

Jasmina opened her eyes in disappointment. No, she couldn't sense the relic, but perhaps if she found Jaz she might be able to. She could only make guesses about this type of magic. "Where is Miss Liliput's cameo?"

Trouble finally made an appearance from beneath the bed, her wiry brown hair sticking out at all angles. How did she manage to achieve such a look?

"I got it," said the gnome, hopping onto the bed and caressing the cameo pinned to her generous bosom. With her brown dress and hair and skin, she looked like something the earth itself had coughed back up.

"May I have it, please?"

Trouble's knobby hand covered the jewel. "It's mine."

"It's Miss Liliput's…"

"It's stolen."

Jasmina leaned forward. "And I intend to return it to the rightful owner."

Trouble pushed out her lower lip. Nuisance had backed up as if he wanted nothing to do with the confrontation. Jasmina took a deep breath. She didn't have time for any of this, truly. How many more annoyances would she be forced to endure?

"Consider it payment," she said.

Those brown eyes narrowed distrustfully. "For what?"

"For him." Jasmina nodded at Nuisance.

"He's not worth it."

Jasmina stifled a laugh. The little woman deceived herself almost as much as Jasmina had with Sterling. "The sooner I return the brooch, the sooner I can find my twin, and then my life will be back to normal. And then Nuisance will want to return home."

"Will you?" Trouble turned to Nuisance, who appeared to consider the question gravely.

"Well, I wouldn't want to follow anyone boring. I suppose I'd go back beneath the toadstools. But why don't you come with us tonight and see how much trouble humans can get into? Then you'll see how much fun it is."

Trouble considered for a moment, then handed the cameo to Jasmina.

Jasmina shook her head. What had she done? Now she had two garden gnomes following her.

⚜

It seemed that Trouble prevented Nuisance from interfering with Jasmina, because no one in the baron's house had a dream of a little man telling them their brooch was being stolen. She had no difficulty returning Miss Liliput's cameo.

But she'd had to wake Aunt, explain her plans, and jog the older woman's memory for where Blanche lived. Then she'd had to change into her chimney sweep's clothing. She'd borrowed a horse from the stable, since she'd never manage both tasks tonight without it. The spell she cast hid them but couldn't muffle the sound of the horses' hooves on cobble-stone, so she took as many dirt roads as she could.

Occasionally she saw flashes of red, and heard the tinkling sound of Trouble's giggle. It comforted Jasmina as she left the almost-respectable district where Blanche lived and made her way toward the church-yard. Riding this horse felt nothing like riding her were-stallion. With Sterling she'd felt as if she were a part of him, one being flying along the London streets. She sat atop this horse like a lump of clay.

Jasmina glanced around and pulled back on the reins. What had made her guide the beast to Sir Sterling's flat? She glanced up at his darkened window and breathed a sigh of relief. He didn't appear to be home; he was most likely already beneath London, searching the Underground for her twin. She kicked the horse into a gallop, no longer caring who might hear the pounding of hooves.

He would be furious that she'd gone unaccompanied into the Underground. That she'd risked her life without him there to protect her. But he wouldn't understand that her life was no longer important if she couldn't have him in it. And she'd never admit to him that she couldn't risk having him choose the illusion over her. She would find her twin herself and perform the reversal spell, and by the time he found out he wouldn't be able to do a thing about it.

But when Jasmina entered the old churchyard her determination wavered. It looked scarier by starlight, with shadows lurking behind every gravestone, the stone gargoyles seeming to come alive to blink and leer at her. She felt slightly better when she reached the inside of the chapel. She closed the old door, left her horse to graze on the grass, and headed for the crypt. Yes, Sterling had been here. Fortunately he'd left the hole uncovered, for she hadn't even thought about how she might move the stone covering by herself.

Starlight illuminated the unusually fogless evening, whereas the inside of the hole looked dark as pitch. Nuisance and Trouble suddenly appeared at her side, staring into the opening alongside her.

"You're not going down there?" squeaked Trouble.

Jasmina took a breath, summoned a dim ball of light, and clambered over the edge.

"Told you," said Nuisance. "Nothing stops a human in pursuit of disaster."

"Don't be ridiculous," said Jasmina with

exasperation. "I've been sneaking in and out of places for years. I have my magic to aid me, and if I encounter anything *disastrous*, I will get out of there, I assure you."

Jasmina knew even the dimness of her magical light would shine like a beacon inside the tunnels, but she didn't have Sterling's were-sight to prevent her from stumbling over the edge of a path or falling into a pit. And there were several, as the tunnel widened into open caves periodically before narrowing again. She never saw Trouble or Nuisance, but she felt them, and that gave her the courage to go on when the walls seemed to close around her too tightly.

She couldn't remember the path they'd taken through the mazelike passages when Sterling had guided her through them. But she didn't need to. She followed the same mysterious, insistent tug that she'd felt when they'd searched for Angel. And it led her unerringly to the Underground City.

Jasmina gasped at the stench and gave herself a few moments to become accustomed to it. She heard the faint sound of gagging behind her. By the smell of Nuisance's breath, she wouldn't have thought the odor of the city would have bothered him. Perhaps it was Trouble.

Thank heavens she wasn't alone.

She cast a spell of illusion over herself and became a man horribly covered in red scabs. She hoped that would be enough for the locals to avoid her, but she wasn't going to take any chances. Despite the drain on her strength, she also cast a don't-notice-me spell. She doubted anyone of royal blood would be down here to see through her spells, but she might encounter a shape-shifter, so she kept to the outside walls, until she came to an opening that seemed incredibly familiar to her. It looked no different than the thousands of other tunnel openings that surrounded the walls of the city, but somehow she knew she'd seen it before.

Was it the passage that had led to Angel's prison?

No. This one looked infinitely larger, as if an entire troop of men could march through it. Jasmina took a last look back at the city, unaware that she searched for a handsome man with a head of jet-black hair until her heart twisted when she didn't see him. He was somewhere in the Underground, she just knew it. But she had as much chance of encountering him down here as she did in the teeming city of London above.

She needed to stop being such a goose and get on with it.

That tugging sensation grew more insistent, until she couldn't ignore it any longer and plunged into the opening. The passageway widened even further until she trod a dirt path twice as wide as the most elegant London avenue. Jasmina hugged the walls, trying to keep to the shadows, looking for any niche or cranny ahead of her to hide in just in case she encountered someone else. Her spell didn't make her invisible, and she vividly remembered the ragtag group of men from the last time she'd been Underground.

Flashes of memory that couldn't have been her own led her to side tunnels that paralleled the main one. Her luck seemed to hold because she didn't see another soul until she reached the end of the passageway. And then she saw too many.

A cavern almost as large as the one that sheltered the Underground City opened before her. It sloped downward and she could see across to the other side, where a black castle stood. The back of it appeared to be flush with the wall of the cave, and on each side of it flowed a waterfall, the white froth gleaming against the black stone. Between her and the castle lay an army, their individual campfires twinkling in numbers that rivaled the stars in the night sky.

Jasmina breathed a soft gasp of terror. Sir Artemus had told her not to worry about the army, but she doubted that even he had imagined the true size of it. There weren't enough shape-shifters in the whole of London to beat such a force. She thought of Sterling fighting such a horde and shuddered.

"Hide," Trouble snapped from the boulders above her. Jasmina had just enough time to wiggle under an overhanging rock when several men marched into the cave behind her, carrying supplies. As they filed past she noticed that their backs all looked the same. Same brown hair and physical shape and gait. Did they only make copies of the same man?

But no, they met up with another group of soldiers with blond hair. But all the blond men looked alike as well. Could the relic only make so many copies of the same person? She remembered what Angel had said about trolls and elves losing their wits when duplicated. Maybe the same happened with men when too many copies were made?

Jasmina had to get out of here and tell Sterling and Sir Artemus where to find the army before it grew any larger. As she crept from beneath the rock and headed back out the passageway, a sudden wave of nausea gripped her and she fell to her knees. Jasmina gritted her teeth and rose again. She took another step away from the cavern and fell again, this time writhing in agony.

The gentle tug that had led her here had now turned into a painful compulsion that she couldn't ignore.

"Trouble," she hissed. A spiky head popped up from a tumble of rocks. "Find Sir Sterling. Show him how to find the army." Jasmina didn't even bother to ask Nuisance. He wouldn't want to miss out on any of the fun. But perhaps Trouble might oblige her.

When Jasmina stood again she turned back to the cavern and the black castle. Her pain vanished and the same gentle tugging returned. Her feet took over, leading her into side tunnels surrounding the larger cave. Each time she emerged to crawl along a shelf above the heads of the army, she noticed she came closer to the black castle.

Eventually she emerged beneath one of the waterfalls. Jasmina fought the tug that drew her on and slowed her pace along the slippery surface. On one side of her the water made a sheer wall of glowing white; its force created a wind that blew off her cap and sent stinging spray into her face.

Jasmina's heart raced as the passage ended in a solid wooden door. She recognized that door, even though she felt sure she'd never seen it before. Now that she appeared to have reached her goal, the compulsion to keep moving forward eased. She took a deep breath of the humid air and placed her hand on the doorknob.

If it had been warded, the protections were removed, because she didn't feel the tingle of magic as she opened it. A narrow stairway lay just inside and Jasmina took the steps slowly, glancing out the narrow windows that overlooked the cavern and army below.

Another door waited for her at the top of the stairs. She recognized this one as well, with its heavy carving of trolbats and cave spiders. Her heart beat a staccato rhythm in her ears as she suddenly realized what lay beyond the door. A bedchamber. With a lovely carved tester bed hung with velvet curtains and heavy medieval furniture and embroidered tapestries covering the black stone walls.

What was happening to her?

Jasmina carefully pushed open the door, drawing aside the tapestry that covered it, and stepped inside.

Jaz sat on a cushioned bench with a small harp across her lap. Green eyes identical to her own looked back at her, and she had the sensation of being in two places at once.

"You've finally come," said her illusion.

It was the last thing she'd expected Jaz to say. "You sound like you've been expecting me."

Her illusion lifted her chin. It made Jasmina feel out of sorts to see her mannerisms copied. "Naturally."

"Why?" snapped Jasmina. Really, the other woman's prim attitude grated on her nerves. And where was the mindless illusion she'd expected to find?

"Because we are two parts of the same whole. It was only a matter of time until we became one again. Merlin's Relic is powerful, but it can't alter nature forever." Her illusion ran her fingers over the harp, sending a haunting crescendo of sound into the room. "I've managed to learn a great deal about the relic in the past few weeks. I was confused when you first created me, and it took a while before I could unscramble your memories in my own head. We might have been apart, but our minds have always been linked. How do you think you knew where to find me? Our connection gets stronger as we're drawn back together… it will make you ill if you try and fight it."

That's why she'd felt sick when she'd tried to turn away from the castle! And the weakness she'd been experiencing since she'd cast the spell… was that a result of being split in two as well? But then Jasmina remembered how familiar it had felt making love to Sterling, and the implications shook her. The visions she'd had of him, that she'd thought were only her imagination… those flashes of memories that couldn't be hers. "Are you saying that every dreadful thing you've done will become a part of me?"

Jaz flicked the harp strings in frustration. "You don't realize exactly what I've done for you, do you?"

Lady Jasmina saw red. "I know perfectly well what you've done. You've ruined my life! Because of you I've lost my best friend, my position in society, the respect of my parents—"

"And you've fallen in love with the man of your dreams."

Jasmina's mouth hung open, for she couldn't argue with that statement. She quickly snapped it shut, adjusted the threadbare sleeves of her shirt and slowly sat on a bench. Where was the evil twin she'd expected to confront? She should have realized that since Jaz was a copy of her, the woman would have some common sense. "Indeed. What else have you done for me?"

The woman's bowed lips quirked, in a way that Jasmina was quite sure she'd never managed herself. "Why, I've brought you to the relic, haven't I? Someone had to keep an eye on it since you allowed it to fall into evil hands."

"I beg your pardon?"

"Well, I suppose that wasn't entirely your fault." Jaz plucked a few chords. "You didn't really know what you had, did you? You had no idea of the power of the relic. But I do, since I was born of its magic." She set aside the harp. "It would be jolly fun to sit and get to know each other, but that would be rather pointless, wouldn't it? Since we are the same person."

"Perish the thought," said Lady Jasmina as stiffly as she could. "I would never run about Spellsinger Gardens, cavort with tree nymphs, and flirt with other ladies' intendeds."

Jaz waved a dismissive hand. "I just had a bit of fun, something your life was sorely lacking until I came along. And have no fear, I only made love to one man—our Sir Sterling."

Jasmina felt furious and strangely relieved all at the same time. How dare this imposter make her think they shared anything in common? "You kidnapped a child!"

"I kept her safe." Those green eyes glittered. Jasmina felt her anger split in two and decided that she looked unattractive when she was angry.

"Do you think," continued Jaz, "that it's been pleasant pretending to be a part of this Brotherhood?

That I've enjoyed being the master of my own destruction?" She cocked her head, studying Jasmina intently. "But I rather think I would like being you again. You've changed enough that we might have a bit more excitement now."

Jasmina's head began to ache. This interview hadn't quite gone the way she'd imagined. She'd only thought to get rid of the illusion before Sterling had a chance—

Jaz's perfectly arched brows rose, and she answered as if she'd read Jasmina's mind. "Don't you see? He doesn't have to choose." She sighed. "But never fear. I will take you to the relic." Her green eyes narrowed and despite the round face, she looked a great deal like Aunt Ettie. She rose and crossed the room, lowering her voice. "You must destroy it, lady, before it destroys our world."

Her illusion wore a gown of emerald silk that whispered when she walked. Jasmina glanced down at her damp, dirty chimney-sweep outfit, convinced that anyone entering the room would think Jaz was the lady, not her. And how did she think a mere earl's daughter could destroy something as powerful as one of Merlin's Relics?

Jaz knelt before her and took her hand. "You don't understand what this relic can do. The duchess thinks she does, but I assure you I have not told her everything. Because you made a copy of yourself and I am the proof of it, I led her to believe that's all the relic does. But in truth, it enhances any spell, makes it infinitely more powerful. And a duchess can change matter. I have managed so far to make her fear its power so much that she hasn't attempted any other spell... but I don't know how much longer that will last."

Jasmina shivered from her twin's touch. She felt so warm and real, not like an illusion at all. She closed her eyes in sudden sorrow. She'd had every intention of destroying her illusion, but now, faced with a woman who appeared entirely real... she couldn't be sure that she wanted to do it.

"Lady Jasmina," her illusion said, "there is more at stake here than my fate or yours. If the duchess were to use the relic to cast a spell to light a fire, half the world would be incinerated. *Do you understand?*"

Jasmina's eyes widened and she nodded. How had she gotten tangled up in all of this? How would she have the courage to try to destroy such a powerful relic? She took a deep breath. It didn't matter how she felt. When things had to be done, she had always found a way to manage it... and this would be no exception. "How do I destroy it?"

Jaz smiled and loosed her hands. "Don't fear. Since I was created by it, I know the relic's secrets. And just think, when you destroy the relic, it will not only get rid of me, but the army below. You will save thousands of lives."

Before Jasmina had a chance to protest that she might not be so eager to dissolve her illusion anymore, Jaz explained to her exactly how she might go about destroying one of the most powerful relics of magic on earth.

Seventeen

STERLING LAY NAKED IN HIS BED, HIS ENTIRE BODY taut with anticipation. He had only spent a few hours tonight searching the Underground, worried that she might come to him again and he wouldn't be there. That he would miss his opportunity to brand her as his own. As she had branded him.

He had allowed her to take control last night. He would have done anything to get the lady to lower her walls enough to make love to him. To protect her vulnerability she needed that control. But, ahh, it had almost killed him.

Sterling rolled over and punched his pillow. She probably wasn't even aware of her own motivations. He thought that he might know her better than she did herself. Except that she'd surprised him with her seduction, as if she were an experienced lover and not an innocent. Perhaps she had a natural aptitude for it. The thought made him smile, and the smile stretched into a grin as he imagined how he would return the same sweet torture she'd given him.

He would explore her body in ways that she couldn't

imagine. And not with his hands, but with his tongue. He'd spread her lovely body out upon his bed and when he grew impatient with looking at her, he'd kiss her senseless so she'd forget her fears and then he'd start at her ear, licking his way down to her toes and then back up again. He'd kiss her where she'd never been kissed before, until she writhed beneath him and begged him for more. But he wouldn't allow himself to give in to her pleas for mercy; he'd continue to stroke her inflamed skin with his tongue until *he* couldn't bear it anymore.

Only then would he plunge inside her, making her his, demanding that she acknowledge their union of flesh with confessions from her heart—

Sir Sterling Thorn groaned and sat up, his groin aching like fire. Damned if he would lie around dreaming of her like some young schoolboy. He'd go to her himself, wait beneath her window and pound the street with his hooves, and if she didn't come out he'd climb up to her room and fetch her. Lady Jasmina belonged to him now, whether she would acknowledge it or not.

He'd just managed to stuff himself into his trousers when he heard a sound at the window. He shook back his hair and stared at the open frame, his hands fisted at his sides to prevent himself from snatching her the moment she climbed into the room.

Bloody good thing he controlled himself. For it wasn't his lady that climbed over the sill, but the spiky-haired little female gnome.

"What are you doing here?" he asked, his voice betraying his frustration.

Trouble didn't appear to notice. "I've come with a message of dreadful tidings." She smiled with such impish delight that Sterling's eyes narrowed. It must be bad, indeed. "I took the horse she left in the chapel and rode all the way here by myself. She seemed quite beside herself when she asked me to go to you, so I figured it would be all right. But the beast was so afraid of me he wouldn't go where I told him and—"

"Who sent you?" Sterling slowly uncurled his fingers.

Trouble scrambled atop the bed and stared up at him with those huge, liquid eyes. "Why, the Lady Jasmina, of course. Nuisance didn't want to leave 'cause he didn't want to miss anything—"

"Where is she?" demanded Sterling.

"Oh. My. Well, she went to the Underground to find her twin, you see. Odd though, the way she seemed almost forced to go into that tunnel toward the black castle. And we had to be careful, 'cause in the cavern there's an army—oh, that's what she sent me to tell you about. The army. Now, why would someone create an army unless they planned some devilment?" Again she grinned, clapping her hands with glee.

Sterling finished buttoning his trousers and pulled on his shirt. "I want you to take me to Lady Jasmina, Trouble. Can you do that?"

"Perhaps." Her hands settled on her hips. "But my lady seemed more worried about that army…"

Sterling filled his pockets and boots with as many weapons as he could. Whatever had possessed Jasmina to go to the Underground without him? Her need for control might very well get her killed. He turned back to Trouble, studying her with a frown. He would much rather get Jasmina back and then worry about the army, but he had a feeling that Trouble wouldn't help him until she carried out her lady's wishes. Who could have imagined that the gnome would be so loyal?

"We'll send Sir Artemus a map." He held out his arms to the gnome. When she hesitated, he added, "He's the prince's closest advisor." Mention of the prince seemed to appease her and she jumped into his arms.

Sterling had Trouble draw a map, which took more time than he wanted to spare. He woke the message sprite assigned to his building, who flew off with his message quickly, although a bit unsteadily. The little man appeared to be slightly drunk, but Sterling hadn't expected any less based on the quality of his lodgings. He just hoped Artemus would credit the message.

As soon as he entered the street he shifted to stallion and galloped faster than he ever had in his life. Trouble clutched his mane and whooped aloud at the recklessness of his flight. He didn't bother to wonder how Lady Jasmina had managed to find an army or whether the black castle Trouble spoke of might indeed be where Jaz had been hiding out. He had no doubt that Jasmina had walked right into the maelstrom of this Brotherhood, and he needed to rescue her. They'd already tried to kill her twice, and just because nothing had happened recently didn't mean they'd quit trying. What might happen to her if this time he couldn't be there to protect her?

"Confounded woman," Sterling muttered as he shifted to human and climbed down into the chapel's crypt.

"Foolish girl," he mumbled as he jogged through the tunnels.

"Keeper of my heart," he sighed when he entered the Underground City. He raised his voice. "Which way, Trouble? You're in the lead now."

The spikes of hair on her head shook with a self-important nod. She led him to a tunnel opening that looked no different than thousands of others, although it was one of the larger ones. Sterling kept to the shadows, using all the stealthy skill he'd acquired doing reconnaissance in the army. When he reached the end of the tunnel, he joined Trouble behind a tumble of rocks and examined the army spread out in the cavern below. He mentally separated the troops into companies and battalions and finally corps just to count them. He swore softly at their numbers.

Sterling's nose twitched. The stink of relic-magic surrounded the entire cavern, and he fought the urge to sneeze.

"Duck," hissed Trouble as a soldier neared their tumble of rocks. Sterling heard the sound of splashing and grinned, moving with such speed that the soldier didn't feel a thing. He dragged the man behind their hiding place and changed into the ragged uniform.

"There's a way around them to the castle," suggested Trouble.

Sterling thought about it for a split second. "It'll take too long."

"Nuisance will be sorry he missed this."

"Stay hidden and there won't be anything to miss."

Her face fell, and Sterling tried not to let that bother him too much as he made his way through the throng of soldiers. It felt like wading through a fog of sweat and smoke and fear. All very familiar from his days in the military, and it must have reflected in his demeanor, because he wasn't challenged as he made his way across the cavern.

But his confidence wouldn't get him through the gate to the castle, where soldiers showed papers to gain entrance. But luck appeared to be with him again when a supply wagon joined the line. Sterling slipped behind it, shifted to stallion, hunching his head and withers to appear as small as an ordinary beast, and kept to the back of it as if by a lead.

He made it to the stables inside the outer bailey, the smell of relic-magic so overwhelming that he couldn't quite pin the source of it. Sterling stared up at the massive stone keep and wondered how he would find Lady Jasmina when he saw a flash of red from the corner of his eye. Sterling shifted to human and crept out of the stables, looking again for that telltale hint of color.

His luck changed when he climbed the wall of the inner bailey. A shout rang out. Halfway to the keep he dodged bullets. His were-speed kept him alive the rest of the distance.

Nuisance waited at a side door of the keep, Trouble already at his side. "That last one almost got you," he sang.

Sterling had felt the bullet whiz past his shoulder and nodded. "Where is she?"

The male gnome grinned and disappeared inside

the keep with Trouble. Sterling followed them on a mad pace up worn stairs and cobwebbed hallways, and then through a hidden door that appeared to lead to hidden passageways. The sound of pursuit faded behind them. The odor of relic-magic grew stronger.

"You've done well," whispered Sterling as he made his way through the dark tunnels to a thin beam of light at the far end.

"I'm a gnome," replied Nuisance. "I'm good at skulking."

And so he was. Sterling placed his eye over the hole of light and blinked. Because of the ancient feel of the castle he hadn't expected to see a room of such opulence within it. What looked like a Roman bath—complete with a columned pool and nude statues—adorned the center of the room. Ornamental trees and shrubs surrounded the walls, and the ceiling had been painted with clouds to make it appear as if the room stood outdoors.

Sterling had but a moment to note the surroundings. His attention became immediately fixed on the woman in the pool. The Duchess of Hagersham. A young girl scrubbed her back, while another woman had her engaged in conversation.

Jaz.

He didn't stop to wonder how he knew it was the illusion, because Lady Jasmina herself appeared and captured his entire attention. She slipped from behind one statue to another until she reached a gilt-edged table with clothes scattered atop it. She crouched behind it and patted the clothing, then slowly pulled down a piece of satin and worried at the folds of it.

"Hey, I want to see too," whined Nuisance.

Trouble shushed him, but Sterling barely noticed the exchange.

Jaz had maneuvered her body between the duchess and the table, partially blocking Lady Jasmina from view. She plucked at the strings of a small harp as if displaying a newly composed tune.

A flash of silver caught his eye, and he glanced back at Jasmina. For a moment the smell of relic-magic overwhelmed him, and he didn't need to see the jewel she held to know that she'd recovered the relic.

Clever woman. Or should he say women? For surely Jasmina and her illusion had both planned this little foray. A bath was probably the only time the duchess allowed the relic off her person.

Sterling blinked. No, wait. He couldn't think of them as two women. He barely had the skill to handle one of them. Bloody hell, he felt confused again.

Lady Jasmina had just started to crawl away from the table when a door on the opposite wall opened and the Duke of Hagersham walked in. Sterling whispered under his breath for her to keep moving, to get behind the statue, but Jasmina froze at the sight of the man. Sterling remembered the way the duke had pawed her, so he couldn't fault her for the reaction.

The duke stared blindly in Lady Jasmina's direction for a second. "I say," he sputtered around a mouthful of scone, "did one of your pets get loose, my dear? I swear there's a naiad crawling near that statue."

"What are you talking about?" said the duchess, rising from her bath and knocking the soap from her maid's hand. "Jaz, move out of the way so I can see—"

"How do you get this door open?" Sterling demanded.

"Jolly good, it's about time," answered Nuisance, and the hidden door popped open with a snap.

Sterling vaulted into the room, brandishing his blades. The duke had started toward Jasmina, his hands raised to cast a spell, but he hesitated when Sterling's body came between them. Ah, he remembered that Sterling would be immune to his magic.

Another man appeared in the doorway, breathing hard and with a red face. "I just received a report that several men have stormed the castle…" The man's jaw dropped at the sight before him. Sterling recognized him: the Marquess of Ogreton. The bounder who had stolen his sister. Sterling couldn't control the rage of his were-self. Within seconds he'd shifted to stallion, slicing the air with his hooves and screaming with rage.

Lady Jasmina rose to her feet and backed into a headless statue. The naked duchess pointed at her. "She's got my relic."

Jaz stared in dismay, as if trying to decide when the situation had gotten out of her control. The duke quailed for a moment, staring at Sterling's flashing hooves in horror, until he caught a glimpse of the soldiers the marquess had brought with him. As they poured into the room, a smile of grim satisfaction lit his face. "Not this time, Thorn. They'll cut you down before you lay a hoof on me, and then I'll have the lady and the relic—if she survives the crossfire."

He was right. If the duke gave the order to shoot they might hit Jasmina. Several of the soldiers already had their gun sights on him. Sterling dropped his front hooves slowly to the marble floor and shifted to human, covering Jasmina's body with his.

"Just a small spell," she whispered, her hands clutching the relic.

"No!" shouted Jaz, as if her illusion could hear Lady Jasmina. Or as if they shared each other's thoughts. "The relic's too dangerous—don't risk it." Jaz dropped her harp and drew a knife from her silk sleeve. In one fluid motion she held it to the throat of the duchess. "No one move."

The duchess opened her mouth to speak and a thin line of red grew at her throat.

The duke took a step forward. The marquess grabbed his arm and signaled to his men to hold their positions. "Do you want to get your wife killed?" he snapped at the duke.

The Duke of Hagersham shrugged, his attention centered on the illusion. "Jaz, don't be a fool," he said. "What about the Brotherhood? What about our bid for power, with you at my side as my queen?"

The duchess rolled her eyes, then glared at her husband. The marquess gaped, and several soldiers looked disgusted. Jaz ignored them all. "Do it now, Jasmina."

Sterling glanced at Jaz, her face so like his own Jasmina's, and yet so incredibly different. He reached out and touched Lady Jasmina's cheek. "What does she want you to do?" he whispered.

"Destroy the relic."

The duchess heard her and started to struggle. The sound of shots being fired and the clash of swords came from deep within the bowels of the castle.

"Do it," commanded Sterling.

"But how can I destroy Jaz?" Jasmina pleaded.

"Bloody hell, we'd eventually merge anyway," answered Jaz, cutting deeper into the duchess's throat as the woman continued to struggle. "Don't make me kill her—just quit thinking about it and do it!"

Tears gathered in her eyes, but Jasmina opened her palm and began to stroke the ugly little figures that surrounded the jewel. They came to life at her touch, peeling away from the silver frame and scampering around it. Jasmina whispered something to them and silver eyes blinked, silver hands reached down at their feet and miniature books opened, their silver pages gleaming with words that Sterling couldn't read.

But evidently Jasmina could. She began to read each book as it opened, and a dark shadow started to swirl inside the garnet. Sterling felt the hair rise on the back of his neck. He hoped she knew what she was doing, for he'd never felt such power before. It couldn't harm him directly, but he feared for his lady.

The sound of battle reached the doorway, and the men who had been held frozen by Jaz's knife moved as a group of shape-shifters fought their way into the room. They shifted from human to animal while they fought—flashes of panther and wolf and bear. A few shots rang out, but the fighting was too close for guns; the sound of steel and feral growls rang across the polished floors. Sterling had a moment to notice the golden head of Sir Artemus before his attention was torn away by a shout above him.

The grinning face of Nuisance popped up where the head of a marble statue should be. "They're sneaking up behind you," he laughed.

Sterling spun just in time to deflect a knife aimed at his back. Jasmina's back was protected by the statue, but the duke snuck to her side and grabbed her hair, pulling her away from that scant cover. She stopped reading the little silver books and closed both hands over the relic while he dragged her away. Sterling shifted to stallion and used all the beast's fury to pound into the marquess. The knife that should have been planted in Sterling's human back fell to the floor from the marquess's lifeless hand.

Sterling turned on the duke, who had hauled Jasmina a few feet toward the bathing pool. He saw the duchess twist out of Jaz's hold and wrestle the knife away from her, but Sterling didn't have time to worry about the illusion.

Sterling screamed a challenge and charged the duke, who pushed Lady Jasmina in front of him as a shield. The sound of booted feet and the cries of dying men faded as Sterling focused on Jasmina. The duke smiled and waved his knife in front of his lady. She suddenly looked very small and vulnerable. "Another step closer and I'll slit her throat as easily as her illusion tried to cut my wife's."

Sterling shifted to human, holding out his hands in surrender. "Just let her go. You can have the relic, just don't hurt her."

The duke's hawkish nose twitched. "Like I said, Thorn, I'll have them both. Now back…"

His words ended on a gurgle. His eyes widened and Jasmina barely had time to twist out of the way as he fell like a stone. Behind him stood the naked duchess, a red line of blood across her throat and covering the knife she held in her hand. "That will teach you to betray me," she snarled.

Jasmina cried out as she noticed her illusion slumped over the edge of the pool, and she jumped in, the relic still firmly in her grasp. The duchess strangled a curse and tried to follow the relic. Sterling caught her arm and yanked her backward, sending her flying into a statue. She smacked her head against the base of it and lay still.

The shape-shifters fought with their backs against the pool, the number of their enemies trapping them. Jasmina stood just behind them, ignoring the fighting as she gently lifted her illusion by the shoulders. "Are you all right?"

Sterling waded in after her, just in time to see Jaz grimace. "The duchess fights dirty," murmured the illusion, clutching the bloody wound in her side. "Would you hurry up and finish the spell? This really hurts."

Jasmina looked up at him, her eyes swimming with tears. "I only have one more book to read." He nodded, took Jaz into his arms and watched Lady Jasmina open her trembling hand and begin to read.

Sterling realized he didn't want to lose either of them. He tightened his grip on Jaz, remembering her familiar warmth and passion, and stared at Lady Jasmina in confusion. He was bloody well fed up with feeling this way.

"What is she doing?" demanded Sir Artemus as he fought off two soldiers while trying to keep an eye on Jasmina and the relic.

Sterling grinned at the opportunity to direct his annoyance at someone. "You know," he said rather conversationally, "you're completely outnumbered. To your left."

Sir Artemus swung his sword in that direction and blocked the blow. "I'd appreciate a little help," he growled.

"Why should I bother?" Sterling felt Jaz shudder in his arms and his heart twisted. He hoped Jasmina would hurry. "It will all be over soon, anyway."

"Not if I can help it." Sir Artemus shifted to lion and pounced on four soldiers, bringing them down with a growl of fury. A few other weres shifted into their animal-shapes, and soon howls and grunts and roars mixed with clashing steel.

The relic in Jasmina's hand began to smoke, red tendrils curling up from the center of the jewel. Jaz felt lighter in his arms and when he looked down at her, she smiled and touched his cheek. "You won't be confused anymore." Her face shimmered and she no longer felt real to him. She'd become nothing but an illusion.

Sir Artemus shifted to human and glanced triumphantly over his shoulder. "*Now* what do you think about our odds?" His golden brows rose as he saw the smoking relic in Lady Jasmina's hand. "What is she—stop!"

"It's too late," said Jasmina, wincing as she dropped the relic into the pool. The brooch hissed when it touched the water, the curls of red smoke branching out along the bottom of the pool, turning the entire bath into a writhing fury. The illusion in Sterling's arms coalesced into a mist of blue, curling for a moment around his shoulders before it wrapped around Lady Jasmina, enveloping her in a cloud of sparkling color.

"Oh," breathed Jasmina, as the mist that used to be Jaz melted into her body.

Sterling waded through the water and gently clutched her arms. "Are you all right?"

"My side hurts. And I have some of her memories." Those huge green eyes widened. "What a wicked girl." But she smiled on the words and reached up to touch his cheek. "She was so very brave... and she loved you as much as I do."

"Jaz... Jasmina?"

"Yes," she answered, and Sterling saw just a hint of Jaz in Jasmina's eyes.

The sounds of fighting grew dim as swords clattered to the ground from suddenly insubstantial hands. The duplicate soldiers created by the relic dissolved into different-colored mists. They swirled about the room, seeking the man they'd been copied from, swooping out the doors if they couldn't find him.

Sterling leaned his face into Jasmina's hand and kissed her palm, fighting the urge to kiss her breath away. First he had to get her somewhere safe. He glanced around the room. Only a few bodies lay about the floor: a couple of shape-shifters, and soldiers who had merged with their other selves, their numbers now sorely depleted.

"She didn't have to do that," growled Sir Artemus.

Sterling snorted. "Yes, she did. You didn't stand a chance against that army, lion-man."

Sir Artemus scowled, wiped his sword clean, and waded into the pool. He picked up the relic, staring at the blackened silver and the cracked jewel. The water, which had calmed to a dull red sheen, suddenly rippled. "I didn't have to fight the whole lot of them."

Sterling led Jasmina out of the pool and draped a cloth about her wet shoulders. The water rippled again and this time he felt the entire castle shake. "What do you mean?"

Artemus pocketed the relic. "I had four hours to find Lady Jasmina and the relic before the combined magic of the aristocracy pulled this place down."

"There's more fun?" shouted a tiny voice from above. Both men looked up and scowled at the two gnomes ensconced in the crystal chandelier hanging in the middle of the ceiling. Nuisance whooped when another spasm rocked their perch.

"The prince couldn't risk an invasion." Sir Artemus gestured for his men to leave. "I think our time is about up. After you, Lady Jasmina."

She followed the shape-shifters and Sterling stayed close behind her, deflecting several sconces and paint-ings and loose stones from pelting her head while the castle seemed to fall apart around them. When they reached the main hall, the stone floor trembled and split, swallowing several men. Sterling shifted to stal-lion and Jasmina didn't hesitate, vaulting onto his back with a leap strengthened by terror.

Sterling bolted out the castle door, water and mud swirling around his hooves. He vaulted over anything that got in his way. A stalactite slammed into the earth beside him. He veered to the left, changing direction again when a boulder rolled across his path. He leaped over a chasm that opened suddenly before him and hit the ground hard on the other side of it, grateful that Jasmina clung to his back like a burr. His chest heaved from exertion by the time he reached the other side of the cavern, and he hoped that his friends would be as swift.

He snorted with relief when a golden lion reached his side, followed by the rest of the surviving shape-shifters. Their numbers had only been reduced by a few.

The Underground City looked deserted, as if the citizens had fled at the first sign of a rumble, even though the spell had been directed at the one cavern only. Sterling followed Sir Artemus through a different tunnel to reach London, this one wide enough for his were-stallion. They exited into the world above through a cathedral.

"The prince will want to question you," said Sir Artemus, his voice echoing along the arched walls of the massive building.

Sterling shook his head and walked out the double doors, taking the street that led to his home.

"I suppose it can wait until tomorrow," the were-lion shouted over the noise of galloping hooves.

Sterling barely heard his words. His lady had molded her body to his and he flew along the empty London streets, only concentrating on getting her alone. Jaz had been right. He didn't feel the slightest bit confused anymore.

He reached his building and shifted, catching the Lady Jasmina in his arms. She made a soft sound of protest. "What's wrong?" he whispered, ready to do battle with that wall of propriety.

"My side."

Ah. Jaz's injury. He took the stairs two at a time, carrying her into his flat and placing her carefully on his bed. Sterling quickly took off her clothes, shaking his head when she pulled up the blankets to cover herself. As if he'd never seen her nude before. He lit a candle and inspected the injury with a frown, then grunted with relief. "It's red and purple, but the wound is closed. Do you suppose you received only half her wound because she was just a copy of you?"

Jasmina shrugged, exposing her smooth white shoulders. "I suppose so. I only have some of her memories, and they come at the oddest times."

Sterling started. "What do you mean?"

Her luminous eyes watched him as he placed the candle on the table. "I mean that we were always connected, although it only became obvious to me at the… end." Her voice lowered to a husky softness. "I have memories of you that aren't my own."

Sterling sat on the edge of the bed. That explained a few things. Sometime during the night she'd lost her cap, and he started to pull the pins out of her hair. "Do you remember this?" He ran his hands through the soft mass of white-gold curls and she pushed her head against his palms when they reached her scalp, nearly purring beneath his touch.

He stood when his body responded to her pleasure and removed his clothes. "Or this?"

Jasmina stared at him with her eyes glowing in the candlelight. "I don't need Jaz's memories to know every inch of you."

He sat back down on the bed and reached for her.

"No, you don't, do you? But the one time we've been together I allowed you to make love to me. It's now my turn, lady."

Eighteen

JASMINA SCOOTED BACK AGAINST THE HEAVY OAK headboard and clutched the blankets up to her chin. Sterling gently pulled them away. "Now, Jaz, you won't be letting your prudery get the best of you, will you?"

He saw something flicker in the depths of her eyes and she let the blankets go, allowing him to slowly uncover her glorious body. Sterling ran his hand up her leg to her thigh. With a groan Jasmina spread her knees, unwittingly bucking the air as if begging for him to touch her where she'd receive the greatest pleasure.

He shook his head. It was going to be an adventure getting used to the two sides of her nature. "Ah, no, lady. I won't rush this. Not after all we've been through."

Sterling leaned forward and kissed the top of her head, then trailed kisses down her cheeks, across her mouth. She laced her fingers in his hair and tried to keep him there, but he slowly unwound them and fisted her hand with his own. "Don't fight me for control tonight. You will lose."

For a moment he thought she might argue, but then her lips quirked and she bowed her head meekly. As if he would fall for that. If he let up for a moment she would wrestle for control, and his heart beat faster at the thought, but he wouldn't allow it. He pulled her up a bit and placed her hands on the headboard. "Don't let go," he commanded.

Her knuckles turned white. He hoped that the wooden frame would bear up. Her breasts hung full and heavy with her body half upright against the headboard, and he couldn't stand the temptation a moment longer. He kissed them tenderly, first one swollen bud and then the other. With her wound, he didn't want to be too rough, but when she groaned his good intentions quickly fled and his tongue laved her nipples, and then his mouth suckled, and soon he felt lost in the sweet feast of her bare flesh.

"I won't let go," he heard her pant, as if scolding herself.

Sterling smiled and trailed his tongue down the valley between her breasts, across her belly, and straight to the heart of her. Such dedication deserved a reward. He nuzzled her wiry hair and licked at the treasure hidden within it. The lady bucked and then gasped in outrage. He glanced up at her.

"What on earth do you think you are…" Her voice trailed off as an entirely different expression crossed her features. "Oh. Never mind."

Sterling buried his chuckle between her legs and quickly became lost in the sensation of her. The hot, salty taste of her. He'd wanted to make this moment last, but as she writhed beneath him, the demands of his animal nature took control. Perhaps after he'd made love to her many, many times, he'd be able to conquer this overwhelming desire.

But he didn't think so.

Sterling rose to his knees and stared into her eyes, proud of the hunger he saw there. She was so very close to the edge. He picked up her legs, lifting her body slightly off the bed, pulling her toward him. Jasmina didn't release her death grip on the headboard. He hoped she had the strength to hold on.

Sterling placed the tip of his shaft against her flesh. Never had anything felt so absolutely exquisite. He leaned forward, burying half of himself inside her, taking it slow so he wouldn't hurt her. Her heels hit the back of his bottom, pushing him deeper inside.

Sterling leaned back, refusing to let Jasmina have her way until he wanted it. Her eyes were wild with desire, and bloody hell, his were-nature responded with equal passion. He moved his knees closer to her and transferred his grasp to her hips, the feel of her bottom beneath his fingers pushing him over the edge. He arched into her, at the same time pulling her hips toward him—and he felt surrounded by her flesh. By her heart and soul.

Frenzy gripped him and he rocked her up and down against his groin, pulled away and then plunged in again, seeking that threshold of pleasure that only Lady Jasmina could give him. And when it came he groaned with the force of it, half-aware that her own release shook her body in union with his.

"Let go," he finally rasped. Jasmina tore her cramped fingers from the headboard and he gathered her into his arms, her legs still wrapped around him, his shaft still inside her as she sat on his lap. He kissed the hair away from her face and stroked her back. He couldn't afford to show her any mercy. He would have her promises before she came back to earth. "You are *mine* now."

"I know."

"I will tell your father that we are to be married."

The stubborn woman stiffened in his arms and pulled slightly away. "No. Please, Sterling. He can be so stubborn, and I need his approval. Please allow me to tell him."

Blast, but he loved the way his name sounded coming from her lips. How could he deny her anything? "When?"

Her brow furrowed. "Soon, I promise."

Sterling hid a small grin of relief from her. He knew that she craved approval from her family and he doubted she'd get it. But he could at least let her try. "Do you love me?"

Those brilliant green eyes blinked at him and she touched her soft fingers to his rough cheek. "You know I do."

"Then I will wait for you to speak with him." He turned his head and caught her fingers in his mouth, suckling one of them for a moment. She shivered and he felt himself grow hard inside of her. Jasmina removed her wet finger and traced his left nipple. Bewitching girl. He lowered his mouth to her neck. "But I won't wait for long."

⁓

Sterling gritted his teeth while his new valet tied his cravat in an elaborate knot. It would take him a while to get used to his newfound wealth; the prince had rewarded him generously for his part in the recovery of the relic.

"May I brush your coat, sir?" asked the valet, his nimble hands putting the finishing touches on the knot.

"It's fine."

"But sir, I see several specks of…"

Sterling shot a quelling look at the little man. Angel had hired shape-shifters for their household staff, most of them fellow prisoners from her time in captivity. Even with such quick hands, his new valet would never have been hired in any other household and longed to prove his worth. Sterling tried to be patient with the odd-looking were-monkey, but he'd had enough. His new, fashionable clothes were itchy and he longed for his old favorites. Perhaps when he returned to Witchshire…

Sterling scowled as he strode to the door, his valet leaping out of the way. He wouldn't leave London without his lady, and she couldn't seem to find the right time to approach the subject of their marriage with her father. Not that she felt afraid of the old boy; she just thought that if she could find the right moment, she would gain his approval.

Sterling snorted and tossed his head, taking the stairs two at a time. Her father would never accept a baronet for a son-in-law, and he'd tried to get Jasmina to see that. But she could be so stubborn…

He glanced in the mirror at the foot of the stairs and adjusted the cuffs of his dark blue velvet coat, trying to stifle the smile on his lips. Truth be told, he liked Jasmina's stubbornness and her prim and proper ways.

Each time he broke through them he felt as if he'd conquered her all over again.

He went to her every night in were-form and carried her to his new townhouse to discuss their situation. Sometimes it took hours and sometimes only a few minutes for their discussions to turn into passion. And afterward he would tell her of Witchshire, and his plans to invest his new fortune into his vineyards. She seemed to be enthralled by country life, and he tried to make it seem as enchanting as possible. Sterling was determined to never make her regret the loss of her father's affection. If only he could convince her that she could be happy without her family—

"You don't need to tell me who you are thinking about," said Angel from the drawing room doorway. Sterling turned and regarded his sister. She looked lovely in a new pink walking gown, tiny white feathers stitched along the hem and neckline, her shiny black hair swept up beneath a hat decorated with more feathers. He smiled in genuine pleasure, proud of the way her cheeks blushed pink with good health.

"I've given her enough time."

Angel shook her head. "No, Sterling. You must let her decide when she's ready. Lady Jasmina is so fiercely independent with her decisions." Her voice rang with pride.

He smiled and took his sister's arm. "I won't wait forever—never mind. Where are we off to today?"

Angel let him change the subject, her pale blue eyes lighting up with anticipation. "The British Museum. There is a new display of artifacts from Turalee. It's quite the rage; anyone who's fashionable, or wishes to be, will be there."

Sterling listened to her chatter on about the fabled island with its mountains mined by dwarves while they drove to the museum. As always, her presence soothed him. For so long he'd worried that he'd never see her again. Now her mere existence at his side brought him a measure of happiness.

And that happiness would be absolutely complete when he could wake up in the morning with Jasmina by his side.

The new exhibit must be popular. When they pulled up to the museum they had to weave their way through a throng of carriages. The crowd seemed to follow them as they made their way to the upper salon that housed the Turalee collection.

Magic animated the museum, so Sterling wasn't surprised when a mummy made its way along a branching corridor. "Has anyone seen my coffin?" asked the moldy voice. "It's covered in gold and has the hieroglyphs of my house." The voice rose and quivered. "I must find my resting place."

A few curious guests followed the living advertisement to the Egyptian antiquities room, but Angel seemed determined to see the new exhibit.

"Oh, look, Sterling. It feels just like walking into a real mountain."

Angel stood just inside the door of the room, and it did indeed appear as if she'd stepped into an enormous cavern. It resembled the Underground too much for his comfort, but it would be some time before he allowed his sister out of his sight again, so he followed her.

Little men with long white beards and glittering black eyes pounded on stones that shimmered with jewels. An ethereal voice followed them through the exhibit, educating them on the habits of the dwarves who mined the mountains of Turalee.

"Look, the wyrms are coming out," whispered Angel.

Long, sinuous shapes slithered out from beneath rocks and out of narrow tunnels, weaving their way around the feet of the animated dwarves and making them stumble and curse. The wyrms had no eyes, just long silver tongues that flickered out to test the air, and scaled bodies that truly looked as if they could pierce through stone.

Angel marveled at their dangerous beauty while Sterling fervently hoped that the creatures no longer existed. Most of the animations had been created by dead artifacts, using a bit of the magicians' imaginations to recreate them. He hoped that was also the case with the wyrms. He could only imagine what chaos they would cause in the Underground.

But Angel appeared to be delighted, and he had to admit that the outing had distracted him from his thoughts of Lady Jasmina. As they rounded a curve in the walkway, he thought for a moment that he'd conjured her up. But the emerald eyes that stared back at him weren't her exact shade, nor the face quite so young and soft. "Miss Forster, what an unexpected surprise."

Jasmina's aunt blinked at him for a moment before her sharp features wrinkled into a smile. "Why, Sir Sterling, what a pleasure it is to see you again."

She hadn't snubbed him. Interesting, that. But

Sterling supposed that with another were on her arm, it would be the height of hypocrisy. "And Sir Artemus. Haven't you had your fill of dark caverns?"

"Quite." The were-lion grunted. "By the way, you might be interested to know that we have rounded up all the conspirators of this so-called Brotherhood. Mostly disinherited younger sons and daughters, but they won't be abducting shape-shifters anymore."

Sterling already knew that, but he realized that Sir Artemus had not blurted it out for his benefit. Angel let out a ragged breath of relief and turned to stare at a dancing wyrm.

Sir Artemus cocked his head at Sterling and suddenly grinned. "My fiancée insisted on seeing this exhibit. Like you, I dance to my lady's tune."

Sterling knew the man baited him, but he scowled anyway. Did everyone in London know that Jasmina kept him waiting? No, he felt sure Henrietta hadn't told anyone else.

"Your fiancée?" said Angel. "That's wonderful. Let me be the first to congratulate you."

For a moment Sterling stared at the couple in bewilderment while they accepted his sister's felicitations. "How did you manage that?" he finally asked.

"I assure you it wasn't easy," said Miss Forster. "Lord and Lady Kraken were quite opposed to the idea."

Sir Artemus growled.

"But since I'll just be a drain on their resources when they make their Grand Tour, they eventually came around." She gave Sterling a piercing look. "And I'm much too old to require their approval."

Sir Artemus smiled at that and patted Henrietta's hand.

"Their Grand Tour?" Sterling remembered Jasmina mentioning something about that, but she'd never brought it up again, and he assumed their plans had changed.

"Why, yes. They will be shipping off to the Continent in a couple of days. I believe that my niece thinks the trip would be an opportune time to broach certain subjects with her father."

Sterling felt Angel and Sir Artemus staring at him.

"But I believe," continued Henrietta, "that her father thinks to change her mind about some of her wishes. He hopes to put her in the path of, shall we say, eligible gentlemen?"

Sterling fisted his hands. Sir Artemus chuckled and Angel clutched his arm. So the old man thought to change her heart? He almost wished that Jasmina would go on this tour, just to prove her father wrong. His initial anger faded as he realized that this might have been Jaz's intention, and she'd been too afraid of his reaction to reveal her plans to him.

Sterling shrugged, making Angel sigh with relief and Artemus scowl with annoyance. Miss Forster just seemed confused.

"I wish them a safe journey," Sterling said, giving a short bow. "It was a pleasure to at least see *you* again, Miss Forster. Come along, Angel."

Sterling's words made Sir Artemus chuckle as he led his fiancée away, even though she appeared to want to continue their discussion.

Sterling didn't feel as confident as he tried to appear, however. He would have a talk with his lady tonight and he fully intended to punish her for not telling him about the trip. It would be a gentle punishment, however. One that would eventually have her begging her apologies between gasps of pleasure.

Then he would make it clear—in no uncertain terms—that she would not leave London without him. Although he sympathized with her, he had waited long enough. He'd been far too patient. She would speak with her father tomorrow, or he would speak to Lord Kraken himself.

Having made the decision, Sterling felt infinitely better. As they journeyed through the Egyptian, Assyrian, and Gorgonian exhibits, he kept his good humor by imagining the sweet tortures he would tantalize Jasmina with.

Until they reached the gardens. It appeared that he was destined for unwanted encounters today.

The museum had recreated the specimen collections from Sir Hans Sloane, most of them plants of medicinal value. Angel appeared fascinated by the wide variety of plant life, the unusual colors and shapes of many of the leaves, and the slightly ridiculous claims of healing properties that their signs boasted. Sterling was less fascinated; if the plants had been real and not magical illusions, and if they'd included varieties of grapes he could cultivate within his vineyard, he would have been more interested.

So when he heard his name, he turned around with eagerness, welcoming some distraction. His face fell when he beheld the party before him.

"Well met, Sterling," said his brother, those jackal eyes gleaming.

His stepmother just nodded, smiling uncertainly.

Her fashionable new clothes looked slightly worn. Perhaps Cecil had only parted with enough funds to allow her a small wardrobe.

His fiancée, however, wore a fancy new dress and bonnet, adorned with pearly shells that clinked when she curtsied. "Won't you introduce me, Cecil?"

Sterling tried to remember her name. Miss Blanche something. He knew he'd met her before but apparently she'd forgotten. Or she just hadn't acknowledged his existence in his shabby old clothing, for her eyes went covetously from his elegant silk coat to his gold pocket watch to his shiny leather boots.

"This is my brother, Sir Sterling Thorn," replied Cecil. "And our sister, Miss Angel Thorn. This is my wife, the Honourable Blanche Thorn."

Blanche nodded and held out her hand. So, Cecil had managed to get her to marry him after all. Sterling viewed her hand in the same manner as he had the museum's wyrms. How dare his brother call Angel his sister? He'd given up that right when he'd stolen her inheritance. But he glanced at his stepmother and sighed. She looked scared to death that others would witness this encounter.

Sterling took Blanche's hand and bowed slightly over it.

"Why, Cecil," she said, "you didn't tell me your brother was in London."

Sterling cocked a brow at Cecil, curious as to what he might say. After refusing to acknowledge his existence for so long, why the sudden change of heart?

"I just recently became aware of it myself," Cecil lied. "Apparently he has done some service for the

Crown and is a favorite of our prince consort." His voice was tinged with envy and a bit of disdain. As if the honor might be a doubtful one.

Sterling felt surprised that he wasn't angry. He felt only… amusement. "I suppose my brother also failed to tell you that we are shape-shifters as well?"

Blanche pursed her mouth, a pout that did nothing to enhance her looks. "How unfortunate. But I suppose that some things just can't be helped."

Sterling threw back his head and laughed. How perfect that Cecil had married a woman who despised his brother's nature, but not his money. He half-shifted to stallion, just to see the look on her face. Angel refused to shift to her swan-shape and join in the fun. She just looked decidedly uncomfortable. Sterling frowned and quickly sobered, keeping to his human form. He realized that Angel had the right of it. It no longer mattered what Cecil or his wife—or even his stepmother—thought of them. He knew whom he could count on.

A man could make his own family.

Sterling took Angel's arm, deciding to put an end to this, when Cecil stepped forward, his pointed ears twitching. "I say, Sterling, do you think I might have a word with you?"

Sterling hesitated.

"Please talk with him," whispered Angel. "It's time."

Sterling stared into his sister's face and nodded. For her sake, he would try to come to terms with Cecil. He walked away with his brother, leaving the three women to stare at each other uncertainly. Cecil stopped beneath the shade of some umbrella-like tree, the leafy fronds tapping the top of his hat. "I'd like to ask a favor."

Sterling started in surprise. It was the last thing he'd expected. "You've got some jolly nerve, brother. I'll give you that."

Cecil waved a long-fingered hand. "Yes, I know. I should have believed in Angel like you did, but I couldn't."

"Because you compared her morals to your own."

"I deserve that," mumbled Cecil.

"Then why don't you return her inheritance?"

His black eyes widened innocently. "Surely she doesn't need it any longer. Not with your recent good fortune."

Sterling snorted. Of course Angel didn't need it, but that wasn't the point. It would be the honorable thing to do. "Just tell me what you want."

Cecil spoke quickly. "There are several balls that we haven't been invited to, and if you could just mention us to the prince I'm sure we'd be put on the guest list."

Sterling tossed his head in surprise.

"Don't you see," whined Cecil, his face twisted with intensity, "if we can only manage to get introduced to the right people, our social position will be assured."

Perhaps that's why Sterling never cared about such things. Because his brother cared too much. "On one condition."

"As long as it doesn't involve money."

Sterling shook his head in amazement. Did the man think of nothing else but money and his social position? "No. I just want the truth."

Now it was Cecil's turn to look surprised. "About what?"

"Our father. I want to know why he cut me out of his will—out of his life."

"You're still wondering about that? Bloody hell, I've told you over and over again. It's your own fault." Cecil rubbed his nose, as if considering his next words carefully. "You just didn't know how to work the old man, Sterling."

Sterling turned on his heel to walk away.

"Wait a minute," cried Cecil. "What about my favor?"

Sterling spun, his hair slapping his cheeks. "I told you I wanted the truth."

"Damn it, man," panted Cecil. "It doesn't matter anymore, does it? You've got more money than our father ever had."

"I don't care about the money, I never did. I only care that Father and I didn't have a chance to reconcile our differences before he died." Sterling took a deep breath. "I just want the truth."

"The old man isn't worth it," sneered Cecil. He held up a hand when Sterling started to turn away again. "But do you give me your promise as a gentleman to get me those invitations if I tell you?"

Sterling nodded.

"Oh, all right then. Yes, I manipulated the old man to leave everything to me. I *needed* that money more than you did. Besides, I was the one who took care of him, jumped when he told me to jump while you went off to the army. I *deserved* it."

Sterling felt tired. Tired of hearing about money. He'd only cared that something had stood between him and his father, and now he knew for certain it had been Cecil. He gave an inner breath of relief as a burden lifted from his shoulders. It was comforting to know that he might have reconciled with his father if not for Cecil. That they hadn't hated each other so much, after all.

The wind sighed through the exotic bushes and Sterling could hear the muted sound of voices again. He needed to get back to Angel. She'd been gone from his sight long enough.

"Will you keep your promise?" asked Cecil.

Sterling nodded again.

"Do you hate me?"

The question brought Sterling up short. He didn't think his brother cared about his feelings. He studied Cecil, the pointed face and long ears and greedy eyes. Surprisingly, he didn't hate him. He only felt pity for a man who valued money and social position above love and family. And he realized that Cecil and his stepmother could no longer hurt him. They just weren't capable of giving unconditional affection.

"No, Cecil. I don't hate you. But don't ever ask me for anything else again, understand?"

"Yes, yes. Just get me those invitations." Cecil scurried off, his face alight with anticipation at telling his wife the news. Sterling smoothed the hair back from his face and started to follow.

"Oh, that was jolly good," said a squeaky voice from within the leaves above Sterling's head. "Do you have any more brothers?"

He shook his head.

"Aw, too bad."

Sterling hadn't seen Nuisance or Trouble for the past couple of weeks; he'd mistakenly thought they'd returned to their toadstools. He looked up and caught a flash of red against the blue sky. For some reason he no longer felt annoyed by the gnome's eavesdropping. Just oddly comforted.

He found Angel studying a plant that sported long, spiky leaves, her face creased in concentration. "Look, even its little babies are all spiky. Rather like some people, isn't it?"

"No, Angel. People don't have to be like their parents."

"Truly?" Her blue eyes danced. He kissed her on the forehead. She laced her arm with his. "Did you have a good talk with Cecil?"

"We talked."

"Do you still hate him?"

Sterling snorted. "I never did, Angel. But don't expect him to be a part of our family. Some people never lose their spikes."

"Oh."

They walked silently through the crowd of people until they reached their carriage. As Sterling handed her up into the shiny new conveyance, she gave him a sidelong look. "When will Lady Jasmina be a part of our family?"

He smiled while she gathered her skirts about her so he wouldn't step on them when he took his seat. "Funny you should ask me that. For I have just decided that if a man can make his own family, so can a woman. And it's time I made Lady Jasmina aware of that fact."

Nineteen

JASMINA STOOD IN FRONT OF THE CHEVAL GLASS IN HER bedroom and studied her reflection. Pale hair, wide green eyes, bow lips. The same innocent and proper looking woman stared back at her, but she no longer felt that way inside. She had a lover she visited every night, a lowborn man she thought of constantly and lusted after with a wanton disregard for her upbringing.

Her cheeks flushed and she covered them with her hands. A memory crept unbidden into her mind... the exhilaration of dancing with tree nymphs beneath a starlit sky. When Jaz had joined with her, she'd felt like two people, an uncomfortable feeling that had gradually faded except for these brief flashes of memory. How would she ever reconcile these two parts of her character?

Jasmina sighed, dropped her hands and smoothed the front of her embroidered muslin gown. She might as well admit that Jaz had always been a part of her, a part she had hidden beneath her upbringing and station in life. Merlin's Relic had just allowed that part of her the freedom to do as it wished. And despite how she tried to return to her old lifestyle, Jaz would not stay hidden anymore. And Lady Jasmina didn't really want her to, because she'd fallen desperately in love with Sir Sterling Thorn and was not only determined to have him, but her father's approval to the marriage as well. She needed all the help she could get.

She had just managed to get her father to speak to her without the walls crawling with flames when Aunt Ettie announced her betrothal to Sir Artemus. She didn't want to deny her aunt happiness, but couldn't Aunt have waited a bit longer? Father had renewed his visions of a fiery hell with vigor.

And tomorrow Father intended to depart for the Continent and Jasmina had no intention of leaving Sir Sterling. So she had to confront her father today.

"You'll never guess who's here," said Nuisance, interrupting her thoughts, as usual.

Jasmina's heart skipped a beat. Had she summoned Sterling with her desire? But no, he wouldn't come here. He'd promised to give her time to gain her father's approval to their marriage. But what if he'd found out about Father's plans to take her to the Continent and had decided to take matters into his own hands? That would be disastrous!

"Who is it?" she asked, unable to mask the annoyance in her voice. Jasmina thought that once they had recovered the relic and she'd joined with her illusion, the two garden gnomes would return to their homes. Or transfer their attentions to someone else. But they hadn't, and it filled her with dread. What awful entertainment did they still predict in her future?

"You'll never guess in a million, zillion, quadrill—oof!"

Trouble removed her elbow from Nuisance's rib and scowled at him. "Just tell her."

But a knock sounded at the door, and the two gnomes disappeared in a blink. Aunt Ettie stuck her head around the jamb. "You'll never guess who's here."

Jasmina resisted the urge to tear at her hair. "Would you please just tell me?"

Aunt sniffed. "Well! It's His Royal Highness, the prince consort himself."

"What? What in heaven's name is he doing here?"

Aunt Ettie stepped over to the wardrobe and began to search through Jasmina's gowns. "Where is that green silk? Trouble, get out here and make yourself useful and undo Lady Jasmina's buttons."

The gnome popped out from underneath the bed, shaking dust from her wiry hair. Jasmina waved her away. "Have they called for me?"

"Not yet, but when they do, you must look presentable."

"Trouble, go find out what they're saying," said Jasmina without a hint of remorse at the unladylike request.

"She's not going without me," replied Nuisance, crawling out from under the wardrobe. Aunt Ettie gave a startled sniff but didn't stop tossing dresses onto the floor.

"Aunt Ettie, you're making a mess," protested Jasmina. "Of course you may go with her, Nuisance. Heaven forbid I should deprive you of your fun."

"For a human," said Nuisance as he followed Trouble out the door, "you're a jolly good sport."

Jasmina waved her fingers and spelled her dress. "There. Look, Aunt Ettie, will this do?"

"Of course not, dear. Royals can see through your spells."

"But only if they cast a counter spell first."

Aunt Ettie turned, the green silk held triumphantly in her hands. "And if he does? Will you risk Prince Albert seeing you in that old muslin?" She spun Jasmina around and popped buttons out of their holes with surprising speed. "Besides, I have a feeling you should look your very best today."

"Aunt…"

"No, truly, it's just a feeling, that's all. Now, quickly. It takes forever to do up all the laces in this gown. Where is that silly maid when you most need her?"

Despite their haste, it took nearly a half hour to get Jasmina into the gown, an elegant concoction of ruffles and lace that would be more appropriate for a royal ball than the drawing room in her own house. When Aunt had arranged Jasmina's hair to her satisfaction, she prodded her over to the mirror. Jasmina felt her mouth quirk in a wicked smile. "That's an enormous amount of cleavage, Aunt."

"It might be necessary."

"I beg your pardon?" Jasmina turned and gently grasped her aunt's shoulders. "What do you know that I don't?"

A knock at the door made them both jump.

"Enter," huffed Aunt.

The door opened. "Pardon me, miss," said one of the downstairs maids. "But yer father is asking fer ye in the formal drawing room."

"We'll be right down," answered Aunt, pinching Jasmina's suddenly pale cheeks. A moment later the two gnomes appeared in the doorway.

"You'd best hurry or you'll miss him," panted Trouble.

"And it's good news," added Nuisance, looking terribly disappointed.

Jasmina couldn't imagine why the prince would visit. He had offered a reward for her part in the destruction of the Brotherhood, but she honestly couldn't think of anything she wanted other than Sir Sterling, and the baronet was one thing she couldn't ask for.

Aunt Ettie ushered her out the door and down the stairs. They met the prince at the landing just as he was leaving. Both of them quickly dropped into deep curtsies. Prince Albert didn't say a word, although Jasmina could have sworn that the man winked at her before descending the stairs to the ground floor.

Jasmina snapped her mouth shut and marched into the drawing room, puzzled by the entire affair. Her confusion quickly turned into astonishment when her father crossed the room and enfolded her in a rare embrace.

"My dear. I wish you had told me sooner, although I understand the need for secrecy. I'm honored that the prince trusted me enough to tell me now."

Mother sat beside the tea tray, her rose gown surrounding her like the petals of a flower. She gazed at Jasmina with eyes that sparkled with happiness.

"Wha-what exactly did he tell you?"

Father released her, closed the doors to the drawing room and resumed his position next to the fireplace, one booted foot propped on the stone hearth. "Oh, come now, daughter. I admire your modesty, but you know perfectly well that you're a heroine to the Crown. The prince has confided in us, so you may drop the ruse."

Jasmina heard Aunt Ettie sniff and the crinkle of her skirts as she took a seat, but Jasmina stood firmly rooted to the floor. Why had the prince suddenly decided to tell them about the relic? Because it had been destroyed and there was no longer any danger to the Crown?

Mother rose from her seat in one fluid motion and took Jasmina's hand. "He told us about the spell, too. The master pointed out that you couldn't have known you held one of Merlin's Relics when you cast that spell, so don't fear that we blame you for it." Her eyes grew glassy with tears. "And we should have known that you would never behave in such a scandalous manner. It was that imposter all along!"

Jasmina opened her mouth to explain that Jaz was not just an illusion, but a part of her that had been released by Merlin's Relic, when her mother jangled a set of keys beneath her nose.

"I believe these belong to you. Can you ever forgive me for thinking you unworthy of them?"

Jasmina stared in puzzlement at the household keys while her mother pressed them into her hand. They felt cold and hard on her palm. "I can't believe he told you."

Father cleared his throat. "The prince told us that you would accept nothing in repayment for your bravery." His voice rang with pride. "So he felt it was the least he could do to let us know what a wonderful daughter we have. Although he wouldn't give us all of the details… and asked us not to pressure you for them." His voice trailed off and he looked at her expectantly as if he'd like to anyway.

Jasmina just stared at him, too overwhelmed to dissemble. With just a few words the prince had given her back her old, well-ordered life. She had her parents' respect and affection, along with control of the household; and with their support she knew she'd eventually regain all of her old friends and acquaintances.

Father's magic responded to his joy, the walls sparkling with bursts of multicolored light that danced over family photos and candle sconces. The sweet scent of jasmine floated on a light breeze, accompanied by the sound of children laughing and music tinkling, her mother's magical contribution to the atmosphere in the drawing room.

Jasmina carefully walked over to a velvet chair and let her knees collapse beneath her. She should be overjoyed. She had everything she thought she'd ever wanted handed back to her on a silver platter. But she only felt a cold ache in her heart, because in order to keep it, she would have to give up the one thing she now wanted most in this world.

To be married to a baronet.

She longed for that other part of her nature that only Sterling could release. She couldn't continue this charade of the dutiful daughter during the day and a passionate temptress at night. Jasmina wanted to become someone else entirely, to acknowledge her love for a shape-shifter and allow the two sides of her character to reach a common middle ground. But the only way she could do that was to be honest with herself and those around her. Starting with her parents.

Jasmina opened her mouth but before she could speak, a commotion from the entry hall made them all turn toward the drawing room door.

The door cracked open and the butler popped his head in, as if afraid to fully enter the room.

"I told you we didn't want to be disturbed," barked Father.

The butler swallowed. "I know sir, pardon me, sir. But there's a gentleman at the door who insists on seeing you."

Both of the double doors suddenly swung wide open and Sir Sterling Thorn stood on the threshold, resplendent in black coat and trousers, not a worn hem or ragged seam in sight. His equally new black boots had been polished to a shine, and a garnet-studded stickpin fastened his cravat.

"It's about time," mumbled Aunt Ettie.

Jasmina's stomach flipped. He looked so incredibly handsome that tingles of excitement raced through her body and she stiffened her spine in response.

"What is the meaning of this?" demanded Father, his sparkling illusions transforming to sharp daggers of light.

Sterling tossed his black mane of hair. He had left it loose, making him look wild, despite his fashionable new clothing. Jasmina had a suspicion he'd done so on purpose. Now, why hadn't he waited to let her speak with her father as he'd promised? She might have had a better chance at avoiding this messy confrontation.

Sterling boldly walked over to her and raised her hand to his lips. "My apologies, lady. But I'm bloody well tired of waiting."

"He's tired of waiting," whispered a tiny voice in glee.

Mother cocked her head with a frown at the tall urn that sat in the corner of the room, but Father ignored the faint voice entirely. "How dare you touch my daughter?"

Sterling straightened to his full height, a good head taller than her father. "I dare even more than that, sir. I am here to ask for your daughter's hand in marriage."

Mother gasped, Father turned beet red, and Aunt Ettie clapped her hands.

"I forbid it." Father's voice lowered to a growl. "Do you hear me? I forbid my daughter to marry an animal. Our family name has already been soiled enough by Henrietta—I will not have two beasts in the family." His fist pounded the mantel. "I will not!"

Sterling ignored her father's anger and turned to Jasmina, going down on one knee before her. "What say you, love? Your father has forbid my suit, and although I would wish it otherwise, you are forced to choose. Will you marry me?"

Jasmina stared into his dark blue eyes, drowning in his gaze. She saw a hint of doubt there, as if he wasn't quite sure she'd accept him. Was that why he couldn't wait any longer, because he was afraid she might not have him? Didn't he know that she loved him with all of her heart?

"I will not allow it," bellowed Father, this time sounding a bit confused.

Jasmina glanced at her father's angry face. Sterling

was right; she would have to choose one or the other. And although she loved her father dearly, Sterling was a part of her soul. "I would be honored to be your wife," she said as calmly as she could, despite the turmoil she felt inside. Her hand trembled and Sterling squeezed it gently, helping her to rise, giving her his strength.

"I will see to it that you will never procure a license," threatened Father. "You will never marry my daughter."

Sterling pulled a paper from his pocket, his handsome face showing nothing but pity, and handed it to Father. "It is too late. The deed has already been done."

Jasmina frowned, staring at the wrinkled document. A sudden flash of a new memory made her nod. "The signatures are valid, Father."

A giggle broke the silence of the room. So, Trouble also spied on them, but she hid beneath the settee where Aunt sat, and Father must have assumed that the laughter was hers, for he suddenly directed his fury at Aunt Henrietta. "You! This is entirely your fault, allowing my daughter to associate with animals. Accepting the offer of marriage from one yourself. If you had protected her from such scoundrels it would never have come to this."

Aunt Ettie's eyes flashed dark green fire, and her lips narrowed frighteningly. She rarely got angry but when she did—

"Don't," whispered Jasmina.

"I suggest you see to your own marriage, Horace, before you disparage my choice of a partner," Aunt Ettie said, deadly calm.

Mother gasped. Father stared from one to the other, his illusion of lights whirling about the room in a dizzying display. "What are you talking about?"

"I've often wondered," continued Aunt, "if you turn a blind eye to your wife's sticky fingers or if you are indeed that stupid."

Mother shook her head, her blonde curls slapping her cheeks.

Aunt Ettie turned to her and softened her voice. "With Jasmina and me gone, you'll have no one left but Horace to protect you, Lucy. It's time you told him."

"Told me what?" asked Father, leaving his station by the fireplace and sitting down next to Mother.

"Really, Horace, it's nothing," crooned Mother. "Just a silly old habit of mine."

Aunt Ettie threw a look at Sterling and cocked her head at the door.

"Come with me," he whispered, tugging on Jasmina's hand. She watched her parents over her shoulder with a worried frown. But then she remembered how Mother had surprised her when she'd handled Father on Jasmina's behalf, and she sighed, knowing that her parents would be all right.

Sterling led her through the entrance hall and opened the door. Jasmina hesitated, knowing that once she crossed that threshold she might never be able to return. "Do you think Father will ever accept our marriage?"

Sterling descended the steps into the street, turned and tossed his head at her. "You've made your own family now. Does it matter?"

Jasmina smiled and lifted her chin. "I would hope that he will wish to be a part of it, but no, my love. It doesn't matter because you are my life." *And my heart and soul*, she finished silently.

"Pssst." Nuisance's head popped up from behind the umbrella stand, followed by Trouble's pointy coiffure. "We couldn't let you go without saying goodbye."

"Goodbye?" Jasmina tried not to sound too over-joyed. "What do you mean?"

Trouble grimaced. "He means that there'll be more fun here—what with your mother's little habit and all—than spying on you."

"Oh." Jasmina glanced back out the door. Sterling had shifted to stallion, his magnificent black coat looking almost blue in the sunshine. He pawed the cobblestones with impatience, demanding that she come to him.

"I don't know why, but I think I will miss you," said Jasmina.

Nuisance grinned and wiggled his bulbous nose. A small tear slid down Trouble's pudgy cheek. "We'll miss you too," she said. "It's just too bad that your life just won't be interesting enough for us anymore."

"Maybe not for you," replied Jasmina as she sailed down the steps. "But for me, it's more than I could ever have wished for."

She threw her arms around her stallion's neck. "Do you know that I think I fell in love with your were-self first?" she whispered. He snorted and leaned into her embrace.

"Well, I never!" said Lady Wiccens as she watched them from her front step.

Jasmina laughed and stepped back, Sterling knelt, and she clambered onto his back. Her husband snorted, then leaped forward in a gallop, finally, at long last, taking her home.

Epilogue

Jasmina sat on a bench at St. James's park beneath the shade of her umbrella, watching her son run a race with the other children. Young Oliver's hair was as black as his father's and it shone almost blue in the sunlight. But when he turned to wave at her, her own green eyes sparkled from his young face.

"May I join you?" a familiar voice asked from behind her.

Jasmina caught her breath, then nodded. Her father settled on the bench beside her and she decided that other than a few new wrinkles, he looked the same as when she'd last seen him six years ago.

"How… remarkable that we should meet like this," she said.

"Not really. I've been watching you all these years, you know."

She hadn't known. She'd thought her family cared as little for her as Sterling's did for him. Only Aunt Ettie had stayed a part of her life, and although she visited them occasionally, she rarely mentioned Mother and Father to Jasmina.

"How is Mother?"

"Quite well. She misses you."

Jasmina blinked back sudden tears. She couldn't count all of the times she'd wished for her mother's advice over the years, especially when she'd given birth to her son and felt so lost when trying to raise him. Loving Sterling made her happier than she'd ever been in her life, but oh, how she'd missed Mother and Father. And she desperately wanted her son to know his grandparents.

Father cleared his throat. "Your husband has been good to you."

"Yes. He is a wonderful man."

"I met with him today."

Jasmina tried to hide her astonishment.

"Asked him over to my gentlemen's club. We had a long chat."

She couldn't speak, too numb even to feel the happiness that should have been coursing through her.

"He's a fine lad," said Father, watching the children race around the duck pond. "If he were as old as the rest of them, he'd beat them…"

Oliver had made it halfway around the pond when he shifted to stallion. Father made a strangled sound. Jasmina cringed; then a spark of anger inside her made her quickly lift her chin. In all the years she'd been married to Sterling, she'd never once felt ashamed of his nature, and she wasn't about to start now, especially when it concerned their son. If her father wanted back into her life, he would have to accept their shape-shifting abilities.

Her father leaped to his feet. "Look at him go, Jasmina! He can fly like the wind."

When Oliver won the race, Father applauded and Jasmina smiled up at him.

But when her son shifted back to human one of the larger boys engaged him in fisticuffs. Jasmina rose to her feet to intervene, but her father gently grasped her arm. "No, let him fight his own battles."

Jasmina sighed. He sounded just like Sterling.

The boys finally broke up and Oliver came stomping over to his mother, his left eye red and swollen. "They said I cheated," he told her. "But that big chap used his magic to trip us, so I said it was fair for me to use my shifting too."

"The other lads are just jealous," said Father. "Because they can't turn into horses too."

Her son gave the old man an appraising stare. "Who are you?"

"I'm your grandfather. And it's far past time we got to know each other. Shall we go for a walk?"

When her father took her son's smaller hand into his own, Jasmina stiffened her spine and tightened her control. But then she smiled and let the tears spill down her cheeks as they walked away.

Jasmina felt him behind her, with that heightened awareness that hadn't dimmed in their years of marriage. Her skin tingled and when Sterling placed his warm hand on her shoulder, her stomach fluttered.

"They make quite a pair, don't they?" he said as he sat next to her on the bench.

She nodded, unable to speak. Her husband gently wiped the tears from her cheeks, his fingertips eventually tracing a path to her lips. Jasmina's mouth opened on a sigh.

"I suppose it would be entirely improper for me to kiss you right now." His blue eyes sparkled in the sunshine, a challenge revealed in their depths.

Jasmina extended her umbrella over his head, then lowered it, covering them both within its shelter. "Entirely," she murmured, and leaned toward the heat of his lips.

Enchanting the Lady

by Kathryne Kennedy

Their magic lives within each one of them...

In a Victorian England with a rigid hierarchy of magic, lion shape-shifter Sir Terence Blackwell is at the bottom rung of society. Only Lady Felicity Seymour, who has no magic, no inheritance, and no prospects, may be willing to judge the man strictly on his own merits...

However deeply it may be hidden...

When family pressures push Lady Felicity into a terrible fate, she has only Sir Terence to turn to. As the two outcasts are propelled by circumstances beyond their control, they are forced to explore the unseen depths beneath society's facade. And what they discover about each other is more real and more beautiful than they ever could have imagined...

"Kennedy has totally enchanted us with this book. It's like reading an adult version of **Beauty and the Beast** *with a bit more spunk."*—Yankee Romance Reviewers

"Casts a magic spell on the audience from the moment the heroine expects to fail her test and never lets go until the final magical revelation."—Midwest Book Review

For more Kathryne Kennedy, visit:

www.sourcebooks.com

The Fire Lord's Lover

by Kathryne Kennedy

If his powers are discovered, his father will destroy him...

In a magical land ruled by ruthless Elven lords, the Fire Lord's son Dominic Raikes plays a deadly game to conceal his growing might from his malevolent father—until his arranged bride awakens in him passions he thought he had buried forever...

Unless his fiancée kills him first...

Lady Cassandra has been raised in outward purity and innocence, while secretly being trained as an assassin. Her mission is to bring down the Elven Lord and his champion son. But when she gets to court she discovers that nothing is what it seems, least of all the man she married...

"**The Fire Lord's Lover** *showcases Kathryne Kennedy's deft craftsmanship... A Tolkien-esque world combined with an eighteenth-century historical romance produces a satisfying tale with twists you'll never expect.*"—*Jennifer Ashley,* New York Times *and* USA Today *bestselling author*

For more Kathryne Kennedy, visit:

www.sourcebooks.com

The Lady of the Storm

by Kathryne Kennedy

There's a thin line between duty and desire...

Giles Beaumont is stuck in a role he never wanted, trying to safeguard a woman of incendiary powers who doesn't think she needs a protector.

Cecily Sutton has no idea of the enormity of her true task and no inkling of the effect she's having on Giles. But somewhere along their perilous journey together, they'll have no choice but to uncover the deep, dark connection that binds them one to the other...

Lose yourself in renowned author Kathryne Kennedy's gorgeous love story set in a lush world made of equal parts wonder and danger.

"Sizzling... Kennedy's exquisite world building and terrific plotting make this a must-read"—Booklist
Starred Review, Top 10 Romance Fiction of 2011

"Romantic and emotional... a wild reading experience."—The Long and Short of It

For more Kathryne Kennedy, visit:

www.sourcebooks.com